Ferret

The Reluctant King

L.K. Samuels

Published by

**Freeland
Press**
P.O. Box 22231
Carmel, CA 93922
www.freelandpress.org

All Rights Reserved, Published 2019

Printed in the United States
ISBN (Print): 978-0-9615893-2-5
ISBN (ebook): 0-9615893-2-9

This novel's story and characters are fictitious.

L.K. Samuels
Ferret: The Reluctant King

1. Fiction 2. Historical Novel

Cover design by Rick Holland at Vision Press. www.myvisionpress.com
Formatted by Mike Dworski.

Name: Samuels, L.K.
Title: Ferret: The Reluctant King

Website for author: www.lksamuels.com

First published, Feb. 2020
Second edition, Sept. 2020

Acknowledgements

Nobody produces a book all by themselves. There are many who assisted in the final publication of this book. First and foremost was my editor, Gregory Bales, proofreaders Jane Heider and Linda Blumenthal, and formatter, Mike Dworski. Moreover, Rick Holland did a wonderful job designing the book cover.

Through the decades, others have read chapters and provided insight towards the storyline and characterization. Chapters were even read and critiqued at a writer's class at Orange Coast College in Costa Mesa, California. They all helped and I appreciate everyone involved.

Preface

Ferret: The Reluctant King was a labor of timeless love, an odyssey that started over 45 years ago in the early 1970s. I started putting pen to paper back in college when I came across the history of ancient Ireland and the English Levellers. I was fascinated by the dispersed political structure of ancient Ireland, where their high kings were more figureheads than powerful chieftains. Interestingly, the Levellers of England seemed to be expressing similar thoughts about the decentralization of power, and are considered one of the first socio-political movements in the world to espouse the liberal concept of equal natural rights. This rich history was not well known except by a few historians, including a dear associate of mine, Kenneth Gregg, Jr., who often lectured and wrote on these topics.

But a number of problems stunted my effort to write a historical novel. My handwriting was almost illegible; so, I borrowed a manual Underwood typewriter. Even an electric Selectric II IBM typewriter was laboriously slow when cutting and taping new copy over old copy. I needed a system that could save my copy. In the late 1970s, I was able to save my manuscript on a large Compugraphic 7500 typesetter. Later, I transferred my book to an IBM clone and printed my proof copies on a dot matrix printer. What an ordeal!

Meanwhile, I did extensive research on Irish and Dutch culture and history, along with the Levellers movement in England. I took a research trip in the mid-1980s to southern Ireland, mostly studying in Cork's main library. I researched old Irish archival books and became acquainted with a few historical slang books. As the years passed, I continue to work late into the night to revise and expand my book. I found a good editor/proofer, along with a book cover designer. Then I attempted again to find a willing publisher, which had always been my greatest stumbling block. By late 2018, I found a way to get my manuscript published.

I still wonder if I would have travelled down this long road if I had known beforehand that it would take almost a lifetime. At least it shows that if one is determined, any arduous journey can end at the desired destination.

Foreword
IRELAND, 1697

In 1691, war erupted between Ireland and England. Like most wars, it was political. William of Orange dethroned the Catholic King, James II of England by invitation of the English Parliament. James fled to Ireland and sought assistance from the Catholic Irish to regain his throne. Ireland rallied behind the deposed English king to fight the hated Protestants and to gain independence from England. Unfortunately, James was a poor military general, and the Irish lost battle after battle. By the next year, 1692, they sued for peace.

Although the Treaty of Limerick guaranteed the Irish the right to exercise their Catholic faith, religious and economic laws were handed down to punish them, causing terrible hardships.

Roving bands of starving Irishmen continued to attack British outposts in the mountainous and swampy interior to regain control of their small country. In the wild backcountry, the Irish still had some control over their destiny.

L.K. Samuels

Part I

Chapter 1

An old man paced back and forth in the dark cell. He stopped, reached for the wall, dug his fingers into wooden poles and squeezed. He knew the wood was too thick to break with his hands. But that did not really matter. He knew he would never see the real criminals face an iota of justice. No, the murderers would never be convicted and executed in front of a cackling crowd. The guilty were never punished. That was the simple cruel fact of life. And he was going to soon prove it beyond all doubt.

"*Droch-chrioch ort!*" he swore in Gaelic under his breath. He gazed at his rawhide hands and age spots. He felt ancient and worn out. His body drooped with a weariness that kept sinking into hopelessness. He feared he had little energy left to fight the pigheads of authority. And why should he? The world was devoid of justness. There were no innocents, no beloved God; only the wicked evil and betrayal that fed upon the flesh of the meek. Fight for what? That was a good laugh.

Feeling queasy, he pressed his cheek against the rough bark and closed his eyes. He let out a feral growl deep in his throat and banged his head against one of the thicker poles. Why had he been so stubborn and foolhardy? There was no way out; his fate was sealed tighter than a tomb chamber. He knew he should have gone deeper into the hinterland, far away from those who delighted in calling themselves civilized. He was a bona fide fool. That was without a doubt.

Suddenly, the old man heard a commotion outside of his small cell. It sounded like a brood of squawking hens scurrying from a red fox. He found a narrow gap between the lashed pinewood poles and pressed his face close to the wall. Squinting, he caught sight of the fort's courtyard. There they were—a whole regiment of the King's men, British regulars cleaning their shiny bayonets. Standing next to them, a pocket of officers milled about the fort like cattle—probably the dreaded Sixth Regiment of Foot—the same murderers who had been responsible for destroying his people. It gave him some comfort to know that they would surely be first in line to burn in Hell.

He twisted around and peered into the darkness. He knew his day of reckoning was coming. That was not so surprising. He had excelled at making enemies. In fact, he took pride in it. Why not be judged by the enemies one had made? That was his golden rule. And as he reckoned it, his half-witted antics had made him slightly more popular than an overflowing piss pot.

Bowing his head, the old man steepled his fingers together and slouched against the wall. If only he had moved on, settled somewhere in the upper Mississippi River Valley, or put down roots in New Orleans with the French. That was what a smart fellow would have done. But no, he got caught inside a web of deception. Should have known better.

The jail door flew open. He turned around and faced a hulking man with dark stubble on his face, shadowed by a dozen red-coated troopers. The big man immediately offended him; he was blocking all of the precious sunlight. Something had to be done. The prisoner backed away and groped around for a possible weapon. Finding none, he fingered his long gray hair and cocked his head to the side. Sure, he could accommodate an uninvited guest. Back against the wall, he wiped his sweaty hands on his black-stained deerskin shirt. He had been a man of some girth before months of prison gruel. Yet, he thought he still had enough grit to break a few bones. Let them come hither. He was ready for them, and for all the other knaves who curried favor with the English dogs.

"Ya have an important engagement. And it ain't with the King!" The big-gutted jailer let out a belly laugh, pulled a club from his buckskin breeches and took aim.

"Go to *Halifax*! I am an Irish king!"

"Why ya bloody hang-dog, I'll—"

In a burst of energy, the jailer rushed the old man, pinned him against the wall and struck him on the head, causing him to tumble like a logged tree. Immediately, the jailer dragged the captive outside into the bright sunlight, next to a water barrel. A sentry grabbed the dipper and splashed cold water across the prisoner's face. The old man got up on one knee, then the other, teeth clenched, right fist balled up. As he slowly stood, his lips stretched into a wide defiant grimace that flung a tirade of profanities at the jailer. That was exactly what he wanted—the more cursing, the more gratifying.

With a broad surly face and a pale index finger, the prisoner beckoned the man to step closer and try again. The jailer's face exploded with rage. With the speed of a charging bull, the brute rushed forward, wielding his club. The old man blocked his assault and sent the man plummeting to the ground. The jailer got up and charged again. After exchanging a few hard swings, the prisoner rammed his elbow into the jailer's face. It had little effect. Another blow sent his adversary reeling backward, crashing into a squad of armed soldiers.

Drawing back, the old man reached down and picked up a handful of sunbaked dirt. He let his fingers enjoy the warmth of the soil before letting it sift out of his hands. With a sense of pride, he brushed the dirt off his hand and nodded. The fray had been pretty one-sided, mostly in his favor. He found it a rather enjoyable spectacle for a man of his age.

The jailer stood, dazed and flustered. He spat blood and chipped teeth. Wrenched with pain, he pointed his stubby finger at the prisoner. "Why ya slimy weasel. I'll show ya who's in charge."

"The name's Ferret. But I will answer to 'your grace' if you prefer." Moving back inside the cell, Ferret braced himself into a corner, beaming with the fervor of a wild-eyed man. He knew how to fight the big boys; all Irishmen did.

"Better come out or I'll have your head spiked."

Ferret shook his head. He had taken a liking to his dark puny cell. It was uncrowded, and the roaches scurrying across the floor were far better company than any Englishman. The jailer stroked his fleshy chin and eyed the prisoner apprehensively.

Ferret tugged on his beard, imitating the jailer.

"Why ya goat-sucking bastard!" The jailer lunged at Ferret, swinging with his right fist. Much quicker, Ferret blocked the punch and hurled himself at the jailer like a hell-bound daredevil. They tumbled to the dirt floor amid a choking blanket of dust. The jailer picked himself up, growled, and prepared to throw another punch. Too late. Ferret grabbed the man's shirt collar, rammed him against the pinewood poles, and bit off a piece of his ear. Screaming and clutching the side of his head, the jailer ran outside. After taking a moment to chew on the ear, Ferret found the texture too rubbery for his taste and spat it out.

"He bit me ear!" The jailer screamed. "He's a bloody weasel! That's what he is!"

More men, British regulars with tomahawks strapped to their belts, surged into the cell. They lashed at Ferret like a nest of rattlesnakes. One clung to his body, trying to hold him down, while another beat him with a club. Ferret buckled under their weight.

The redcoats bound the prisoner's hands, dragged him outside, dumped him face down in a twisted heap, and backed away. They appeared none too pleased to have a go with a man whom they considered possessed by demons.

Lightheaded and bruised, Ferret attempted to stand. Instead, he slumped to his knees, fell headfirst to the ground, rolled over, and stared up at the sky. He cursed the broiling sun as if its bright light was punishing him like the fury of a scorned woman. For a moment he wondered if even nature was conspiring against him, but the dull pain came from his hands. The bloody rope had been tied too tightly, cutting off the flow of blood. It was an odd sensation: the sun was hot and yet his sweating hands tingled with the sting of ice. He struggled to loosen the ropes but failed. There was nothing he could do. They were digging deep into his flesh, numbing his fingers and hands. Might lose a finger or two, if he lived that long. Soon his whole body would turn to cold stone.

Regaining his strength, Ferret tried again to stand. When he got to his feet, he looked up and glanced at the sun with defiant triumph. Nobody would ever outshine him. He thought back to how Indians treated the mentally deranged. They would avoid anyone they suspected of having the falling sickness. Seen it happen with the Cherokee. Heathens feared crazy men; they would flee in holy terror because they believed madness was contagious. He was beginning to think they were right. He had to do something. He began working up a mouthful of spit. Next, he blinked his eyes rapidly and frothed with a bemused smile. He could feign craziness. He was already halfway there.

"Get a-moving!" A runty soldier shoved Ferret forward, ignoring his antics. "And do not think you can befool me. You're surely the devil incarnated and you will pay for your bloody crimes." Another redcoat clenched the old man's hands and pulled him toward a scaffold.

Ferret swallowed his spit and limped ahead. He could barely see: his left eye was swollen; his right eye was coated with clumps of dirt. Still, he could sense a multitude of people closing in, gathering about, ready to mock him and scourge him. He could see fuzzy outlines and silhouettes shifting all about him. Then he heard cackling geese, hissing, squabbling, and honking. But they were not geese; they were human voices, hundreds of commonfolk, chattering at each other for no good reason.

He squinted and focused on a gaggle of stupid, gawking faces. They were staring at him; hundreds of colonists, pushing and shoving, mostly Virginian farmers clad in rough leather, beaver hats, and tall boots, along with a sprinkling of black-capped Dutch traders puffing on two-foot-long pipes. Farther away, blackamoor slaves gazed from behind their masters, while black and white children raced in circles, chasing dogs or playing hot cockles. He silently watched the menagerie and dreamt of better times.

Dreaming. It was the only nice thing about life. Did not cost one penny. He could just sit back and fantasize about a peaceful Ireland of green pasturelands, quiet landscapes, big-hearted gentlefolk, honest kindred and carefree life of plenty. It was the perfect daydream. But that's all it was, just a hollow dreamfest. The real *Eire* had died long before he had been born.

Breathing in deeply, Ferret eyed the gallows. Behind it were the poorly built main barracks of Fort James, Virginia, surrounded by tall, spiked walls to ward off Indian attacks. To his left was the main gate, standing wide open but jammed with busybody colonists and trigger-itchy soldiers. He tried to get a better view of the gate. It was the only way out of the fort, his only chance to escape.

Deriding and taunting the prisoner, several young colonists moved closer and poked long willow sticks at Ferret. He lurched at them and growled. He had bitten one ear off already. He wondered if Virginian fingers might taste a mite better. He would never find out; they suddenly stumbled backward.

To Ferret's right, three British drummers began rattling their pigskins in unison. It was a ploy to torment and annoy him. They had done it to Irishmen for centuries. He wanted to put his hands over his ears to block out the horrible racket, but his tightly bound ropes had other plans. Instead, he flashed the drummers an evil eye.

"Halt!" A young English officer hurried over and stood in front of the scaffold stairs. He scowled at the prisoner, then smirked. "Fine day for a hanging!"

"'Tis a splendid day indeed," Ferret said and popped a lopsided smile. "I for one shall enjoy every second of it. Wouldn't want you to miss it, me laddie. But if you grow faint-hearted, just look the other way. I'll understand."

The officer's face flushed red. "Get this buffoon under the gallows."

Suddenly, a black-robed man confronted Ferret. It was Judge Locke, the man who had sentenced him to death. Locke clamped his hands over the prisoner's for a long time, as if they were about to pray together.

"I am sorry," the judge said softly. "The Lord will look after you. I will see to it."

"Ha!" Ferret looked straight into the magistrate's eyes. He prepared a special volley of spit just for this vile blackguard, then he saw a soldier lift the butt of his flintlock. He swallowed the spit.

"Remember," Locke said as he continued to clasp the prisoner's hand, "the Lord works in miraculous ways."

Ferret's face lowered. What was the judge jabbering about? Judge Locke would live and he would die. Nothing very miraculous about that.

"Get climbing!" a soldier commanded from behind.

Ferret broke free of the judge and shambled to the makeshift, pine-hewn stairway that led up to the gallows. A hemp noose swayed in the morning breeze. He leaned against the railing and noticed how rickety it was. He would never have allowed such a weak railing in his kingdom.

Ferret trained his eyes on the hooded executioner, who kept scratching his forearms. It was hard to fathom—all of this lavish proceeding and fuss over the likes of one puny Irishman. Some might be flattered. It was not every day that the English allotted such expense for a hoary vagabond. Usually, they just shoot Irishmen in the back, toss a few rocks to mark the body and think nothing of it.

"Move along." A soldier growled as he shoved Ferret with his flintlock.

Ferret turned and scowled at his British tormentors. There was something odious and repulsive about English ways and their ill-begotten traditions. So formal, prissy and clean—even their brass buttons were shiny and spotless. But there was more to these men than fancy garments; more than collarless redcoats with yellow lapels and cuffs; more than silly-looking grenadier hats that peaked above the head like a mountain, or pig-tail queues that swung like an old plow horse's tail. No, these were men of hollow conscience, willing to obey orders without considering their consequences; these were the same sort of men who ruled *Eire* with an iron fist and hot lead. He remembered watching a Brit bayonet an Irish woman from Macroom because her pudding had turned rancid. The soldier had treated the woman like a poke of raw potatoes. That was who they were—soulless men who killed strangers because they were under orders from afar. To the English, murdering strangers was a mere duty. The Irish were different. Clan fought clan to satisfy justice, not to exterminate those they disliked.

"Come on, now! Move!" the soldier ordered.

Ferret remained deep in thought. *Eire... Eire... Eire.* His father had been murdered in his homeland by the same army of cutthroats. It happened near Macroom. Had to be the worst day of his pitiful life.

"We don't have all bloody day!" The soldier shoved Ferret in the back, causing him to fall to his knees.

"Criminy! See here!" a Scottish colonist shouted. "He's an old man. Show some respect for age. Could his crime warrant such ill treatment?" The colonist slipped his smoking pipe into his wide belt. "What did he do anyway?"

The soldiers ignored the question.

Swiftly, two soldiers came up from the rear, grabbed Ferret, and dragged him up the steps. They dumped him on the scaffold flooring, underneath the noose.

"Who did ja murder?" one man suddenly yelled. The question rippled through the crowd. It appeared that nobody knew the answer.

An old, thin woman pushed her way through the colonists until she was in front of the platform. She faced the gathering crowd and rasped, "Listen to me! This prisoner be falsely accused." She lifted her right arm and pointed to the prisoner. "He was convicted in a secret court. Is this English justice?"

"Shut up!" a portly colonist bellowed with scornful contempt at the woman. "Ain't no skin off my teeth!"

A tall, well-dressed black man in white sleeves confronted the fat colonist. "Sir, I would refrain from interrupting. 'Twould be most unhealthful." The black man raised his heavy arm and displayed a massive fist. The fat colonist quickly turned silent.

The old woman, facing the scaffold, shouted again. She tried to catch the prisoner's eye. "Hear me, prisoner! The Lord will keep you from harm's way."

Ferret, still lying on the floor of the gallows, peered over the edge. The woman acted as if she knew him. *Who is she?* She looked familiar, mighty familiar. But all his companions and kindred were long ago dead and buried in unmarked graves. The men without consciences had massacred them. This enraged him to the point where he wanted to set the entire world ablaze with fire and brimstone. To him, everyone deserved to be jabbed by Satan's pitchfork for all eternity.

"The Lord protects those who protect themselves," the old woman shouted as she pushed closer to the gallows.

Who is she? She seemed so boisterous and saucy. Her shrill voice pricked like a thorn. Her gray hair ceded to a few streaks of wavy red, like... Ferret shook his head in disbelief. Not possible. His wife had died decades ago in a fiery pit of burning hell. Still, this woman spoke with a beautiful Irish brogue like his beloved Heather. He wanted to reach out and touch her hair and see for himself. But he knew his hands were too tightly bound. The British had made sure of that. They were always so prim and proper.

However, after shifting his body to gain a better look at the agitated woman, Ferret discovered that the rope had become loose, as though it had become undone all by itself. That was a silly notion. Ferret pulled against the rope and it began to give way. How was this possible? It had been tighter than catgut on a fiddle. The rope must have been cut. Impossible! The last person to touch his bindings was Judge Locke. Something was not right. He slowly swung his eyes to the left and then the right, gazing intently at what he could not see. It was infuriating. Something was afoot and he did not have the slightest clue.

He needed to concentrate. He quickly stared down at his bound hands trying to avoid alerting anyone. He had to find out if he was indeed free of his restraints. But before he could make that assessment, the executioner loomed closer and pulled out a black hood. Ferret looked up. The end was at hand. Darkness would soon befall him. He had to act.

At that moment the old woman yelled out again, but her words were lost among the clamor of the crowd, who were turning restless. Ferret squinted at her and wondered if it could really be Heather. Then he noticed her eyes. They had the same fiery look of...

Ferret fought back tears as he returned his attention to the rope. It could not be Heather. Not even possible. Ferret struggled to come up with something fast. He needed more time to think. Luckily, the executioner backed away to accommodate several British officers. There were still a few more formalities to get through.

Major Mountjoy, a tall, skeletally thin officer, climbed up the scaffold with a number of high-ranking officers. Taking his time, he strolled over to Ferret. He turned to one of his men, perturbed. "What is the prisoner doing on the floor?"

The soldier smirked and shrugged his shoulders. "Must have fallen, Sir!"

"Well, get him up! This is an official hanging, not a drunken alehouse."

The soldier rushed over and carefully lifted Ferret to his feet. The gentleness surprised Ferret, wondering if such a man would grant one last wish to a condemned prisoner.

"Could I confer with that woman down below?" Ferret whispered, trying to point out the woman with his bound hands. "There must be something I can do to make it worth your while."

The soldier grinned. "Not possible. But when you get to where you're going, I'm sure there'll be plenty of women to chatter your ear right off."

The executioner walked next to Ferret and looped the noose loosely around Ferret's neck.

Mountjoy breathed in deeply, pushed away a few strands of hair from his forehead and tidied up his uniform. He inched over to the scaffold's edge and began to address the gathering crowd. "Hear ye, hear ye! Charges against the prisoner will be read forthwith." He stepped aside to allow his superior officer to read the formal charges.

General Williams walked to the scaffold's edge, glancing back at Mountjoy. Williams was a recent arrival from London, sent to investigate reports of rampant smuggling activities. He was eager to impress the other officers. Despite a smallpox-scarred face, he appeared healthy. He rearranged his white wig and carefully broke open the wax seal on a roll of parchment. He waited for the colonists to quiet down.

"I once hanged a twelve-year-old pickpocket," Williams said in a low tone, attempting to amuse Mountjoy. "Hanging the bloody ragamuffin did wonder for the township. It made everyone think twice before pinching an apple."

Mountjoy nodded respectfully. "I'm sure everyone will enjoy the hanging, General."

"Of course they will." Williams faced the crowd, lifted up the document and began to read. "His Majesty, King George II, hereby grants the authority to local magistrates of the Commonwealth of Virginia to render a decision concerning charges of treason against one Sean O'Neill, also known as Ferret."

"Ferret?" the crowd roared.

The clamor halted Williams's reading. He watched the crowd with bewilderment.

"Ferret's been dead for years," a Dutchman cried out. "Murdered by Injuns. Whole township burned by savages."

"Nay, nay!" the old woman shouted. "All lies to cover the truth. King Ferret fought redcoats, not Indians."

Williams turned to Mountjoy, appearing somewhat confused and

12

shaken. "I had expected an enthusiastic crowd of loyal subjects of the King. This is quite insufferable. What is going on here?"

"Well... ahh..." Mountjoy stuttered with quick breaths. "That trial... Well, you see, we felt obligated to hold it in secret. Nobody was to know. We felt it was critical to do it that way. We could not let the populace know beforehand that this Ferret miscreant was still alive. Besides, almost nobody should have known about the hanging."

"Then you should not have announced it!"

"Sir! We had to post a few notices. English law and all that," Mountjoy said apologetically. "We dare not infringe on the King's laws. The risk is too great. The commonfolk bicker about everything we do here, and they have the power, or should I say the black powder, to do something about it. Still, I was ordered to make an example of someone in Virginia."

Williams frowned. "Why didn't you hang a local man?"

"Sir!" Mountjoy nervously rubbed his clean-shaven face. "Mayhap you do not fully comprehend the situation here. We're no longer in the Old World. We cannot antagonize local Virginians. To do so would risk open rebellion. 'Tis a regular hornets' nest." Mountjoy paused, looked over his shoulder and softened his voice. "Do you realize that there have been three uprisings since Bacon's rebellion? They've attempted to boot out the Royal Governor more times than I can count."

Mountjoy wiped his forehead as the crowd pressed closer to the scaffold. The colonists were quickly shoved back by a marching row of redcoats who forcibly displayed their steely bayonets. This only provoked a greater chorus of mocking jeers.

"You must understand," Mountjoy rang out, "a scraggly rabble of colonists burned Jamestown to the ground over some silly argument. I chose Ferret because he had recently been captured. I thought he was unknown in these parts. I was apparently mistaken."

Williams took a quick glance at the ugly crowd, then turned back to Mountjoy. "My report will not be complimentary."

"With all due respect, Sir. Who cares about your bloody report? We might not leave here alive. Every colonist is armed and a dead shot."

"My God, they're still loyal Englishmen! Right?"

"They are wild men of the forest. Little better than feral bastards. They owe no allegiance to anybody."

"Nonetheless," Williams said, "I will still proceed whether they listen or not." He stomped his foot to get the crowd's attention. When the loud chitter-chatter of the crowd subsided, he lifted up his official paper and spoke with a strained, nervous voice. "The court, in the year of Our Lord 1748, has rendered a verdict in accordance with the laws of England and Virginia's House of Burgesses. The charge is treason against the authority of the Crown and Parliament. The verdict is 'guilty as charged.'" He looked up from his document and glared. "Punishment will be carried out immediately. To be hanged by the neck 'til dead!"

Ferret bowed slightly and smiled. The crowd cheered for the prisoner's disregard for authority.

The crowd's reaction continued to perplex Williams. His mouth flopped open as he stepped back a few inches. His eyes glanced around warily, as though he was preparing an emergency plan to make a discreet retreat. Before he could act upon his jitters, he noticed that the crowd's attention had refocused on an old, one-armed man trudging to the gallows stairway. Williams was amazed to see the colonists suddenly turned silent and solemn.

Several British officers quickly saluted the thin and frail man as he prepared to climb the stairs. He wore a tattered white wig and an outdated officer's uniform crowded with medals of honor. He trembled as he climbed the steps. With a hoarse voice, he shouted, "Hang the cur and be done with it." His words were ignored by the crowd, but the old man continued to curse the prisoner. Reaching the platform, he hobbled up to Ferret and joyfully poked his cane at the prisoner's belly.

"You old skull," Ferret huffed. "Worms ought to be burrowing through your head." He was unimpressed that Cromwell had lived so long. He knew from firsthand experience that evil often outlived good.

"Let the worms starve," the major general whined with a high-pitched shrill. He waved his armless stub in the air. The scar across his face was red from exertion. "I shall enjoy sweet vengeance at long last."

"Sorry to disappoint you," Ferret chortled. "The world's a hollow wilderness, and I stand here deprived of my anonymity. I have no desire to live."

"What?" Cromwell lurched back. He clenched his fist tightly and brandished it in the air. "You cannot cheat me of my victory. You'll die and I will be immortalized." Within moments, Cromwell went into a coughing fit and struggled to breathe. Something was blocking his throat. He inched over to the edge of the platform, eyed the gawking colonists, and spat into the crowd. He shuffled away with a joyful look imprinted across his face.

The crowd screamed in indignation.

Cromwell's smile widened.

Ferret shook his head. "You can't vex me. Little matters anymore. 'Tis impossible to get a fart from a dead man."

"Well, I will enjoy your demise nevertheless." He rubbed his neck and looked up to the heavens. "Oh Lord, castigate this man for his hideous crimes."

"Crimes?" Ferret snarled. "'Tis the likes of you who take delight in watching flowers wilt and children die."

Enraged, the old general knocked the wooden tip off his cane, exposing a long spike. He swiftly jabbed Ferret in the thigh. The crowd roared and surged up against the scaffold like a wave. Dozens of red-coated soldiers forced them back.

"This be British justice?" a Scottish colonist screamed.

Mountjoy marched up to Cromwell, grabbed him around the waist and pulled him away. "Sir," the major whispered in Cromwell's ear, "you may jab him all you like after he is properly hanged. But not sooner. We must follow the rules."

Cromwell feigned remorse. "Aye, we mustn't forget the cursed rules!"

"So, this is a proper hanging?" Ferret moaned as he cringed in pain. The blood streamed down his leg and splattered on the floor boarding.

Williams squinted at the old, testy general and then turned to Mountjoy. "Who is this man? I was under the impression that I was in charge of this execution. I demand to know what he is doing here!"

"Becalm yourself," Mountjoy said. "That's Major-General Cromwell.

He commanded the military forces below the Carolinas. His gallantry led to the defeat of the Yamasee uprising thirty years ago."

"Then he has no business here."

"Sir!" Cromwell gasped. "I was an exemplary commander and a decorated war hero. I would be careful as to what I say in public."

From the corner of his eye, Williams glimpsed a figure hovering next to his prisoner. Turning around, he saw one of his soldiers attempting to bandage Ferret's wound.

"Are you daft? We don't bandage the dead!" Williams immediately kicked the soldier out of the way. "This is not the land of hang-dog louts."

William's patience had reached its limit. With narrowing eyes and tightening lips, he rushed over to the edge of the platform, faced the crowd, and glared down at them. "I may have the devil to pay, but I will proceed with this hanging forthwith." He cleared his throat and boomed in a commanding voice. "If anyone else interferes with this lawful execution, the offender will spend a fortnight in the stockades on water and roaches. Have I made myself clear?" He turned and eyed the executioner, nodding his head to signal him to press on with the hanging.

Acknowledging the approval, the executioner walked behind Ferret, unfolded a black hood and prepared to slip it over the prisoner's head. At that moment the crowd turned unruly. They heckled and howled with loud catcalls. Some hissed shouts of "shame" and "pox on your soul!" Others began to throw spoiled fruit and rocks.

Suddenly, a shiny object landed at the prisoner's feet. Ferret glanced down. It was a dagger. He cast a brief glance all around him, realizing that a conspiracy was afoot. Could be a dirty hoax. Surely someone was planning to shoot him if he tried to escape. Old trick. But that made no sense. He'd be stone dead either way.

Ferret knew he had to act fast. The best opportunities were always short-lived. He would have to worry about the puzzling mystery later. He broke the rope around his wrists and ducked from under the noose. Next, he lunged at the executioner, knocking him off the scaffold, and scooped up the dagger. He wielded it in a defense posture, aiming the blade at the startled soldiers.

Williams motioned to the guards to capture Ferret, but he was too late. Dagger in hand, Ferret jumped Mountjoy and clamped him in an arm-lock. He swung Mountjoy around before the soldiers could fire, tickling the major's throat with the blade's keen edge.

"Easy now!" Ferret said with a lift of his brow. "I've got a reputable hostage. I would hate to see him become damaged goods."

The stunned soldiers stood frozen in silence, not moving a muscle.

"Stand down!" Ferret barked.

The redcoats slowly lowered their flintlocks.

"Now be so kind as to pull back," Ferret said with a newly invigorated voice. "Or so help me God, I'll carve him up like a turnip."

"'Tis another conspiracy brewing. My God, don't let him escape, again. Not again!" With a sniff of defeat, the general hobbled to the stairway, stopped, turned, and glared at his longtime nemesis; finally, he retreated from the scaffold.

"Look here, my good fellow," Williams said without thinking. "You must surrender."

"Why?"

"Well. 'Tis the King's law. And the King…"

"The King! I was once a powerful king," Ferret uttered with a sad smile. "A fancy, fat-headed king to be sure." He slowly shook his head. "Was not too proud of it. Never wanted any of it." He bit his lower lip and gazed at the tarnished knife. It was no ordinary dagger. It resembled the one he had found as a child before the battle of Macroom, just hours before his father was captured by Cromwell's henchmen. He tried to block the memories, but they came flooding in without mercy—the dying villagers, the blazing fire, the never-ending bloodshed. He had lost his world, bereft of everything but a river of tears. He thought he had buried them for good. Now it looked as if he would have to relive them once again.

Chapter 2

The scrawny, painfully thin boy recoiled in agony. Something in the dirt had slashed his hand. He had been grubbing in the ground for something to eat and had not been paying attention. Can't get much stupider than that, he thought. Just plain thick-headed. He figured that he must have knocked heads with a sassy rock, the kind that talks back with a sharp-edged tongue. He rubbed his injured hand and sat in pain, seesawing back and forth. The day had not gone well. A storm was brewing on the horizon and he still had to scout for his father.

He hated rocks. These cursed buggers blotted the land like the prickly blackberry bushes. The rocks were everywhere, and it seemed to him that they were good for nothing, unless the heedless wanted to get bloodied and bruised with every unlucky encounter. He had once overheard an English officer bellyaching about *Eire*. "Ireland is nothing more than a quarry with a spattering of moss and grass between layers of hard rock," the man had said. No truer words were ever spoken by an Englishman.

Cradling his hand, the boy began to realize that the deep gash was far too thin, deep, and long for a mere scrape from a rock. He leaned back, lifted up his hand and began to suck on the wound. This gave him comfort. He wondered if he had found a better food source. Then the thought hit him: could he satisfy his hunger by feasting on his own blood? He would never need food again! But the notion was too perfect. He knew that nobody ever got something for nothing. And besides, there was this little problem of cannibalism. Eating human flesh was wrong, even if it might keep a person alive.

He stopped sucking and tried to stanch the flow of blood. Wiping the bloody hand on his long and bulky goat-hair cloak, the auburn-haired boy turned and retraced the area where he had been injured. He reached out and searched for the half-buried object. Within moments he found the culprit. At first, he wanted to inflict revenge, pound it with his fist, punish the thing that had given him so much discomfort. But that could hurt him more. Instead, he fingered the dirty object and soon concluded that it was not a rock. It was something else, something foreign. What was it? This was a head-scratching puzzle.

With his uninjured hand, he dug deeper into the thin soil, but the thing refused to budge. He kicked it a dozen times until his feet throbbed. There had to be a better way. He could smash the object with a rock, but that might damage it. God knew how many things he had demolished in a fit of rage. He decided that to act smart meant doing things that led to less work and pain. That seemed so obvious. But not everyone took kindly to such a notion.

Again he looked around, inventorying what was at hand. He found a fairly strong stick and jammed it beside the object. If Archimedes could move the earth with a lever, he could find something to break free something stuck in the ground. He pushed against the object. It loosened slightly. Finally, with a sudden snap, it broke free. The boy quickly crawled over and pulled out a long, thin, metal blade. He had unearthed a real treasure, an ancient dagger caked with loam. It was no ordinary belly slasher. This was a weapon fit for a king.

With a sense of triumph, the boy lifted the blade high overhead, slashing the air as if he were in the thick of battle. Good weapons were scarce in *Eire*. He remembered a time when his father's men charged into battle, wild-eyed, bellowing with indignation, armed with only clubs and stones. It had been a daring attack, but most of the men fell in the heat of battle. Somehow his father had cheated death. Some called it a miracle. He called it the Lord's promise to return *Eire* back to its people.

The weapon excited the boy. It fed a desire to kill all outlanders, to slaughter all Englishmen wherever they could be found. Although he had been taught that killing was wrong, he knew good people did it—some even bragged about their murderous handiwork with glee.

He began rubbing and picking the dirt off the dagger. It had Celtic symbols on it. After applying an ample amount of spit, he discovered a carved animal head on the hilt. At first sight, it resembled a squirrel, but the snout was too long. After a deeper cleaning, he was sure the symbol had the distinct features of a ferret—the noble pet of kings, poets, and scholars.

A chill overcame the boy. He sat up on his knees and crawled under the tangled branches of a large oak tree. There was something in the air, something amiss. He had an uneasy feeling that he was being watched. He wrapped his cloak tighter and rearranged the rags around his feet. He glanced at the valley below and for a moment thought he heard the rumble of English pigskins in the distance. With a tight grip around a branch, he leaned over a steep cliff's edge to get a better view of the wide valley below. He saw nothing of interest—just the lazy river meandering through a scraggly forest and the fast-moving clouds above. It was peaceful. Not like Macroom had been the night before.

He trained his eyes on the river again. It was shallow in most spots, black, murky, and stagnant. Most commonfolk considered it evil, possessed by a demonic force lurking in the shadows. The villagers had placed stepping stones across the river's entire span, allowing them to cross without touching the dark water. But Britons were indifferent to the danger. They would march through the inky water and come out alive and unaffected. That was how he first knew they were the defiant legions of the Unholy One.

He had taken a fancy to Macroom, a small village of thatch-roofed cottages ringed with rock walls. Stones tied to the thatch kept the hovels from blowing away in windstorms. But it seemed to him that what kept the village together were the wild and rambling stems of the blackberry. They wove and intertwined throughout everything, entangling the commonfolks with one another. It had been this way since before the reign of Christianity, at least that was the lore recited by wayfaring bards and village elders.

The trees did their part too. The grove of white oaks surrounded the village as if they were standing guard against all enemies. The oaks were essential to move from one cottage to another. With branches burrowing into the damp earth, they made excellent pathways, despite their haunting and twisting images which resembled his grandmother's rheumatic fingers. Since winter months were muddy months, getting around was limited. But anyone with a strong grip could leap across the trees' branches and bare roots or swing from branch to branch to avoid ankle-deep mud. The woodland chambers high in the treetops shielded nimble children from angry parents and early bedtimes. For the whole village, the oaks were barriers to the bitter north wind, preventing ice from bonding to walls and roofs.

A recent arrival to the village, the boy found Macroom a refuge. His stay there was to be temporary, safe from the treacherous streets of Cork. At least, that was what everybody thought. He could see now that this was a big mistake. As it turned out, he had not fled far enough into the hinterland. Trouble had followed him like stink follows dead fish.

The boy lowered the dagger and blankly stared toward the sky. It was not his fault when bad luck came knocking. He had been off frogging that afternoon. He had just caught a big croaker when the river suddenly exploded into bright flames. He stood there on the shoreline perplexed, wondering how water could suddenly catch fire. He reckoned it was witchcraft, at first. But he had to fight such silly notions. He knew that superstitions were tricky things that were usually rooted in folklore, gossip, and ignorance.

As the flames grew stronger, he found himself weakening, unable to move, fearful that Judgment Day had finally arrived and that the fires of Hell had burst through the surface and were about to engulf the countryside. There must be a reason for this. He backed away from the river and fell. Before he could get up, he turned his face and discovered that the Netherworld hadn't arrived, at least not yet. The water was not burning. There was nothing unearthly or hellish. It was the work of mortals—Cromwell.

The boy sighed softly and closed his eyes. The misty wind sprayed his face. He knew what to expect. The cold blast was hurling a North Atlantic storm his way, a tempest to be sure. It would be invigorating. Nothing like watching black thunderheads with white crests race above the highlands with thunder echoing in the distance. He took a deep breath. The rain was so fresh, sweet, and clean—far better than the smell of burnt flesh. If only he could forget the past and pretend that goodness still inhabited the earth.

But that was not how it happened. He remembered screaming at the top of his voice and then running toward the village. He leaped over a hedgerow, sprinted past a herd of sheep, and scrambled under a thicket of blackberries, trying to ignore the stinging cuts. When he had reached the edge of the village, he stopped, afraid to witness the calamity. He had known what to expect. They all did. The villagers had talked incessantly about what would happen if they got caught. They said they did not care. One elder, a blacksmith with a fondness for weapons, scoffed about the danger, opining that they could defend themselves against anything. That seemed pretty cocky. Sean had a feeling that the English subscribed to a different opinion.

After he saw the flames engulfing the village, he got down on his belly and slithered next to a small hut loosely chinked with peat. He continued and soon came to a rock wall, shimmied up, and peeked over. It was the worst of nightmares. Tears rolled down his cheeks. The screaming of the villagers made him shiver. The village courtyard was awash in a sea of red. Bodies littered the ground. The British foot soldiers were stabbing them with their bayonets, making sure they were dead. Others found amusement in disemboweling the fallen.

He remembered seeing the burning church. The front oak doors had been barred by poles and ox-carts. Soldiers were throwing torches onto the church's roof. Smoldering hands, black and blistered, wildly flailed out of small windows. In desperation, a mother pushed her baby through one window as the smoke thickened. The child fell headfirst onto a flagstone walkway, screaming. Several soldiers ignored its cries and walked away.

The soldiers.

He had watched them laugh and joke with the air of arrogant noblemen. One soldier with a large swagger and a pronounced stutter downed a bottle of whiskey. Others shot blindly into the sky. Those who hadn't gotten their fair share of merriment set more cottages on fire. One tall soldier, part of the Dutch Guards, wore a cheeky smile of a conqueror as if he had the power to do anything he liked to the helpless. Two drunken men slung their flintlocks over their shoulders and danced a jig like fairies, carrying on as if they were at a solstice bonfire to celebrate the returning sun. Sickening was too mild a word.

What had bothered him the most were the villagers' wails and screams. He could not get that tormenting sound out of his head. Their piercing shrills had grown more frantic, more intense, more blood-chilling. He wanted to help them, but he had no weapon or plan of action. He was useless. He should have done something. He had warned the villagers of what might occur. They had ignored him, treating him like a halfwit urchin. What they were doing was reckless and illegal. They knew it. Most Catholic masses had been forbidden since the English invasion. Nobody ever listened.

The boy folded his left arm across his chest and shook his head. He must forget it all, the past was the past; nobody can bring back the dead. He pulled away from the ledge. There was nothing to see below. He had hoped to watch in glee as the English army fled in hot retreat. He knew his father's army wanted to avenge Macroom and punish Cromwell. It was just a matter of time before his people would collar the blackguard, and put him under the sword. That would be justice.

But Cromwell always seemed to be beyond the reach of justice. His name had sparked fear and hatred among Irish hearts for generations. Winston Cromwell was more than just another Englishman sent over to destroy the Irish. Ordinary Englishmen had done that for centuries. This one was different. Winston Cromwell was said to be a grandson of the late Lord Oliver Cromwell—the man who had beheaded King Charles I, invaded *Eire*, and slaughtered half of its population. The young upstart had all the marks of another tyrant with a black heart. Many feared that he was trying to live up to his family reputation.

A grand reputation was Cromwell's inheritance, and he guarded it with jealousy that bordered on obsession. Within months of his posting in Cork, he campaigned to wipe out the last remaining rebels in his territorial dominion. After that, he had plans to uproot the few remaining Irish farmers and replace them with English and Scottish settlers. He was stealing everything he could lay his grubby hands on. At his bequest, harsher laws were enacted, forbidding any common folk with a drop of Irish blood from owning land, cattle, horses—anything of value. The

Irish had become outcasts in their own country. Thousands of Irishmen had already fled overseas. There was little reason to remain behind.

Though he was young in years, Sean had never known peace. He couldn't imagine a time when he might. Pushing his shoulder-length hair out of his eyes, Sean glanced at the threatening clouds and admired the dagger. A faint rustle of grass stirred behind him. A hand grasped his shoulder. The boy quickly twisted around. It was his brother, Brian.

"Let me go!" the boy pleaded. "Leave me be. I'm scouting for father. *Fag an ait!*"

Brian grinned. "Sean, ya're just moonshining. Ya always do. Dream of this, dream of that. That's all ya ever do, ya weasel! Dream and pass water. Ya're useless!"

"I hope you get Jolly Rant and die! You puckfist!" Sean yelled.

Brian dropped to his knees. "Ya'll die first, brother. I saw it in me dreams."

Brian was always teasing Sean. Like most Irishmen, he was a prophet of doom and gloom, a dispirited soul. Nothing was ever right. He could not decipher subtle differences. He saw everything as black and white, dead or alive; there were no shades of gray. But Sean knew that was not the real world. His old schoolmaster Aristot had taught him that.

"Have you sighted any Britons?" Brian asked with a smirk.

Sean frowned at his brother and crossed his arms. He was spying for his father, and not for his oafish brother. It galled Sean that anyone would question his loyalty. But that was Brian's crude way. You were either with him or against him, and if you were with him, you were still a target of his abuse. It was better to be his enemy just to get better treatment.

"No," Sean said. "But the approaching storm stirs like a—"

"Ya got words up yar arse-gut," Brian said.

"You're just jealous."

Brian grinned again. "Ya're right, ya little oxhead. Now stay awake!" Then he leaned over the ledge and looked himself.

"You don't believe me?"

"I trust not the oak nor the man who beheads it."

Sean shook his head. If only he were older and bigger. Everyone said he was puny for his age, but that was foolish thinking because nobody kept records of birthing dates. Father had figured his age at eleven or twelve years, but he also said that was just a wild guess.

"Looks quiet," Brian mumbled. Then he caught sight of the dagger. He reached over and grabbed the knife. "What be this?"

"An ancient dagger," Sean said excitedly. "See the markings on the hilt? It must be from Ui Neill dynasty, or older. It could have been iron-forged at Tara—a royal blade of the High Kings!"

Brian shrugged. "Who cares whence it came? 'Tis a weapon! Where did ya steal it?"

"I found it over thither. 'Tis mine!"

"A little tyke has no use for a belly slasher." Brian tested the dagger's dull point.

"'Tis not yours!"

"Needs a bit of grinding. Otherwise, it be in decent shape."

Sean reached up for his dagger. Brian blocked his advance, knocking his brother to the dirt, face first. Sean slowly sat up and rubbed his head; his lips were caked with mud while blood rushed down his chin.

"Listen, ya little weasel." Brian snarled, loosely pointing the blade at Sean. "I'm larger and the elder. I claim ownership. When ya reach the strength of manhood, ya'll learn what it takes. Like all men of standing, we take what we want. The bloody Brits do. Why not me? The strong will inherit the world; the meek hast no need of it. Ya might learn that someday—the hard way." With that, Brian strutted away.

"Thief! Prigger! I hope you get Jolly Rant and die." Plopping down near the mountain's ledge, Sean sulked, crossed his arms, and gave out an exasperating sigh. Nothing ever turned out as it should. The world was a hell-bound bog of misery. If only he had no brother.

Sean scooped up a handful of rocks and looked for an easy target. Finding none, he simply threw them over the cliff. By happenstance, he peered down into the valley, trying to forget what his brother had done. As his face sagged deeper into despair, he suddenly caught sight of something out of the corner of his eye. Something was moving down below. He leaped up, stood still, and shaded his eyes to get a better view. There they were. A whole column of redcoats had just entered a clearing. Nearly twenty soldiers were marching in an irregular formation, while a few stragglers rambled about as if they were in deep slumber. The more lively ones carried flintlocks; most wore outdated and rusted gorget breastplates. Their breeches were bare-brown leather and their waistcoats faded to a dull burgundy. To Sean's way of thinking, the soldiers behaved more like a beaten army than troopers on the hunt.

After meandering into an open meadow, the parade of disheveled redcoats came to a halt. A heavyset man in an officer's uniform found a fallen tree, took his time to circle it and finally located a flat spot to sit down with the clumsy grace of an unwieldy cow. He reached into his pocket and pulled out a silver timepiece. He snapped his finger to signal the drummers to perform a drum roll. All that did was scare a flock of birds. The fat man rubbed his neck, looked around, and took another glance at his watch as if he was waiting for someone. The oddness of the scene left Sean both baffled and worried.

After several minutes of loud drum beating, the fat man motioned for the drummers to cease. He attempted to stand up but failed, collapsing back onto the log. He whistled for assistance. Two regimental soldiers rushed up and with great effort pulled the officer off the log. After catching his breath, the officer moved to the head of the line and barked out a series of orders. He folded his hands behind his back, and with his men strolled across the river and finally disappeared into the dark forest.

Sean scratched his head in disbelief. The soldiers were going in the wrong direction. They had no chance of victory. Parading halfwits with banging drums were no match for the cunning of his father, Black Fox.

With the threat removed, Sean resumed his daydreaming. His attention focused to the fierce North Atlantic winds that had begun to rake the land. Sniffing the winter air, he felt at ease. This was his kind of weather, his domain. He imagined himself general of the tempest, commanding the element. With one wave of his finger, he conjured an army of lightning, thunder, and hail. With victory assured, he would tally the toll, calculate the destruction, and order the wounded to shelter.

Suddenly, a bright flash lit up the sky; a loud boom followed. It was gunfire, not thunder. It had come from Black Fox's encampment on the hilltop above.

He leaped up and started to run. Ascending farther up the mountain,

Sean struggled through the dense forest, plowing through thorn bushes that blocked his path. As he drew closer to camp, a salvo of gunfire boomed louder and the gun smoke grew thick. Racing faster, he stumbled, fell, and slammed into a fallen oak tree. He looked up to see a clearing alive with hundreds of English soldiers and a few surviving villagers from Macroom.

He rubbed his eyes in horror. It was happening all over again.

Chapter 3

Out of breath and panting, Sergeant-Major Stuffleton lumbered ahead of his small force of twenty armed men. His uniform was tight and ill-fitting. Suddenly, he stopped and took in a great gulp of air, almost doubling over. In desperation, he lunged for a nearby tree branch and hugged it until he could regain his balance. The men stopped and watched with amusement.

After a series of violent coughing fits, Stuffleton regained some strength and walked off in search of a flat and dry resting spot, somewhere that he wouldn't be poked, jabbed, or muddied. He thought he had found one near the riverbank, overlooking the stagnant water—a polished, bowl-shaped boulder. Pulling out a white handkerchief, he carefully brushed the dirt and leaves aside and fingered its smooth surface. That was not enough to suit his fancy. With the refinement of a high-society gent, the officer gently laid the lace-edged cloth on the rock, turned, and sat with a sense of relief and grandeur.

Before Stuffleton could engage in another struggle with gravity, his small detachment of regulars drifted away and gossiped. They milled around aimlessly, looking painfully disinterested in being there.

One thin-bearded soldier elbowed his sidekick. "I dare say, old lard-bottom seems to have dragged us on another one of his wild goose chases."

"Quite possibly." Another soldier nodded. "But that's better than finding the goose."

"I wager lard-bottom wouldn't know a goose if it bit him on the buttocks." A third soldier scoffed. "If he did, we would be advancing instead of retreating away from the rebel stronghold."

"That's fine with me," the first soldier said. "I have no desire to tangle with one of those Irish devils."

Too distant to hear his men's chatter, Stuffleton wiped sweat from his forehead with his long sleeve. He fished out a slice of pastry hidden in his coat pocket. He wolfed it down and grumbled to himself that he was not going to move another inch, no matter what Cromwell wanted him to do. He nervously tried to unbutton his stained white collar, but it had worn off long ago. He glanced at his men, then at the hillside above.

Suddenly, one of his men shouted something about hearing distant gunfire.

"No, you didn't!" Stuffleton said. "I didn't hear a blasted peep." He repositioned his body to find a more comfortable seat on the rock.

"I heard it too, sir," another soldier said.

"Don't be daffy," Stuffleton huffed. "Nothing's out there. If you hear rumbling, 'tis just God's thunder clappin' the sky."

"There it is again," several men agreed in unison.

One of the sweaty-faced soldiers approached Stuffleton. He wore a worried look and tilted his head as if he could sense danger ahead. "We ought to go back. I think that would be most prudent, sir."

"I'm not moving one bloody muscle," Stuffleton said. "We don't have time to chase after ill-boding ghosts or things that don't concern us."

* * *

From the hillside above, Black Fox and most of his men watched Stuffleton's column with keen interest. He moved behind a rocky outcrop and squinted at the enemy. He bit his lower lip and tapped his fingers on his right leg. He was not sure of the significance of the rudderless antics of the redcoats in the valley. There had to be more of them. Accidents didn't just happen this way. Someone wanted him to be distracted by the soldiers' erratic behavior. That bothered him. There must be an overall purpose. But what was it?

Before Black Fox could gather his thoughts, his second-in-command, Ligan O'Connor, a bulky man whose face was surrounded by a jutting beard and shoulder-length hair, confronted him. "*Beagan luais, siul beags!*" O'Connor shouted. He shook his fist in the air. Clad in a cumbersome black cloak, he wore a pot-iron helmet similar to those of Imperial Rome, but without the plume. Hogbacked and stiff moving, he always found something to complain about. The men called him *seanbhean*—old woman.

"How many times must I repeat myself? Speak the King's English. How can we defeat our foes if we don't know their language and culture?"

"I don't want to!" O'Connor growled.

Black Fox draped his right hand across the shoulder of his old friend and took him aside. "Listen to me with both ears. We must know what we fight."

"I do. They have throats to slit. All the knowing I need."

"Aye. That's the general rule of thumb. But we need a precise strategy to do just that."

"You must listen, me Black Foxy. An attack is nigh. Feel it in my gut. Cromwell roots around like pig for truffles. Something wrong."

"Perhaps," Black Fox began to rub his neck, "but why would they send old lard-bottom after me? He can barely buckle his belt. Most of his men are probably miles away shooting game for food. But, come to think of it, that alone is suspicious. Stuffleton's best marksmen couldn't hit a caged animal with a saker cannon."

"Don't treat me like a lubber. You know something sinks wrong."

Black Fox sighed. "Aye. The proof is in the pudding." He motioned for one of his warriors, MacFhinn, a man of few words and loyal deeds. "Check our encampment and fetch back a report with haste. I fear treachery."

MacFhinn bowed with the weight of years and respect. He hurried off to the rebels' makeshift camp which recently overflowed with refugees from Macroom.

Black Fox returned his attention to the fat Englishman below, who remained seated on a boulder, staring downstream, oblivious to the world of hurt around him. Black Fox squinted with a small furrow in his brows. The Englishman was as big as a full moon but appeared to him as only a blurry red figure. Black Fox's eyesight had worsened in the last few years. He felt he had a duty to conceal that fact from his men. He could not show any weaknesses. Leaders could not afford defective traits in times of war. If only he could obtain one of those fancy refracting spyglasses. Pity. The English had so many useful devices; even their language was more precise and efficient than cumbersome Gaelic. This would not matter if the English would just mind their own business and take care of their own. Why did they have such a craving to humble their neighbors?

Chewing an oat stalk, Black Fox leaned against a tree stump at the cliff's edge and tried to relax. He chewed gingerly; he could barely eat without losing a shard of tooth. He collected every bit of fallen tooth just in case the tooth-drawers might find a way to put them back into place. He shook his head. He was such an old, poor stupe; he knew that what came out never could be put back in.

He poked a finger through a hole in his threadbare English breeches. He thought about how he enjoyed English apparel—the strong leather jack-boots and the breeches with button-down waistcoats. His men despised such clothing, especially feathered hats. To dress in English fashion had once been a sign of wealth and good taste in Ireland. Those days were long gone. Now, the Irish in the backcountry distrusted all men of foreign dress and decorum.

Black Fox tried to avoid thinking about the war and how things had deteriorated. Supplies were nonexistent, his men were exhausted, his cause was hopeless, and his position as leader was never secure. His men had nothing left to fight with. They had withered to bare bones and had submerged so low into despair that they resembled an injured plow horse too weak to make it back to the stable at night.

Suddenly, there was a bright flash and a loud boom—cannon fire. Black Fox's men gathered around him. They bickered among themselves. Black Fox knew they wanted to attack without forethought, plans, or common sense. He resisted that temptation. He knew something was amiss; that he was being played. That took no great brain power. He only wished his men had some.

Kerry McGuff, a large intimidating man with a grotesquely hooked nose and dark eyes, confronted Black Fox. Speaking in rapid-fire, he demanded that Black Fox launch an immediate attack or resign his authority. "Me fearless Lord." McGuff's eyes popped out. "'Tis time to do what must be done! *Amas m gan choinne?*"

"Nay!" Black Fox said. He stared at McGuff. "I will not make any move until I know where to set down my chess pieces."

McGuff's eyes widened. "My *túath* will disown you!"

"I need more time."

McGuff's narrow lips displayed a scowl with no intentions of yielding ground. Considered hot-blooded and quick to anger, he never trudged about without carrying a stone battle-axe in one hand and a claymore in the other. When irritated, his eyes would bulge and his fire-scarred neck would twitch, giving him the appearance of a wicked dwarf. He commanded the largest of the tribal clans, and his disheveled men were pledged to follow his orders alone. Black Fox could ill afford to antagonize him. Unfortunately, his military tactics, like his weapons, were woefully out of date.

McGuff stepped closer, almost touching the tip of Black Fox's nose. They locked eyes and exchanged glares.

"I must warn you. I'm not backing down," Black Fox said. "You'll get a chance to avenge Macroom. But I prefer to stalk silently and attack unannounced. 'Tis more gratifying."

"Not for me clan."

Black Fox rolled his eyes and let out an annoyed groan before running his fingers through his graying hair. "So that's it. We fight until we all die?"

"Better to die than to be shamed."

Black Fox shook his head. Before the war, he had been considered not only the best warrior in Ireland but a man born to noble heritage. Some claimed he had the bluest of blood; others said he was the last true heir to the Irish throne. He knew it to be mostly true. His bloodline dated back to the High Kings of the O'Neill clan that had once ruled most of Ireland. But nobody in any position of power would acknowledge it.

He touched the heavy silver chain draped around his neck. It held an emerald *Brehon* ring, which supposedly betokened one's true bloodline to the last true over-king of Ireland, bestowed on his clan hundreds of years ago. In this sense, his royal heritage gave him an edge over lesser-known chieftains. Although he was recognized throughout every village in Ireland as the rightful king, few believed he would ever wear a crown. The way the last war had gone, he doubted he would ever be elevated above the rank of court jester.

"Can't you see?" Black Fox asked. "'Tis a ploy. They want us to attack Stuffleton and his small band of misfits. They beg us to attack."

"I see well enough. Do you?"

33

Black Fox looked away.

"I see a warrior fearful of his own shadow, hesitant to attack while murderous Britons wander free in *Eire*! *Criffan*! *Mo chraoibhin!*" McGuff's tone shifted from defiant to frigid. "Some menfolk not crafted of heavy stone."

"I am! Don't you understand? Thy enemy is impatience."

"Impatience is all we have left." McGuff snarled, suddenly breaking out into a humorless laugh. With a jerky movement of his body, he turned, huffed and stomped away.

Black Fox was losing battles on all fronts. He was almost fifty—an old man by any standards. His nights were sleepless, moody, and guilt-ridden. His body was plagued with pain and fatigue. His headaches were becoming more frequent, and the right side of his face was often numb. But his illness was the least of his worries. He had become detached from his men. He felt he had lost their confidence and loyalty. It was a bad omen, especially since he had little faith in their abilities. He had been taught that a leader should be willing to die for his men. He felt like dying, but not for his warriors. He wondered why he was still fighting at all. The war had been lost years ago. Ever since Winston Cromwell's arrival from England, the war had deteriorated into small-scale cattle raids. What was next, stealing chickens from henhouses? Yet he had put too much into the fray to let go. His pride, his honor, and his reputation would not allow him to surrender. Capitulation would make him worthless. Better to be dead. Maybe McGuff was right. Maybe suicide was the best way to part from earth.

McGuff soon returned with a dozen battle-ready men. "Time to decide our fate. If your heart fears bloodletting, I will lead me men to the Lord's greater glory." He paused. "But I ask consent, Lord Cormac O'Neill."

"Only if you can muster a majority vote to bless the attack."

McGuff smiled and raised his sword.

Black Fox knew his demand for a vote was an idle threat. Most of his men wanted to assault the British forces and chew off their limbs and heads. He could not change that, but he did wonder if the British attack on the village had some alternative motive besides killing more Irishmen. Were the British antics leading his men down the primrose path, putting them in an untenable position? That was when the thought struck him—maybe there was a conspiracy afoot. Murdering the villagers and burning the church might have a bigger purpose, part of a well-planned military strategy to flush his men out of hiding. Did not matter now. Good suspicions or not, McGuff and his men could only see the small picture. They wanted to do something simple, something mindless. Take revenge and jump into the fire pit with sword and flintlock in hand, to show that they could act as brutally and savagely as the outsiders. He was afraid they were being led like lambs to the slaughter, and there was nothing he could do.

Black Fox's men erupted into war cries. They were excited over a chance to even the score. Some ran off to prepare for battle. Others performed a short ceremony by praying together in tight huddles and boasting of past victories in battles. A few howled like wolves at a full moon concert.

Wolves!

It was a good word to describe his men, Black Fox thought. They resembled the hairy Norsemen of ages ago, pillaging savages fitted with battle-axes and swords too heavy for most Englishmen to lift. Their hair was greasy and matted, weaving in and out of their flowing beards. Many romped about half-naked and barefoot, looking for any excuse to disrobe at any moment. Sure, they had wool tunics, but they were so loose as to be almost useless. If someone told them to display some modesty, they would growl and roar with an inferno of indignation.

Black Fox glanced down. The worst was the painted faces. His men would smear on gobs of red and orange pigments, getting it all over themselves and others. The ritual was mostly symbolic. They would decorate each other whether a battle was imminent or not. The point was to look fearsome and powerful in the face of the enemy. That was a good laugh! They had almost no modern weapons to scare anyone. Swords and spears were almost useless against long-range flintlocks. That was the sad truth. He had a few men lucky enough to tote flintlocks, but most could barely load them or aim them properly. Usually, they would cram too much powder down the barrel, in hopes of a grand explosion. Like a ruddy bomb, the gun would explode in their faces. He suspected it was British policy to abandon guns in the field so the Irish would misuse and misfire them, thus killing more Irishmen at little danger to themselves.

He recalled an incident when his men had captured a storehouse stocked with hundreds of leather boots. They needed footwear, but nobody wanted them. Sure, they were of poor quality, like most supplies from England, but his men were always complaining about stubbing their toes on the rocky ground. Only one of his warriors, a young orphan from the boglands of Meath, had taken an interest in the boots. It was good to see someone willing to try modern English attire. Within moments, the young lad explained that he had a better use for the boots. He sliced one up, skewered the pieces of leather on sticks and roasted them over a fire like slabs of tough beef.

Suddenly, Black Fox detected a disturbance. He turned around and soon found himself in the midst of commotion. McGuff had taken charge of calling for a vote. He stretched out his arms and demanded the authority to lead the attack. In quick fashion, the chieftains stood, raised their weapons, and grunted a few words about the glories of victory. In total, nine of the ten chieftains had agreed to launch an assault. Only Ligan O'Connor refused to raise his weapon. He explained to the war council that he was abstaining, that he could not in good conscience take sides against Black Fox.

Black Fox sighed and shook his head in despair. Is this what it had all come down to? After years of fighting, his talents were being thrown to the wind. McGuff and ignorance were the only victors. It was just a matter of time before he would be asked officially to resign from his position. That was what it had come down to. So common. Ireland was rife with tribal infighting. The only gift the Brits ever gave to the Irish was to bring them closer together in their hour of anguish. That was a remarkable feat. But he could now see it as a Trojan horse. It only gave the redcoats more targets in which to cut down the Irish in greater numbers.

He sighed and looked at the ground. He recalled one battle leading up to the siege of Derry. The tribal elders disagreed over whether to attack. Almost half of the tribes refused to take part. The battle went ahead as planned. He and his clan just sat down on a grassy hillside and watched the English mow down the Irish forces. His clan had treated the battle like spectators in a bear-baiting ring—simply out to have a good time.

And yet, Black Fox understood the reason to honor tribal traditions. The Irish hated to be told what to do. At every level, a sense of independence was paramount. To the Irish, nationality was not the measure of all things. An Irish overlord could be just as wicked as a British overlord. That's why every chieftain's power was limited. If a chieftain had become unpopular, it was probably due to his incompetent and abusive ways. Nobody wanted to live under that kind of brutal ruler. So clans and tribes often switched their allegiances or formed new ones. They had the right to go with the best to elect their leaders. It had to be that way; they had to be chosen. Otherwise, the only way they could get rid of a mad-dog bully was to drown the bastard in a river of blood.

As Black Fox refocused his attention on the valley below, Ligan O'Connor approached. His face wore the same serious expression as before. *"Cromwell tioranach scafar. Tioranach! Drochbhlath air!"*

"Speak English," Black Fox said, annoyed. "And aye, I know Cromwell is a liar. Tell me something I don't already know, old mate."

O'Connor frowned. "You let McGuff utter our native tongue."

"He is now the bearer of the scepter. But don't worry. I haven't outlived my usefulness. There is surely more to come."

McGuff returned in time to overhear Black Fox's admission to O'Connor. He beamed with a confident smile. "Good to see you know your place. Preparing to join us in battle, my dethroned lord?"

"See here!" O'Connor stepped in front of McGuff. "How dare ya. Foxy be direct heir of high kings. Ya should bow and lave his bare feet."

"As I have been told," McGuff said, "I too have royal blood gushing through my veins."

"Ha!" Ligan chuckled. "Not from a bog-squatting dwarf."

Black Fox stepped between the two men before they could come to blows. "First things first! Let's slaughter the English. After that, we can slay each other in the ignoble name of honor. Right?"

McGuff sheathed his sword and gnashed his teeth with a growl. "I suppose Cromwell would make a better adversary."

O'Connor leaned to one side and glared at McGuff. "We must settle afterwards."

"Good day, gentlemen!" Black Fox walked away, determined to put some distance between the two hotheads. He did not get far.

Still vexed, O'Connor tagged after Black Fox as if he were a lost puppy. "You never listen to me!"

"Sometimes," Black Fox chuckled with a serious undertone, "I think I'm the only one that does. Now, what is it? Speak up—as if I don't know already."

"Ya can't go after Cromwell. He be too strong and God-fearing."

That posture took him by surprise. "Cromwell is no different from any other blackguard," Black Fox said. "I understand Puritans and Englishmen well. They be bloody pretenders, fakes, cloaking their frailties in dogma. They pretend sainthood during the day and toast the devil at night. It takes only a small poke of gold to disrobe their hood of piety."

Other men gathered around Black Fox to listen.

"I have never found a true Puritan," he continued. "'Tis my belief that each man always draws a line betwixt good and evil. But when examined closely, that line is more crooked than a sow's tail. And they do that because a crooked line is more convenient to overstep. Give me a man who says he is honest and I'll show you linen so soiled that no soap can cleanse it. Give me Cromwell's trousers and I'll show you mountains of dung." The men guffawed with delight.

Before he could resume his speech, MacFhinn pushed his way through the crowd, dropped to his knees, and bowed. He was out of breath. Finally, he took in a big gulp of air and spoke with a tone of fear. "Lord, the English besiege us! They have invaded our camp."

At that moment, more gunfire rocked the air. Everyone turned to the sound. Several men unsheathed their swords and prepared to rush toward the sounds of the gunfire. They shouted "Attack!"

"Hold fast!" Black Fox said. "We march as one, in order, on... on McGuff's command."

Everyone crowded around McGuff. He asked for complete silence, sank to his knees and recited a short prayer to assure victory.

Black Fox looked down in reverence, but his thoughts drifted to the poor condition of his men. He studied their weathered faces and stick-thin bodies. They had followed him for almost six years. Back then they had numbered in the thousands; they were young in spirit, swollen with pride, patriotic fervor. They boasted that they would sunder the British Empire in days. Only a handful remained. He felt sick.

* * *

McGuff motioned men forward through stands of dense pine and oak. Sticky vines tore their skins as they struggled to move forward. It took some time to reach the hilltop encampment. As they neared the edge of a clearing, his men fanned out behind rocks and trees. From his angle, Black Fox could see British forces advancing from two fronts against the panic-stricken villagers. There were hundreds of redcoats. Never had he seen so many lobsters in such close quarters. His mind went numb. It was suicide to attack, yet he felt they had a duty to do more than to worry about their own well-being. They had to protect his people, no matter the consequences.

Fires swept across a camp of tents and crude huts. The village men, armed with scythes and two-pronged pitchforks, formed a defensive circle around the women and children. Meanwhile, the soldiers were dragging a man through their front line in full view of the villagers. It was Tralee, the Irish chief from Macroom. An English officer ordered his men to drop the chieftain at his feet. Drawing his pistol from his belt, he took aim at Tralee's head and pulled the trigger. Tralee fell forward, dead.

The villagers roared in outrage. Over two-hundred strong, the village men charged. The soldiers took careful aim and fired a volley, cutting down a third of the men. When the smoke cleared, and to the surprise of the English, the villagers were still coming. Caught off guard, the British worked frantically to reload, pouring gunpowder into their barrels and packing it down with rods. They were too late. The village men crashed into the front line, stabbing, clubbing, and biting the invaders. Overloaded with powder-bags, backpacks, blankets, and food, the British were easy targets for the light-footed Irishmen. The villagers seized the fallen soldiers' flintlocks and pikes and chased the fleeing Britons.

Black Fox could see what the villagers could not: soldiers hiding in the forest on the other side of the clearing. Cromwell had set up a trap with the villagers as bait; he was not interested in farmers, shepherds, women, and children. No, the British hoped to destroy the last remnants of the Irish army.

Taking a closer look at the battlefield, Black Fox noticed several officers on horseback riding to the edge of the clearing. One wore a stunning breastplate, adorned with a golden sash and topped with a lavishly plumed hat. It was a bad omen. High-ranking officers never rode near the battlefield unless victory was completely assured.

A small cavalcade of dragoons galloped to the rescue of the retreating foot soldiers. They slashed with their swords at the villagers. Then a fresh column of foot soldiers charged into the melee and forced the villagers back to their original encirclement.

Suddenly, a shot rang out to Black Fox's right. It was McGuff. More shots followed. McGuff leaped up, howled a battle cry in Gaelic, and brandished his sword. He ran at the enemy; the others followed.

"Fall back! Fall back!" Black Fox shouted. Nobody listened. They no longer had a proper army. The Britons pulled back a short distance, halted, and knelt in a precise two-line formation, their weapons aimed at the Irish horde. McGuff ordered a frontal attack, swooping toward the enemy like a windstorm blowing through the grasslands.

"Fire!" rang out the command, and dozens of Irish soldiers fell. The suicidal onslaught continued. Outmatched and outwitted, the Irish fought gallantly, throwing themselves against the wall of red and the gray steel of their swords.

Four columns of soldiers marched quickly out of the forest into the clearing. Dozens of grenadiers followed, hurling fused bombs overhead. To their left, one hundred pikemen with ten-foot spears ran ahead of a contingent of mounted dragoons.

"'Tis our fate to fail," Black Fox whispered. He was alone, except for Ligan O'Connor.

"Aye," his friend said. *"Nil se ar do rogha fein."*

"Was the choice ever ours?" Black Fox shrugged. "Was it?" He turned away and unsheathed his sword. "You see, our lives belong to the watchman of death. Or is it the other way around? I could never get it right."

Ligan gave a weak smile, tipped his bowl-shaped helmet, and charged into battle.

The English had almost encircled the Irish. Black Fox soon broke through the British line. He felt it was his duty to turn the tide of battle, except that it was hopeless, but everyone had their unrealistic dreams. That was what made men do the impossible.

Killing two Englishmen with quick swordplay, he fought his way to the battle's center. He tripped over McGuff's body. He felt no sorrow. Nothing mattered much now; he had outlived his own era.

Jumping atop a large tree stump, Black Fox retook command. The battle had degenerated into a tight circle. Its diameter dwindled every second. Lowering his sword, Black Fox attempted to swallow but could not. He felt like his throat had been already cut.

Chapter 4

Major-General Cromwell leaned over his saddle to get a better look. He murmured over and over again, "There's no escape this time. Absolutely no escape." He savored his words. This time he had proven himself to be a man of undoubted courage and determination. Accolades would grace his victory.

With a self-confident smile, he began to relax. He looked down at his uniform and flicked a bit of lint from his brass breastplate. Next, he stroked the plume of his hat, although he hated the fuzzy softness of feathers. They would shed all over his uniform as if he were some abandoned statue, appreciated only by pigeons. Still, the problem with the feathers was minor compared to his whole uniform, which was coming apart at the seams. All the army-issued clothing in Ireland reeked of shabbiness.

"Sir," a pale-faced officer said, "the battle bodes well."

Cromwell did not reply. No response was required. The battle had been won before he had engaged the enemy. Victory was no stranger to him.

The officer pleaded for him to reply. "Does it not, sir?"

Cromwell nodded. He began tapping his fingers on his breastplate. The metallic ring made him feel invincible. Imperial Roman generals wore similar breastplates, including the great Julius Caesar who wore his magnificent armor when he paraded the streets of Rome after defeating the Gauls.

Tightening his grip on the reins, Cromwell kicked his horse and galloped within thirty yards of the battle. There he stopped and surveyed the last remaining hotbed of fighting. His soldiers had surrounded the Irish rabble and were preventing any possible escape. Cromwell watched a wounded Irishman, armed with a flintlock, break through the encirclement. For a brief moment, he felt a touch of sympathy, knowing full well that it was futile for the Irish to continue. But there would be no escape. His forces reinforced the breech and pushed the man back like a crashing wave on a steep, rocky beach.

Cromwell was a tall man. His breeches were as tight as his morality was rigid. He was already Major-General of Cork. He was young for his high position; he was slightly past the age of twenty-eight. He knew he was a man of destiny, a man who could change history and accomplish great feats in troublesome times. Caesar had achieved much in the years before he became a battle-wise general. The Roman Senate, fearing his ambitions and skills, ordered him to conquer Gaul with a small, insignificant army. Gaul's tribal armies were three times as large and well armed, the terrain was treacherous, and reinforcements from Rome were scarce. Nevertheless, Gaul and the surrounding territories soon fell to Caesar's genius. Could Winston Cromwell, grandson of Lord Oliver Cromwell, do less in Ireland?

The north wind grew stronger. Cromwell watched one of his grenadiers light a grenade and heave it into the Irish vortex. A scruffy peasant picked it up and threw it back. The explosive rolled into the English ranks, blowing apart three of his most loyal men. With a thud, a severed leg landed in front of him. Cromwell lurched backward, startled, almost falling off his horse. *God! What a sight!* He shook his head in anguish. He had known one of the men, James Bradshaw, a dear schoolmate at Oxford. What a waste of good fighting men, dying in the hellhole of Ireland! There could be no greater sadness for a proper Englishman.

Cromwell turned away and tried to ignore the battle. He had met Bradshaw at Oxford's Bodleian Library and soon developed an affable friendship. They both had nothing but contempt for Oxford and for education in general. In their points of view, the other schoolmates were fools, gullible, believing whatever the professors preached from the shrine of conventional doctrine. It would never cross their small minds to question assumptions or theories; almost nobody could think for themselves. His schoolmates were content to memorize text in order to graduate, wholly satisfied with placating the Oxford dons. Theirs was not an education; it was intellectual self-abuse. A halfwit could be taught to recite the works of great authors, but after all had been said and done, he was nevertheless a halfwit—an educated halfwit.

Still, Cromwell had learned something useful at Oxford—the marvelous ideas of Machiavelli and his conjecture that war is not about victory but about controlling the citizenry, molding them into a greater whole. And in that vein, true leaders had to be just as merciful to the plebs as they were stringent. Order was the remedy; discipline the cure. This struck a clarion chord in his soul. Never before had he encountered such clear thoughts on ruling and statecraft. Like Machiavelli, he wanted to capture the hearts and minds of the people he would rule. He wanted loyal citizens to follow him as the Apostles served Christ. His citizens would readily obey because of his strong leadership, not out of fear of torture or execution. They would lay down their lives for him in devotion to his divine rulership. What more could a ruler wish for?

Suddenly, Cromwell caught sight of the glistening blade. He tilted his head ever so slightly and watched a brawny Irishman impale two of his men—right through their abdomens. He could see that the enemy was making one last attempt to break through the encirclement. It failed, but another of his officers fell, his head split open by a heavy Irish sword as he protected a fellow officer. Cromwell was touched by the sacrifice. He felt honored to command such brave and devoted men. They were the backbone of England, unlike the indolent ministers in London who controlled the army without any idea what was going on in the Irish countryside. Viceroys had fancy notions, but few solutions. They signed edicts and required troops to enforce policies that failed because the viceroys did not have firsthand knowledge of the situation. The viceroys cared not what the local subjects thought. Their edicts were often pure horse dung.

Cromwell spurred his white horse closer to the shrinking battlefield. He stopped and noticed his frayed sleeves. Without thinking, he pulled on a loose thread, but the thread did not break. Instead, as he tugged, the seam unraveled—so rapidly that he feared he would soon be sleeveless. Such cheap material. England's foreign policy toward Ireland was just as threadbare, denuded of logic or common sense. Still, good or bad policy notwithstanding, he detested the fact that he would be blamed when another rebellion erupted or another English settler was found murdered in his bed. The Viceroy in Dublin would replace him, leaving undisturbed the policy responsible for the disorder.

As Cromwell watched the courageous Irish perish; a sense of pity surged inside of him. He hated to see a defeated army squander men so wastefully. In his mind, war had always been grossly overrated as a tool of governance.

As the fighting waned, Cromwell was approached by Colonel Henry Winchester, who wore a white-powdered wig, satin clothes, and gold rings. Medals and ribbons swung across his broad chest. Winchester moved his horse alongside Cromwell and waited for him to acknowledge his presence. He appeared slightly intoxicated.

"Yes, Colonel, what is it?"

Winchester took a pinch of snuff and then spoke in a clear, stern manner. "Sir, we have the rapparees encircled. The engagement is ours!"

"Is it?" Cromwell huffed with a slight scowl on his face. He knew that Winchester detested him and his whole ancestral lineage. That was obvious since they first locked eyes on each other. And who could blame his dismay? His grandfather, Lord Cromwell, had offended many in England, especially the nobility.

It was no secret that Winchester had taken full advantage of the current situation in England, proclaiming himself a diehard royalist. It was a safe position to take. The British monarchy had made a full recovery since the beheading of King Charles I. Still, Winchester usually kept his opinions to himself unless he had indulged in too much cherry brandy. When that happened, the colonel's true colors flowed freely like an oversupplied river—spewing verbal abuse at Parliament, affluent upstarts, and coarse plebeians.

"Well?" Winchester waited for a more cogent reply. None came.

Instead, Cromwell gazed silently at him. The colonel and his ilk were the same men who controlled the Viceroy and the political machinery—effete aristocrats, wealthy but useless. And Winchester was less than useless; he was broke. His family had lost their fortune, and he was obliged to accept a military commission in Ireland. Cromwell hoped he could make the colonel's stay long and unpleasant.

Winchester cleared his throat. "Yours was an excellent strategy, if I may say so, sir. The bout is ours. The dogs have cornered the Fox. Your eldfather, Lord Oliver, would be proud. Very proud, I daresay."

"The battle remains in doubt, Colonel."

Winchester turned in his saddle, puzzled. "Sir? The rapparees are outnumbered, outmatched, and outgunned. 'Tis only a matter of time before we dispose of the bodies. Like in Drogheda, sir. I heard that they sold the survivors to slave traders in the West Indies. The Crown made a pretty penny. If you wish, I could arrange the matter."

"Mawworms have affected you, Colonel," Cromwell said, raising his voice. He reached over and caressed his horse's mane gently. "I will not kill or enslave the survivors of this battle."

"Pardon me, sir, but why not?"

Cromwell squinted at Winchester with one eye. "Tell me, Colonel. What are we doing in Ireland?" The question was nearly treasonous. Everyone wondered, but no one dared ask the question openly. "Are we here to murder every last bog-trotter and devil-dodger?"

"Sir, we are here to civilize the land. 'Tis our Christian duty to tame the hinterland."

"And what have you tamed, Colonel? Have you stopped the smuggling or the selling of supplies to the enemy?"

Winchester squirmed, gritted his teeth and then finally looked around with an embarrassed frown. His unusual restraint was short lived. He raised his index finger and directed it at Cromwell. "God-a-mercy! Are you questioning my loyalty to the King? You should be the last man to make such accusations! It was your eldfather who murdered King Charles at Whitehall. Most disloyal act ever conceived. And I do not say it because I am a royalist and you a Parliamentarian. Nay, I say it because I disapprove of men chopping off the heads of their leaders!"

Cromwell smiled. "Indeed."

Winchester's faced flushed red. "I guess it serves no purpose to reenact the civil war here, sir. But I *am* loyal."

"I do not question your loyalty. I only ask to whom you give your allegiance! Why have none of my subordinate officers seized Black Fox and destroyed his lair before now? Is it stupidity or a conspiracy? In one month, I have done what you failed to do in four years. Understand me well, Colonel! There are many opportunities and temptations here. Diogenes would have to search a thousand years to find a handful of honest Englishmen in Ireland."

"Sir, I refuse to listen to this rubbish." Winchester prepared to depart.

Cromwell seized the reins of Winchester's horse. "Hold fast, Colonel. If I were a suspicious man, I might wonder how a man of your modest commission affords a bevy of satin attire and gold rings."

"Bosh!" Winchester shook his head violently and galloped away.

Free from the rants of a lesser mortal, Cromwell turned his attention back to the battlefield. He quickly spotted the folly of an Irishman. The man was silhouetted against the dying sun as he commanded his shrinking forces from a large tree stump. For a moment, the man resembled Moses preparing to cross the Red Sea. Cromwell permitted himself a thin smile. The British sea of unwavering resolve was impregnable; this time the Irish would not escape the deluge.

A young lieutenant rode up to Cromwell from the rear lines. The officer was young and thin as a scarecrow. With trembling hands, he awkwardly reached over and gave Cromwell a rolled piece of parchment—a message that Cromwell had been expecting.

"Good work, Lieutenant Townsend," Cromwell chimed. He dismounted and unrolled the parchment across his saddle. On it was the crude sketch of a man's face. "Our spy has done his job well I must say."

"So much blood," the lieutenant said with a catch in his throat. "We're a might close to the action, sir. A stray shot could strike you."

"I have seen this face before." Cromwell paused, finding it difficult to put a name to a face. He prided himself on never forgetting the facial features of anybody, especially someone close enough to gut him. In a flash, he suddenly remembered the man on the stump. Cromwell turned and stared at the man depicted in the sketch—Black Fox. So here was the man the English army had been hunting for an eternity. Why had it taken so long to track down one petty malcontent?

"Sir! General Hawkins was killed from a farther distance. I suggest—"

"Your work is done here, Lieutenant Townsend," Cromwell said. "Has our spy been rewarded?"

"Aye, we left the reward in the church as instructed, sir! 'Tis amazing how a small poke of gold doubloons will loosen the tongue."

"Greed is an incessant illness for which there is no cure. That is what makes it so useful, Lieutenant." Cromwell turned, rolled up the parchment and focused his attention back to the battle. Two fresh columns of his troops had marched from the rear and melted into the turmoil of red coats and gray cloaks. Fewer than fifty Irishmen remained fighting. The others were wounded, dying, or dead. Like fish in a shrinking net, men piled upon men, all converging toward a receding center. "Lieutenant, you may go. I must end this carnage." He turned to his fighting men and shouted, "Hold back! Let them surrender!"

The British soldiers froze like jammed gears in a watermill; swords and spears paused in midair as if time had stopped. Cromwell strode to the front line. He knew that such tactics were irregular, and he enjoyed the thought that his men never knew what he would do next. Must keep everyone guessing; that was an important trait of the truly great men of history.

One curious English soldier turned his head to watch Cromwell approach. Cromwell whipped out his hand and slapped the man's face lightly without breaking his stride. "Face front!" he said. "'Tis better for the neck and your life."

Cromwell stopped just short of the front line. "Throw down your weapons!"

The Irishmen reluctantly dropped their arms and waited.

Cromwell did not look directly at Black Fox. He would first disgrace the rebel leader in front of his own men. "I will be brief, so listen well," he said. "I will set free every rogue here and now. But only if someone, anyone, identifies the rebel chieftain."

Cromwell stood and waited impatiently. He was sure his offer would pry open someone's lips. His generosity was unparalleled. Nobody in their right mind would be so lenient to the bog-trotting Irish.

Chapter 5

Major-General Cromwell's offer was met with silence. "Come, come," he demanded. "I know the blackguard is called Black Fox. Nobody else needs to die. Just identify your leader. 'Tis a simple request!"

Black Fox remained fixed atop the tree stump. He shaded his eyes with his right hand and looked toward the horizon. Then he twisted around and looked behind him. He repeated it again and again, attempting to look far and wide. Some of his men followed suit. After he surveyed the entire battlefield, he shrugged his shoulders. Some of the British soldiers sniggered. Everyone knew the man on the stump was Black Fox.

Cromwell's face flared red as he stared at Black Fox. "You're a damn fool! You tempt death, but you will not cheat it."

"But it's so delightfully fun to tempt death," Black Fox mocked in a teasing tone.

"And it is equally delightfully fun to call forth the hangman?"

"I see we are in agreement."

"No, we are not!" Cromwell said. "Death will not give me what I want."

"Then we have hit a bloody impasse."

"Indeed."

"Well." Black Fox bowed to Cromwell. "I see I must take the first step and introduce myself. For all practical purposes, I am the one you seek."

"So, you admit to your traitorous actions."

"No, I admit to being the one you so desperately desire."

Cromwell stepped back and took a breath. This was getting him nowhere. He was beginning to lose his mental clarity. His taste for victory was being tainted by this flippant Irishman. He knew that the defeat of the rebels was mostly a hollow victory. It would provide him with little long-term satisfaction. Still, he had put an end to the last major source of disturbances in his district. But then again, the rebels were mostly engaged in oafish cattle raids. No, the real threat to his authority came from a more devilish source. That was the real battle.

"You are a rather petulant insurgent," Cromwell said.

"Me? An insurgent?" Black Fox leaned back. "That's a good one. I believe you've it all backward."

"Do I?"

"I'm not a usurper of lawful authority. How could the Irish in their own land be insurgents to outsiders?"

"A rather labored theory, I must say. But that is not up for debate." With a simple hand gesture, Cromwell ordered Black Fox to be brought in front of him. Two soldiers marched up, seized the rebel's sword, grasped him by the arms and dragged him away. After the soldiers deposited their prisoner in front of Cromwell, they withdrew.

The Major-General's face brightened as he gazed upon his captive. At least he had done what nobody else had done. That had to mean something. With a cocky smile, he strutted around his captive, inspecting Black Fox like a trophy. He felt like a prosperous merchant salivating over the joy of achieving a bargain deal. He stopped in front of the prisoner and studied him. "What to do now?"

"Oh, that's easy." Black Fox grinned and straightened his shoulders.

"It is?"

"Aye. Admit your defeat."

"Me?"

"Don't be coy." Black Fox casually brushed dirt from his shoulders. "I will be the first to say that your men put up an admirable fight, but I'll accept your surrender nonetheless." He reached for Cromwell's sword.

Playing along, Cromwell's eyes narrowed slightly. "Oh? And I suppose we will get favorable terms?"

"Quite amiable. If you scurry back to England, all will be forgiven. Easy as making water."

"My superiors would balk at such lenient terms. They are accustomed to victory."

"Remarkable. I've roamed Ireland for nearly six years, and I've seen more English backsides than victorious eyes."

"Ireland is under a new landlord," Cromwell said, trying to maintain his good-humored sarcasm with his brazen counterpart.

"Pity. I had already selected an enchanted castle."

"Sorry to dash your hopes, but you've been evicted. Time has run out."

"What you mean is that you've unfairly altered the lease again."

"Well, in a manner of speaking," Cromwell said with an amused tone. "The English are very good at that. We are rather demanding proprietors."

"Aye, and we're always penalized with heftier payments."

"Not for long." Cromwell turned and ordered his captive to be put under the noose. "'Tis time to make more grist for the mill."

Several soldiers rushed up to Black Fox, bound his hands, and pushed him to a nearby oak. They lifted him onto a small makeshift platform of rocks. They swiftly looped the noose around his neck.

With his officers standing nearby, Cromwell turned, took a few steps, stopped and proceeded to address his men. "I have a queer announcement. I have decided to release our prisoners after returning to Cork. I know it is unorthodox, but blood cannot be washed out with blood. With our victory today, the war has ceased, and with it our military objectives. We need not take revenge. For if we hang an Irishman today, someone will slit an Englishman's throat tomorrow. A hanged neck for a slit throat is no bargain."

Murmurs of outrage rose from the ranks. Nobody in past memory had shown such clemency towards captured Irish rebels.

Winchester pushed to the front line, shoving everyone out of his way with the fury of an enraged bulldog. "This is utter nonsense. All the prisoners should be hanged immediately!"

Cromwell knew that a more decisive battle was just beginning. He had to identify the traitors among his own ranks. If he could not root out corruption, his career would languish and stagnate until he was replaced, like all of his predecessors. Given Winchester's reactions, he was beginning to feel uncomfortably naked. As he faced his troops, his back laid bare to most of his less reputable officers. He wondered if that would be his own undoing.

Cromwell bit his lips and clenched his fists tightly. He had to get Black Fox to cooperate or his plans would come to naught. Sporting a stern face, he moved closer to Black Fox. "You have heard my intentions to release your men, but not my conditions. So here they are. By law, you and all of your men must pledge an Oath of Supremacy to England. Secondly, you must name the British traitors who supplied you. You have no army; therefore you have no need to protect their identities."

Black Fox stared at the darkening sky. "All things considered, 'tis a fine day for a hanging."

Cromwell had expected stubbornness. Any leader worth his salt would refuse the first offer. Still, he began to understand that he had just created a difficult dilemma for himself. If he hanged Black Fox, he would never unveil the identities of the British traitors. If he spared Black Fox, he risked losing any possible respect from his own men. It was all too easy to get caught in one's own cleverness.

There has to be a way, Cromwell mumbled to himself, trying to think through the problem. He began to entertain the thought of shipping Black Fox to London and letting the authorities deal with him at Tyburn, where pirates, religious heretics, and Irishmen were popular fare for a good hanging. But that would not solve his dilemma. He had to deal with this rebel here and now. "Speak up. What is your reply?"

"I would rather march with lemmings to the sea."

"I'm sorry," Cromwell said, "I can only offer you a stretched neck." He ordered the noose be tied around Black Fox's neck.

As the final preparations were made for the execution, Cromwell's thoughts drifted to other matters. England once had its own wild and barbarous men, most notably the radical Levellers of the late 1640s. They had argued that even common people should decide their own fates; they barely believed in any form of government at all, something they called a republic. London had been overrun with these madmen during the civil war. They would have leveled society if their demands of freedom for all individuals had come to pass. Even his grandfather had been swept up in this whirlwind of republican lunacy. But finally, Lord Cromwell came to his senses, seized control of England, and imprisoned many Levellers. Unfortunately, some had escaped to Ireland and the New World. Maybe some of these rebels were their subversive heirs.

As he gazed at the horizon, Cromwell began to think of Ireland as a good refuge for the Levellers. The country was almost ungovernable. The people had never had a feudal system with serfs and lords, never had to bow to authority or a true king. The Irish were uncontrollable, disrespectful, and nomadic, following their cattle and sheep wherever the grass was greener and the water purer. Such a peasantry was impossible to tax, conscript, or instill with a sense of allegiance.

While Cromwell's back was turned, Winchester and two other officers moved closer to Black Fox. One officer drew his pistol and aimed it directly at the rebel leader. Black Fox winked at the slow-moving assassins. Cromwell suddenly snapped out of his musings and faced Black Fox, failing to notice Winchester's actions.

"Are you winking at me?"

Winchester and his companions slowly moved back into formation.

"Something's in my eye," Black Fox said.

"I'm sure you find this all very entertaining. I wish there was some other device to persuade you."

"Better terms might awaken my tongue." Black Fox held up his bound hands and gave an irresistible look of innocence. "I'm not some fanatic papist praying for martyrdom. I just had this hankering for some excitement."

Cromwell was surprised. Was it possible that his captive was an erudite deist? A rare breed in Ireland. Bloody shame, he thought, to extinguish a sharp-witted mind simply to punish the disobedient body.

Just then, a small column of English soldiers burst into the clearing. They were led by a disheveled, heavyset man who found it difficult to maneuver around the heaps of dead bodies scattered across the battlefield. Upon reaching Cromwell, the bulky man stared dumbfounded at the condemned prisoner, rasping with a nervous voice, "My Lord! Black Fox in the flesh!"

"I see no introductions are required, Sergeant-Major Stuffleton," Cromwell said sarcastically. He was more than vexed over the fat man's appearance. He rubbed his neck and crinkled his lip. "Why are you here? You were supposed to attack from the other side of the mountain, engaging in a frontal assault, and draw their fire. But my scouts reported no such gunfire or attack."

"Sir, I beg your pardon, but weren't we to engage the enemy together?"

"God-a-mercy! My orders were explicit. I had you repeat them. Remember?"

Stuffleton shrugged his shoulders.

"You're either a thick-headed fool or an inept spy. Look at yourself. You're unshaven and unkempt. You evade the truth like a gypsy beggar. If the enemy were attacking Kinsale, you'd be merrymaking in the alehouses of Mallow. You defend where Irish rebels do not attack. You attack where rebels do not defend. You would make a better ballocks papist than a soldier."

Before Cromwell could continue, one of Stuffleton's buttons popped open, unleashing his sagging belly. Cromwell covered his face with his hand and turned to two nearby soldiers. "Do something with this imbecile. Anything. Arrest him!"

Two small men approached the huge Stuffleton and grabbed his arms.

Stuffleton refused to budge. "You cannot arrest me. I'm with the Scottish detachment!"

"Fine! I will promote you to my stockade detachment." Cromwell sneered. "Most of them are already from Scotland. What a criminal breed, I dare say."

"Great snakes!" Stuffleton gasped in a hoarse, guttural voice. "I'll get ya for this, ya hang-dog!" After another round of cursing, he shifted his weight forward and began shoving his way through a throng of soldiers, dragging the smaller men behind him.

Cromwell sighed. It would seem that he could trust nobody in this land of death, deception, and dishonor. Shaking his head, he glanced out towards the empty battlefield and thought he saw something move. It looked like a child running toward them with the speed of a frightened deer. What was next? A plague of swarming locusts?

Chapter 6

Sean scrambled across the battlefield, over the bodies of fallen horses and men. He knew what was happening. From higher up the hill, he had spotted his father's misfortune—surrounded by the enemy, placed under a tree, while over his head dangled a short-noosed rope. He knew what the English were about to do. It was the only thing they knew how to do.

He ran faster. He had to save his father. He slipped in a pool of blood and fell, landing eye-to-eye with Ligan O'Connor's corpse. Ligan's eyes were wide open, and for a moment, Sean thought he was still alive. Was nobody impregnable? Was nobody spared? Sean turned away.

He caught a glint of light shining off a dagger held in the stiff fingers of nearby fallen man. It was the dagger he had found an hour earlier.

A horrifying thought struck him. If it were the same dagger, then the body must be... No! He leaned over the Irishman and wiped smudges of dirt from the dead man's face. It was his brother. "Brian!" Sean yelled and pulled at his brother's shirt, pleading with him to get up. He cupped his hand in front of Brian's nose. Nothing. He threw his arm around Brian's chest and dragged his brother until he could drag him no longer. He stared at his brother's face. Not dead—sleeping! He touched Brian's hand and felt the icy flesh. A large black stain soaked his brother's cloak. Then he noticed a spear tip protruding from Brian's back. Tears burst from his eyes.

Sean wanted to run somewhere, but his body was frozen in place, paralyzed. It was as if a heavy iron chain had been wrapped around his arms and legs. He stood up feeling weak in the knees, wobbled backward and forwards, and felt ready to heave everything in his stomach. He fought back nausea and the urge to vomit; he had to concentrate on what to do. A thought started to pulsate through his throbbing head. Father! He could still save Father! Sean grabbed the ferret-hilt dagger as anger surged through his entire body. He knew what to do now. What lay directly ahead was a red wall of sullen blackguards. He was not about to let them escape his wrath. He would kill every last one. He brandished his knife overhead, screamed, and ran straight to the redcoats.

As Sean neared the English, a soldier turned around and watched in disbelief as the child led a lone attack.

"He's got a knife," someone muttered with amusement.

"Aye, he does indeed." A thin-faced soldier slowly drew his pistol and waved it menacingly in the air. "'Tis a belly slasher, to be sure."

Only ten yards away, Sean stopped, frozen. He had to be daffy to assault a whole prigging army. This would not get his father rescued. His old schoolmaster would have belittled him for eternity for such a foolish blunder. He had to get far away fast. His tender age gave him no special protection. The English were merciless. Why was he making so many mistakes? This one would probably be his last.

The lean soldier trained his sight on his stationary target and fired. He took a step forward and lowered his weapon. His face glowed with a thin smile of satisfaction. "Got the little tyke!"

Sean stumbled backward. He had been hit. He looked down and saw blood flowing across his cloak. He tried to brush away the blood. That wasn't working. His hand turned numb; his body could not stand properly. Legs were becoming weak. The circle of red kept growing and growing. He closed his eyes and dropped to the ground.

Cromwell quickly rushed over to the soldier who had fired his weapon. "What is it this time?"

"Nothing much." The soldier pointed to the fallen boy. "The tyke flashed a dagger. Thought I'd better take a pop at him. Put him out of his misery before... well, you know the adage: nits will become lice."

"I see," Cromwell said with a solemn nod. "No harm done, but inform me beforehand next time."

"But it was in self-defense," the soldiers said. "I knew what I had to do."

"Fine, but there are protocols," Cromwell interjected.

As the two continued to converse, Sean stirred. He tucked his knife inside his cloak, applied pressure to his wounded shoulder to stanch the bleeding. He struggled to stand up, finally found footing, and dashed towards them again.

"A bad shot, soldier," Cromwell said after watching the boy bolt past.

Quickly, Sean raced through the soldiers' ranks, unopposed. He leaped at his father, clinging to him with his last ounce of strength.

"Son!" Black Fox moaned with anguish. "You should not have come. I'm now beholden to their merciless souls."

Cromwell smirked as he approached his captive. "'Tis true. It appears that I do have something to offer. Now you will tell me all that I require to cleanse this land of corruption. Otherwise, the boy's future becomes... let's say, cloudy."

Black Fox gazed warmly at his son. "It appears that choices are luxuries I can no longer afford."

"The names!" Cromwell thundered.

"One of them is right—"

A shot rang out. Sean felt a jerk, and then his father's body went limp. Blood dripped onto Sean's forehead and then trickled down his face.

"Cut him down!" Cromwell shouted. "Get him down!" Without waiting for someone to follow his orders, he seized a knife, reached up, and cut the rope himself.

As Black Fox's body dropped, Sean slumped to the ground. Closing his eyes, he curled up like a dying spider. He had only barely registered what had happened, but he knew it was too horrible to think about.

Cromwell put his hand over Black Fox's mouth. "Damn! He's dead!" He whirled around at his men. "Who fired that shot?" He rushed over to a smoking pistol that lay on the ground. In a sudden spurt of anger, he kicked the weapon into the thicket. "Who? Who!"

No one came forward.

Cromwell clenched his fist. "Somebody better confess!"

When nobody declared his guilt, Cromwell took off and raced back and forth between columns of soldiers, searching for a man without a pistol. "You're all damnable hangdogs! Someone bloody well better confess, or I'll hang the lot of you!"

Coming out of his stupor, Sean crawled to his father's cold body and embraced him one last time. That is when he saw it hanging around his father's neck—the emerald ring that represented the royal power of the high kings of Ireland. He had to have it; something, anything to remind him of his beloved father. He reached over and broke the chain. Looking over his shoulder, he shoved the ring into his pocket.

Suddenly, he was filled with rage. The Brits had destroyed everyone he held dear. They would pay. He would slaughter every last slag of them. He jumped up, reached for his hidden dagger, but immediately bumped into Colonel Winchester. The colonel lifted the boy up and shook him like a floppy rag-doll. Sean squirmed and struggled; he was unable to reach his dagger. With a swift leg movement, he kicked Winchester in the groin. Winchester howled, released the boy, his cheeks puffed out like an enlarged bagpipe.

Back on the ground, Sean tried to run again, but he did not get far. This time he was blindsided and crashed into a solid wall of flesh—Stuffleton.

Stuffleton bristled with indignation as he growled in a low tone.

Sean tumbled to the ground. Somewhat dazed, he sat up, shook his head, and mumbled. "I can never get away."

"Well," Stuffleton huffed and moaned, "I guess we're both caught in the same net." He flashed an evil eye at the two soldiers guarding him.

Before Sean could get up, Cromwell grabbed his arm and reeled him in like a hooked fish. He seized the boy by the throat and shook him violently. "Who are the traitors? Who?"

Sean pulled out his dagger and slashed at Cromwell, slicing him deeply across the face. The impact knocked the general to the ground. Stunned, he sat, holding his bleeding face.

Laughter rippled through the soldier's ranks as Sean arched his back and brandished his weapon like a Roman gladiator, ready to fight the next challenger. He dared the soldiers to attack him. He shouted, "Are you all lily-cowards?"

The soldiers roared with laughter.

Sean lowered his weapon, confused. He didn't understand the joke. As they laughed, however, he realized that he had been given a brief opportunity to escape. He wanted to fight, but he knew he was outnumbered and outmatched. He darted through the guffawing soldiers and vanished like a rabbit into the underbrush.

Chapter 7

Hurtling into the underbrush, Sean tripped, lost his balance and tumbled headfirst down a deep ravine. Wild blackberry thorns and rocks gashed at his face and arms as he rolled down the embankment. He clutched at branches, but they ripped through his palms, burning his hands. He finally plunged into a deep pool full of reeds and peat moss.

He could not swim, and his worst fear was to sink beneath the murky water. Monsters lived there. They would bite off legs, arms, heads, and take the soggy remains to the netherworld. He splashed violently until his arms hit something mossy and soft. Clawing at it, he struggled up a mushy, half-submerged log, inch by inch, until he flopped onto the riverbank, exhausted.

He knew he could not rest. The redcoats would never stop pursuing him until he had been captured. But he was too weak to stand, so he rolled onto his stomach and slithered through a maze of tree roots and tall horsetails. The sky had darkened and he could see nothing, no stars, no moonlight, only brilliant flashes of lightning etching out momentary silhouettes. Large, cold drops of rain pelted his face.

Sean leaned against an old oak. He fingered the wound near his shoulder blade. It was less serious than it felt—merely a grazed shoulder. The English were definitely poor marksmen. He tore strips from his cloak and applied it to his wound. That stopped the bleeding, at least for a while. After a short rest, he decided it was time to escape the ravine and find better shelter.

With difficulty, he attempted to climb up a patch of loose rocks along the riverbank. The stones were wet and slippery as ice. He came to what looked like an abandoned pathway, and started to climb up the steep bank. It soon came to a dead end, but he continued onward and upward, found an insecure foothold. He reached out for something to catch his fall, but there was nothing to grab. With another misstep, he fell and landed back into the shallows of the pond.

Shivering in the icy water, the weight of his plight was too much to bear. His head was spinning to the point where he could not tell which direction to go or what to do. He inhaled deeply, barely managing to take in short gulps of air. He had to get out of the deadly water; with his last spurt of energy, he hauled his body onto the rocky shoreline.

He almost started to laugh. What was the rush? He knew he was getting nowhere. It was as if life was mocking him for trying to escape its cruel grip. He decided to rest and block out any negative thoughts. He began to place his hands on top of a pile of rocks, fingering them with the delight of a small child. He found them surprisingly round and glassy smooth. He dredged up a handful and examined them more closely. In the flashing streaks of lightning, they appeared ugly and devoid of life. Just like him. If only he had died. If only that bullet had slammed into his head. Everything would be better. Let the dogs chew on his bones. Let the crows peck out his eyes. That would have been more merciful. At least his pain would end.

As he began to calm down, he collapsed backward, against a steep and muddy embankment. He stared at the stones again, slowly rolling the smaller ones between his fingers. He closed his eyes and took a deep breath. Life had been much better ages ago. There was once hope and dreams. His father had assured him that he could drive out the invaders and fix everything. Father was wrong.

Everything seemed wrong.

Ferret threw the stones back to where they belonged, into the dead of blackness. His father had once found similar stones, nearby the seacoast outside of Cork. Except they were lifeless and dull, their natural state. And that was because they were brutally bone dry. But his father had wanted to make a point. With a thin hint of a smile, he bent over and dipped the stones into the clear water. Suddenly they changed. They were now beautiful, sparkling like gemstones, bursting with the colors of a rainbow after a spring rain. Suddenly the stones had gone from plain to flashy glamour. He knew that his father was trying to share a few pearls of wisdom: that beauty often concealed profound and deep-rooted ugliness. His father's parable was silly. The water had simply bathed the stones into colorful beauties. Nothing was really special. There was nothing special about anything. Life was a cruel jape. There was never going to be any glimmering light beyond the darkness, just momentary beauty that ended when the watery elixir evaporated.

Hearing twigs breaking, Sean turned and attempted again to claw up the embankment. He glanced back as lightning flashed overhead. Haunting images of gritty shapes rustled behind him—tall, dark figures with quivering arms, ready to pounce on him. He climbed faster. After crawling to the top, he stood there, teetering, almost falling to his knees. Quickly, he reached out and caught an oak branch. He had to get away, get his body into gear. No time to dither, no time to think. Move.

Finally, he stepped forward, and staggered out into an open field, but made so little distance that a frog could have outraced him. He had to move faster. The noise behind him was growing louder. Instead, he was moving slower. His body felt heavy. Head pounding, feet sinking under each step, his eyes blurred. He could not breathe. If only he could escape somewhere.

* * *

Sean opened his eyes and shivered. He was on his back, cold, lightheaded, and weary. The rain had stopped. He must have fainted. He sat up and looked around. There was no one behind him. The thought should have given him comfort, but it made him feel dejected and despondent. He had escaped, but from what? He was trying to get away, but to where? The thought made his head spin and his stomach wrench. His doubts were crushing him. He had to come up with a plan. Any plan would do. But why should he search for shelter or a warm fire? That was a futile and laughable plan. There was nothing out here. Nothing at all. And even if he did find something, there was little reason to oppose the harbingers of death.

Sean looked up for a long time in silence. Faint slivers of lightning fanned out to the south. The storm and its blustering winds had passed, and cold stars pierced the crystal sky. He was in a meadow, lying on wet grass and shamrocks. He felt the chill, but he also felt peaceful and warm. It was a strange feeling. He leaned his back against a rock and pulled out his dagger, accidentally cutting his thumb. The sharp sting gave him comfort as if reassuring him that he was still alive. He watched the blood ooze for several moments without attempting to stop the flow. Who needs blood, he thought? It was just something to give more pain.

He slit his thumb again, and the pain seemed less severe. He wondered if it would ease with each passing slice. He pricked the palm of his hand. Then he did it again until a regiment of tiny redcoats dotted his flesh. At that moment he realized that only he had escaped the talons of death. He had nobody now. An empty, hollow feeling inundated him. Even his mother had died, during childbirth. He had killed her too.

Half dazed, his mind raced over recent events. Was he responsible for his father's death? Could he have prevented it? Could he have cut him down from the tree? Instead, he had done nothing at all. He fingered his dagger. One quick thrust would make his suffering go away forever.

It seemed that death was the only way to end the void of emptiness. At least it would take him where all the others had gone. He would not be left behind again. But was it wrong? A fiery priest once warned about people killing themselves—that it was a most unholy of sins. Declared that these sinners would be consumed in the fires of Hell. As things were going, even that was better than living.

Suddenly, he heard something—a voice? He looked around and spotted a distant glow from beyond the trees. What should he do? He glanced at his dagger, and then back at the light. Must be the murderous Britons searching for him. He stood up and threw out his chest. This time would be different. He would make sure they found him.

Gripping his dagger tightly, Sean got up and dashed toward the light. He ran down a narrow footpath overgrown with tall reeds. Beyond a cluster of abandoned thatched-roofed huts was a small castle-like dwelling of gray stone. He paused and scanned for enemy soldiers but saw none. Light from a taper shined through a cracked window.

Sean edged closer to the building and peeked inside through a slight opening in the door. A small fire in the hearth cast deep shadows along the undefined borders of the large room. Several white moths fluttered around the flickering candle on the windowsill.

Pushing the door open a bit more, Sean at first thought the room was empty. He entered just a few feet and sniffed the musty air. The room reeked of spoiled meat and moldy hay. Suddenly, a long-robed, humpbacked woman with sunken cheeks crossed in front of the fire, her lanky body silhouetted against the firelight. She was singing to herself while stirring the coals with an iron poker. She pushed a small, flat loaf of bread on the floor closer to the flames, then turned and peered at Sean.

"Mo chraoibhin?" The woman spoke in an old Gaelic dialect that Sean barely understood.

"No. I was just passing by," he said.

"Anglican! Anglican lad," the old woman squeaked in broken English.

"Nay, ma'am, I'm Irish. I got English from my uncle in Cork."

"So! *A ghiolla seo...* come inside and honor a poor old woman. 'Tis nice and warmful."

"I cannot." Sean glanced past the door, outside into the darkness.

"Come, laddie. Thou wilt not come to harm. If ye have lost thy way, ye cannot travel till dawn." The woman lowered her hood, revealing white, straw-like hair. Her thin cheekbones were pitted with penny-sized smallpox scars. Her mouth curved downward in a permanent scowl, displaying a toothless grimace. As if remembering better days, she simpered, "come. Come. Dry thy cloak. Sit a spell and fill thy belly with bread. Hospitality be my profession."

The old woman's cajolery made Sean uncomfortable, but it had been so long since he was dry and warm.

The woman placed a loaf of bread on a dirty linen tablecloth that draped to the floor. She sat down, pulled out a long knife and cut several slices of bread. With a trembling hand, she tossed a piece to the boy.

Sean hesitated, not sure what to do, but soon succumbed to his appetite. As he ate the tough bread, he studied the old woman. Her wrinkled face and the age spots on her hands reminded him of his eldmother in Cork. That gave some comfort.

"'Tis better now, me laddie?"

Sean nodded.

"Well, I beseech ye to stay the night. Thy company be most agreeable."

"If it pleases you. I shall not bother you longer than forenoon."

Turning to the hearth, Sean stretched his hands out to feel the fire's warmth. The woman approached him from behind. Without words, she took off his wet cloak and hung it on a pole near the fireplace. His inner shirt was thin and soaking wet; it clung to his body, showing his pink flesh. The woman was surprised.

"English inner garments? How fancy-dancy."

"From my uncle."

"Thou art well fed," she said approvingly. "Fattened like a weaned swine in summer." She fingered the red stain and bulge of rags across the boy's shoulder and offered him a wool blanket. Standing naked in front of her, he gratefully accepted it, and wrapped his chilled body.

Sean slouched on a low, straw seat in front of the hearth, his long hair cascading down his back. He closed his eyes and wondered why he was trying to comfort his body since he had no plans to live long.

The woman began applying strips of white flax to his shoulder. It was a good feeling to know that someone cared about him. It seemed that strangers often did more for him than his own kindred. He felt he could sleep in that chair all night.

Yet the solicitous old woman disturbed him. He recalled warnings about old women living alone in the wilderness. It was said that they were witches and would do unspeakable horrors to lost, wandering children. But he was no child. He could fend for himself. Let the old biddy do what she will; the Lord will protect the innocent. Sean began to doze.

Clang! Sean's eyes popped open as he twisted around, looking for English soldiers. There were none. The old woman had dropped a long, rusty knife on the table and appeared embarrassed.

"Dear me," she said. "I be clumsy as ahh..." She fumbled for words. "How do a young nipper of a lad come to be so far from thy abode anyway?" She pulled nervously at her wrinkled chin.

Sean started to answer, but the woman continued, speaking faster.

"And a schooled lad with an Anglican tongue, at that. Ye got important kinship somewhere I suppose? Aye?"

"Nay, I have no one." He hid his face and lowered his head. "I once had a father, and mama, but..."

"No one, ye say? Orphaned like a motherless fawn. Ye could disappear, and no folk would know different."

"Well," Sean said, "almost no one, except my uncle in Cork. He traded with the Britons during the war. But my father disowned him long ago."

"Good," the woman said, pursing her lips. "I mean, me dear laddie, traitors need to be scorned, as ye rightly did. I know about traitorous kindred. Poison of the earth, say I." She ambled to the door and pushed it shut, dropping a wooden bar into place. Returning to the table, she picked up the knife and sliced more bread. Sean slid his chair to the table.

The woman's face turned sour as she talked. "Thou mayest choose thy friends, but kindred be stuck to ye very skin like warts and welts. Never stomached me kindred. Blood or no blood, they be dreary goose-heads nonetheless.

"I once had a man of sturdy grit, until he turned rancid like old milk. Me man thought his duty was to God and *Eire*. Instead, the oxhead died for naught defending the dethroned English King, James II. Thence I descended into widowhood. Was treated no better than a harlot of the night."

"He fought the Britons. 'Tis no cause for shame."

"Shame? Me man was befooled. 'Tis shame enough. He joined with foolhards to fight other foolhards. Many an Irish overlord hath come to me. I remember well. They plead for gold to battle outlanders, then they ransack me domicile to pay for it. Fancy that! Our own overlord robs us to prevent looting by foreign dogs. 'Tis a wicked world, say I. Do not speak to me of defending *Eire*. God-a-mercy!"

"But Britons are murderous curs!"

"Spake with the pride of an old falcon and probably with skin as tough."

"I know no one who loves the English. Even Uncle Madoc speaks ill of them in private."

The woman hissed. "Madoc, ye say? Madoc O'Neill of Cork?"

"Do you know him?"

The woman's eyes narrowed. "The Lord told me this day would come. Know I of him? Madoc murdered me husband after the battle of Bony. He spoke witness against him. A pox upon his soul!" She lunged at the boy and slapped him. "Fie on thee!"

Jumping back in surprise, Sean crashed against the table, accidentally pulling off the cloth and revealing something white beneath. He crouched down and dragged it out from the dimness.

"What hast thou done," the old woman cried, wide-eyed, leaning over the table. "Leave it be!"

Sean lifted the small, round object into the firelight and then dropped it in horror. It was a child's head, dry-skinned and moldy green, its hollow eye-sockets staring at him.

The old woman smirked, cringed, and rubbed a rosary attached to her robe. "'Tis not such a nasty habit. Foodstuffs be scarce and orphans many. I cannot pawn myself like a fancy wench."

Sean backed away and raced for the door.

"Shelly, Shale," she muttered, "none the wiser." She clenched a long knife and held it between her flat breasts. "One more sacrificed! 'Tis all I ask." She glanced at the boy. "The lad be unwanted and abandoned, oh Lordy. Only thee and I have need of this lad. Thou mayest have him after me; I the flesh and thou... the soul. Life everlasting."

She twisted around, slowly, almost dancing, caught up in her wit. Suddenly, she wept loudly, then cackled as tears ran down her cheeks. With one hand, she made the sign of the cross, bowing her head as she prayed. "Bless thee, bless thee. 'Tis the true *bodkin* of Christ." She looked up at the boy and hummed a prayer in Latin.

Sean struggled to lift the bar from the door. The old woman struck, missing his neck by an inch, her blade embedding deep into the door. He dropped the blanket and ran to the table, naked. She reached for him, but her long crooked fingernails only snagged Sean's bandaged shoulder, loosening a handful of bloody rags.

The woman grasped the knife handle with both hands and threw her weight into it, twisting it free from the door. "Thou sweet laddie. Most foolhardy it be to depart from the warmth of me goodwill."

"I'm Protestant, not Catholic," Sean said. "I would make awful company for supper."

"I don't think ye taste be any different. Lordy knows, I'm not one to be choosy." She stretched across the table and took another slash at him. Again the knife missed its mark, instead gouging the table's surface. She cursed the knife as if it had a will of its own.

Snatching his dagger and clothes, Sean rushed back to the door. The woman freed her knife and cornered him. They faced each other, each brandishing a knife. Sean jabbed first.

Surprised, the woman stepped back and swore. "Ye vile polecat!"

Sean pushed the bar up and pulled it toward himself. This time, it tumbled to the floor. He tried to open the door, but he saw he was too late. The old woman's knife was raised. This is it, he thought. He would end up as soup bones in a cauldron and then be thrown out for the pleasure of wild animals. The woman cackled insanely. Sean closed his eyes.

Suddenly, someone pounded on the door.

They both froze and stared at each other, unsure what to do.

The door began to open. The woman shuffled backward, still holding the knife over her head. Sean, clenching his dagger in one hand and his garments in the other, also moved aside.

A tall, British soldier with sandy-blond hair entered the room. He gaped at the woman's knife. "Fine greeting for an officer of the Crown." Then he drew his pistol.

The woman screamed, "Leave me be!"

"Sorry to interrupt your festivities," the soldier said. "But apparently, someone forgot to send me an invitation." He glanced at Sean, still naked. "Your guests are dressed formally, I see." Then, bending over, he picked up the small human skull, sighed, and poked his fingers through the eye sockets. He glared at the woman. "This cannot continue! May the Lord pity both our souls." His pistol flashed.

The woman dropped her knife and fell.

"'Tis a poor day when children become fit for foodstuff," the soldier murmured as he gradually lowered his head and swallowed.

Sean drifted closer to the redcoat, his mouth hung agape.

The soldier stepped back and eyed the child. "She's in the Lord's hands now, and I believe His hands will be rather full." Then he pointed his smoking pistol at Sean. "Come here!"

Sean sidled closer and hid his eyes behind his bundle of garments. He felt as though he were leaping from one fire pit to another. Somehow he would have to do it again. Somehow he would have to outwit this soldier who had saved his skin.

"'Tis a mighty lucky lad, I daresay," the soldier said.

"I've had better nights," Sean said.

"Well, my word, the tadpole understands the King's tongue." The soldier clicked his teeth and winked, then lowered his pistol. "Can you dress yourself as well?"

Sean pulled on his inner garment and draped the damp cloak over his shoulder, hiding the dagger.

"Poor woman." The soldier knelt next to the woman's body and gently closed her eyelids. He cleared his throat and gazed at the boy. "Now, what shall we do with you?"

Sean shrugged and slowly reached inside his cloak. He would not go back to Cromwell alive, and neither would this lobster man.

Chapter 8

Sean followed the soldier outside as if attending his own funeral procession. He felt sure he was to face a firing squad, and if he were lucky, a freshly dug grave. But, outside the cottage, he only saw a blazing torch on a staff. No armed men, no dragoons, no Cromwell. He fought the impulse to run; the mere hint of flight would result in a bullet-riddled body and his head spiked on London's Gate. He kept trying to look around without looking around. Where were they? It would be a pity to disappoint the red-coated Jack sticklers.

"Mighty far beyond the pale for an English-speaking laddie," the soldier said as he crouched down and faced the boy. "Are you English or Irish?"

Sean did not reply. This was some stupid ploy. Cromwell's men would jump out at any moment and put him in fetters, or shoot him on the spot.

"Well?" The Briton slid his pistol into his black belt. "Likely an orphan, I wager."

Again, Sean did not answer. He folded his arms and looked straight ahead. He knew they were hiding somewhere.

"I know you're not deaf," the Englishman said with a cheerful tone. The man was tall and incredibly handsome and appeared to be in his early thirties. He had an engaging smile, a friendly demeanor, almost cordial, and yet distant. Like all Englishmen, the soldier was clean-shaven, sporting a strong chin and rosy cheeks. His light brown hair was combed back neatly into a long ponytail. His trousers were too tight, his sleeves too short, and his red coat too large. To most observers, he apparently was cursed with a shabby tailor who suffered from poor eyesight. Despite his lighthearted talk, his watchful blue-green eyes were bloodshot, like those of a restless man desperate for sleep or peace of mind. "Come on, laddie. Talk, nod, or dance a Scottish jig! I don't have all bloody night."

"Stop playing dumb," Sean finally said. "You know who I am."

The soldier leaned forward and slightly cocked his eyebrow. "I do?"

"Aye. And you know it."

"Well, then I must be a soothsayer, and you must be a soothsayer too, that is, to know that I can foretell events."

Without moving his head, Sean chanced another glance through the corner of his eye. There must be more soldiers lurking about. What were they waiting for?

"Are you lost?"

"Let's end this cock-and-bull chatter!"

"Why? This guessing game is such jolly fun."

It was bad enough to be captured, but intolerable to be played the fool. Sean gazed up into the soldier's kind and fatherly face. "Where are the rest of you?"

"Ah, is this some sort of Socratic question? I mean, if all of me is not here, then the rest of me must be somewhere else."

Sean tilted his head to one side, frowning. This Englishman was no ordinary buffoon, but why go to such effort?

Suddenly a twig snapped. Expecting the worst, Sean whipped out his dagger and prepared for battle. The soldier followed suit. He jumped up, spun around, and drew his pistol with blinding speed.

A short, dark-faced man wandered into the circle of flickering light, wearing a droll grin, a black, wide-brimmed hat and a large pack on his back. Outfitted in a plain brown robe, he resembled a chubby monk.

"Why, ... it's only Paco!" said the Englishman. He put away his pistol and scolded his companion as if he were a child, waving his finger in the air. "You should be more careful, Paco. I nearly shot you! Bad Paco!" Then he reached over and snatched the boy's weapon.

Sean looked down at his empty hand, astonished. The soldier's movement was so fast that only a ghost could have seized his weapon. Angered, Sean lurched at the Englishman, jumped up and grabbed for his blade. He was determined to retrieve his property, but the soldier kept lifting it higher, just out of his reach, enjoying the strife like some vapid dolt. "Give it back! You bully-rook English prigger!"

The soldier pushed the boy away, turned, and examined the blade's hilt in the torchlight. "My, my... it looks like a ferret's head. I once owned a ferret, a wild one at that, back in London. Perhaps I should say he owned me. A fierce beast, he was. Very independent. I found him with three legs. He'd chewed the fourth right off when it was caught in a trap. Ferrets hate captivity." He glanced at Sean. "And if you must know, we're not Englishmen. Paco's a Spaniard. A halfwit to be sure, but that's better than any Briton."

Sean stopped jumping and stood motionless. He cocked his head in disbelief. There was something peculiar about this soldier. Why was he bad-mouthing the English? Must have been touched by the lunatic rays of the moon.

The short fat man approached Sean and stuttered. "Me P-P-Paco." His right eye twitched uncontrollably. Taking the boy's hand, he sniffed it like a dog, drooled, and nodded with a faint smile.

Sean jerked away with a gasp. He was not sure whether the Spaniard was human or some ungodly half-breed. He had heard stories of vile creatures of the night taking over men's bodies and plundering the countryside. "What ails him?"

"Just about everything. One leg is shorter than the other. Of course, you could say one leg is longer. He's half deaf and half Moorish. Had part of his tongue ripped out in London after losing a court trial. He makes dull company, but an excellent pack animal."

Paco removed his hat, bowed and beamed with an exaggerated grin. His head gleamed in the torchlight. *"Siii... Paco! Yo soy Paco."*

Confused, Sean approached the soldier. "Are you an English officer?"

Paco suddenly became agitated and disappeared into the underbrush.

The soldier chuckled. "You've scared Paco, me laddie. He is easily frightened by wild boars and Britons." The soldier walked to the dense thicket. "Paco, come back. There are no English here."

Paco refused to come out.

"Come! Are you hiding or making water?" He faced the boy. "He gets a bit confused at times."

"So am I," Sean said. "I thought you were searching for me."

"Searching for you? My word, why would I do that?"

"I've been lost and—"

"I don't search for lost children. I avoid them."

"Then you're alone?"

"Aye, if you don't count my footman." The soldier gave the returning Paco a pat on the head. "Don't fear me, laddie. I'm harmless."

"That's what that old woman told me."

"I'm a little less hungry and far fussier about my choice of edibles." The soldier laughed, then gave a hand signal to Paco who immediately dropped to all fours. The soldier began fastening supplies to the Spaniard's back. "I had a good horse awhile back, but I lost 'im. Now I have this hoofless pack animal." He slung goatskin water bags across Paco's shoulders. Next, he strapped heavy sacks, a bedroll, and pots around the Spaniard's neck. "Doesn't he make a dandy mule? Unfortunately, if I leave him for a minute, he unpacks himself and wanders off."

"Don't you want to question me?"

"About what? Questions are not in my line of business. I'm a merchant—a tradesman—but I've met with hard times, as you can plainly see."

Sean glared at that man with a suspicious scowl. "'Tis a queer merchant who dons the official red coat of England's king, and carries few wares."

"You've cut me to the quick, laddie!" The soldier displayed a sheepish grin. "Poor huckster I am, righto. Few wares to hawk, and dressed inappropriately." He chuckled, brushed his coat, and tugged at his wrinkled shirt collar. "Terrible workmanship. I prefer a French lieutenant general's uniform, but they are hard to come by without a bullet hole or two." He put a finger through a hole in the collar. "See? Clean shot."

Sean's eyes narrowed with suspicion.

"Let me properly introduce myself, my little ragamuffin." He swept off his plumed tricorn hat and bowed. "I am commonly known to the country folk as Strongbow. As for the uniform, it is a ruddy good disguise that I had the pleasure to borrow. And I borrow much, for I believe that nobody really owns anything. I'm not saying you shouldn't. All I'm saying is that once you own something, you are in danger of having someone else take it away. Can you keep a secret?"

Sean folded his arms and shook his head.

"Well, neither can I. That's why I'm on the run. I'm too honest. The English have a price on my head. That's why I've taken to soldiery. I mean, what's a more splendid trick than to hide from the wolves by running with the wolf pack? So off I went in search of myself. Someday I just might find me."

Just then, Strongbow noticed Sean's bloody cloak. "My Lord!" He knelt and pulled the cloak open. Sean's wound had begun to bleed again. "You've been shot!"

"So?" Sean winced in pain. He stepped back and huffed out an angry breath. "You need not vex over me." With a quick jerk, he rewrapped his cloak and flung a cold stare at the man. "Just let me bleed!"

"Not upon my watch!" Strongbow began ripping strips of cloth from Paco's tunic. When the Spaniard realized what his master was doing, he sprang away, bags and black iron pans banging.

Strongbow moved closer to the lad, but the boy refused any help, holding out his hands to block the bandaging. "Come, come, my little acolyte. Even a mouse deserves a crumb from the table."

"'Tis a waste of time."

"'Ods bodikin! You are asking me to forsake my conscience. That is a mighty big request from a little titmouse. For you see, the dictate of conscience is most demanding. It follows you like a fiendish shadow, day and night. There is no place to escape; no region to hide. No man can run from himself. I must not neglect my Christian duty."

Sean glanced down, his face sagged with the weight of sadness. He realized that to discard one's life to the reaper of death was unfair to others. Every life had some greater value and one must not squander the gift of life. At least, that was what his father had once explained to him. But who needed a gift that only brought misery? Who needed to live in pain? From what he had seen, life had no meaning or purpose. Nothing much mattered.

"Why so sad?" Strongbow asked.

"Life is so... truly vile."

"You must not lose hope."

"I'm afraid that hope is lost, dead and buried."

"Well, laddie," Strongbow smiled as he raised his eyebrow, "let's see if we can exhume it. I am sure I can find a shiny shovel. Then we can dig it up and resurrect the corpses of hope. Breathe new life into this cruel world. What say you?" Strongbow's grin widened.

Sean blinked in surprise, not sure what to say. Was this stranger a fully mature mooncalf?

"Well?"

"My tongue is slow and heavy."

"Mine is not." Strongbow grabbed the boy's arm, threw open his cloak and studied the gunshot wound for a moment. "The injury doesn't look too serious." Strongbow muttered as he began dressing Sean's injury.

"Why must you fret over me?" Sean stood still but continued to voice his doubts. "You didn't fuss over the old woman. You just shot her!"

Strongbow continued tying the rags around Sean's shoulder. "See here! That old hell-hag was brainsick. Misery accompanied her like nits on the unwashed. Everybody from Macroom to Cork knew the rumors. But 'tis far worse in other lands. Look at España. Why, ... I hear that crones bake pies out of orphaned babes at night and sell them at next day's market. Makes Ireland look downright civil."

"How did you know I was in danger?"

"I was sleeping in one of the abandoned huts and heard a commotion. When I peeked through the window, I saw her chasing you. That is, chasing you like a hungry ghost."

"But you murdered her!"

"You ungrateful codling," Strongbow said. "I saved your thick skin. Murder! Really! You talk as if you wanted to die."

"My schoolmaster in Cork taught that it is wicked to kill someone because they're peculiar."

"Mighty queer schoolmaster." Strongbow shook his head. "Protecting the defenseless isn't wicked, laddie."

"She had only a knife, and you a pistol. That seemed sort of... unfair."

"Fine! So murder it be. I surrender. But I'll tell you this. Fancy thinking will not keep you alive. I am one of nine brothers. Of them, only three reached manhood. I believe I am the only one remaining. I do what I must, be it stealing, killing, or whatnot. I will survive."

"'Tis the nature of any animal to fight if cornered," Sean said. "But I am not an animal. What of you?"

"I saved the wrong soul! The old witch should have sliced your ear to your belly." With that, Strongbow squeezed the rag tightly, finishing the last knot.

Sean winced from the sudden onslaught of pain.

"You've been pixie-led by a befuddled master. Not many schooled tadpoles here in the bogland, let alone a lad of your tender years. I've met a goodly number of schoolmasters. They preach up a storm and get you all excited over something you cannot remember an hour later. I hope I never bump into yours. Sounds like he could talk Saint Gabriel into a life of sin."

"What are you going to do with me?"

"Nothing." Strongbow huffed. "If you want to be among the pious, try a monastery. But my path offers more promise. You may come along if you can pull your own weight."

Strongbow returned the dagger to Sean. "What is your name, laddie?"

Sean paused. He was suspicious of Strongbow, and he knew Cromwell was still searching for him. "Why should I tell you?"

Strongbow slapped his knee in delight. "Spoken with the wisdom of King Solomon. Every man ought to mask his true identity." Then Strongbow leaned forward and almost whispered. "Want to know a secret of life?"

Sean nodded.

"A wise man knows when to wear the mask and when to show his true face. That bit of knowing will get you far. But I need to call you something. Anything."

Sean glanced at the dagger's hilt. "Ferret. Ferret!"

Strongbow grinned again. "'Tis a splendid name. Indeed it is. Particularly, for a lad who slinks about with the mischief of a devious weasel!"

Chapter 9

A few days later, Strongbow, Paco, and Ferret arrived at the edge of Kilmore Forest, a region of dark woods, white ground fog, and unsteady ground. One of the last unpopulated woodlands, the region was considered to be haunted by evil spirits. Rumors warned that any foolhardy adventurer who entered the forest would never return.

"We must take care. Kilmore is hexed," Strongbow said with a grin, determined to spread his own unique version of the rumors. "Neither Irish nor English will enter here. The threat is too grave, the danger too high. They should expect a swift and merciless death."

"So why should we enter?" Ferret asked with a serious look on his face.

"Well, 'tis the perfect hideaway."

"But what of its ghosts and spirits?"

"Possibly the danger is somewhat... exaggerated."

"So bravery has little to do with it?"

Strongbow's forehead cockled into deep folds. "Listen. It takes men of grit and stout constitution to enter this ghoulish land."

"I'm no chit to scare at your pleasure. I'm not afraid of fairy tales or anything else."

"I would be. Some things cannot be killed."

"Like what?"

"Like acts of kindness."

"You cannot kill such a thing."

"Exactly," Strongbow said with a broad grin as he walked deeper into the forest. "Kindness is a sort of force, a sort of trust that makes people respect each other. Without kindness and trust, what do you have?"

Ferret eyes narrowed to glassy slits. "So, I should trust whatever you say?"

"Well, let's just say I'm more trustful than most."

"Most of whom?"

"Aye, that's the rub." Strongbow pushed forward, leaving the boy and Paco a few steps behind. Strongbow found the boy exhausting, and not only peculiar but overtly suspicious of everything and everyone. That was borderline dangerous, at least to those who had the habit of being too honest. But the boy had other disturbing traits. Strongbow realized that his young traveling companion was a powder keg ready to ignite at the slightest provocation. He had known many a brave man, goliaths with nerves of steel, and yet they dreaded Kilmore Forest. They would rather have another go around with the Spanish pox than to enter Kilmore Forest. But this prickly ragamuffin would tread where muscular angels feared to go.

As the last rays of sunlight faded and a misty fog blanketed the ground, Strongbow stopped and peered around. He knew the dangers of the peat bogs. They could appear anywhere in the forest, hidden under dense layers of moss, pine needles, and grass. They were deep ponds filled with frigid stagnant water. Men and horses alike had been sucked down and disappeared without a trace, leaving only bubbles to mark their graves. After searching for dryer ground, he decided to camp for the night in a small meadow of chest-high grass and thick patches of bulrushes.

Striking a flint rock to iron, Strongbow produced a shower of sparks to light a wad of tinder. After the fire started burning, he proceeded to cook a pot of soup-like stirabout, made from barley, oatmeal, and mostly water. Without fresh milk, it was almost indigestible. To augment the porridge, he passed around a satchel of biscuit crumbs. Ferret took numerous handfuls, but Paco reached in with both hands and stuffed his mouth full. Strongbow simply watched the two gorge themselves on what he considered stale and probably wormy bread.

After the soft glow of twilight had petered out, Ferret moved over to Strongbow and sat next to him. He poked a stick into the hot coals and stirred the embers to make them burn brighter, hoping to get more heat. After attending the fire, he reached for his father's gold ring, pulled it out, and slipped it on. He wanted to examine it in the firelight.

It quickly caught Strongbow's attention. He had heard about such a ring and understood its significance. He assumed that it was just another well-crafted forgery. But if not, it meant the boy had either stolen it or had some claim to royal blood. Still, the royal ring represented a coterie of pompous men with fat bellies and wallets who dominated the commonfolk to suit their personal interests. They would sell their souls for a poke of gold. Strongbow considered such prigmen the bane of society, rewarded with titles, privileges, and bribes by the Crown. Most of the peasantry loathed these selfish cronies for conspiring with other aristocrats in political games of deception and thievery. He had always despised the highborn. He turned to Ferret. "That's a mighty exquisite ring. Is it a *Brehon* ring?"

"'Twas my father's." Ferret scratched the emerald with his fingernail to dislodge some grime.

"Laddie, do you understand what this means?"

Ferret shrugged.

Strongbow frowned. He doubted the ring's authenticity and the boy's possible nobility. Still, he had learned long ago not to disparage princely dreams and lofty aspirations. That is all that most people had in their wretched lives. Why steal hope for a better life? "You could be our future king!"

"I think not."

"Of course, a king requires more than royal blood and a golden ring. He needs an army."

"With an army, who needs royal blood or a ring?"

Strongbow was taken aback and was at a loss to come up with a more astute answer. "Well,... that's not important. What's important is what others think. I mean, the royal ring is a symbol of authority, like the great scepter of the English throne. With it, everyone will be your loyal friend. The Irish throne could be yours for the taking."

Ferret slipped the ring off his finger. He tossed it to Strongbow. "It did not befriend my father."

Strongbow held it up to the light and admired it. "It has been said that the Tyrone clan holds a *Brehon* ring in waiting. I'm afraid it's only a well-worn myth."

Ferret peered at Strongbow. "Are you Strongbow Tyrone?"

"None other."

"My father once spoke about your escapades. He said you were the gentleman's thief. And that you demanded tribute from anyone on the highways. He said a snake would make a better companion."

"I should take offense," Strongbow smiled, "but little offends me these days." He stood up to his full height, brushed bits of grass and dirt from his breeches, extended his affable arms, and launched into an oratorical speech. "I consider myself more of an honest man than a dishonest wood-kern. Like many Irish chieftains, I lay claim to a wee bit of Ireland. I exact a tariff on any wayfarer who enters my territory. Consider it a road toll. Someone must repair the roads. Only an abundance of shillings can perform such a noble feat. But if road fees dishearten you, well, 'tis the price we pay for civilization."

"Have you repaired any roads?"

Strongbow laughed and evaded the question. "Anyway, that is my true legacy." He briskly turned away with a gesture of impatience and distaste, feeling a bad taste in his mouth. He wondered if he should have deserted the boy long ago, especially an irritating one with a hoity-toity posture.

As the fire slowly died down to glowing embers, Strongbow crouched with his back to the boy. He reached for his belongings, pulled out a few supplies, and rolled out a wool blanket across the ground. Next, he fluffed up some bags and garments for a pillow and dropped back to the ground. He faced Ferret with a glare of defiance. "Your name befits you. You lurk about like a shifty weasel, prying into every nook and cranny to besoil my good name. If you want proof of my integrity, I will give it freely. Recently, I captured a thief, a prigman of notorious bad manners. I chained him to the sheriff's door in Cork. Why? Because this freebooter had been robbing the gentry using my good name. Duty and honor bound me to disable the impostor."

"More like eliminating the competition," Ferret said in a quiet voice while grinning slyly.

Strongbow tossed the ring back to Ferret. "You're quite a saucy lad. Mighty cock-sure of yourself. Perhaps you do bathe in royal blood." He pulled the blanket up under his chin and plopped his hat over his face.

Like a dog, Paco circled his pile of sacks and blankets several times before he finally settled down. With a yipping howl of ecstasy, he leaped into the pile and excitedly rolled around as if his bedding held a half-rotten carcass.

Ferret had no bedding or supplies. All he could do was to gather piles of dry leaves and clumps of grass. He scooped them up and then dropped them over his body, trying to find a way to sleep. He sensed the damp coldness that seeped into his skin and chilled the body to the bone. *Eire* was infamous for its biting cold climate that was rarely warm enough to comfortably unclothe oneself indoors or outdoors. He was never going to fall asleep; the noise from his chattering teeth was going to keep him awake until dawn.

Strongbow also found it impossible to sleep. A band of crickets loudly serenaded the silent night air, chirping as if their lives depended on bellowing the loudest sounds. Strongbow drummed his fingers on his chest, thinking back to his hardships growing up in a poor land with little comfort, especially for anyone small, dutiful, and submissive. He had many challenges in growing up. He had once lost a tooth for talking back to his father. Children were expendable, the last ones fed and the first ones to die. During his early years, he firmly believed his parents held a deep affection for him. As he became increasingly skeptical of how things work, he could see the ailment gnawing at the bowels of society. Everything he was told was a cock-and-bull story. He soon understood that he was just another slave bred to work on the family farm.

Trying to find a comfortable spot on the ground, he began to wonder if he should have handled this saucy child as his father would have, with a stiff backhand to the face. It was good enough for most children. Or was it? He had not turned out so well himself. A highwayman was not the epitome of honor. He had abused and mistreated many, but he had little choice. The English had closed down everything. He was too notorious to become an impoverished renter of someone else's land. Backbreaking hard work in the field was never his cup of tea. Perhaps his father had not smacked him hard enough.

Strongbow rolled on his side and saw Ferret shivering under a mountain of leaves and grass. He got up, found a spare blanket, and threw it over the boy. If this pauper ever became a princely king, it could not be said that Strongbow Tyrone had allowed the boy to freeze to death.

As he pondered how to handle the lad, an owl flew low just above his head, shrieking like a mythical banshee. It gave him the shivers. The Irish considered owls a bad omen, harbingers of death. To hear an owl hoot is a warning of impending death in the family. Strongbow glanced about and got the feeling that someone was watching him from a distance. Maybe a murderer followed him and planned to rob his purse. It was an absurd notion; fairy legends were fit only for children and their fanciful imaginations. Even so, he pulled his weapon closer and gripped his blanket tighter.

* * *

Sunlight stung Ferret's eyes the next morning. He rubbed them, threw off his blanket, stood and scanned the surroundings. It took a moment for him to realize that the camp was completely deserted; he was alone again. A queasy feeling swept through his stomach. Strongbow and Paco were nowhere to be found; their equipment and supplies had vanished. Even the campfire's ring of rocks, half-burnt wood, and ashes had magically disappeared. He had half expected this to happen; throughout his life, he had been discarded like a pile of trash. Nobody could be trusted to do the right thing. Despondent, he gazed up into the hazy sky. There was nothing left for him here.

Just as Ferret walked away, a hollow voice rang out from the trunk of a distant hazel tree. All sorts of fears assailed him; it could be a clever trap, an advance party of Cromwell's cutthroats, even another hungry witch with a larger knife.

"Fair morning!" Strongbow suddenly popped out of the opening and ambled toward Ferret, his hands clasped behind his back, looking guilty.

Ferret swung around and with sullen eyes peered at Strongbow. "Were you going to cast me aside?"

"Me? How can you believe such rubbish?"

Ferret just stood there silently like a ghost, saying nothing, his watery eyes filled with hurt and confusion.

Strongbow approached Ferret. He swallowed and then looked down with an apologetic face. "Sorry, laddie. I didn't mean to give you the wrong impression. I felt it was vital to move our encampment last night.

84

You see, I'm at a disadvantage here. Adversaries abound like fungus on dead trees. I understand it not one bit. But heed my words; enemies have the habit of appearing out of nowhere. And they rarely forgive my past deeds."

Ferret nodded slightly and gave a tentative smile.

"I would never abandon a fine mate. Never!"

Ferret nodded again, eyed his blanket on the ground, bent over and picked it up. He handed it to Strongbow. As much as he hated to admit it, he was wrong. "I'm usually the one who's left behind and duped," Ferret said in a mournful tone. "Perhaps some people can be trusted."

"Well, well, imagine that. I was actually right after the fact." Strongbow almost sang his words in harmony.

"Aye, but 'tis the exception," Ferret said as he pepped up a bit. "Trust is harder to find than a comet in the sky. I blame it on England and her ongoing invasion of *Eire*. We have been soiled and defrauded by outsiders. The English make us pay for our own chains. Why are we prisoners in our own land?"

The question took Strongbow by surprise. "Hard to say. I suppose they have no other choice."

"But we do," Ferret said. "We're not moon-blind cattle. I say we must take flight from this cursed isle. 'Tis time to abandon our motherland."

"Oh, hold on there!" Strongbow reached back and rubbed his neck. "That's one ruddy tall order." He quickly realized that to abandon Ireland would imperil his gainful employment. He had done quite well relieving aristocrats of their onerous valuables. He felt that this was almost his duty. For the most part, the upper crust was simply sponging off the Crown which, to his way of thinking, justified his untimely withdrawals of their valuables. He was just stealing back what the stealers had stolen. He was just repeating the glory days of Robin Hood.

"Shall we leave?" Ferret asked impatiently.

Strongbow lingered on the thought for a little longer. He had noticed a worrisome trend. His revenues were decreasing every year. He suspected it was due to the higher tariffs imposed by the British on Irish trade. It did not take a soothsayer to foretell that less Irish imports would shrivel the supply of local wealthy patrons. He likened his situation to a small puddle drying up on a hot summer day. But then again, Irish summers were often cold and foggy.

"Well?"

"I must be honest. I've gotten accustomed to prigging the tainted moneyed and the tax collectors right here. It would be a crime to abandon my demanding clientele." Noticing Ferret's frown, Strongbow added, "I only thieve from those who have too much."

"And who has too much?"

"Certainly not I." Strongbow reached into his pocket and jingled a few coins. "See, the devil may dance in my pockets."

"When the devil's blind."

Beaming, Strongbow slapped Ferret on the back. "There's never enough, by Jove. I'm not ashamed to say that a poke of shiny five-guineas is my bedfellow. Men simply chatter, but gold speaks. Bear in mind that only the money-bags publicly oppose stealing. And that is because they're the only ones with assets worth pilfering."

"Stealing is stealing. And I would never lower myself to the level of a scurvy swagger."

"You're a ruddy pepperbox, all right." Strongbow gritted his teeth with a cringe. He felt an overwhelming urge to slap the urchin across the face but restrained himself. He had never met a child so insolent and discourteous. He was sure that the boy had to be drowning in blue blood. "I wager that your schoolmaster taught you all of this loony claptrap."

"He is the most learned man on the isle," Ferret said. "Aristot is a self-taught polymath and reformer."

Strongbow recognized the name. "I've heard about this wretched wizard. He was imprisoned by both Irish and English. Seems he makes enemies of everyone. Just like me."

"He's no sorcerer," Ferret said. "He taught me to read the classics in Greek and Latin. I learned why the Athenians lost their democracy, why Plato's philosopher-king notion has no merit, and why Aristotle's metaphysics ring clear and true. Yet, they all pale in comparison to Locke's self-governance ideals."

"You've been bewitched. That's plain to see."

"'Tis no puppet-play," Ferret said. "The follies of rulership plague all and always. I shall not be seduced by its dark side. I want no part of it."

"You may have little choice, your highness," Strongbow said, sweeping his hat to his knees in an elaborate bow.

As Strongbow and Ferret sparred, Paco had plucked and skewered two woodcocks and dropped them into the fire. He roasted them until they were black and crisp.

With a quick rise of his hand, Strongbow silenced Ferret. "We have better pursuits." Reaching down, Strongbow picked up a small tree branch, swung it at the fire, and knocked the fowls out of the red coals. Examining the over-cooked meat closer, he joked that they were the recipients of burnt offerings.

Everyone sat on the ground and ate. Still captivated by Ferret's strange tutor, Strongbow waved a half-chewed leg at Ferret. "I must say that many rumors abound over your schoolmaster. I heard that he single-handedly provoked a war in Wexford. Got a whole township to revolt against a British outpost. But, at the last moment, his heart jellied, and he called it off. He fussed that the Irish chieftain was no better than the King of England."

"The chieftain was a bully-rook. Why spill blood to replace one bully with another?"

"Did you know that your Aristot befriended the biggest bully of them all—Lord Oliver Cromwell? The same Cromwell who butchered the Irish some fifty years ago. The most wicked of all despots, I daresay."

Ferret shrugged. "'Tis no secret. Absolute power corrupts all menfolk, even the purest of heart. Aristot once confessed his guilt to me. He has since learned that good intentions often spill over into bad consequences. He revealed to me once that it was impossible to do good without releasing evil."

"Well, so you say. But someone must grab the reins and destroy evil and injustice."

"But that was what Aristot thought he was doing," Ferret said. "He failed. He failed miserably. Violence and revenge are poor weapons to fight evil. Only mercy can vanquish evil."

"Oh, mercy! Well, that's not what I've been told, laddie boy." Strongbow ran his hand over his head and found it difficult to respond. He was not sure how to answer such a bold and sweeping statement. For him, mercy was for the weak-kneed and weak-hearted.

"Listen up, me little weasel. I have a better way to put this. The English have committed many acts of cruelty for which revenge must be sought. Eye for an eye, tooth for a tooth. You can't tell me you don't harbor murderous thoughts against them? That you wouldn't love to slit their throats at night? Be honest."

Ferret's face fell. He stood, and moseyed over to a pile of gear. He reached down and picked up a few pots, looping some of the roped ones around his neck. He looked up, and there was sadness in his eyes. "I've said too much. I've distracted you. Shouldn't we go?"

Strongbow grinned. "Laddie, I relish distractions. That's all we really have in this forsaken world."

Chapter 10

After another day's walk, Strongbow, Ferret, and Paco approached Raca, a village where Strongbow insisted he had once lived. From atop a ridge, they surveyed a broad valley of yellow oxeyes and tall grass sloping gently toward the river. In the distance, two spiraling pinnacles towered in the center of the valley, like tall islands in an ocean of green.

Raca was a simple hamlet, occupied mostly by peevish women, half-naked children, and lazy shepherds. It was where Strongbow had come to marry a woman famed for her outward beauty but ill-reputed for inward ugliness. Strongbow had tried to forget Eileen but often failed. He knew there was little point in dredging up bad memories from the failed past.

Taking a goatskin bag from Paco, Strongbow drank deeply. The liquid felt good, smooth as English Northdown ale.

England.

The dreariness of Ireland had never suited him. His father, along with most of his kinsmen, had sailed on a sloop to Plymouth. It was a common adage among the Irish that it was better to live in a foreign land than under foreign rule in your own. But their timing had been poor. Plymouth was then inundated with forlorn Irishmen, most preparing to depart for France, Spain, or the British colonies of America.

Strongbow had drifted to the gaiety of London. He became a professional gambler, using his charm and wit to exploit the many bored merchant-venturers who spent their time playing cards and drinking. Eventually, he had won a prized freeholder estate along the banks of the Thames, bustling with gardens and servants. For a while, he lived a charmed life among the wealthy, privileged, and military elite, but he lost the estate to the monarch and the pawnshop. He reckoned that the former owner had struck a deal with the authorities, accusing the Irish upstart of cheating at whist. The worst part was that an English civil court had declared him an outlaw, thereby stripping him of any legal protection. Anybody could abuse, rob, or kill him without repercussions. His friends deserted him. They had to. It was illegal for anyone to aid or abet an outlaw. He had to leave England.

Strongbow had always regarded the English as brazen and cocky, confident that they were right and everybody else wrong. And yet their attitude toward the monarchy was puzzling. They seemed to bow down to royalty like docile lambs. The English king did not have to horsewhip or cudgel obedience into their subjects, like foreign despots in savage lands. Such tactics were unnecessary in England. British commonfolk were as eager to obey as the rulers were to rule.

Strongbow recalled an incident where a London printer had published a book without applying for a license. The authorities cropped off his right ear. The man considered himself lucky. If he had printed Milton's *Areopagitica* instead of Chaucer, he would have lost two ears and had his nose slit and forehead branded. But even he seemed grateful that someone was preventing unapproved books from reaching the public. Thereafter, he rebuked his own careless and unlawful actions and told everyone that they must obey the crown, and if caught, pay a heavy price. Strongbow felt discouraged over this blind obedience to authority by the English. He could see that the best slaves are those who think they are free. The Irish had no such illusions.

When he returned to Cork, Strongbow had an arranged marriage to a fifteen-year-old half-Welsh girl. Eileen was a picky, argumentative woman who wouldn't have been satisfied with the Prince of Wales. Within four years, Strongbow left her. After the way she treated him, he would have rather lodged in the boglands and supped on tainted gruel.

The problems started after a few years. His wife failed to bear children, considered the lifeblood of family farmlands and homesteads. She blamed him, he blamed her—they both felt ashamed. To live without children was a sign of doom and despair. It was regarded as a death sentence since there would be nobody to provide loving care for old and withering couples. He had to leave. There was nothing to hold them together. The last he had heard from village elders was that she had died of the pox. The only other news was more hearsay than fact. Years ago he came upon an old acquaintance, a tooth-drawer from Wexford, who told of a rumor that Eileen had given birth to a child eight months after he had abandoned her, a healthy blue-eyed girl. The tooth-drawer claimed the child had been born without a right thumb. Nobody from the village confirmed the birth.

Strongbow brushed off his uniform and descended the ridge toward Raca. He led the party down an overgrown footpath to the monastery, which family lore said had been built before the birth of Saint Patrick. The courtyard was choked with tall bindweed. Earthen mounds and stumps of trees checkered the grounds. Remnants of dead ivy stained the walls. It was just as he remembered.

It was at the monastery that Strongbow noticed something curious—the absence of smoke from village chimneys. Something was terribly wrong. As they hurried down the hill, he could see that large acres of grain fields near the village lay abandoned. Rows of oats and rye had shriveled in the sun. In adjacent fields, swarms of blackbirds devoured what had not already been dug up by wild boars. Half the countryside was starving, and yet here food rotted on the stalk.

They were almost running to a cluster of stone huts on the edge of Raca. Bullet holes pocked the charred walls of most dwellings. Everything had been torched. It was as if the Romans had eradicated the village to prove that they could cause greater destruction than their sacking of Carthage.

Accelerating their pace, Strongbow, Ferret, and Paco rounded a corner and saw a dozen dirty laborers tearing apart the huts with pickaxes. They were loading the building stones into carts and hauling them away. Nearby, women in tattered dresses sat under a Union Jack, watching their children play hide-and-seek.

Strongbow rushed up to a crowd of commoners and confronted a leather-faced man. In his best English accent, he asked, "What happened here?"

"Don't rightly know, sir," the man said. "It was deserted before we arrived." The poorly dressed man spoke with a Cornish accent. His eyes narrowed with suspicion. "See here!" The man's voice suddenly raised in anger. "We're freeholders. We have title to this here land, papers from Dublin. Want to see 'em?"

"No." Strongbow backed off. Turning, he bumped into a young woman breastfeeding her baby. He mumbled a short apology.

The woman eyed him coldly. "'Tis our land, now," the woman blared. "All legal and proper. Right?"

"I'm sure it's yours." Strongbow tipped his hat, turned, and walked toward a burned-out hut. As he stopped in front of a destroyed hut, the breastfeeding woman raced after him. Reaching him, she tugged on his uniform, trying to stop him from entering the structure. "Sir," she almost broke down in tears, "you ought not to look inside. It will cudgel your heart. I know they were Irish, but it is a most gruesome sight."

Ferret glared at the woman and her baby. She cracked a thin smile, but he refused to return the goodwill gesture. He understood that these transplants from England and Scotland were taking over the land. Ferret was in no mood to smile at anyone.

"We tried to notify the authorities," the woman said softly. "No one had bothered to report it."

Strongbow stared at the woman and clenched his fist. "Madame, I know what happened here. I assure you it will not be forgotten."

The woman bowed and backed away.

Strongbow continued down the rocky and rutted road. He wove in and out of half-collapsed buildings. Finally, he stopped in his tracks and glanced around. This was the building. He stepped inside the blackened doorway of a one-room cottage on the edge of town. There, he hesitated and stared down at something in the dirt. Ferret had caught up with him by this time and watched Strongbow stagger out of the sooty hut, his face in his hands. He silently fell to his knees.

Ferret wanted to rush up and console him, but he knew that deep grief demanded solitude. It was a comfort denied him when Black Fox was executed. Right after his father had died he wished never to speak to another human again. Now, he realized that he was not alone, that the injustice of life was not reserved solely for him. He moved toward the doorway.

Strongbow suddenly jerked Ferret back. "'Tis not something you want to retain in memory." Strongbow's voice quavered, his lips trembling.

Ferret broke free of Strongbow's grip. Nothing could be as dreadful as witnessing one's own father die like a cow on a butcher's hook. He wanted to stare horror in the face. He slowly crept inside and saw five half-buried skeletons, their bones charred. It must have been a hellish inferno. Two were small, no doubt children. He realized that these remains were likely Strongbow's only remaining clan. He slowly withdrew from the burnt-out cottage, his head lowered, and leaned against the charred wall.

Paco had finally arrived, looking bewildered and a bit scared. Strongbow stood up, embraced his old Spanish friend, and wiped his sooty hands on Paco's shirt. He took off his red-plumed tricorn hat and raked his fingers roughly through his hair. He then lifted his hat up in the air. "This feathered hat was a gift from my father. I prize it ever so much. But he is gone. He succumbed to the plague in France. I was in London. When his death was made known to me, I felt as if it had never taken place. Distance does that. Somehow I think of him as still alive, enjoying the exciting life of Paris. 'Tis a grand device to block the lingering effects of heartache."

"We should go," Ferret said. Dwelling on the dead never did any good. He had traveled to the underworld of misery for only a few days and felt a desire to remain there forever, never to return to the living.

"I should not have forsaken her," Strongbow murmured. "Poor Eileen."

Ferret found it uneasy to listen to Strongbow's mourning. Pains of the heart should be private, locked away, kept behind stone walls where nobody could intrude. He did not want anyone to know of his own grief or fears. He thought someone might use them against him, as his brother once did.

"She was a sharp-mouthed shrew," Strongbow said. "I should feel no sorrow, no heart-sore. But I do, as if I lost a valuable boot or hunting gun." Strongbow stopped and hesitated for a moment. "That's it! I have merely misplaced her, and if I search hard enough, I will find her again, someday. What do you think, laddie?"

Ferret said nothing. He inched closer to Strongbow and looked up at him with a worried expression. He wished he could say something comforting, but he knew that silence offered more condolence. And yet that in itself seemed so sadder than sad.

Chapter 11

A wind chilled the air as the last rays of sunlight plunged behind the hilltops. Ferret wrapped more rags around his hands. He wondered what to do next. He had no idea where they were going, but wherever it was he wanted to get there fast. Any shelter away from the biting cold would do, but Strongbow had become listless.

"We must find shelter or we'll freeze," Ferret said.

"There's a cave over yonder." Strongbow pointed back to the hillside. "Not far, nor much to offer. 'Tis like Ireland. Some say we're an ill-favored land of not-so-plenty. But I look at the brighter side. 'Tis really a land plentiful with not-so-much."

They passed the outskirts of Raca and came upon a mound of brownish rock guarded by dense undergrowth. A path had been cut through. They approached the opening and found a wooded gate hinged on old shoe leather.

"'Tis my old hideaway. Few know of its whereabouts," Strongbow whispered. "I've arranged to meet an old associate here, a potbellied Scotsman who always had a flea in his ear and fire in his belly. Most ill-tempered man of the cloth I've ever known."

Strongbow made his way down the path and squeezed into the cave. He motioned for Paco to follow. Paco refused to go inside, afraid of the dark cave and its narrow entrance. Ferret barged through the small entrance and saw a faint beam of light straight ahead, so dim that he could only navigate by pressing his hands against each side of the cold cave wall. As his eyes became more accustomed to the murky light, he encountered mats of spider webs clogging parts of the cave tunnel. Most of the webs had been pushed aside. He presumed that Strongbow had done it, but the cave had become so wide by then that only a whole regiment of soldiers could have dislodged them. Pressing onward, he soon noticed the glow of burning torches. The light was unnerving; it cast an eerie light on the high, jagged ceiling of the cave. As he turned a corner, Ferret thought he heard voices.

Suddenly, someone stepped in front of the boy and shouted, "Who goes thar?" Dressed in a large, brown frock, the man blocked Ferret's way and held several torches above his head. The fiery light blinded Ferret, forcing him to shield his face and eyes with his hands. He could only discern a stout figure with big feet.

The fat man glared down at Ferret. "Not another stray chit. They plague the land like pesky ship rats."

"Not that particular chit, I would wager," another voice rang out from the back section of the cave. "The laddie may be one of the chosen ones."

"Oh?" The fat man swung around to confront the new intruder. "What did ja say, heathen?"

"Don't you recognize me?" Strongbow asked.

"I wish I could say no." The fat man lowered his torches. "Ya might be the devil incognito?"

"I will never tell." Strongbow laughed with a hearty roar.

"Ha, . . . well, ya still not worth a turd in my book."

"Well, upon my soul. I see that my old Badger hasn't changed one bit after all these years. Wonders never fail to surprise."

"If ya had a soul." Badger exploded with an elated chuckle. His scowl shifted to a lopsided grin.

Without further words, they embraced and slapped each other on the back.

With a quick shift of his body, Badger stepped back and blinked in amusement. He had just noticed Strongbow's English uniform. "Great snakes! Ya've enlisted with the English again. Red coats must be fashionable amongst thieves."

"Who else dons them?"

The two laughed as they walked deeper into the cave, leaving Ferret behind.

Badger had dropped one of his torches, allowing Ferret to pick it up and follow. After walking 30 yards, he came upon a wall covered with hand-carved messages. He stopped and studied the old writing. The text appeared to be in crude dog-Latin and spoke about a strange blazing light up in the sky. It warned about God's displeasure against those who bear the mark of the beast. It went on to tell of God's fury and the pouring of the blazing light into his cup of wrath, or something to that effect. Ferret surmised that the strange light must have been a comet, meaning that the message came eons before the arrival of Galileo. As for the beast, he thought it might be a reference to English outsiders, who had been beastly to the Irish for centuries. He found it curious that God's divine wrath so far had been unfulfilled.

Strongbow and Badger entered a small, high-ceilinged room illuminated by torches and dozens of long-necked candles. Strongbow sat next to a wobbly table littered with chipped brown earthenware. A bleached skeleton with a red handkerchief around its neck sat in a chair across from him. Strongbow nudged Badger with his elbow. "One of your most devoted mates?"

Badger lifted up the chair, skeleton and all, and set it far away from the table. "I'm particular about the company I keep." Badger groaned as he sat in an old straw-lashed chair that creaked with his every move. "But ya be my exception, Strongbow."

Badger poured ale into Strongbow's clay mug and rested his elbow on the filthy table. He frowned with a look of desperation in his eye. "Much has gone awry."

"Like what?" Strongbow innocently asked.

"Why, ya old fart! Do ya know that I'm on the run? Cromwell had me arrested and detained. The man suspects everyone of deception."

"Of course, you'd never stoop to deception." Strongbow laughed.

"Don't give me the cockbrain drivel! I was a spy and a God-fearing one too. I abetted the Irish more than any Scot."

Strongbow lifted his empty mug, begging for another round of libations. Badger obliged, refilling Strongbow's mug to the brim. They both toasted with the clinking of mugs. "I must say," Strongbow said, "let's hear it for crafty spies and merry old Scotland. Now, where's the grub?"

Badger frowned again, then pointed to a sack of rotting oats, an almost empty hogshead of ale, and baskets of old dried fish. He poured more ale for himself.

Strongbow glared at Badger and attempted to imitate his friend's scowling face. "Seriously. This be it?"

Badger shrugged and looked resigned.

"Well, I guess we should all leave and dine in Cork," Strongbow bellowed with a sense of humor. "There's plenty of edibles there."

"Not on my life," Badger said. "They'll likely dine on us."

Strongbow sat up straight, eyes wide open, and met Badger's grimace. He appeared to be enjoying his battle of wits with his old friend. "Come, come. I have a wonderful plan to make us wealthy. And if you join me, you could be my jovial Friar Tuck."

"I'll fry, that be sure." Badger grumbled. "Ya didn't listen to me. I was arrested by Cromwell. God-a-mercy, I escaped. Now I'm an outlaw."

"You're in good company."

Badger rubbed his stomach. "Odd's Bodkins! Cork be far too dangerous. Cromwell will cleave our skulls and pluck our bones. He's determined now, since executing Black Fox."

"Executed the Fox, you say?" Strongbow mumbled and leaned back in his chair, appearing unsurprised.

"Aye," Badger said as he guzzled his ale. "Last true rebel leader. Palsy day for *Eire*, that's for sure."

Entering the room, Ferret approached Badger and stared at his pudgy face. At first, he froze but soon inched his way toward Strongbow. Not wanting to be overheard, he cupped his mouth to Strongbow's ear and whispered. "Don't trust him. He's a turncoat," Ferret clamored. "I saw him near Macroom with Cromwell."

"Well," Strongbow turned toward Ferret with a look of amusement, "that is not so perplexing. That's because he was under Cromwell's command."

"We must capture him and tie him up!" Ferret demanded in a louder voice.

Badger suddenly stopped eating. He pointed at Ferret and glared at Strongbow. "Who's the brassy codling?"

"An orphan I found along the highway," Strongbow said as he poked at a piece of wormy fish. "He accuses you of hobnobbing with Cromwell. What say you?"

"I was doing no such thing," Badger roared, "I was spying on him. I'm no pawn of the English. I escaped from his clutches. Sure, I joined his bloody band of cutthroats, but briefly. I took the spot of a Scottish replacement, a sergeant-major Stuffleton. The poor dolt happened to have died on his way to Cromwell's command. A real tragedy if I ever saw one."

Ferret stepped back, not knowing what to think. Nobody was what they appeared to be. It was like the dull, dark stones that momentarily turned beautiful when wet. The water was hiding the innate ugliness of the world. His father had been right. Everyone had a hidden, dark side, and it would only be exposed when subjected to the hot light.

"I would not trust him," Ferret said.

"I'll slap that dung-faced brat to New Spain," Badger bellowed and reached for Ferret's face with his flabby arms. Ferret backed against the cave's wall. Light from the torches fully illuminated the boy's face. Badger took a closer look at the young intruder. "Wait a blasted minute. Ya him! The crackbrain boy with the dagger!" He turned to Strongbow, horrified. "Charged the whole regiment, the wag did."

Strongbow cocked his head and glanced at Ferret with a sparkle in his eyes. "I thought you were against killing others."

Badger pounded the table with his fist. "The lad assaulted Cromwell. Gashed and bloodied the general's face. Ya got a hell-bred polecat nipping at your heels."

Strongbow grinned. "Lord 'a Mercy! It seems I have found my successor!"

"I'd rid myself of the lad," Badger said. "Cromwell has put a price on his head."

Strongbow's grin widened. "Does he not search for us all? We all would make a merry band in Cork."

"Not Cork! Ya be like the wind-blown dandelion. Who knows where you'll fly off next?"

"Cork is rich with merchants to rob—for Ireland's sake, of course."

"Horse piss!" Badger's belly quivered like jelly. "Ya rob men by day and squander the spoils by night. Ya're an Englishman at heart—stayed in London too long."

"I can deal with Cromwell." Strongbow propped his boots on the table. "'Tis like plucking flowers in God's acre."

"You blasphemous ragman. Ya be worse than a freethinker." Badger shoved a long, wooden crucifix in front of Strongbow's face and then slammed it on the table. Just then, two figures emerged from the darkness. One was a young man, gaunt and thin, wearing a frayed cloak of tawny wool. Behind him tagged a child, no more than four or five years of age, clad in a one-piece cloak. The child cringed at Badger's voice.

"This be MacMacken," Badger said. "He served with me since we departed Scotland. His mother was a Pict Highlander, and this shame weighs heavy on his soul. Doesn't it lad?"

MacMacken shook his head.

"Notwithstanding," Badger said, "MacMacken's father hewed a true and loyal Scotsman out of him."

"Who's the child?" Strongbow asked.

"Some beggar child. Orphaned, like half of *Eire*."

"Boy or girl?"

Badger reached over and flipped up the child's garment. "Has no divining rod, so 'tis a girl."

Frightened, the girl scurried behind the hogshead barrels and began wrapping tatters of cloth around her small cold hands.

"We found her wandering in the village. The English settlers were feeding her like a stray cat. They dumped her on me because they had little food to spare. Now the runty whelp follows us everywhere we go." Badger began to eat strips of dried beef. "She must be deaf-mute. Won't say a word. We can't take her with us."

MacMacken sat and joined the small feast. Swilling a tankard of ale, he plopped several sacks of old rye onto the table. He attempted to pick out the worms but found too many. He gave up, reached for a blackened loaf of bread and scraped off the mold. With a few swallows, it was gone. Next, he lifted up a string of dried, smoked fish and sniffed it. Shaking his head, he tossed it over his shoulder.

Badger, who was less finicky about his cuisine, stuffed his mouth. "To your health." When he began to make another toast, his clay mug cracked and ale trickled down his arm. He plugged it with his thumb. "If only we had hot buttered rum to warm our jolly selves, we'd all be as merry as elves." He reached into the sack and poured rye into his mouth, worms and all. "The Britons be a venomous race of serpents that spew wickedness from their tongues with the ease of barristers." Bits of food and drink sprayed from his mouth.

"Hear! Hear!" MacMacken cheered, pounding the table. "Sing another Scottish ballad."

Strongbow brushed crumbs from his uniform. "Tell us something we don't know!"

Badger grimaced and belched. "What more do ya want! Ya're a fine mate, to blow the thunder out of my sails."

As Badger, Strongbow, and MacMacken drank, Ferret edged toward the table to filch one of the grain sacks. Suddenly, the girl tugged at his cloak. She unwrapped the rags around her hands and pointed to her quivering mouth. Ferret understood—she, too, wanted food. He noticed the girl's right hand was thumbless and wondered if it were a natural deformity from birth. He grasped her disfigured hand. The girl did not object; she permitted Ferret to touch her as if she enjoyed the attention. No scars—it seemed God must have wanted her to have only nine fingers. She quickly rewrapped her hand.

As Ferret and the girl feasted on the grain, MacMacken spoke of an Irish spy employed by Cromwell.

"'Tis true," Badger said. "Cromwell has a most devious spy in Cork; one of his most steadfast cronies. Sold a sketch of Black Fox to Cromwell. A viler traitor was never born."

"Has to be true," MacMacken said. "How else was Cromwell able to snare Black Fox at his den?"

Ferret stopped chewing, his face flushed red, and his eyes blinked rapidly. He tensed up. His attention was now focused on Crowell's mysterious spy in Cork. He listened closely to what the others were saying about the turncoat responsible for his father's demise. Immediately he made up his mind. That was where he had to go—Cork. Uncover the man's identity and make him pay for his crime.

"Then again," Badger blabbered as he chewed, "all of *Eire* teems with spies. 'Tis why Cork be most unhealthy."

Strongbow taunted him: "Spies like you?"

Badger growled. "God's thunder! Ya stubborn goat-sucker! Don't ya lock bullhorns with me again! And take yar chit with ya. Lordy knows ya've assembled the ragpickers of the earth. That boy be yar worst problem. Best to dispatch him along the way."

"Why?" Strongbow took a big swig of ale.

"Because the boy is the son of Black Fox," Badger blurted out.

Strongbow spewed ale into Badger's face. "What?!"

"Ah, son of a bitch!" Badger wiped the ale off his frock and face. "This be too much. I'll see you in Ulster, Hades, or with St. Peter, whichever comes first, I care not the damnedest." Badger took one last swallow of ale, whisked the grain sacks off the table, and stomped away.

Strongbow stared at Ferret and hesitated. "Hmm... be this true? Was your father Black Fox?"

Ferret looked up with wide eyes and calmly nodded. He thought back to what Strongbow had said about his dead wife. He too wanted to think of his father's death as ancient history—like it never happened. And if it never happened, then why get all excited about it? Fate was not something that acted on its own. What was done was done. But he could not stop thinking about revenge.

"He was a devilishly smart fellow," Strongbow said somberly. "I had some dealings with the Fox in the past. Ireland will miss him."

MacMacken stood and gave a pleasant farewell to Strongbow. He announced that come morning, he and Badger would depart for the coast. They both agreed to leave the girl child behind and let her fend for herself.

Strongbow took another long gaze at Ferret and laid a hand on his shoulder. "I'm sorry, laddie. I'll do what I can. But I'm afraid it will never be enough."

* * *

The next morning, Strongbow poked Ferret as he slapped dirt off his uniform. "Up, you slugabed! The sun lingers for no man." He raked back his hair with his fingernails. He found a tick crawling on his neck, plucked it off, and squeezed the little bloodsucker against the wall.

Ferret got up, rubbed his eyes, and wondered how Strongbow knew it was morning. They were too deep in the cave for sunlight to penetrate. He thought that some people must have inner timepieces and could wake up at any time they wanted. He had no such ability, but he wished the dawn would come later.

They found Paco outside the cave, shivering in an early morning mist, pacing back and forth like a caged animal.

Badger had departed with MacMacken earlier, leaving the girl behind as planned. She, too, was outside not far from Paco, sitting on the soggy ground and playing in little pools of muddy water. Ferret knew he could do nothing for her. He had his own problems and had to take care of himself first. Still, the thought of abandoning the child—only a baby, really—left a bitter taste in his mouth. The girl would starve like countless other orphans who wandered the countryside.

The girl approached Ferret and reached up to him with her muddy hands. Her red hair was tangled and matted, her pale face streaked with drool, and her legs smudged with dirt and grass stains. Her blue eyes begged for attention.

With a rag, Ferret tried to clean dry blood and dirt from her forehead. That was a futile effort. Next, he reached into a small poke and gave her a handful of oats, nearly all the food he was rationed for the day. She wolfed down every piece. Then she burped and began to hum tuneless rhymes to herself. He was sure nobody would rescue such a useless urchin. She was so small, thin, and ugly.

"What will become of her?" Ferret asked as he draped a blanket across Paco's shoulders.

Strongbow said nothing.

"She could come with us."

"We do not have enough food."

"I know," Ferret said. "But we cannot leave her behind. That would be pitiless."

Strongbow handed several pots and coils of rope to Ferret to carry.

Ferret hated to admit it, but nobody cared about people who had nothing to offer. He himself had often been mistreated for that reason. That fact was a festering wound. If only Strongbow would become beholden to her. He thought there must be some way to convince him.

Ferret crouched down to the girl's eye level and tried to comfort her. She reached out and hugged him, reluctant to let go. He decided that they had to take her along. No other course of action could dispel the guilt that was seeping into his heart.

"She won't be much trouble," Ferret said.

"She will be unable to keep pace," Strongbow said impatiently. "She'll delay us. Leave her be and help pack." Strongbow tied the last supplies on Paco's back.

Ferret bit down on his fingernails and kept weaving in and out of intense reflection. He had to do something. But what? The orphan was no kindred to him. He had no obligation whatsoever to help her. Why was he so concerned about helping this child from nowhere?

"She won't eat much," Ferret said. "I will watch over her."

"We only have enough for one meal a day for the three of us."

Strongbow started down the path, followed by an overloaded Paco. Ferret lagged behind, unsure what to do. He looked back. The girl was following him. There was nothing he could do. He knew she would never survive the winter night out in the open.

Suddenly, the girl fell into a puddle of icy water and squealed.

He ran to her and peered down. "You're too much trouble." He shook his head.

She reached up with her frail arms, begging.

Ferret hesitated, then he dropped his pots and pans and lifted her in his arms. "We cannot take you. You cannot come with us. You understand?"

As he carried the girl, she played with Ferret's hair and gurgled. Soon, she twisted from side to side and became fidgety. She was too much trouble. Ferret set her down and walked ahead. After a few yards, he peered back and saw her tagging behind like a donkey, sampling the grass at every fencepost. This was unacceptable.

Ferret gritted his teeth and hurried down the pathway. He was not going to wait for her. He could not share his single daily meal with a child too stupid to keep up.

He remembered what an elder yeoman had told him about French peasants; they were fortunate to eat three decent meals a week. The less fortunate would go mad with hunger, and with bloated stomachs and hollowed eyes ate dirt to kill the hunger pangs. That was not going to happen to him. Let the girl be on her own. There were plenty of dead children alongside paths and roads, so many that nobody had the time to bury them. What was one more? Let wild dogs tear off her legs and arms and gnaw her bones.

Although Ferret moved further ahead, he continued to look over his shoulder. When the girl slowed down, so did he. Finally, he stopped and waited for her. "'Tis no game. You must keep up."

She nodded.

"I'm not your keeper."

Within minutes, the girl ran off and began to play hide-and-seek. When Ferret would twist around, she would dart behind a brier thicket and peek at him, sometimes waving in delight.

Picking up his pace, Ferret hiked ahead and soon lost sight of her. But again, after a while, he waited for her to catch up. When she did not come, he backtracked and found her sitting in a patch of violet bindweeds.

Reaching for his coil of rope, Ferret lifted the girl's sack-like dress and tied a loop around her waist. "*Stad*," he ordered and tugged on the rope. She refused to stand. He started to panic. The thought of being abandoned by Strongbow horrified Ferret. So he dragged the girl behind him as she tossed stones at him. "I'm not your *mathair*." He picked up the child, shortened the rope, kept it taut, and forced her to follow. When she became too tired to walk, he carried her. This was one orphan who would not be left to the dogs.

* * *

A few days later they entered Agora, a small seaport on the eastern coast. They headed for a small, gothic-looking cathedral at the center of the town.

Except for the stone-built cathedral, all the buildings of Agora were makeshift, constructed of thin wood, hemp canvas, and sticks. The entire town could be taken apart, moved, and rebuilt. Many such Irish towns were movable, allowing the inhabitants to follow their sheep and cattle herds according to the seasons.

Agora was prosperous. The streets were choked with carts brimming with sacks of grain, barrels of fruit, slabs of pork, and foreign goods. The inhabitants were well-fed and jovial. They wore silk and otter furs. Merchants bustled about, trading and mingling with English gentlemen, ship captains, and clergymen. Many wore fur coats and feathered hats, and all appeared unarmed. Unarmed! The thought was perplexing. All the Englishmen Ferret had known feared to work unprotected when dealing with Irishmen. Ferret gawked at the wealth he saw. How was it possible? How could they be so well fed? A cheese merchant strolled by. He was heavily perfumed. His stench of sweat and sweetness was so potent that Ferret felt compelled to bat away the odor.

Suddenly, Ferret felt a tug on his rope as the girl lunged at a barrel filled with fruit. Before she could reach the food, Ferret reeled her back. English justice was merciless and swift. Stolen goods could result in a lopped-off hand, even for a small beggar child.

Coming to the cathedral, Ferret stopped and looked at the black mold caking the tall stone archways. Its courtyard was strangled with weeds and high-climbing vines. A heavy lock and chain at the front entrance frustrated Strongbow's attempts to break in. After a barrage of curses, he stomped to the rear of the cathedral and discovered a small door sealed by several large planks. Strongbow hurled the boards aside, barely missing the girl's head.

"Get that tit away!" Strongbow roared. "How many times do I have to tell you? Leave her behind."

"She followed me."

Strongbow rushed over to the girl and lifted up the rope that connected her to Ferret. "Then what's this?"

Ferret simply shrugged and ignored Strongbow's uncaring remarks. This all seemed so unfair and tragic to him. He could not simply let the orphan girl wander the hinterland by herself. Nobody would help. Ferret had promised to share half his food with the waif. That did not satisfy Strongbow, who warned that hunger pangs would eventually override his generosity.

Strongbow turned back to the opening and crept through. The others followed.

Inside the sanctuary, Strongbow walked toward the altar. Shafts of light beamed down from the half-rotted roof sixty feet above. Pools of water reflected the sunlight like broken shards from a looking glass. He splashed down the center aisle, past broken pews gauzed with cobwebs. The area was enclosed with carved wooden walls, furnished with a few small tables and long rags on the windows. Strongbow appeared to be searching for something.

The girl wandered until she discovered a bowl of old, green crabapples in a large box. She popped one of the fruits into her mouth, then another. Unable to eat so many at one time, she tried to hoard them inside her cloak, only to watch them slide down onto the floor. When Ferret drew close, the girl sat on the floor to guard her nest of fruit like a jealous hen protecting her clutch of eggs.

When Ferret picked some up, she pushed him away. That was not what he had expected. He thought she should be grateful to him, and share. Ferret reached under her legs and grabbed several of the bruised crabapples.

Sitting cross-legged, she stuck out her tongue at Ferret.

"You greedy gully gut! Give some to me."

She spat a half-chewed glob of crabapple in his face.

He wiped his face with his hand. Strongbow was right. Hunger made people crazy. But he realized that hunger was not a good reason to seize the girl's crabapples. Let her have what she had found. The crabapples were small, old, and probably bitter.

Moving away, Ferret noticed three books on the altar. He reached up and picked up the largest, a leather-bound tome. He opened the cover. The words were in Latin. They said something about holy books.

A voice cracked like a bullwhip: "Drop it!"

Ferret looked up. In front of him stood a flabby-bellied priest. It was Badger.

Badger rushed over and snatched the book away, grumbling. "This be the holiest of holies. Only God's anointed clergy may gaze upon His sacred words. Yar eyes would sizzle like hot wrought iron if ya read a single passage. And then yar eyes'd bleed red. Only men of the cloth may interpret the Lord's words."

"But what if a clergyman misinterprets what's written?" Ferret asked innocently.

"What bibble-babble. Heretics like ya will not get past the gates of Saint Peter. How can ya understand? We're the infallible ones."

"Luther disputed that long ago. The Bible is for everyone's eyes."

Badger's mouth foamed. "Martin Luther! That blasphemer spewed lies to the ends of the earth."

"He did not," Ferret said.

"Do ya doubt my authority?"

"I wish not to. But when I get to heaven I shall ask him," Ferret said with confidence.

Badger snickered. "Fine, what if Luther went to Hell?"

"Then you may ask him."

Before Badger could wring Ferret's neck, Strongbow stepped between the two. "Let's not start a civil war. The boy is just an inquisitive lad. No harm done."

"The devil dwells in his soul!" Badger snorted and wheezed. "Ya've corrupted this lad, no doubt."

"No doubt," Strongbow said in a sarcastic way.

"So why did ya follow me here?" Badger grumbled.

"I could ask you the same!"

"I'm here to meet with my fellow clergymen."

"Fancy that! I too have an appointment. That is, with something more important."

With a smirk, Badger asked, "Like a poke of gold?"

Before Strongbow could answer, two priests stepped out of the dimness. One was MacMacken, now robed in gray. The other was a short, middle-aged man with a kind face. His thin arm swung limply as if it had no bone to support the flesh.

Badger pointed to the older priest. "That be Father Yeats. But more importantly, why would anyone hide gold here?"

Strongbow shrugged. "What better place than a cathedral? 'Tis deserted, and churchgoers are forbidden to enter."

Father Yeats drew closer. He was cradling his lifeless arm. "Colonel Winchester found the gold behind the altar yesterday. I saw him take it from under the floorboards near the altar."

Strongbow walked over to a church pew, dropped into the seat and slouched like a sack of meal on a saddle. "I've been made the fool." After fuming for few minutes, he stretched his boots up over a pew railing. "But I will not leave without my payment."

"You must!" Father Yeats's voice became strained. "Winchester is paid handsomely to permit this port to operate. Cromwell suspects him. Our situation is delicate."

"You mean your smuggling operations are in danger."

"We all benefit from our... associations with the colonel."

"Very good," Strongbow said as he kicked over the pew railing, causing dust to fly. "'Tis impressive when a crook can justify his own crimes."

Father Yeats raised his eyebrows. "Crime, is it? Smuggling is no vice. We barter Irish flax for Spanish grain with nobody the worse: no killing, no robbery—just a fair exchange. Can your profession make the same claim? I know you prig the highways like the most common of thieves."

"That's not my only talent."

"So you also bare your skills at the brothel?"

Before Strongbow could reply, the thunder of horses' hooves disturbed the silence. The main church doors were burst open and a dozen dragoons armed with flintlocks surged inside. They were led by a tall, slender corporal carrying a pistol.

Without warning, Strongbow whipped out his own pistol and aimed it at Father Yeats's chest. "You're under arrest!"

The corporal pointed his pistol at Strongbow's head. The other men backed him up, lifting their weapons. "Caught at last!" He quickly seized Strongbow's pistol.

"Indeed," Strongbow said to the corporal. "But for what?"

"You're wanted for treason, Colonel Winchester."

Strongbow flinched in surprise and fumbled for a response. "Me? Winchester? How delightfully preposterous."

"Well?"

"Listen here," Strongbow said, "I would wager good odds that I'm a wee bit smaller than that pompous elephant with an inflated sense of self-importance. But if you were to locate the scoundrel, I would be the first to blanch his bones in boiling oil."

The corporal looked again at Strongbow, thought for a moment, then lowered his pistol. "True, you don't seem to fit his portly and conceited features." He began to scratch the back of his head nervously. "It seems we have a mutual foe!" Then he added, "But why are you, an officer, in this banned cathedral?"

"I've just apprehended these papist spies. They are unregistered and most dangerous."

The dragoons swung their flintlocks at Badger, MacMacken, and Father Yeats.

"And they are bloody thieves to boot," Strongbow said.

The corporal stroked his stubbled chin. "And, by God, who are you, Sir?"

"Major Strongbow. You are...?"

"Holbrook. Corporal Jonathan Holbrook, Sir."

"Corporal Holbrook, I have captured these unregistered priests, possibly Jacobites infiltrating the King's lands. I believe the swag-belly is a Jesuit, as wicked as they come. The other one, I discovered, stole parishioners' tithes in Waterford. Not one pittance was given to the Church of England."

Holbrook looked dubious. "I see by your insignia that you are from the 8th Dragoons of Parliament's armed forces. Are they not stationed in Londonderry?"

"Your sharp eyes are a credit to your uniform, Corporal. I'm on a secret assignment, commissioned by London to uncover a hideous plot, the details of which I cannot divulge. Completely hush-hush, as you can imagine."

"I am imagining a lot, Major," Holbrook said, his dark brows knotted.

"Corporal," Strongbow said, "I will not have suspicion cast on my authority by a lower-ranking officer. And likely a non-commissioned one at that. You fail to realize the importance of these clergymen. They might be the vanguard of a secret invasion of Ireland by French of Spanish forces."

"But, Sir..." Corporal Holbrook softened his voice and straightened his stance. "These circumstances are most irregular!"

"Corporal, your provincial attitude shocks me," Strongbow said with raised eyebrows. "To disobey a superior officer is a serious offense. Would you risk your life for a superficial suspicion? Would anyone of you?"

Holbrook glanced down. The corners of his mouth dipped into a dismayed frown. "I assure you that I do not question your authority. 'Tis only that..."

"I would never risk stretching my neck on a gallows because of a fanciful doubt. Never!" Strongbow uttered forcibly.

"I understand." Holbrook returned Strongbow's pistol.

"Good. Now, I have need of your assistance. I must deliver my prisoners to Cork. Four or five of your men will do splendidly."

Badger's face turned white. His eyes darted back and forth between Strongbow and Holbrook. "I'll not be taken to Cork alive."

"So we'll take you there less than alive," Strongbow said.

"Ya would like that, wouldn't ya?"

"Did you hear me, Corporal? I require five of your best dragoons."

The corporal began to perspire. "Sir, I have in all one dozen men at my command. I cannot spare one soldier."

"Come here." Strongbow beckoned the officer with his arched finger. They moved away from the others, stopping in front of the smashed altar.

Holbrook spoke first in a low tone. "Major, even if I could relinquish all of my dragoons, you would be inviting disaster."

Strongbow quickly noticed that the man's eyes were bloodshot and ringed with dark bags. "My lord, are you ill?"

"I've not slept for days. You see, I am in distress. Four of my men have already deserted since departing Cork. One scurvy knave attempted to choke me in my sleep. I have only a two-day's supply of food for a four-day mission. For ammunition, I have thirty rounds remaining."

"That's so!"

"It gets worse," Holbrook said. "My men have not been paid for two months. They are jittery, hot-tempered, and contemptuous of authority. Morale has sunk to the lowest ebb I've ever witnessed. Some of these men were crimped into the military. Others were loaned from petty lords who were required to send someone. They sent criminals. All pressed into service and told in no uncertain terms that they had to join or rot in jail. These be unsavory men."

"Give me at least one," Strongbow said.

"Very well!" Holbrook strode back to his men. He faced one soldier, grasped his arm and pulled him forward. "This is Frank Sterns. I suggest you hog-tie him at nightfall and let one of priests guard him instead." The corporal coughed into his hand, concealing a weary grin. "Good day, sir." He swerved around and departed in haste, followed by the remainder of his men.

Strongbow studied the soldier. "You come highly recommended. Let's see if you measure up to your reputation."

Sterns smiled. "I'm sure I will, sir."

Chapter 12

Strongbow drummed his fingers on the church pew as he carefully examined Frank Stern. "You're under my command now. Is that clear?"

"Aye, sir!" Stern's bald head covered liberally with ringworm sores, he scratched vigorously while trying to remain at attention. He had a nervous tic, and there was a nasal quality to his voice. He dropped his pistol, apologized, and then dropped it again. He reminded Ferret of a jester in a troupe of roadside performers. This soldier was much less than he had expected from Cromwell's legions. He was a clown, but one who made no one laugh.

Strongbow strolled around Stern several times and studied him with the intensity of a papal inquisition. "What do you know about Colonel Winchester?"

"Nothing. He's a deserter. Ran off with some lower-ranked officers, I hear."

"And the gold?"

"What gold?" Stern asked.

"What gold?" Strongbow repeated, disheartened. "Don't they tell you anything?"

"Well, just hearsay. And that is usually unreliable."

"I must be blessed with the luck of the Irish." Strongbow lowered his head and gently squeezed his earlobe.

"That bad, sir?"

With a frustrated growl, Strongbow kicked over a tall wooden church pew to his right. He seemed to enjoy destroying church furniture. It still gave him little satisfaction; the bench was heavily damaged. The enclosed wall had already half-collapsed into the aisle. He turned back and faced Stern. "Bad? 'Tis worse than bad. The robber hath been robbed. Why is my destiny so elusive?" He drew in a deep breath and released it slowly. "Let's try another approach. Tell me why Corporal Holbrook treated you so... let's say, discourteously?"

"I'm a royalist," Stern said proudly. "Holbrook backs Parliament. 'Tis a somber difference, to be sure."

"I see," Strongbow said, turning to Badger. "Bind his hands."

Stern's forehead furrowed. "What? You're not serious! My commander was just playing a bit of tomfoolery."

"I'm not." Strongbow swung his pistol at Stern. "There're no devotees of the King amongst us. As for me, I loathe bowing to anyone less scrupulous than myself."

"Sir, this is surely a prank!"

"No doubt," Badger said as he tied the soldier's hands.

Stern's eyes blinked rapidly. "Major Strongbow, indeed!" His voice rose. "God-a-mercy! You're an impostor!"

"The real impostors are the English," Strongbow said. "They act as if the Lord Almighty dwelt within their household. And when they discover a neighbor of a different creed, they murder him in the dead of night. The English speak of liberty and then defecate on the rights of freeborn commoners in every land. Tyranny lurks in their hearts like boils on scarred flesh."

Ferret was astonished by Strongbow's strong words. He had thought his friend only cared about relieving people of their money and embellishing tall tales. Was he just mouthing another person's diatribes?

"Bosh!" Stern shook his head. His face turned red. "You're a prick-eared liar. Ireland squats in filth and chaos. The Irish sleep with oxen and sows on dirt floors of dung and piss. They're half-naked, shoeless. They haven't a tuppence to their bastard names. Most live without chimneys and gnaw on raw meat. Everyone on this isle desperately needs our help. I've seen more civilized savages in Guinea."

Strongbow was unimpressed. "By all means, we'll confine our livestock, build chimneys, and burn our meat. 'Twas decent of you to civilize us. Now you may sail back home with the comfort of having tamed another backward people."

Then, with a wry smile, Strongbow shoved his pistol closer to Stern's face. "On second thought, we cannot set you free. You just might try to help another land of savages! We cannot bear to see you go through such trouble again, can we?" Strongbow pulled a cowbell from Paco's pocket and hung it around Stern's neck. "Just belling the cat. I hope you take no offense."

Badger yanked on Stern's rope and led him like a cow around the church grounds. With some assistance from Father Yeats, Badger eventually lashed Stern to an archway for the night.

To Ferret, it seemed heartless and pointless. The soldier had done nothing to hurt them. Ferret realized he had probably been crimped into the military against his will and likely hated his service in *Eire* as much as the Irish hated his presence.

Ferret watched Stern and his struggle to break free of the ropes. On the surface, he loathed all Britons or any foreigner who would invade and ravish another land. But he knew that acts of injustice were not confined to one nationality. A king and his ministers never counseled with the populace. So how could the subjects of the king be held responsible for their government's action? The people had no choice but to follow, escape, or die. That was the real crime. Mistreating this defenseless soldier would accomplish nothing. The real criminals resided at the palace of Westminster.

* * *

When the morning sun invaded the dark church, everyone awoke. Ferret was first to rise. He quickly tied the rope around the girl and rushed outside.

Immediately, he had a feeling that something had changed. It was far too tranquil for this flourishing seaport. Peering through the church's gates, he realized that the village had disappeared, its makeshift buildings and boisterous people all gone. Only the monastery and several courtyard walls remained, looking desolate and windswept on the empty bluffs. Ferret suspected that the arrival of Holbrook's dragoons the day before had alarmed the residents. It signaled to the town folks that their prosperity was near its end. To government officials, smugglers were viewed as pirates, who engaged in criminal acts destined to lead to a hanging. That would frighten anybody away.

Searching through wet rubbish, Ferret found a few half-rotten pears and prepared to eat them all. Suddenly, the girl nudged him and pointed to her mouth. At first, he resisted, thinking back to the unshared crabapples. Despite his hunger, Ferret poked his thumb into the fruit and broke off the lion's share for the girl. She smiled with gratitude. Maybe she would learn from his example.

After devouring the pear, the girl slipped the rope from her thin hips, as if she were undressing. She handed the rope back to Ferret.

"You'll get lost," Ferret said.

She shook her head.

"Well, you better follow me closely," he said.

The girl did more than follow. She trotted next to Ferret and maintained his pace. Then she surprised him again by reaching up and grasping his hand. He felt strange. He had never gotten used to being touched affectionately by anyone but close clan members. In fact, any type of loving relationship was alien to him. After his mother had died, he had been treated like a hand-me-down, pawned off on distant kinsfolk like a bale of poor-quality wool. His father had been absent for most of his early years, busy fighting English intruders in the hinterland.

But Ferret had become attached to this puny orphan. Walking side-by-side holding hands, he felt like he had a little sister. The feeling warmed and comforted him. Knowing that he now had someone dependent on him was as satisfying as it was troublesome.

Returning to the monastery, Ferret and the girl found Strongbow and the rest of the party preparing to leave, with Stern in tow. MacMacken had been put in charge of Stern and seemed to relish mistreating his prisoner.

Strongbow led his odd band of wayfarers into the wild countryside on a crude road—just a pair of deep ruts barely wide enough for an ox-cart. The road twisted south along the seacoast to Cork. It frequently pushed inland to avoid tidal mudflats.

Badger grumbled and took his anger out on Stern, whipping him with a switch as if he were a slow-moving donkey. Father Yeats objected to Badger's cruelty to no avail.

The girl skipped along, poking twigs at Paco's dangling pots. She would get distracted and follow blackbirds that hopped from branch to branch in the shrubbery. Ferret enjoyed watching her play. When they lagged too far behind the others, he would carry her until they caught up. It was heavy work, but the feel of her arms around his neck compensated for the discomfort. He supposed his mother would have done the same for him.

* * *

Early in the afternoon, they came to an abandoned hut on the roadside. Tired and weary, they stopped for a moment and found a spring-fed stream. The girl was the first to go near the shallow stream. She waded into the middle and splashed the water with fearless delight. Paco knelt on all fours, leaned down, lips puckered outward, and gulped like a thirsty horse. Before Ferret could mosey over and take a drink, he thought he heard a rustling sound in the treetops. He stared up and noticed something stirring above the leaves. Could be birds. He just could not make it out.

Suddenly, the shattering sound of gunfire crackled through the air. A party of armed Irishmen dropped from trees and dashed from behind rock walls. Several pointed their flintlocks at Strongbow and stood motionless while a half-dozen others surrounded him.

"Caught us a Major," one of the highwaymen said after noticing the rank on Strongbow's uniform. "A real peacocky one at that."

He poked Strongbow's buttocks. "A little tight in the rump, don't ya think, Major?"

The other robbers eyed the entourage of children, priests, prisoner, and horses. Father Yeats and MacMacken tried to intervene on behalf of Strongbow but were blocked by the other armed men.

"Now, drop ya weapon," another highwaymen said.

Strongbow complied. He pulled out his pistols and let them drop to the ground.

The ringleader approached with a broad smile and immense self-confidence. He sauntered and swayed his body with the agility of a predator, watchful of both hunters and prey. He stopped, his lips curled in a defiant sneer as he spat on the ground. "I'm Gillian O'Hare," he said with a gruff voice. "And this be our territory ya trespass. Ya will pay us tollage. Pay a lot, I reckon."

Strongbow mustered up a heavy Irish brogue. "Gentlemen. I'm incognito. I'm not really English."

"Nay, ya're mistaken, Major. We're nowhere near Cognito." The man snorted with a barely contained chuckle. "Ya're in the countryside of County Cork."

Stern snickered under his breath. "They think 'incognito' is a place."

Hearing that snide remark, O'Hare ambled over to the bound English soldier and studied him with a mixture of scorn and caution. He fingered the cowbell hanging around Stern's neck. "Ruddy cute. I guess yar a deserter?"

"We ought to free him," one of the freebooters said.

"What say ya to this, prisoner?" O'Hare asked.

Stern hesitated at first, then turned talkative. He rattled on about his ordeal, how he was captured and why. "I'm being tried for desertion and selling secrets to Irish rebels," he lied. He held out his tied hands, expressing his desire to be released. "I welcome your merciful assistance."

O'Hare spat in Stern's face. "I never trust anyone who betrays his own kind!" He flaunted a sickly grin, showing a mouthful of stained teeth. "Ya're a draffsack fool, I reckon."

"I'm Irish!" Strongbow shouted, trying to get the ringleader's attention. *"Eireannach!"*

"Ya *Eireannach?*" Gillian turned and smirked, appearing unconvinced.

Ferret rushed up to the robber, determined to help Strongbow. "He speaks the truth! I'm Black Fox's son and—"

"Get out of me way!" O'Hare blared as he shoved the boy to the ground.

When Ferret sat up, blood was dripping down his chin. The girl rushed to him, unwrapped a rag from one of her hands, knelt on Ferret's lap and gently held the rag up to Ferret's face.

O'Hare tightened the grip on his pistol. "Major, I want ya shillings! Where's ya *piosa m airgid?*"

"I have none. Search me. *Ta an t-airgead gann.*"

O'Hare laughed. "Aye! Money's scarce, ya be right on that one." He started to search Strongbow's pockets.

A flock of birds suddenly took flight and O'Hare turned around. A small regiment of English foot soldiers had assembled into a battle line two ranks deep. They knelt, lifted up their weapons, and fired a volley of shots.

"Rith m!" O'Hare shouted. He swung his pistol around and fired one shot at the redcoats. Before the gun smoke had cleared, O'Hare had escaped into the brush. The other highwaymen were in flight, hurdling over a rock wall, but not before the soldiers had discharged another salvo of gunfire.

Several shots whizzed past Ferret's ears. He grabbed the girl and yanked her to the ground. Two highwaymen were hit and died instantly. Kneeling, the redcoats reloaded and fired another volley.

After the rebels had fled, Corporal Holbrook approached and saluted smartly. "I see we have arrived in time. The rapparees are particularly active in this region, Major Strongbow." He kicked one of the bodies. It was Frank Stern. Holbrook continued. "I would like to say 'poor chap,' but I believe it was Stern who attempted to murder me one night. He had something to do with Colonel Winchester."

"And that was...?"

"Winchester was a smuggler. He was arrested and then escaped. Cromwell has called for his capture, dead or alive."

"And what about Stern?"

"Stern was close to Winchester," Holbrook said. "I believe a conspiracy was a-hatching."

Strongbow picked up his pistols and eyed Holbrook. "Why were you trailing us?"

"We were trailing Stern. I was convinced that he might lead us to Winchester, but..." Holbrook knelt and examined Stern's tied hands, and then he glanced up at Strongbow. "Bound!"

Strongbow managed a weak smile.

Holbrook stood, brushed his pants and holstered his pistol. "Corporal! I'm impressed. I see that you can distinguish a vile character like Stern readily. Sorry about my doubts back at the church. The land crawls with pettifogging impostors, and I thought I heard a slight Irish brogue in your voice. But you have proven yourself quite admirably."

Just then, Holbrook was interrupted by strident screams. He and Strongbow both turned and watched the source of the commotion.

A beautiful, black-haired woman was struggling with two soldiers who had shackled her to a tree. She jerked, twisted, and lunged at a soldier's hand, trying to bite him. She shouted, "*Stad!* Leave me be!"

"Who's the beauty?" Strongbow asked, relieved to change the subject.

"A witch," Holbrook said. "At least that's what the townsfolk in Lismore told us."

"She's much too heavenly to be tainted with Wicca," Strongbow said.

"That she is," Holbrook said, finding it difficult to keep his eyes off the woman either. "But I'm afraid she's too cockish for any man to handle. They say she can make anyone deathly ill with a touch of her finger. She has been accused of bludgeoning her husband to death. She's one woman I would never want to prick. I'm afraid she'll be hung in Cork."

"In Cork?"

"Aye, I'm stationed there," the corporal said. "You should join us. As you can see we are foot-bound. Rebels stole our horses last night. Probably killed them for meat."

"Well..." Strongbow hesitated.

"Splendid," Holbrook said, appearing pleased. That was when he noticed Ferret and the girl. He gave a quick command, ordering one of his men to carry the girl. "Your son and daughter, I presume?"

Strongbow nodded feebly.

"'Tis heartwarming, sir," Holbrook said. "Not often do I see a high-ranking officer caring for his Irish bastards. I have two children in Wrexham, but I still treat them as my own flesh, bastards though they be."

"Aye," Strongbow said with a faraway look.

Chapter 13

Taking a break on a grassy ridge, Ferret scanned the horizon and recognized the hazy outline of Cork. After living in the hinterland for several years with his father, he was coming back to a bleak future. He had left no bridge unburned, no friend unprovoked, no kinfolk unscorned, and no stone unthrown. He was an outcast in the most backward seaport of Ireland. And the worst part: there was no one to blame but himself.

He closed his eyes and tried to forget his troubles. The cool, moist breeze from the Irish Sea tousled his long hair. He began to imagine that he was going to some other realm, a place where he could be left alone and spend time engaged in inspiring daydreams. He opened his eyes and watched Badger and Strongbow quarrel over some trivial matter. They seemed to revel in endless heated exchanges that never amount to anything.

He attempted to return to his earlier pleasant thoughts, but the horrors of Cork kept dragging him back into the darkness of nightmares. He pursed his dry lips and shook his head in disgust. This would not be a pleasant reunion. He wanted nothing to do with the citizenry of Cork. They were disdainful British sympathizers, like his uncle, fat from cheating the Irish out of their land, livestock, and foodstuff. He felt as if he were about to reenter the soulless pit of Sodom and Gomorrah.

Ferret breathed in deeply, trying to gain a better perspective. Instead, he began to smell Cork's distinctive stench of rotting fish, livestock, and feces. The town had been blessed with many river-fed canals, but most townsfolk were too lazy to dig holes and bury their waste. No, they poured their chamber pots into the river canals. Or worse, they tossed their muck into the middle of the street. Of course, this made it nearly impossible to avoid stepping into night soil and arousing sassy botflies.

Along with his companions and Holbrook's regiment, Ferret descended the steep slope of the ridge. On the way down, a heavy band of storm clouds moved overhead and treated them to a deluge of heavy rain. Nobody seemed to mind. Fort Elizabeth's tower was within sight, causing one soldier to sing a rousing tune from an old English ballad. Several men pledged to buy a round of hot buttered rum at the Red Bull alehouse.

Ferret began to worry about getting caught in a flood. Although Cork had been built above the Lee River, the rushing water paid little heed to man's achievements, regularly overflowing the thick stone walls that surrounded the port. Despite the danger, he often enjoyed watching the force of nature plague mankind. Sometimes, he secretly wished the storms would tear asunder every vessel in the harbor, smash the wooden piers, and drag unwary British sailors to watery graves. Other times, he had wished the same disasters would befall his uncle's merchant fleet and warehouses. And when his dreamt-up catastrophes failed to materialize, he started to doubt the Lord's sense of justice. Either God was too weak or uncle Madoc had bribed Him.

As Ferret brooded over his situation, Strongbow meandered over. The chained woman gleamed with the raw beauty of a rose that bore a thorn that could not be extracted. Pale-skinned, she sparkled with an infectious intensity. Her sable hair was braided back in one strand, accenting her long, slender neck and thin face.

With a genial smile, Strongbow tipped his hat. "A most pleasant afternoon."

The woman snapped, "What's so pleasant about it?"

"I've seen far worse downpours."

Ferret listened to their bland chitchat. He wondered if she were a witch, shrew, or harlot. Many Irish women were said to have spiritual powers and could cast spells on the most strong-willed men. He was not sure of that claim. The only witch he'd had the displeasure of meeting had only one skill—a talent to thrust knives at strangers. He had a feeling that even a hot-headed woman would not discourage the English lust for carnal pursuits. They seemed quite susceptible to women, betraying God and country for a soiled and scraggly half-naked Irish wench. Why men would surrender their future for a mere woman was beyond him.

Strongbow pulled his collar up. Rain dripped off his tricorn hat. "What was your crime?"

"I killed me man." The woman chortled with a sickly sweet smile. "Took an axe to the ox-head. My way to bury the hatchet."

"I assume he deserved it."

"I wanted to do him worse!"

"Really?"

"I wanted to eat his rutty liver. That I did."

The woman eyed Ferret and the girl. She knelt next to the girl, who clung tightly to Ferret's leg. "Pretty chit." Turning to Strongbow, she asked, "Part of your brood?"

"I'm not sure if they're mine," Strongbow said sheepishly.

The woman laughed. "Half the bastards in *Eire* be yours, I wager."

"Not quite half."

"I'm Rachel," she said with a malicious smile. "Want to know the truth of it all?"

Strongbow nodded.

"'Twas my right. The hotspur cheated on me. He took me purse. Spent it on Jamaican rum. Then he tried to murder me one night. Defended myself, that I did."

"Commendable." Strongbow muttered with forced enthusiasm, pursing his lips in thought.

"If you believe that, then don't let them imprison me."

"I doubt whether I can do anything."

"Hmm! Just like all the other swaggers." Rachel rattled her chains with obvious delight.

Holbrook walked over and interrupted the two. He pointed to Cork, gesturing that they were approaching the city's main gate. He nudged Strongbow to the side, away from the prisoner, and lowered his voice. "I must report to Fort Elizabeth. I shall escort the priests and have them chained in the tower. 'Tis the law."

Strongbow scoffed. "The law!"

"Indeed." Holbrook's eyes widened with surprise.

Strongbow appeared annoyed and looked away. "The law is often but the tyrant's will, no less and no more."

"Well," Holbrook stepped back and folded his arms, "the priests still defied the authorities. They are unregistered. We are duty-bound to enforce the laws of the Crown."

"Aye, that's the rub. I mean who doesn't defy the law? Most folks cannot make any sense of the King's edicts. If they could, they wouldn't remember it. If they remembered it, they would surely ignore it. That is what men have done throughout history."

"An interesting interpretation," Holbrook said with a smile.

"Don't get me wrong," Strongbow said. "I obey the laws that matter. I don't run naked through thorny hedges, or leap off towering cliffs. These are the real laws that must be obeyed or the body will have a nasty recompense."

"Bravo, sir. You're a true teaser."

"Howbeit," Strongbow said, "I am still under strict orders to take these vile priests to my superiors in London. They are my prisoners."

"I understand. Well, we already have an ample supply of imprisoned clergymen in the tower. Who needs a few more impious souls?" Holbrook touched the brim of his hat. "I must take my leave, but it has been a real pleasure to serve with you, Major." Holbrook and his men left for the main gate, with Rachel in tow.

Ferret tightened his cloak as the rain fell with more force. Badger grumbled about the inhospitable weather. Paco shook himself like a dog, knocking off a tin pot. MacMacken and Father Yeats huddled together for warmth. The girl sat in a mud pool, splashing and giggling. Strongbow stood, indifferent, appearing lost.

"We need shelter," Ferret said. "Too bad my only kin in Cork is my uncle. He's got a dining room larger than a Roman basilica. But he's a traitor to his own people."

Strongbow snapped out of his trance. "A dining room that large? Sounds jolly!"

"Didn't you hear me? He cannot be trusted, and, well, we once had a quarrel and..."

"Just one?"

"He asked me to leave. My father and I disowned him."

"You'll just have to reown him." Strongbow chortled. He removed his waterlogged hat and squeezed the water out of it. As he did, he cast a glance at the Crown's insignia on the front. "That's it!" He flopped the hat back onto his head. "Me laddie, there is an ancient English law about billeting soldiers in private housing. Laws must be obeyed, at least when they benefit us the most. Your uncle's house will do splendidly."

"No!" Ferret said. "He is a man of evil devices. He's sharper than a serpent's tooth."

"Don't worry," Strongbow said. "I can handle even the most ill-mannered cur."

Ferret looked down. He felt helpless as he watched everyone ignore him like he wasn't even there. With a dejected expression on his face, he mumbled. "Will this day ever cease?"

"Don't despair." Strongbow tried to comfort Ferret. "I will handle your uncle with velvet gloves."

"An iron fist would be more fitting." Badger let loose with a haughty roar. "I can grind down the serpent's tooth. Evil can be cleft. Ya just have to barge in and cut it down to size."

"Go on, laddie." Strongbow pointed towards the city's gate. "Let not your heart sadden. We're more than capable to handle any demon taskmaster, even if it were Beelzebub himself."

"But he's worse than Satan," Ferret said.

Strongbow laughed. "Just take us out of this godforsaken tempest and let me work my miracle."

Ferret nodded as he walked ahead, took the lead and began to quicken his pace. He entered through the guarded gate and walked past the drenched and chilled soldiers. Within moments of reaching the water-front, they faced dire circumstances. Heavy rain and high tides had already begun to flood the shoreline of the city. Its narrow, cobblestone streets had turned into a raging river of mud, rocks and downed tree branches. Waterfalls cascaded off tall roofs. Rising water surged over broken walls and swept debris against doors and windows. Half-drowned rats swam past. One gray rat clung to Paco's leg, clawed up, and settled on his hat, squeaking with fright.

Suddenly, Ferret heard a shriek. He turned around and saw the girl struggling to stay afloat. She had been swept away by the rushing water, caught in swirling torrent, heading toward the main canal that dumped into the bay. He ran after her, but he found himself caught in the churning, chest-high water. The current was too strong. He was knocked down by a half-submerged sheep carcass. Pushing it aside, he lunged towards the child as she sank below the water's dark surface.

Frantically, Ferret reached into the water. Nothing. He tried again. Finally, he dredged up her blue-faced, flaccid body. Ferret shook her violently as his feet found the bottom.

Suddenly, the girl coughed and spat out a mouthful of dirty water. She grasped at Ferret, clamping hold of his chest and knocking him off balance. He slipped and tumbled back into the surging water, soon bobbing up and down in the swift current.

Out of nowhere came a loud voice. "Grab the stick, laddie!" At first, Ferret saw nothing. The pelting rain was too strong to see beyond a few feet, but he caught sight of a dangling pole. He reached up and clenched it with his remaining strength. Ferret was slowly pulled to shore, while the girl clung to his back.

"Baths are most inappropriate in rainy weather," Strongbow said as he pulled them out of the water. The girl transferred her trembling arms to Strongbow's thigh, hugging him tightly.

"You're safe now, little mudfish," he said softly.

Regaining his breath, Ferret clasped Strongbow tightly. He was elated to be alive and with someone who cared more for him than his wretched uncle or any absentee father.

"I hope you enjoyed your little swim," Strongbow teased Ferret, "but we can't dally all day. How far is it?"

Ferret took a moment to get his bearings. Then, turning east, he led them through a series of less flooded streets and came to a wealthier parish. He stopped and examined a large ornate door. He was not sure he had come to the right place. It seemed so long ago.

"Is this it?" Strongbow asked.

Ferret took a deep breath and knocked, waited and knocked again. Nobody answered. He turned around and looked at everyone's crestfallen faces. Maybe he had the wrong place. Maybe nobody was home. Just as he was about to turn around and leave, a feeble old woman opened the door. Before she could greet the strangers, everyone scrambled past her, desperate to get out of the cold rain. The woman shut the door and felt around with her hands, confused. Ferret reached out and took hold of the woman's hand. He led her to a stone slab in front of the fireplace, dodging small iron pots placed to catch rainwater dripping from the ceiling. The woman resembled his eldmother, but he thought it impossible. Rumors had spoken of her death from a gruesome illness.

"Who be you?" the woman asked with a trembling voice. She was frail, skinny and almost bald. She shuffled from place to place, barely able to move about without leaning on a convenient wall.

"'Tis Ferret."

Corla tilted her head. "Who? Come to me, laddie. I'm poor of sight in the pitch of winter." Her voice quavered. Without warning, her arm shot out to feel his face. Ferret jerked back, startled. He drew near again and knelt in front of the spindly woman. Her fingers were swollen at the joints and her skin darkened with age spots. She caressed Ferret's face and ran her claw-like fingers through his long, disheveled hair.

"Sean! Oh, little Sean!" The woman moaned with glee. "I thought the Lord had taken you away from me, far away. But the Lord indeed hath been good to me."

"It is really you?" Ferret asked. "They said you had died of canker-rash."

"Don't be silly. I refused to sleep in my deathbed."

They embraced.

A voice roared from another room. A hoary-headed man, short in the legs, bespectacled with thick lenses, and topped with a white silk nightcap, stomped into the large room. It was Ferret's uncle, Madoc O'Neill, a wealthy widower who had two sons overdue from a voyage to the Virginias. He was bundled in a French beaver fur coat. When he took off his nightcap, Ferret saw that his head was covered with scabs.

Frightened, Paco sought safety behind Badger, his dangling pots and pans rattling. The little girl stared, wide-eyed, from beside Father Yeats and MacMacken.

"Who comes prowling at twilight?" Madoc demanded.

Corla spoke up first. "Madoc! Sean lives!"

"Not in my abode!" Madoc rushed over to Ferret, suddenly stopped, and stared down with a disdainful frown. After a moment, he turned to Strongbow and examined him from head to toe. "What do we have here?"

"Obviously, one of the King's loyal men," Strongbow said.

"Well, I assume my nephew has troubled you, sir? But let me be clear. You may do with him as you please. Clamp him in irons. Just begone with him. The little prigger has only ill respect for his elders. I disowned him long ago."

"Actually," Strongbow cleared his throat, "Ferret, as we know him, has assisted us immeasurably."

Madoc turned silent, his face darkened with a horrified, vacant look. He began to scratch his belly with vigor. "That's sheer rubbish!"

"Not at all," Strongbow said with a tone of authority. "You're not seeing him in the right light."

Madoc turned to Ferret and lowered his forehead to peer over his spectacles. That did not satisfy him. He removed his eyeglasses and wiped them on his sleeve. After gazing through the lens, he put them back on and examined Ferret again. His eyes narrowed for a couple of seconds until he started to shake his head. "I see nothing but a saucy child."

"I mean your nephew is a fine, upstanding laddie," Strongbow said. "You should be proud of him."

"That's hard to fathom," Madoc said.

"I will tell you what is hard to fathom." Strongbow inched closer to Madoc. "A man of your wealth and talents should be able to judge character better. Your nephew led us away from danger. And for that noble deed, he was wounded. So, I would take kindly towards him, especially since he is now an orphan."

"What!? My nephew is an orphan?"

"*Correcto*," Strongbow said. "His father perished recently. Your dear brother is dead."

"My brother is dead?" Madoc said as Corla began to sob. "You play me the Jack."

"He died with the last of his men," Strongbow said.

"My brother had it coming. With the outbreak of war, he fled to the outland to resist the English. He cursed me for remaining behind. Well, the world is still unjust, and now he crawls with worms."

"But he's your brother," Corla said.

"I have no heartstrings to pull." Madoc refitted his spectacles. "I knew it would come to this. My brother was foolhardy. He should have known what to expect. Those who play with cats must expect to be scratched. I offered him opportunities. Come and build ships, I said. Come and learn commerce, I said. Come and follow the winds of wealth, I beseeched him. Nay, my brother scorned me like some scruffy seaman without one day's pay to his name."

"I see," Strongbow said, "but we have a bit of a problem. The barracks of Cork are overfilled. I am in desperate need of shelter, along with these men. Do you have something to offer the King's men?"

Madoc's anger subsided. He let out a long sigh and gazed heavenward. "I've housed soldiers in the last war. My policy has never changed. But I want no part of Sean."

"But you must understand. Your nephew warned us of an impending attack by highwaymen outside of Cork. He saved our lives, and he is under my protection."

Ferret closed his eyes as Strongbow's fibs grew bolder. He knew that Strongbow was trying to help again. Yet it rubbed against his past teachings. Aristot had drilled into him the bad consequences of deception and why it would haunt the soul. Ferret wondered if well-intentioned lies were somehow permissible. But it seemed that once one got snug with lying, there was no turning back.

Taking in a deep breath, Madoc's taut body eased up. "Perhaps my nephew has come to his senses. I have been slightly in error." He clapped his hands, and two servants appeared. "Please partake in my hospitality." He ordered one of his servants to stack more logs in the large hearth. Another one was instructed to fetch an abundance of food and ale.

As the fire roared to life, the girl was attracted to its glowing light. She put her hands out to feel its warmth. Madoc noticed her and asked, "Who's the titmouse?" Eyeing Strongbow, he added, "I suppose she's your youngling." He watched her drink from a pot of rainwater on the floor.

Strongbow stood silent, struggling to come up with a plausible answer worthy of the question.

"Didn't you hear?" Ferret interrupted the moment of silence. "My father remarried. She's my half-sister." He looked away, trying to convince himself that some lies had to be told. He knew it was wrong, but he could not help himself. He was willing to go to purgatory or Hell to save her. Eternal punishment was his destiny after judgment day. And if that came to pass, so be it.

"Where is her mother?" Madoc inquired.

"She died of the Spanish pox."

Madoc took off his spectacles and moaned. "My aching noodle! I can see what's happening. You expect me to take custody of her?"

"This girl be your own blood-kin," Strongbow said. "Bereft of parents! We English frown upon ill-mannered gentlemen who shirk from their responsibilities. I understand that you trade much with us?"

"Aye," Madoc said reluctantly.

"Then, I know you will give them decent treatment. You could put the lad to labor in the dockyards. That ought to be worth something, you niggardly skinflint."

Madoc nodded grudgingly, his face flushed with annoyance.

Ferret was surprised—and hurt—to hear Strongbow's talk about his proposal to Madoc. He desperately wanted to stay with Strongbow. He hated his uncle. And yet he knew the girl needed a steady home. He felt he had a duty to stay behind and take care of her. He should never have let her tag along; it wasn't as if she was his true-blood sister. Burdens were like burrs under the skin; they were near impossible to remove.

Just then, the girl stomped her foot to get his attention. Instead, it got the attention of Corla, who shuffled next to the girl and gently hugged her. Placing the child in front of the fire, she stripped her bare and draped a green cloak over her shoulder. She stroked the child's scruffy hair and plucked out head lice. "Oh hinny... oh hinny," the old woman sang tenderly. The child just stared at the fire.

"Remember," Strongbow said, "the lad has done us great service. I want him treated well, along with his sister. 'Tis the British way."

Madoc forced a smile.

Part II

Chapter 14

Madoc was gracious to Strongbow's entourage that night. They feasted with gluttony, drunkenness, and big talk. Ferret wanted nothing to do with the festivities. He knew his uncle would soon regain his senses and launch insults and threats against him. What he had not anticipated was Strongbow's whirlwind departure early the next morning.

"You don't have to leave so soon," Ferret said. "We have plenty here."

"Better to starve than to live a fat slave," Strongbow said with a wink.

His face devoid of emotion, Ferret watched Strongbow saddle up Paco with equipment. He felt betrayed. For the first time, he wished he were the sovereign of a kingdom. With his kingly powers, he could order complete obedience from any subject with the snap of his fingers. Wielding absolute power, he could command his guards to block Strongbow's path. And if his friend escaped, his army would pursue, capture, and clap him in irons. Ferret would keep him close forever. Yet he doubted whether Strongbow would find such brutish acts endearing.

Strongbow pinched Ferret's cheeks. "Why the sad face? Come now. I will return, laddie."

"You'll come back?"

"I'll be counting the hours and minutes—that is, I would if I had a reliable timepiece." He gave Ferret a quick hug. "What could keep me away?"

"What if you die?"

"Die! Upon my soul, why would I do such a thing?" Strongbow retied a loose blanket across Paco's back. "No man would dare take arms against me. The world knows that you would avenge my death with swift and ghastly retaliation."

A grin tugged at the corner of Ferret's mouth. He struggled to prevent his face from blossoming into a full-blown smile.

Strongbow opened the door and strolled out into the bright sunlight. The rain had stopped; everyone was cleaning up the storm's aftermath. Madoc stood outside and supervised his servants as they dragged, then threw fallen trees, dead livestock, and other debris into the canals.

Strongbow stopped and approached Ferret's uncle. He swung his finger directly at Madoc. "Heed my warning, Master O'Neill. I am depending upon your good heart. But if it hardens into ice, I will make sure the king hears of your misdeeds."

"Aye." Madoc's mouth tightened as he nervously scratched his belly with both hands.

Strongbow waved one last time to Ferret as he ambled down the street with Paco, MacMacken, and Badger. Father Yeats mumbled, "Blessed are the children" and hurried after the others.

As soon as Strongbow disappeared, Madoc turned to Ferret and assaulted him with a barrage of abuse. "No ragabash nephew of mine will sit about moonshining all day. You'll work in my dockyard when I say, where I say, and—"

"And what I say." Ferret knew the line by heart. Madoc sang the same song to every new worker in the dockyard.

"If I catch you loafing," Madoc continued, "I'll sling your pin-buttocks out of here. Report to the docks now!"

With a silent scoff, Ferret turned and meandered down the street, not looking back. He immediately headed for the dockyard. Before he had gone far, he realized the girl was following him. He stopped, waited for her to catch up, and then clutched her hand. He felt it was his honor-bound duty to be her brother and protect her. He had to. The city was dangerous. Every week a street waif was trampled by horse cart or ox wagon and died or, worse, became crippled for life—a slow, painful death sentence if ever there was one. To keep someone safe was to never let go of their hand.

Near the waterfront, they chanced upon a large crowd gawking at some type of scuffle or fray. Ferret and the girl squeezed between two large men and reached the inner circle. There they found his old schoolmaster Aristot the center of attraction. He had always looked imposing. A large goiter grew across Aristot's scarred neck, and his white beard almost swept his knees. He towered over everyone, resembling a mythical giant with grotesque facial features.

Ferret hid behind a man carrying a young pig under his arm. He was not sure he wanted his master to see him. Wherever Aristot went, he was certain to get caught up in the thick of controversy. His schoolmaster had ridden alongside Oliver Cromwell as a Roundhead and fought at the battles of Naseby and Langport. After the royalists were defeated, he was appointed a magistrate in London and was one of the signers of the warrant to behead King Charles I. He once confessed that it was the biggest mistake of his life.

Not long after the death of King Charles, Aristot realized that he had been played the fool. The execution was not conducted to destroy the power of the monarchy, but to enhance Cromwell's authority. Soon afterward, his old compatriot turned tyrant and began to jail his allies. Four of the main leaders of the Levellers had been imprisoned in the Tower of London, including the fearless "Freeborn John" Lilburne. They had accused Cromwell of dodging his promise to uphold freeborn rights. That had been a major sticking point. Many in England held sway to the old ideas of an absolute monarchy. They viewed government, not God, as the granter of all rights. Cromwell had betrayed the Levellers' creed that civic authority is derived from the consent of the governed. He had gone back on his word and opposed rights for individuals, saying it would give too much freedom to the people. A number of outspoken Levellers were put on trial for high treason; others were arrested and put to the gallows.

Aristot had watched Cromwell's lust for power grow to the point where his old friend now demanded to be made Lord Protector for life, with his son as his successor. A king could ask for no better. In his darkest hour, Aristot found himself threatened by Cromwell. He had refused to support Cromwell's new power as Lord Protector, and was forced to flee to Ireland. To hide his identity, he changed his name to reflect his admiration for the Greek philosopher Aristotle.

Ferret watched Aristot take charge of two ill-tempered men in an effort to adjudicate a breach of tort law. As the judge, he waved them on, encouraging them to continue their heated exchange. The large crowd thrilled to the spectacle of a possible fistfight. As both men circled each other, they cussed and bickered like ill-mannered children. It appeared that they would soon come to blows. One of the men, whose name Ferret quickly discovered was Clayton, was a short, half-bald man with an impressive potbelly. With his barrel chest puffed out, he wildly gestured with his fisted hands. The other man, Kerry, was lanky and had an immense nose. He seemed less assured of his ability to win a physical confrontation.

Clayton shook his accusatory finger at his foe. "You goat-sucking bastard! Steal me chickens, will you! You grout!"

"Pure lies!" Kerry said.

"Thief, thief, that's all you be!"

"I'm no thief, you thick-headed, scurvy scab!" Kerry bellowed, his eyes flashing with indignation.

The quarrelers stopped momentarily and eyed Aristot. He stared back and extended his long arms outwards. In quick fashion, he clapped his hands with a serious expression on his face. "Continue. You're doing splendidly!"

The crowd cheered like spectators in a cockfight. Ferret watched intently. The girl looked on in wonder.

"Bastard!" Clayton shouted, groping for better insults.

"Lies, all terrible lies, you freebooter," Kerry said.

After a half an hour of sparring, both men glanced at each other and sighed, exhausted.

Clayton spoke with a softer tone, pleading, "Kerry, why did you thieve me chickens?"

"'Em cocks jumped me fence, ate me corn, and dug up a row of turnips. What would you have me do? Starve? Nay, I shoot trespassing fowl and make the most of it."

Clayton stroked his fat chin. "By Saint Patrick, you might have given me some of the carcass."

"Eh?"

"I raised 'em chickens!"

"But I fed 'em!"

They laughed.

Then Aristot lifted his long arms. "'Tis my judgment that sharing would be most unworkable. I have decided to keep the fowls myself. Be they plump?"

"What?" Clayton roared.

"Wait!" Kerry said. "Why should we give them to you?"

Aristot teased. "Do I not hunger?"

"Sure, but we raised them. Why can't I share 'em with Clayton?"

Aristot concealed a faint smile. "Share them?" He paused. "Well, there be similar cases in the *tauth* of Garland. The carcasses were indeed halved, but—"

"But what?" Clayton spoke impatiently.

Aristot turned to Kerry. "What do you say? Shall the chicken be shared with your neighbor?"

"'Tis better than giving them to you," Kerry said bluntly.

"But chicken be my favorite," Aristot said with a sheepish grin. "'Tis best in a loblolly stew thickened with barley and milk."

"By crikey." Clayton muttered, smacking his lips. "That sounds delightful."

Kerry bumped Clayton hard with his elbow. "'Tis our cocks, remember." He went up to Aristot as he continued. "'Tis our fowl. Surely, we ought to be the ones to share it. 'Tis only right."

Glancing up to the heavens, Aristot appeared to concentrate on the issue. He was known to procure long-lasting solutions that would abate deep-seated resentment. He peered down and cracked a thin, confident smile. "So, you each want your fair share. Halving the carcasses is a possible mitigation. What do you say, gents?"

"Half," Kerry sighed with relief, "seems fair to me."

Clayton nodded.

Aristot clapped his hands. "A very wise choice. 'Tis done. Both clans will share the birds equally."

Kerry walked over and pressed a coin into Aristot's hand and applauded his legal judgment. He bubbled with gratitude and expressed heartfelt thanks. "Believe me, we couldn't have done it without you. You be the best tort judicator in all of Cork." He turned to Clayton and grabbed his forearm. The two walked away together and began bickering over whose sow had dug up whose fence.

As the crowd melted away, Aristot was reaching for his flat hat and sheepskin-covered books when he recognized Ferret. "Sean O'Neill!" he said with a surprised look. "Could it possibly be you?" He rubbed his beard and frowned with a curious squint. "The question, I must beg, is why would such an ungrateful lad return to me?"

Ferret hurried over to Aristot to embrace him, but his old schoolmaster blocked him with an outstretched hand. A few moments later, he pulled from his pocket a small animal with piercing scarlet eyes and yellowish fur. It ran up Aristot's arm, sat on his shoulder, and squeaked at Ferret and the girl.

With excitement, the girl cooed in delight. Her eyes were glued to the creature's every movement.

"This ferret bites me when it gets affectionate," Aristot said. "Are you here to do the same?"

"I had to leave!" Ferret said. "I had to escape from my uncle. I had to find my father."

"Do you still search for him?"

Ferret lowered his head. "Father's dead."

"Most unfortunate," Aristot said without emotion. "But your father was a man of violence."

Ferret had expected little sympathy or compassion from "Whitebeard," as he was known by his most intimate friends. In recent years, Aristot had focused on the teachings of Greek Zeno of Citium, an ancient Greek philosopher who taught that man should be indifferent to pain or pleasure and prided himself on being above any emotional fray. His Stoic philosophy left little room for feelings since self-control was necessary to overcome destructive emotions.

"Every man creates his own private hell," Aristot said. "Brutal men believe they may challenge the mighty, and when they fall, they become embittered or befriend a shallow grave."

Ferret's eyes began to tear.

Aristot's face softened. "Have I spoken too harshly? I understand your heartgrief. But your father not only taunted death, but he also attempted to control Ireland by force. Aye, he might have replaced British rule, but not rulership itself. Why replace one ruler with another? They be all cut from the same crude stone, hardened with brunt of weaponry, no matter what nationality bore them. All rulership reeks of the dark side of mankind. It knows no bounds."

Ferret looked up with wet, bloodshot eyes. "I have nowhere to go."

"You must control your feelings." Aristot put his hand on the boy's shoulder.

Ferret did not listen. He was remembering his early tutelage when Aristot worshiped the greatness of human potential. Then, he had expounded that mankind would someday touch the great lights in the sky and that sweet liberty would reign supreme across the globe. Aristot had changed. He had become critical of everyone and everything except, perhaps, his precious Greek philosopher, Zeno.

"Someday I must avenge my father's death."

Aristot's eyebrows arched. "Have all my teachings gone to naught? To harm another human releases your inner beast, allowing him to devour you in an orgy of hate. It will lead to a frenzy of butchery and bloodshed. And it will enslave your soul until a larger beast feasts on your corruptible flesh. Here, put out your hand flat against mine."

Ferret complied. Quickly, the old man pushed against Ferret's hand, almost knocking it away. Ferret pushed back with even greater force.

"Do you not see what you have done? I applied pressure and you resisted. Every resistance begets counter-resistance. Our Lord Christ preached this principle from the Mound. When mistreated, He told us to turn the other cheek—not slap it."

"The truth will always be innately painful," Aristot continued. "Like dry, crusty bread, it can be hard to swallow. But mankind has an affinity for evil. 'Tis a distemper that burrows deep under the skin like an abscess. We all wish to make slaves of others: one man over another, one clan over another, one kingdom over another. Never ending, never ceasing. A world of battle to conquer one's fellow man before he conquers you."

Ferret sat down next to the girl and brooded. He understood that man was his own worst enemy. He could see it almost every day. A monster dwelt within every soul. It would steal, murder, rape, and do anything for a position of power. Everyone knew what was right, but still, they did wrong. Why should he be any different?

Aristot continued. "Your father reminded me of Lord Oliver Cromwell some fifty years ago in London. Lord Cromwell spoke of liberty. He fought the king to free England of tyranny. But after Lord Cromwell's Ironsides had defeated the monarch, he turned ruthless. It was as if the monarchy had never been destroyed. Indeed, nothing had changed."

As Aristot moralized, his frisky pet romped across his shoulders, scurried down his arm, slipped, and clung to the underside of his sleeve. Rescuing the animal, Aristot tenderly stroked its fur as he lowered it for the girl to see. "This beastie was a gift from one of my students. Actually, the boy had to get rid of her. Killed too many of his father's prize chickens, I suspect."

The girl reached up to touch it.

"She bites," the old man said.

Despite the warning, the girl grasped the animal and squeezed it. It bit her arm. She shrank back, screamed and burst into tears. She rushed to Ferret and wrapped her arms around his thigh.

Aristot reached down for the animal and put it back on his shoulder. "Few ever really listen, do they?"

"I listen," Ferret said.

"Perhaps, but even I have difficulty listening to others. Do you know what Lord Cromwell once confided to me?"

Ferret shook his head.

"I befriended him in his early days. The young Lord Cromwell was a man of high principles, a Puritan and a companion of the Levellers. Like me, he spoke of equal rights before the law, and opposed the King. He was filled with passion for liberty for every individual and tolerance for every religious sect. Lord Cromwell was a man of wisdom and insight.

"But after his victory over Scotland's militia, I asked him whether England now blossomed with freedom. He hesitated. We both knew that he had arrested his opponents and censored his critics. I asked the question again. Finally, he said, 'Aye, there be freedom in England. I may do whatever I wish.'"

Aristot sighed. "I remained in England even after that. I had not listened well." He scratched the ferret's ear. Without warning, the animal bit him on the finger, drawing blood. "She gets carried away and thinks I'm toying with her." Aristot paused. "You, too."

"I'm no Saint Christopher," Ferret said. "But what about you and Lord Cromwell? What did he do?"

"The brogger soured and became intolerable. Still today, 'tis hard to understand. I believe that Cromwell foolishly sought power to destroy power. Of course, he lost that war with his conscience."

Aristot pointed to several children sitting in a pool of mud. "'Tis like a child playing in the dirt; he cannot help but besoil his garments. As Cromwell associated with England's powermongers and elite, his temperament became more like them—muddier and corrupt. I, with many Levellers, opposed his invasion of Ireland. We had just freed England from tyranny; to invade Ireland would make us what we had fought so hard against. Day after day we uttered these words, and day by day more of us were arrested.

"After I escaped to Cork, I learned that Lord Cromwell had disbanded Parliament. Could a king do worse? He handpicked another parliament which offered him the title of King. He would have accepted had he not feared the fate of Caesar over a thousand years earlier. Indeed, Lord Cromwell drank from the well of power and became a drunkard. Power destroyed him from within. I say to you, few men can resist such a potent drink. Now, I trust no one. You will understand more when you become seasoned with years."

Just then, a girl approached with some papers for Aristot. She introduced herself as Maureen O'Hara. She was Ferret's age. She had brown hair that cascaded to her waist. Her patched and tattered robe fit loosely, showing bony shoulder blades. Ferret stared; there was something different and disturbing about her. She glared back, hawk-eyed. Ferret turned away. Getting up to leave, Ferret faced Aristot. "I shall return. I have much to learn."

"You do indeed," Aristot said, "but I doubt you will remember it."

Chapter 15

Eight years had passed since Strongbow had disappeared. It was 1706. King William III was dead and Queen Anne had ascended to the English throne. She was pressuring Parliament to prohibit exports of Irish wool to any country except England. All Ireland feared a new age of starvation. Some prepared to leave; others talked of open rebellion.

Ferret tried to ignore the worsening economic conditions. Aristot opposed such nonsense as rebellions, politics, or strife, and Ferret felt obligated to heed his master's wishes. Besides, he had more important concerns. He wanted to leave Ireland for good.

Now almost twenty, he had grown muscular from working in the dockyard daylight to daybreak. He was tall, over six feet. He looked dapper in English breeches, white knee stockings, a billowy silk shirt, and a gold-trimmed tricorn hat. He had grown a stylish ponytail so long that it almost touched the dagger holstered on his wide belt. To compensate for his rejection of Irish fashion he affected a scraggly goatee; his uncle threatened to pluck it strand-by-strand. Facial hair was regarded as a disgrace—reserved for peasants and pirates. Nevertheless, Ferret promised himself he would one day grow a grand beard reaching his kneecaps, with or without anyone's approval.

Ferret often recalled Strongbow's final words. His friend had promised to return. He had heard clergymen make similar claims, preaching that the Almighty would return "someday." That day of deliverance never came.

In his spare time, Ferret searched for his friend in town and in the countryside. One of his best sources was Jonathan Holbrook, now a lieutenant under Major-General Cromwell. Sometimes, as they sat together sipping hot Indian tea at the Red Bull alehouse, Holbrook would provide tidbits of information on criminal activities in southern Ireland. On other occasions, he would read John Locke, oblivious to Ferret's questioning.

Holbrook was different from other military men. His Welsh mother, disillusioned with English authority, had disapproved of her son's enlistment. The Welsh had hated the English since the 1300s for invading their nation. Holbrook had taken much of his mother's cynicism to heart. He had joined the army to escape England. Hoping for duty in the New World, he got no farther than Ireland. While stationed in Ireland, he had studied the *Brehon* laws, which were similar to the English common law but more complex. Holbrook was intrigued with the Irish tradition of an almost powerless High King. Ferret would spar with him over the implications, arguing that his native land never had experienced the slavery of serfdom nor prohibited women from sharing property rights with men.

Such ideas were dangerous. Talk of democracy or republicanism could lead to imprisonment or deportation. Ferret sensed Holbrook's fascination was more than academic. Holbrook asked about unhappy dockworkers and the ringleaders who were inciting trouble. He pried for information about hotheads who might be disenchanted with English rule. Ferret did not take the bait. In fact, he had no idea who were the firebrands nor did he have any desire to find out. He had heard of mysterious organizations and secret meetings, but he felt that such activities would only lead to more death and destruction and could accomplish nothing worthwhile.

Calls for rebellion had stirred the air for years, but they were becoming more insistent. Every month fewer vessels would harbor in Cork. The dockyards and marketplaces seethed with rumors that all Irish exports would soon be banned. Only Madoc's ships, with a near monopoly on the export trade, seemed immune.

Ferret suspected that terrible times were coming. And yet, he could not shake the odd feeling that he had been put in Cork specifically to alter the course of history. He attributed such fantasies to an over-active imagination. He knew he was lucky just to shelter and feed himself and Heather, the orphan girl whom he had rescued.

* * *

One day that spring, Lieutenant Holbrook spoke of a series of robberies that had been committed by a debonair man with a plumed hat accompanied by a rotund halfwit. Without a word, Ferret sprang to his feet and dashed away. The very next day, Ferret saddled one of Madoc's horses and rode to the area where the last robbery had been reported, near Kinsale. He searched for three days, but he found nothing. He decided that Holbrook's report had been hearsay, probably a fake theft to cover someone's gambling debt.

On his return Ferret took a detour across a long stretch of coastal mudflats. It was an unusually sunny day. He wanted to enjoy the splendid sight of sea and sand. But his thoughts wandered elsewhere. Only once had anyone taken interest in him. Strongbow had treated him like a son, lifting him out of the darkness and into the light. The encounter had been brief, but it made him realize that he had been orphaned long before his father's murder.

Ferret's reverie was interrupted when his horse nearly trampled a large man sunbathing on the sand. Ferret stopped, turned his horse around, and began to apologize. The dark-skinned man was in no mood to talk. He glanced up at Ferret and darted up the beach.

"Come back!" Ferret yelled.

The man refused to stop.

His memory might be cloudy, but the man bore a striking resemblance to Paco. Like this man, Paco had always run awkwardly, slow-footed, arms flailing. With a sharp kick of his spurs, Ferret galloped after the waddling barrow of flesh. Just then, another fellow jumped from behind an outcropping of rock. He raised his pistol and grinned. In a flash of spark and smoke, a shot rang out. The lead ball hit Ferret's horse and his front legs collapsed. Ferret was hurled across the sand.

The tall man swaggered over to his fallen victim. He pulled out a sword and loomed over Ferret. "Your purse or your life!"

Ferret looked up from where he had fallen. "I have nothing of value."

"Come, come, gent. Everyone bellyaches about being beholden to poverty." The robber tapped his sword's tip on Ferret's chest.

Ferret refused to flinch. "Don't you recognize me?"

"Should I?"

Ferret stood up and brushed the sand off his clothes. Was his old mate jesting? How could he have forgotten? Then again, everything was a game to Strongbow. His ill-suited humor was his most annoying trademark—always making light of the dregs of life. Nobody could ever get a straight and honest answer from him. Who would want such an intolerable friend?

"Very nice," the robber had lowered his sword and touched Ferret's silk shirt. "A taffeta doublet from India. I can see that you're no boorish peasant, that's for sure."

"I am Ferret O'Neill. Do you remember me now?"

"Good Lord!" Strongbow leaned back. "Little weeds do tower into great trees." He handed his sword to Paco. He beamed and moved to hug Ferret. "Laddie! Where have you kept yourself all these years?"

Ferret backed away. "You know where I've been!"

"I do?"

"'Tis one of the biggest ports in the region. Wouldn't take long to rediscover what you left behind."

Strongbow shrugged. His grin was rosy. "What's a little time among mates?"

"Apparently not much."

Strongbow tapped his lips lightly with his fingers. "My dear laddie, I have just returned from Aherlow Valley, and I have something for you." He untied a bagpipe from Paco's back and presented it to Ferret.

"More stolen loot, no doubt." Ferret knocked the gift out of Strongbow's hand.

"What the devil!" Strongbow huffed with indignation. "I'm bestowing a pricey tribute and you're offended?"

"You gave your troth. I believed you. I thought you were dead."

"Just wait a little longer. I might still rise from my tomb."

"You wield humor like a limp weapon."

"Don't be such a fusspot. Some Jack Stickler you turned into!"

Ferret bit his lip. So this is how it was. Strongbow had challenged him on the battlefield of ill humor. Walk two paces, turn, and fire a sharp-edged word. Ferret rolled his eyes and scoffed. "I guess nothing matters. Right?"

"That's my bloody excuse for living."

Ferret glanced at the ocean. He had always taken the world too seriously. That was hard to overcome. But Strongbow was a common
rogue who pinched money from unsuspecting gentry. Could anyone
expect noble deeds or thoughts from a freebooter? "I guess we all live
on borrowed time. Who needs eternity? I mean the Creator will sort it
out after the last harvest. So, it all comes down to the luck of the draw?"

"I'm not a bad seed," Strongbow said, "just a little misguided."

"That's not for me to decide. A higher court will make the final call.
But I am sure you can bribe a judge to arrive at a better verdict." Ferret
walked back to his dead horse.

Strongbow followed. "Sorry about the horse."

"Were you aiming at me?" Ferret dropped to his knees next to the
horse, touched the bullet hole and rubbed the blood on his fingertips.

"It was a warning shot. I meant it to pass overhead."

"Not the sharpshooter you once were," Ferret said. "The decrepit
always hide their intentions behind lies."

Strongbow unsheathed his sword again. "You indeed make an artful
weasel. Someone ought to teach you to respect your elders."

Ferret reached for his own sword, a basket-hilted Spanish weapon
embedded with green semi-precious stones. He saluted Strongbow with
his sword. "Let see if your swordplay is as good as your marksmanship."

"You cannot take me, laddie! I'm known as the diviner of cold steel."
Strongbow bowed and then quickly lunged at Ferret.

Ferret held his ground and blocked the sword with his own. The two
blades clashed in a shower of sparks. On Strongbow's second strike,
Ferret pushed back and almost knocked his old mate to the ground.
Strongbow found himself stumbling back a few more steps, halted his
retreat, and began to gasp for air. He put up his unarmed hand and looked
up at Ferret. "Let's try that one more time."

Ferret nodded with a wide grin.

Gripping his sword tighter, Strongbow launched another thrust at
Ferret, whirling his blade more carefully. Ferret repelled the attack as if
his left hand was tied behind his back.

Strongbow recoiled and frowned. "My, my, you're not the child I
once knew. You're a regular war-wolf." He stared at Ferret's fancy

sword. "Where in the name of heaven did you procure such a magnificent weapon?"

"It's one of Madoc's. My uncle's fencing instructor told him to get a sparring partner. I became his moving target. If I wanted to live, I had to surpass his skills. So, are you going to jabber me to death or fight?"

Strongbow's eyes flared into an angry glare, his body stiffening. With a running start, he lunged at Ferret from another direction, taking several swings, missing Ferret by a wide margin. With shortness of breath, he backed up and almost tripped over a piece of driftwood.

Ferret seized the moment and stormed forward. With little effort, Ferret knocked Strongbow's sword out of his hand and pinned him against an outcropping of rocks.

Mouth agape, Strongbow shook his head. "Why are we sparring?"

Ferret tapped his sword tip on Strongbow's chest. "I believe it was something about teaching me a lesson."

"I hope you learned it well." Strongbow chuckled. He pushed the blade away, picked up his sword and walked back to Paco. "But we shall leave horseplay to horses."

Nothing ever turned out the way it was supposed to, Ferret mused. If he thought God would return in glory at high noon, a blizzard would come instead. He almost felt as if he had lost the scuffle. It was hard to win a fight with a man who thinks he can never lose.

Ferret lowered his head. When he was a child, he would have died for Strongbow. He would have done anything that a loyal son was expected to do to please a dutiful father. But Strongbow was no one's father. Why had he gone out of his way to befriend a destitute child?

* * *

Ferret remained in Strongbow's camp for several days trying to find an excuse to explain the loss of his uncle's horse. Meanwhile, he watched Strongbow rob rich merchants, just like the legendary Robin of the Hood, except this Robin kept all the money for himself. Ferret found Strong-bow's pilfering escapades amusing, almost enchanting. His old mate had turned thievery into a genteel art form. Such was his reputation, and he was proud of it. In a fastidious ritual, he would courteously bow to his victims, threaten them with a pistol, and plead for contributions to some fraudulent charity—usually a refuge for indigent highwaymen. On special occasions, he would dazzle them with playful swordplay, careful never to injure anyone, except, as with Ferret's horse, by accident.

Although opposed to stealing, Ferret knew that most of the wealthy enjoyed special favors from the English crown. Only certain merchants were allowed to do business, while other tradesmen were restricted, barred, or banished. Moreover, Cork's affluent families were from England and had made their fortunes by confiscating land from the King's opponents in every part of the empire. Behind every affluent man was a history of sanctioned pillage. To Ferret, there was a sense of justice when Strongbow robbed the robber barons.

When Ferret had seen enough, he walked back to Cork. Strongbow offered him assistance at first, but soon reneged and instead gave a half-hearted promise to visit him in Cork. Ferret knew it was a lie.

Months passed without any further Strongbow sightings. When Ferret queried Holbrook about robberies in the south, the reply was disappointing. They had ceased.

* * *

Madoc dismissed the loss of the horse with little more than a few well-chosen curses. He even ignored the few dents on his sword, saying that it must have fallen off the wall. It was unlike Madoc to forgive anyone. Something else was gnawing on his mind. Ferret had a feeling the distraction concerned his uncle's two sons. They were long overdue from their voyage to the Virginias and the Carolinas. One returning sailor reported that he had seen them in Boston Harbor, but that had been so long ago that most believed they had died in a shipwreck. Madoc often lamented alone in deep bouts of melancholy. At other times Madoc behaved intolerably, thundering at his workers for any little mishap. When trouble arose, no matter how insignificant, he would snap at anything within reach like a blind street dog. However, despite his terrible bark, Madoc lashed only with words.

It was Corla who had the real bite. She would manipulate and bend Madoc. Although small and brittle, her shrill voice could deafen ears and sear the soul. She was nervy, excitable, and often irrational. She had been overjoyed to take charge of the girl when she and Ferret had arrived in the house. It had taken her only a few hours to christen the child Heather, after a long-dead daughter. They would dally together on the floor like sisters, playing tip-cat or handy-dandy.

Corla demanded that Heather be educated, which was not uncommon in Ireland. Irish traditions accorded many rights to women. Madoc objected to the expense. He argued that it was pointless to spend money on a deaf child. Corla's demands grew more insistent. After a few epic crying fits, Madoc finally agreed to hire the cheapest tutor he could find. When the tutor examined Heather, he discovered that the child was neither deaf nor dumb. Heather could speak all along. She spoke slowly, her mouth trembling as she uttered a few simple words.

The tutor that Madoc hired was a grim-faced, middle-aged man named Henry Dodgebury, whom everyone called "the Dutchman." Born with an abrasive personality, Dodgebury would feign quick half-smiles only to complain about what he just smirked at a minute later. Dodgebury was humorless; he dressed in black from head to toe. He objected to the nickname "Dutchman" because he was a native Zealander. Small children were frightened of him because his eyes were recessed so far back that he appeared faceless in dim light. He suffered from frequent colds and continuously coughed into mucus-stained handkerchiefs.

The Dutchman's presence increased Madoc's problems in the community tenfold. His neighbors begged to allow their children to sit in the back and observe. Along with an onslaught of small bribes and sweet words, loaves of black bread and freshly churned butter were delivered to Madoc's doorstep. Madoc gibed that he could water his Madonna lilies with the tears shed during one encounter.

Madoc's eventual surrender resulted in a circus of undisciplined and dirty children marching through his carpeted hallways. In short order, they were banished to the servant's entrance. In the classroom, they pouted, cried, twitched, and fidgeted restlessly. The trouble prompted Dodgebury to demand additional money for the extra workload. Madoc

L.K. SAMUELS

instituted a small fee for the Dutchman's services and for repairs to the makeshift school room. Since hard money was scarce, a three-notched tally stick was collected from each child each month. When the dock-workers got paid, they redeemed the tally sticks in coinage.

The Dutchman's reason for his abrupt flight from his homeland was never elaborated, beyond a few laconic words about "religious persecution." That was all that anyone knew, except that he boasted of excellent teaching credentials. But the tutor's fervent Calvinism became an increasingly sore subject. His sect had a reputation for harsh discipline and an outlook that despised the enjoyment of life and simple pleasures. The tutor once bragged about a Swiss boy who had hit his mother and was executed by the local Calvinists as a lesson to disobedient children.

To keep an eye on Dodgebury so he might not poison his Catholic pupils with Calvinism, Ferret would attend the Dutchman's tutoring sessions when work at the dockyard was light. When parents asked questions about the sessions, Ferret's answers were usually ill-received. One father booted the tutor over a railing and into a muddy pool with warnings that the bottomless sea was next. Another parent threatened to blot out his eyes with a hot poker. The Dutchman was undaunted. Although the parents disliked and distrusted him, they had little choice. Since the educated populace had abandoned Ireland during the war, teachers were mostly unavailable. It was said that only the foolhardy came to teach in Ireland, elevating the Dutchman to the unenviable position of "better him than nobody."

It was during one of the Dutchman's lessons that Ferret discovered something about the Netherlands that sounded too incredible to be true. It happened just after the schoolmaster performed another round of punishment on an inattentive boy. The tutor had crept behind the child's back, opened a large book near his ear and slammed it shut. The boy fell to the floor in terror while the other students sat in silence.

With a willow stick gripped in his hand, the Dutchman stared down with a sour face. "Someone ought to beat the devil from your draffsack soul. A bit of pain does keep the mind from wandering." The schoolmaster slapped the stick into the palm of his own hand. "Agony can surely heal body and soul."

151

Walking back to the front of the class, the schoolmaster spoke with scorn of men who searched the heavens with powerful telescopes, condemning Huygens for his "discovery" of Saturn's rings.

"He exemplifies," the Dutchman grumbled, "men who attempt to disprove the Lord. For the Lord has already given us all we need to know in the Holy Writ. To question the universe suggests that we question God's authority. Leave unknown mysteries to the Lord. If we seek to understand the unknown, we will be damned to eternal unhappiness. Only the Divinity understands what can never be understood."

This was too much for Ferret. He glared at the Dutchman. "What's wrong with seeking the truth?"

Stone-faced, the Dutchman swelled up his chest. "You must subscribe to the freethinkers. Woe to the lout who exposes blasphemous ideas to innocent children!" He walked toward Ferret. "Truth comes from authority. 'Tis what keeps men civilized. You wish to destroy that? You wish to level society?"

"Perhaps." Ferret stood his ground. He often felt an urge to see society leveled to its foundations, to start over from the ground up. It seemed to him that society was built on weak and faulty footings. "I search for my own truth, in my own way, and no king, noble, or clergyman has authority over me."

The Dutchman cocked his head and clasped his hands together as if to pray. He looked up to the heavens, his bushy eyebrows spiking from his forehead like black pine needles. "I do not oppose open discourse. Many Calvinists pride themselves on tolerance. And so do I, as long as heretics speak their tripe in some other region of Hell." He coughed and spat into his handkerchief.

"I once dwelled in Rotterdam," the Dutchman continued. "I saw the horrors of loose authority. 'Twas a hotbed of sacrilegious discord, anarchy, and freethinking. Profanity so vile, so lewd, that it put tavern matrons to the blush. The whole of the lowlanders be in free-flowing chaos. Citizens do what they want, think what they will and salivate in selfish wealth. Rotterdam reeks with the rot of Sodom." His voice became strained. "I had hoped that Cork remained untouched, unspoiled

152

by the greed of self-glorification. I erred! Lucifer is well fed in this backwater port."

Ferret listened intently. Rotterdam was a free land without murderous kings and callous tyrants. In a flash of clarity, he saw a tunnel of light opening up to a spacious new world. The Promised Land did exist; if only he could find a way to get there!

Chapter 16

While carrying a heavy bale of wool across a ship's narrow plank, Ferret gazed at the horizon where the bright sky melted into the dark water. Far beyond lay the Netherlands, a country so mysterious that God could only have conceived it in a moment of inspiration. How could such a small seafaring nation built on mudflats and salt marshes become free and independent? The Dutchman had criticized his motherland for things that any Irishman would envy—liberty, free thought, prosperity. The possibility was almost too mind-numbing to comprehend.

Ferret knew that *Eire* would never flower again. Conditions grew worse each day. Sumeria, Assyria, Greece, and Rome had all crumbled into hopeless dust. Great nations lived once, and then, like a rose, shriveled up and died. Ferret believed he was witnessing the final disintegration of his homeland. Impoverished families roamed the streets, begging for handouts from other penniless citizens, exhausting charities and bankrupting the church. The countryside around Cork had become a barren wasteland, denuded by hungry hordes who had left little greenery for sheep and cattle to graze. Each morning funeral wagons gathered up the dead like freshly cut lumber, to be dumped in the river. The indigents' hollow eyes reflected lost hope and pervasive gloom, prompting one clergyman to proclaim that people could live on nothing but hope for a better day.

Ferret was thinking about how much longer he could stay. Life was like a ship at dock. The water's surface was calm, but waves always inched the ship farther from the dock. Its only constraints were two ropes that prevented the vessel from drifting away to the unknown. Ferret watched the ships try to escape only to be held back, again and again, imperiously. When it came to his turn to break free, he wondered if he would be able to cut the line and sail away. He knew he had to leave someday, but only when the time was right.

Just then, foreman Josh Cockston shouted from the dockyard. "Come here, me fart-gutted weasel." The sweaty-faced man took off his hat and ran his grimy, stubby fingers through greasy hair. He was Madoc's favorite foreman: hot-tempered, irreverent, and disliked by one and all, a man of little distinction and even less sense. "Give thar message to your uncle." He thrust a scrap of paper into Ferret's face.

Sure, he could deliver a message to his uncle. The problem was that Cockston would dock him for the lost time. So much for fairness in a perfect world, Ferret thought, clenching his teeth.

The foreman soon turned his attention to a twelve-year-old boy who was struggling to carry a bale of wool. He grabbed the youngster and shook him. "What did I tell ya to do?"

"'Tis too heavy," the boy said.

Cockston cuffed the boy on the head, knocking him to the ground. Next, he dragged the boy to the water's edge and threatened to toss him into the dark water. "No back talk." He growled as he firmly clenched the boy's shirt. "Obey me words or ya'll sup with 'em sharkies."

The boy was too scared to move.

Ferret felt compelled to do something. He pushed his way to the foreman's side, faced the bully, and blocked his pathway.

"Get outta my way ya nick-ninny!"

"Apologize to the boy."

"I do what?" Cockston burst with a loud, uncontrolled belly laugh. At that point, most of the dockworkers ridiculed Ferret over his requested apology for a measly boy. They howled in derision, mocking Ferret as if he uttered the most absurd thing possible.

Ferret could see that he was getting nowhere. Instead, he reached into his pocket for a copper coin and dropped it on the wooden planks. "My word, someone lost their coinage."

"Where?" the foreman demanded.

Ferret pointed to the ground.

"Upon my soul." The big man squealed, his eyes drawn to the copper coin as if he had sighted a treasure chest of gold. "My, my... there's an unclaimed farthing. Won't last long, no sirree." Cockston dropped the boy and lumbered past Ferret, bent over and struggled to sweep up the nearly worthless coin. The task was daunting; he grunted and groaned as his over-spilling gut strained in the endeavor.

Ferret's opportunity arose much sooner than he had anticipated. Reaching over, he grabbed Cockston's ear and twisted it with relish. "Someone ought to teach you better manners."

"Let go or I will bury ya alive!"

Ferret wrenched the foreman's ear harder.

"Madoc will hear of this. So help me!"

Ferret released the man, stepped back and waited for the onslaught from an obstinate man with a bullheaded rage. Instead, the sudden release caused Cockston to fall backward. He tripped over a coil of rope, stumbled past bales of wool, and plunged over the wharf's edge. Ferret rushed over to the edge of the pier and watched the foreman bob up and down in the choppy water. It gave him comfort to know that the boy would not be dining with the sharks and denizens of the deep. Ferret turned to the boy. "If he ever threatens you again, holler. I seem to have acquired some skills at disarming bullies."

As Ferret comforted the boy, Cockston continued to barely tread water. The absurdity of the situation was almost comical. Every time he attempted to shout obscenities, filthy water would flood into his raunchy mouth. But the situation was becoming dangerous. Almost nobody knew how to swim. This realization forced a half-dozen dockworkers to scramble over to assist their floundering foreman. Each time they hoisted him up with a rope, his fingers lost their grip and he tumbled back into the cold water. Finally, a rowboat came alongside and hauled Cockston in with a fisherman's net. Ferret shook his head with a grim frown. The foreman could have drowned. This possibility made Ferret realize the enormity of what he had done—after this, he would be lucky to get past the gates of Hell.

The skinny boy slowly approached Ferret and gazed up with curious eyes. He rubbed his bruised arms and let out a pitiful whimper.

Ferret glanced down.

"Why?" the boy asked.

"Ahh... You mean why did I help?"

The boy nodded with some reluctance. "Nobody ever did that before. Nobody hearkens to me. Why you?"

Ferret was taken aback and unsure of how to respond.

The boy waited for an answer, his wide eyes trained on Ferret.

"You were being unfairly treated. Someone had to do something."

"Nobody ever did before."

"Someone must shine the light in the face of darkness. 'Tis our civil duty."

"You ought to be running the dockyard, sir."

"I would rather captain a vessel and escape this bedeviled isle."

"Would be a crime for you to forsake our land. Not many have your touch of mercy. May the Lord bless you and protect you." The boy lowered his head, turned and returned to his work.

Blessed? The thought struck a funny chord. Ferret felt more cursed than consecrated. There was little to appreciate or admire in *Eire*. He took another glance at the boy. At least someone appreciated his effort. That was saying a lot, given the ungodly state of affairs.

* * *

Arriving at Madoc's with the note from the foreman, Ferret tiptoed inside, careful not to disturb Heather. Constantly suffering from many ailments, she had grown weak and haggard. Her face and arms had taken on a green tinge. She often looked as if she might vomit at any moment. Most feared that she had consumption, but a physician proclaimed it a case of "green-sickness," which frequently assailed females after puberty.

As he searched for Madoc, he heard a strange voice echoing through the hallway. Ferret crept to the dining room and peeked inside. Two men were talking business. One was Madoc and the other wore the uniform of an English officer.

"We have a little problem." The officer shifted his body to another position, allowing the sunlight to accent a long scar across his face. The scar was unsightly, reddish and bumpy. It would cause people to stare with slack jaws. Ferret recognized his own handiwork. It had to be Major-General Cromwell.

"There has been a new edict from the Crown," Cromwell continued. "I have been ordered by London to halt all wool exports from Ireland immediately."

Madoc lowered a bottle of wine he was about to pour without filling Cromwell's wineglass. "What?"

"Wool has been banned completely. 'Tis contraband to all Irish merchants."

"That's more than a little problem!" Madoc said. "By crikey, that's a bloody outrage. You cannot be serious. Cork will starve. Twenty years I have labored to build my fleet and business. Twenty years! How can they forbid exports of wool? 'Tis all that Ireland exports! I'll be ruined!"

Cromwell grinned as if he had cornered a rat and intended to play with it before feasting. "I must confess that I find this edict somewhat distasteful."

"What are we to do?" Madoc's hand trembled as he poured the wine.

"I have little control over the whims of Parliament, and less influence on the capricious mandates of the Queen. I have no choice but to obey the edict." Cromwell paused and then asked with sheepish glee. "What would you have me do?"

Madoc shoved the glass toward Cromwell. "The last time England tried to ban Irish wool was back in '89. Some did not take well to that decree. Remember the Royal Governor of Waterford? He did not fare well either. His face exploded like a squashed grape after sipping a glass of pinot noir. Rumors spoke of some wretched Irish disease. Others blame a wine of poor quality."

Cromwell studied the wine and carefully lowered the glass. "But I cannot sit by idly-bidly."

"No one profits when trade is choked," Madoc said.

Cromwell turned his attention to a somber painting on the wall. He leaned closer to get a better look. "Hmm… looks expensive."

"Wasn't much," Madoc said. "'Tis a portrait of my grandfather by some obscure Dutchman. Rembrandt, I believe."

"The colors are too dark." Cromwell mumbled as he touched the canvas with his finger. "Nonetheless, my orders are precise. All wool exports have been banned and smugglers are to be hanged from the gallows. That's the Queen's law."

"I'm no smuggler!" Madoc said.

"Of course not," Cromwell said. "You have nothing in common with smugglers. Listen, I wish no part in Cork's demise, or in yours. But pressure is mounting. Irish wool competes too well with English wool. Either England or Ireland starves. But I will be bloody damned before I emaciate Cork into oblivion. I have no wish to rule over a plot of gravestones."

Madoc nodded. He understood Cromwell's dilemma. If Cork perished, the commander would be demoted. If he disobeyed the edict, the hangman's noose would soon tighten around his neck.

Cromwell continued, "I've learned that a new commissioner will arrive to monitor all shipping in the area. He will undoubtedly investigate our excisemen at the dockyard and discover our little arrangement. That must not occur."

"Well, it appears you need my help." Madoc huffed, flaunting a tight-lipped smile. "So I'm invaluable to you."

"Tilly vally! I can handle my own affairs with the utmost success." Cromwell's eyes sparkled with the flare of confidence. "You forget who controls Cork's barracks. I am empowered to assert my authority in any manner deemed necessary. I am empowered to arrest anyone for any reason. I am all the law I need."

"What will you have me do?"

"The solution is simple," Cromwell said. "This commissioner will probably sail on one of your vessels. As you know, most voyages are dangerous. Many have suffered unspeakable accidents at sea. They get drunk, lose their balance, and tumble overboard, never to be found. Most unfortunate." He sipped his wine and smiled.

Madoc cleared his throat. "We do try to prevent such accidents, but they are frequent—sad to say."

"Just remember," Cromwell said, "I prefer wine that doesn't leave an aftertaste. If I cannot depend on a glass of fine wine, I shall search for another winemaker." Cromwell dropped his glass on the stone floor and stomped his boot on the broken shards.

At that moment, Ferret entered the room. He approached Madoc as he held the note tightly in his hand. After he stopped, he glanced at Cromwell and was amused over how tall he was, at least six inches taller. The major-general appeared less menacing than he had a decade before.

Cromwell stared at Ferret. "You look familiar. Where do I know you from?"

"From a land too far to be remembered and a time too short to recall," Ferret said with a menacing glare.

"Excuse him." Madoc waved his hand dismissively. "He's my daffy nephew. Take no heed of his rambling antics."

As Ferret handed Josh's note to Madoc, his eyes were drawn to Cromwell's pistol, which was bulging in his side holster.

Cromwell noticed Ferret's interest and handed it to Ferret, describing it as a finely-crafted handgun, a Wellington.

Ferret studied the weapon. It was beautiful. His index finger began to caress the trigger. All he had to do was point the pistol at Cromwell and pull the trigger. This was his best opportunity to right past wrongs. Yet he hesitated. From what he could gather, Cromwell's plan would keep Cork from wasting away. Ironically, Cromwell was trying to right a wrong, something many might tout as valiant. That mere thought disturbed him. He admitted that Cromwell's plan to murder the commissioner was inexcusable, but he knew the offense could save hundreds or perhaps thousands of lives. It seemed he had stumbled into a gray area of two equally undesirable choices. He hated moral dilemmas. They rattled the soul, darkened the spirit, and cut so deeply that the mind became stuffed with senseless clutter. He had to make a fast decision.

Ferret lifted up the pistol, looked through its gun sight and took aim out a window at a stray cat. He had to admit it. Cromwell's governorship had so far been a pleasant surprise. His father's murderer had won over many commoners, artisans, and merchants. And he had done it by being forthright. It would indeed be a travesty if Cromwell's health were to suddenly go downhill. Ferret handed the pistol back to Cromwell.

Ferret had missed his opportunity to avenge his father's death. He hoped he had done the right thing. He had a feeling he would one day regret this decision.

* * *

Ferret roamed Cork's streets for hours that afternoon. He brooded over whether he would ever leave his country or achieve anything worthwhile. Standing next to a deserted canal, he watched the sun hovering above the horizon, bathing the buildings in a cold yellow light. Waves sloshed gently against the dock. He wanted to be alone; he felt as if he were in a world that had nothing in common with him. He held tightly to the pain of solitude but knew that such emptiness never accomplished anything.

As Ferret wandered, he drew near the Red Bull. Suddenly, he heard a familiar voice. Two hooded figures darted into the alehouse. One of the voices belonged to Strongbow.

Ferret slowly went inside, trying to casually spy from shadowy nooks and corners. The alehouse appeared almost deserted, its wood-planked walls dimly lit with rush candles. As his eyes became more accustomed to the low light, he noticed two figures sitting near the stone-laid hearth, drinking ale, and whispering. Strongbow's back was against the wall, his hood raised, watchful. He was dressed as a wealthy merchant, in fine silk and linen, with a brown velvet cloak that touched the straw-covered floor. Ferret approached from his side.

Strongbow snapped around, twisting to his left side and jabbing Ferret with his pistol's barrel. "Get any closer, mate, and we'll have to get wedlock." In a flash, he lowered his pistol. "Ferret? You cockbrain. I almost shot you!"

"Again! I would hate to see what you do to your enemies!"

Strongbow's eyes glistened as he slipped his weapon under his belt. "What enemies? I have none. At least, none alive." He embraced Ferret. "My stout laddie. You come at a most fortuitous time."

"I'm not so sure," Ferret said as he sat in a chair.

"You came upon me with remarkable deftness. You would make a splendid spy." Strongbow laughed.

The other hooded person watched them intently, drew the hood back—revealing a woman. Her chalk-white face was engulfed by coarse hair, wild and unkempt. Two small warts dotted her chin but did not detract from her beauty. Her tight, low-cut dress showed much of her bulging breasts. She was young; her fiery eyes shined with a fullness of life, or perhaps a touch of madness.

Just then a baby cried. The woman lowered her bodice, revealing a white engorged breast. She gently pushed the baby up to her pink nipple.

Uncomfortable, Ferret leaned away from the stranger and noticed she had no ears, only stubs. The odd sight caused him to gape at the women.

The woman noticed Ferret's repulsed reaction and let out a bitter hiss.

"Don't be alarmed," Strongbow said. "Rachel is sensitive about her ears. They lopped them clean off after the witch trial." Strongbow paused and took a brisk check of the deserted room. "You met Rachel years ago. Corporal Holbrook was transporting her to Cork."

"I thought she murdered her husband?"

"Cromwell decided that her crimes were committed in another district. He sent her back to the local authorities. On the way back she... disappeared."

"Strongbow kept me alive," Rachel cooed.

"You rescued a witch!" Ferret recoiled.

Rachel pounded her fist on the table and cursed. *"Amadan!* No witch, no witch. *Droch-chrioch ort!"*

"Rachel's no witch, my dear laddie," Strongbow said. "She's from the moorlands, in the interior, near Athlone. She lived under the old Celtic traditions. She did not understand English law and—"

"Hate English," Rachel muttered.

"Righto," Strongbow said as he took a sip of ale. "Anyway, she was married to an old pinch-fart chieftain. But she abrogated the marriage years ago. That was her right. But the chief was a lout, a regular vinegar pisser. Disobeyed the *Brehon* laws and refused to give Rachel part of his property."

Rachel's mood changed quickly. She slithered her arms around Strongbow's neck.

"But why risk coming back?" Ferret suspected that Strongbow had an alternate motive. He was always hiding his motives behind a façade. Whatever it was, it had to be something big. Maybe he was behind the rising tensions in the dockyard. Port officials were being assaulted, buildings defaced. Somebody had to be behind the uproar.

Strongbow lowered his voice. "We plan to abandon the sinking ship. We wish to remain dry. You were the one that suggested it. We're taking your advice. In a fortnight we plan to depart for good. No looking back." Again, Strongbow glanced over Ferret's head to see if anyone else had entered the alehouse.

"No leave *Eire*," Rachel protested.

Strongbow ignored her as he continued. "'Tis pigwash, all this official talk of better times for Ireland. I know worse is yet to come. I've heard rumors, and I have heard from those who start rumors. Wool will be banned, and restrictions on beef will follow. Our isle will starve as it has never starved before. We must leave now before it's too late!"

"How do you know this?" Ferret asked.

"Doesn't matter," Strongbow said. "I have comrades in London. We can live the wonderful life of nobility."

"How?"

"I have secured passage on the *Green Sounder*. I believe the vessel is titled to your uncle. The captain is an old mate of mine. He will take us—Badger, Paco, and many more—off this dreadful isle."

Ferret shook his head. "The *Green Sounder* stinks of old age! Its hull's rotted. The ship barely floats."

"'Tis still seaworthy," Strongbow said with a little hesitation. "Better than staying here. Will you come?"

Ferret knew that Strongbow always had his fingers dipped into every stewpot. He would not be surprised to learn that Strongbow had something to do with the turmoil. "Why take me?"

"Because you may be king of Ireland someday."

"King of a country that I abandon?"

"Kings do that frequently."

"With armies in hot pursuit." Ferret snickered. His lips tugged upward in a pensive grin. He never knew what to expect from Strongbow. Though he detested liars and thieves, he knew he would always forgive Strongbow's impulse to swap truth for lies. He reasoned that everyone had their blind spots. He hoped others would forgive his own as often as he overlooked Strongbow's.

"Come laddie. What tethers you to Ireland? Surely not your uncle?"

"Heather is ill."

"Heather?"

"The girl you abandoned at my uncle's abode," Ferret said.

"She's no kindred. No real blood."

"I've never mentioned that to anyone and neither should you. To me, she's flesh-and-blood kin."

"Bring her." Strongbow smiled and took a hearty sip from his tankard. "If you come, it will be like old times. You may chastise me for my scoundrel ways, and I won't nitpick one bit." Strongbow shoved his ale at Ferret and snatched Rachel's mug for himself. "A toast. Let's drink to something, anything."

Ferret took a swig of the dark, syrupy ale. He lifted his tankard into the air. "To the Netherlands?"

"Whatever you wish," Strongbow said confidently. "Wait and see. This time fate is on our side."

Chapter 17

Cromwell rose in the early morning light. Daybreak was the most enjoyable part of his day. He was alone and undisturbed; the rest of the world slept. His day was about to begin and he wanted to be first in line to command it.

Wrapped in a wool blanket, he held a cup of hot bohea tea to warm his cold hands, and watched the sunrise. He found it entertaining to observe merchants in block-wheeled carts stumble and fall on the ice-caked streets. Pathetic. They couldn't control anything in their wretched lives, not even where they were going.

His men knew of this early morning routine and referred to him as the "Window Spy." They feared he would catch a glimpse of them coming back from town after curfew. And he did notice them stumbling back to the barracks, covering their bloodshot eyes from the sunlight. But Cromwell never punished the men. He was no spy. He enjoyed the quiet of the early morning hours and prized his morning solitude.

Cromwell lifted up a carved turnip and examined it. It was creamy purple with streaks of orange. A brood of Irish children had given it to him in appreciation of his superior leadership. "A queer gift," he murmured. It was a local custom to celebrate the eve of Allhallowmas. The turnip had been hollowed out and gashed with a crooked and fearsome face. They had told him to light a candle inside to fend off wicked spirits. He thought of it as a warning. Autumn meant nights of heavy drinking, rabble-rousing, and fear.

Fear was man's worst enemy. Even his fellow Englishmen dreaded the long and cold nights of winter, fearful that God's interest in mankind eroded a little with each passing day. The slow disappearance of the sun was unsettling. Nobody knew for certain whether the sun would return in spring. It had, for millennia—but what if it burned out or blew up? What if he ran out of hot tea? The barest trace of a grin crossed Cromwell's lips. These apprehensions were childish, so pointless that they were unremarkable even for his diary.

Lieutenant Holbrook knocked on the door and entered the room. He doffed his hat and quietly but urgently said, "Sir, I have arrests to report."

Cromwell was displeased. He took a long sip of tea and glanced away. His morning quiet had been breached. He wanted to ignore Holbrook, but his duties had to be performed.

"'Tis early, I know, Sir," Holbrook said, noticing that Cromwell was barely listening. "But we apprehended two unregistered priests last night."

Cromwell's face soured as he gazed at the high ceiling. It was easy to capture unregistered priests. The difficult part was transporting them to London for banishment, prison, or execution. Like clockwork, they would be arrested, read a list of accusations, marched aboard ships, and, within months, reappear, as if by magic, in Ireland—animated, cheery, and often better fed than when they had left.

"Sir," Holbrook said, "one of the priests might be a deserter, a former officer of yours."

Cromwell sat upright in an instant, his interest now piqued. He did not want a priest. He wanted Winchester. His former officer had stolen from the military so thoroughly that it had soiled everyone's reputation. And then, like a ghost, he had escaped everyone's clutches. Cromwell had vowed to one day settle the score.

Cromwell rubbed his face as he unclenched his teeth. Other than Winchester, he could not blame any of his lower-ranked officers for wanting to desert this backward isle. If only he had realized how primitive Ireland was before accepting command. Yet his options had been few. He had been in desperate need of a commission. At first, he had considered a post in the colonies across the Atlantic, but reports from New England and the Virginias noted that over half of the settlers died within the first year. Ireland was less deadly. Cromwell turned to Holbrook. "The deserter's name is?"

"I believe he was known as Sergeant-Major Stuffleton."

Cromwell slouched back into his chair. His eyes narrowed, trying to remember the man, the face and the place, then he grinned. "That fat-skull idiot is a priest? What a mockery. The priesthood must be desperate for new recruits!"

"We found him drunk, wandering near the Red Bull with another papist, a Father Yeats."

Cromwell picked at his scar as he voiced his displeasure. "I want them put into irons and shipped to London. Do not under any circumstances tell the captain that they're men of the cloth. With luck, this time I'll get at least one hanged priest listed on my record. Anything else?" Cromwell leaned back in his chair.

"Sir, when we captured the papists, I overheard something disturbing. The *Sea Weaver* harbored last evening, and her men were bellyaching that Irish wool and beef are to be banned. I told them it was a hoax. Still, the men were mighty vexed. Shout, they did, with disrespect to Queen, Parliament and... you, Sir."

"Me! Outrageous rot! I had no hand in this travesty."

"'Tis true then?"

Cromwell saw that Holbrook had trapped him. This lieutenant was different from his other officers, intelligent and of modern thought. He began to fiddle with the turnip and glanced up. "You would make a fine lawgiver or barrister, Lieutenant. Nonetheless, I am not at liberty to say much. Perhaps some Irish exports might be limited."

"How limited?"

"Your rank does not make you privy to such information. I daresay, you have the boldness of wild Irish blood."

Holbrook bit his lower lip. "I'm Welsh, Sir, and I have heard some of the wealthy Irish merchants refer to you as one of their own."

Cromwell enjoyed Holbrook's gamesmanship. He was wary of the usual mundane complaints and whiny criticisms. "Listen here. I'm well beloved in Ireland. See this?" Cromwell held up the carved turnip. "The children of Cork presented me with this token. I have done much for these people. That, Mr. Holbrook, is why I have an orderly seaport."

"Sir, I do not wish to contradict you, but any honor-bound soldier here could tell you that you're not as beloved as you think."

"Bosh!" Cromwell snarled. "The Irish have given celebrations in my honor. I have hanged very few bogtrotters. I have improved the roads. I have ruled with grace and leniency. What more could they want?"

Holbrook pulled out a paper from a shoulder pouch and handed it to Cromwell. "I'm afraid that this handbill accuses you of banning wool for personal profit."

Cromwell snatched the parchment, unrolled it and read the short declaration. "Why should I care about this?"

"Because the market square is flooded with them."

"Let me see." Cromwell started to read. "I'm being accused of being an arrogant tosspot who profits at the expense of..." Cromwell stopped and glared at Holbrook. "I don't have time to read such utter tripe."

"You need to be aware of this. I know they mean well, but your stave officers and adjutant are most likely keeping you sheltered."

Cromwell sighed. An age-old Saxon proverb suddenly came to mind: "He that hath a head of wax must not walk in the sun." How could this be? How could he have lost his good standing in the eyes of the townsfolk? He had brought order and justice to an unstable land. Nobody could dispute that. Many of his associates had confided in him that he was doing a splendid job. Could they be wrong?

Cromwell lifted up the paper again and read the short declaration in earnest. As he did, he felt an urge to crush the turnip. He had tried to give the region modern and enlightened governance. In return for his service, he gained nothing but disrespect from the Irish. He had hoped to be acclaimed as a great statesman, as a leader, not a tyrant who ruled with an iron fist. But he could see that they thought of him as a corrupt tyrant. He detested corruption and tyrants! "No signers, I see."

"Something must be done," Holbrook said. "Cork is a powder keg set to blow, especially with so many half-starved commonfolk clogging the streets."

Cromwell squeezed the turnip, cracking its skin. Some of the people must still appreciate him. Then again, the Irish were not the noblest of races. He should not expect much from half-breeds and mongrels.

"Sir," Holbrook said, "there are rumors that you need to be made aware of. Other allegations speak of far more serious charges of wrongdoing."

"Lieutenant, don't treat rumors as God's truth. Rumors are worse than lies because nobody can find their source."

"But what if they ring clear?"

"Rumors reek of deception. They are born to undermine my authority. It takes only a small half-truth to spark the rabble. Remember the rout the month before I took command of Cork? A soldier's gun accidentally discharged and killed a passing child. After that, rumors spoke of some Pharaoh-like British policy to murder all Irish children. Took a whole regiment from Waterford to restore order. My predecessor lost his command soon afterward. They shipped him off to the New World, and he died of cholera within the year. I do not like to see history repeat itself at my expense. Order must be maintained. I want more patrols policing Cork. A show of muscle should suppress any thought of disorder."

"Perhaps we should leave our flintlocks unloaded until we need them," Holbrook said. "To prevent any repetition."

"Unloaded firearms?" Cromwell thought for a moment. "'Tis better to leave halfwits in the barracks than to leave muskets unloaded."

"We'll have plenty of time to load them, Sir. We patrol Cork, not the underbrush."

Cromwell stood and laid his hand on Holbrook's shoulder. "These are dangerous times, Lieutenant. Gunpowder has the miracle of immediate respect. But... do what you must."

Holbrook nodded and departed.

Cromwell grasped a spyglass, walked to the window and fully extended its lens. He gazed toward the dockyard. A ship was entering the harbor. He wondered if the vessel carried his favorite English brandy and bohea tea. His supplies were running low.

Chapter 18

A sailor's cry shattered the air: "Ghost ship!"

Dozens of dockworkers ran to the pier to see the mysterious vessel. The more superstitious workers ran for their lives. The ship was barely visible in the fog. It looked like a ship that legend said haunted the seven seas, rising from the graveyard of sunken ships in the depths of the ocean. This apparition, however, was not content to dissolve into mist. This vessel was heading straight for the docks.

Ferret watched, dumbfounded, as the damaged vessel limped into the harbor. It was anything but seaworthy. The vessel's rigging and sails were tattered, the crow's nest had been blown off, and its hull had been repaired with makeshift patches of wood, tar, and canvas. Low in the water, the phantom ship listed to the right, causing its broken topmast to hover overboard. It looked as if the vessel might capsize at any moment.

When the ship was fifty yards out, shouts of "the *Chetney*" jolted the air. Ferret knew the *Chetney* had been lost for countless years. Ferret's cousin Arthur had been her captain when she left; Arthur's brother Leary had been her first mate. Everyone had assumed them to be dead. But here the *Chetney* was! The vessel scraped alongside the pier. Before it dropped anchor, it crashed into the dock. A gangplank was shoved from deck to dock, and a dozen gaunt crewmen fought one another to be the first ashore. One sailor leaped overboard, too anxious to wait any longer.

News of the miraculous arrival of the *Chetney* spread. Townsfolk rushed to the dockyard and embraced the long-lost sailors. Others watched with amazement. Less impressed were the excisemen, who began to haggle over the merchandise believed to be stored within the vessel's hold. One anxious exciseman wanted the tax and shipping fees paid in full immediately. Finally, after most of the crew had departed, a brawny man, taller than the others, strode across the plank with a large duffel bag slung across his shoulder. It was Arthur O'Neill.

A short, bald exciseman buzzed at Arthur like a horsefly. "What be your cargo?" he demanded with a raised eyebrow.

"We have none," Arthur stated with slight amusement.

The exciseman was incredulous. "Take me for a pixie-led blockhead from the hinterland, do you? Your hull lies low in the water!"

Arthur grabbed the exciseman, lifting him up to eye level. The man's toes dangled an inch above the ground. "Are you calling me a liar?"

Just then, Arthur noticed his approaching father, dropped the puny man and embraced Madoc.

Arthur looked at his father with a wry gleam in his eyes. "I understand that you've had your share of problems too. Rumor has it that trouble is brewing in your dockyard."

Madoc froze. "Where did you hear that?"

"Here and there," Arthur said dryly. "Does it matter? Ireland's always suffering under some unbecoming weight of fate."

Madoc glanced around and failed to see his other son. "Where's Leary?"

"I'm sorry," Arthur said quietly. "Leary succumbed to bloody savages." Arthur explained that they had run aground during a tempest so wicked that it seemed to darken the entire globe. Half the crew made it ashore alive only to find themselves in territory where they had to contend with bloodsucking mosquitoes, blistering heat, and Indian war parties. Arthur clenched a handful of his own hair and pulled. He made a slashing motion across his hair. "Savages scalped him before he could gulp his last breath. God-awful sight it was."

Arthur explained that every time they attempted to repair the *Chetney*, they were attacked and driven out by a bloodthirsty tribe called the Yamasee. Only after years of struggle were they able to complete the repairs. Before heading home, Arthur sailed south and reached the territory of Spanish Florida, looking for a seaport to trade their wares for food and supplies. They settled in St. Augustine for three years before sailing home.

Ferret wondered if Arthur's tale was true. He remembered his cousin's preoccupation with plots and conspiracies. Arthur had believed that master conspirators controlled almost everything in the world, from colossal wars to the Pope, and it had been his aspiration to join the powerful elite. This was why his cousin had bragged about never letting an opportunity go to waste. As for misfortunes, Arthur welcomed them, convinced that they were tests to strengthen the will to survive new challenges. He saw them as opportunities to cheat both ill fate and death. He boasted that he had the skill of an alchemist, who could magically transform vinegar into sweet wine. Despite Arthur's fancy talk, Ferret found his story of Leary's death suspicious. One less brother meant one less inheritor when Madoc stood before his maker.

Ferret was determined to keep his distance from Arthur. His cousin had a sullied past. He was volatile, alternately taking the role of part prankster and part bully. Arthur would use threats to intimidate and embarrass outsiders, misfits, and the feeble throughout Cork. But on some occasions, he had become physical. When he was an adolescent, Arthur fought an adversary over the affection of a girl and pushed the juvenile over a cliff. The unlucky lad broke his arm.

During another incident, Arthur had once tricked a man to eat a raw oyster and then argued that the creature would eat away his stomach unless something was done. Arthur gave the desperate man a bunch of hot chili peppers and a bottle of vinegar disguised as beer. The man nearly died. But Arthur's most serious offenses occurred when he was the ringleader of a gang of petty thieves and ruffians. He and his chums would get arrested for breaking windows, selling stolen goods, or disorderly conduct outside of alehouses. Whatever the unlawful act, however, Madoc would rescue his son and arrange to get the charges dropped.

As a boy, Arthur would abuse Ferret with threats and belittlement. If that failed to get Ferret's blood boiling, Arthur would shove, kick, and punch him. Ferret had felt like a rag doll, beaten and mishandled. Madoc would do nothing to stop the onslaught, dubbing it "growing pains." The injustice would continue until Ferret would retreat, hurt and humiliated.

Arthur finally noticed Ferret. "Father, is this one of your pigwash servants?"

Madoc grimaced. "'Tis your cousin, Sean. Remember? Everyone now calls him Ferret."

"He even looks like a ferret—dog-faced, pink-eyed, and yellow," Arthur quipped. He took a half-hearted swing at his cousin.

Ferret caught Arthur's fist with ease.

Amused, Arthur played along. "You've grown a backbone and a dollop of muscle."

"I'm not your chattel anymore."

"Everyone is subservient to someone," Arthur said resolutely, "except those with the biggest whip."

Ferret refused to release his cousin's arm. Arthur's smirk changed to a frown when he realized he could not break free. Ferret wanted to force Arthur to his knees and humiliate him. Such show of force would prove that he had the wherewithal to stand up to any overbearing ruffian. But he had no desire to become a bully-rook or a swaggerer who sought to brag about his toughness and exploits. Ferret loosened his grip, releasing his cousin's arm. "The meek can defend themselves."

"Not in my world!" Arthur gleamed with a sly smile on his face. "But if you seek supremacy, you might try laying claim to your O'Neill bloodline. Become the next King of Ireland. That is, what's left of it."

"Not interested," Ferret said with a shake of his head. He was not sure whether his cousin was serious or playing him the fool.

"Power is rewarding," Arthur said. "It has its perks—fat gravy and clotted cream. Once you have tasted its power, you will find its flavor savory and addictive. Besides, it be rightfully yours; you be no commoner. Take the war to their homeland and slaughter every last Briton in his bedchamber. Cause them to bleed and bring Ireland back to its glory."

"Christ could not be tempted. Why should I?" Ferret turned away. The thought of abusing others for personal gain was repulsive. He knew that Arthur simply wanted to use him until he found someone better. That was one of the biggest flaws of human nature. Ferret knew he was wrong to flaunt his physical strength like an ill-mannered lout. But without bravado, a man would be seen as a coward, a faint-hearted, misbegotten weasel with legs of quicksand. He knew he had to sometimes defend his position with force, whether or not his principles also ended up bruised.

"What is stopping you?" Arthur asked, smugly. "Afraid of Cromwell's military prowess? Perhaps it's because greatness comes from noble deeds and not by highbred birth."

Ferret was dumbfounded. Arthur had just stepped off his half-submerged vessel moments ago. He could not have known about Cromwell's command in Cork—unless he had docked in a harbor up the coast. Ferret cringed at the thought that his cousin had joined a conspiracy even before reaching home. He wished he could decipher the language of Arthur's deceit.

* * *

Corla was first to meet Arthur at the doorway. She demanded the name of the tall stranger who kissed her forehead.

"Who do you think I be?" asked Arthur.

Corla reached out with her good arm and touched the man's face. "How dare you play ragman with me!"

"I'm no ragman. 'Tis Arthur."

Corla's face unraveled. Tears trickled down her cracked cheeks. "You shamed your eldmother. Scampered off to some unknown land without telling me. Hindustan, was it not?" She hobbled over to the hearth for warmth. "Hindustan! Full of damnable heathens."

Arthur followed her. "'Twas the West Indies and Virginy."

At the hearth, she stopped, turned and finally embraced her grandson. "You should have come back sooner."

"I'm sorry I've been delayed."

Clearing his throat, Madoc picked up Arthur's duffel bag and walked through the house to Ferret's room. In quick fashion, he ordered Ferret to move his own belongings somewhere else.

Ferret had expected this outcome. He tried to hide his anger, even though he knew the only room remaining in the house was the attic, and its amenities were considerably less suitable—rough floors, cobwebbed ceilings, and drafty walls. He knew he and Heather were lucky to have a roof at all.

It did not take long for Arthur to affirm his authority. Before Ferret had finished moving out of his room, Arthur entered and fired another barrage of thinly veiled threats, announcing that someday he would be lord and master of everything. On that day, he said, everyone would taste his wrath.

Ferret ignored Arthur's bloated sense of self-importance and ordered him out. Strangely, his cousin obeyed and retreated in silence, but stayed just outside in the hallway. That seemed like an odd reaction but he could not concern himself with his cousin's odd behavior. He had to concentrate on his task at hand. As he busily stuffed a large bundle of clothes into a canvas bag, Heather returned from the market. Immediately she began to assist Ferret, collecting his books and papers.

Arthur suddenly reentered the room and grabbed Heather's wrist. He reeled her close to him, causing her to drop everything she had gathered. For a moment, it appeared that he intended to kiss her.

Ferret rushed up to Arthur, their faces inches apart. "Let her go!"

"I'm just examining my property."

Ferret understood the reference clearly. Arthur's uncivil actions bore a resemblance to an animal marking its territory. It was tactless and crude, but apparently his way of putting both himself and Heather on notice, like a new landlord figuring out how to evict his unwanted tenants.

Ferret stared at Arthur straight on and calmly said, "Heather will be honored amongst our clan. She's no child, indentured servant, bogtrotter or weak-willed woman susceptible to forged charms. She is one of us, my sister."

Arthur backed up. "I would never harm those dearest to me."

"The clan must stick together." Ferret lowered his voice. "That's our duty."

Arthur's disposition changed, and he bowed slightly, grabbed Heather's hand and kissed it. He noticed her thin body silhouetted against the window. He stared at Madoc, who had just entered the room. "Do you not feed this child?"

"She's a little mawkish." Madoc swallowed with a dry, hollow click in his throat. "I mean she eats less than a bereft church mouse."

"I feel less afflicted today, Uncle," Heather said in a soft, reedy voice. She removed Arthur's hand from her side and fled to the corner of the room where she sat in a chair playing with her stringy hair and chewing on a long-nailed finger.

Arthur took a long look and finally concluded that she was a "skinny waif" and not much more.

Ferret had a clear understanding of Arthur's choice of words. *Waif* meant that Heather possessed no value to him whatsoever; she was an unwelcome guest with little time remaining. Kindred or not, Arthur would expel both of them when he took command of the O'Neill estate. Knowing Arthur, Ferret reckoned his uncle did not have long to live.

* * *

The attic was barren of furniture and caked with dust. The ceiling was so low in places that Ferret had to crawl on his knees.

Heather began to sweep the floor, and to lay out moth-eaten blankets for bedding. Her face glistened in the flicker of the candle; she looked like a golden angel. Her face was petite and her neckline slender. He knew that someday he would have to tell the truth about her heritage—that she did not have any. She was old enough now, but he was afraid that if he told her, she would run away forever, upset over all of his countless lies. He also wondered if he wanted more from her than mere sisterly affection. He had noticed Heather's changing body. She was likely past thirteen years of age and certainly marriageable. The days were gone when she scampered around the room wearing only an impish smile.

He looked down her nightgown as she leaned forward to sweep. Her pear-shaped breasts were pale and firm, her pink nipples erect. Ferret wondered who might bed Heather upon wedlock. The thought made him jealous.

Heather noticed Ferret's gaze. "I'm changing," she said. "See!" Kneeling, she lowered her gown to show off her body. She moved closer to Ferret so he could see better, running her hand over her nipples, proud at becoming a woman. "I'm even growing red hair below." She lifted the gown over her head and dropped it across the bedding. "'Tis very curly."

Ferret stared in spite of himself and recalled the old sleeping customs that many Irish still practiced on cold nights. Clans would undress and sleep naked under a blanket in front of a fire. Even if a visitor stayed the night, all would sleep together unclothed. The English had introduced sleeping clothes to the well-to-do, along with some modesty.

Ferret felt a stream of cold air rushing from a crack in the wall large enough to see the dockyard through. When Heather sneezed, Ferret wrapped a blanket around her shoulders. "'Tis a mite cold to bear it all."

She leaned forward and kissed Ferret on the cheek. "I will always love you, brother."

"And I you." Ferret found his fingers creeping under the blanket, soon discovering her chest. He folded his hands around her back and pecked her cheek.

She returned the kiss, but this time fully, on the lips.

He enjoyed the sensation of her mouth on his and wondered how far this would go.

She giggled. "If only we were strangers of blood."

Must not go further, Ferret thought. *This must be only fraternal love.*

"I would give you healthy children," Heather cooed. "I've dreamt about it."

"I'm your brother!"

"Half-brother." She leered at him and tried to kiss him again. "It does not bother me. Many wed within their clans."

He gently stopped her advances. Heather had to remain a blood relative or Madoc would evict both of them. But that was not his only burden. He had never been with a woman before and was unsure what was expected of him. There were no books or instructions, just crude jokes from men in back alleys and stories of carnal pleasure from lusty women. It all seemed to boil down to hot nervous nights of liquor-induced stupor. It sounded coarse, awkward, unnatural. And yet, his desire to prick a woman was overpowering.

She took his hand and kissed it.

"I'm serious!"

"And I'm not?"

"You had better go now," Ferret said as he tried to break free of her grip.

"I'm staying," she said. Like their Irish kindred, they too had often slept in the same bed, huddling close together for warmth, hot skin to hot skin, but with the innocence of children. She would even joke about his "long knobby snake." But now she wanted more than body warmth on a cold night. "Please? I'll behave."

"If you stay on your side."

"And if I do not?"

"You will leave."

Her face fell. "I'll behave." She kissed Ferret lightly on the lips again. "I know how to behave."

Chapter 19

Ferret awoke when he heard a suspicious noise. He scanned the dark attic room. Nothing seemed out of the ordinary. He assumed that the loud, rattling disturbance came from a distant thunderstorm.

Heather's arm was wrapped across his naked chest. She had broken her agreement. He would have to scold her in the morning.

Another rumble shook the room. This one was much louder than before. He listened for the pounding of the storm but heard neither pelting rain nor whistling wind. The sound was like thunder or gunshots. He must be dreaming. Cork was a backwater seaport in a scorned land. If a dazzling spot burned brightly somewhere in the world, this was the farthest point from it.

"Did you hear that?" Heather whispered. She clung to Ferret like a mother to a newborn child.

Ferret removed her arm and tossed the wool blanket aside. He lit a candle, rolled out of bed, and crawled to a small window. Outside, a mob with torches milled in Madoc's dockyard. Men were firing weapons into the air. He glanced over to Heather. "There's trouble brewing at the dockyard."

"'Tis none of your concern." Heather grabbed Ferret's arm and pulled. Instead, Ferret pulled her much harder, causing them to tumble as if wrestling. She tackled him. They struggled for a while, rolling back and forth until Ferret accidentally hit Heather in the face. She fell back, a little blood oozing out of her mouth. Ferret pinned her shoulders to the floor. "Have I hurt you?"

"I'm fine," Heather cooed, "but you won't be if you go outside."

Ferret released his grip. "You know I must go."

"Please stay. I fear danger abounds outside."

Ferret clambered over Heather's body and began to search for his clothes. The candle was casting deep shadows, concealing everything he wanted to find.

Heather rolled onto her side and watched Ferret unearth one of his boots. "You shouldn't have to go."

"I have a duty to my uncle."

"That old skinflint!" Heather huffed, crawled away, then plunged into a pile of blankets. After settling in, she started to play with her long hair, bundling large strands into her palm. She looked up. "If you stay, you can hit me again. I know that is what the beloved do."

Ferret cocked his head in surprise. "What kind of foolishness are you talking about?"

"Menfolk always hit their women. The baker from Albert Quay horse-whips his wife without mercy. I saw it through a window. Isn't that what lovers do?"

Ferret, too, had witnessed several wife beatings. It seemed that men could not help but strike their women, especially when drunk. It seemed to him that some treated their women worse than pigs. It was generally tolerated, provided no one was killed. He found it disgusting. "You don't beat someone you care about."

Heather frowned. She appeared unconvinced.

"'Tis cold and you're still ailing." With a strong hand, Ferret pushed her under the covers, tucking the blanket around her neck.

Heather obeyed without a whimper. "Indeed, you must love me."

Ferret crawled over to the window again. "Looks beastly down there. I'll have to go."

"Watch yourself. And don't trust anybody."

"I'll be as safe as a mother's fawn in Heaven." Ferret searched for his shirt and found it lying next to a large wooden trunk.

Heather glanced at Ferret. "Was she pretty?"

"Who?"

"My mother. She wasn't your *máthair*, so you never speak about her much. But you must know?" Heather asked excitedly.

"Well, she was pretty," Ferret said.

"Pretty? That's all?" She raised her eyebrows and looked pointedly at her half-brother. "There must be more."

Ferret hesitated and searched around. "I must find my other boot."

"I must know who I am."

"You're an O'Neill," Ferret said with a sigh of irritation. "Isn't that enough?" Ferret closed his eyes and summoned up images of his long ordeal with the mud-faced waif. He had to practically drag the defiant child across the wild hinterland. They had near to nothing. They were both bereft of parents and of future. Those facts created in him an everlasting fondness for Heather. Yet his misfortune was far less heartbreaking than hers. He was not an orphan of unknown origin; he could tether his life to a family line.

"That means nothing to me. What was she like?"

"A gentle soul who had a thin, sweet voice. A saint if there ever was one. She was no gimcrack."

Ferret found it difficult to come up with precise details. He had had no real mother himself. A withered old woman, crotchety and hard-hearted was paid to suckle him after his mother had died at birth. For years, he believed that the homely woman with a bloated red face and hairy black warts was his mother. Even her own children found her repulsive, nicknaming her "pug face." She could not recall how many younglings she had birthed since so many had died young. She would sit in a rocking chair and force her children to work from sunrise to sunset, hauling firewood or dumping dirty chamber pots into the river. "'Tis what chits are for," she would say. He had been relieved to discover that "pug face" was *not* his mother.

"Mother glowed like a divine angel," Ferret finally said in a timid voice.

Before Heather could ask more questions, the commotion from outside grew louder. He took one last look through the window. A yellow glow illuminated the low clouds. There were now hundreds of torch-carrying men scurrying about, helter-skelter, piling crates and bundles of wool into a heap. They were setting the wood and wool ablaze. Bonfires brighter than a harvest moon on a clear night leaped high into the sky.

He gently placed his hand on her shoulder. "I must go."

She cupped her hand over his hand. "Be careful."

Ferret nodded, found his other boot, and rolled out of bed. After rushing downstairs, he entered Madoc's large bedroom to wake his uncle. Without knocking on the door, he entered and shouted that there was unrest in the dockyard.

His eyes closed, Madoc sat up and cocked his head. He rearranged his white stocking cap. "Don't be a silly-willy," he murmured, then fluffed up his pillow, rolled onto his side, and fell back asleep.

"Get up!" Ferret shook the bed, then yelled louder. "Bonfires are burning in the harbor!"

Still half asleep, Madoc pulled the covers up to his neck. "Leave me be!"

Frustrated, Ferret swooped up a bronze water basin from the mahogany bureau and poured water on Madoc's face.

Madoc immediately sat up as he flailed his arms wildly. He coughed and spat and finally scowled at Ferret. "What's the meaning of this?"

"There are hundreds of revelers in the dockyard!" Ferret said.

"That's impossible. Not my dockyard!"

"Just go and see for yourself."

"What rubbish!" Madoc moaned as he tumbled out of bed, slipped on his beaver-lined robe, and rushed outside into the street.

As they left the house, Ferret followed behind his uncle. Before he got far, a hooded woman suddenly blocked his way. When he attempted to go around her, she snatched his arm. "Ferret O'Neill?"

"Aye."

"'Tis Aristot. He's gravely ill. He's in need of a physician. I thought I might borrow a cob or two."

Ferret pried her hand from his arm. "Who are you?"

The woman lowered her hood. "Maureen O'Hara. Maybe a few sixpence would suffice. He just turned for the worst."

Ferret remembered her well. She was Aristot's prodigy, strong-headed, well-versed in Stoic teachings, and knowledgeable about most everything. She was living with Whitebeard, learning from him and serving as his caregiver. Years ago, he had visited Maureen, hoping for a spark of affection, but she spurned him.

Ferret had once inquired about her forebears and kinfolk. Maureen was the youngest of thirteen children from a family that made candles, lanterns, and torches. She was descended from a well-known clan that stretched back to the Norsemen's day, known as the Old English. Her forebears had founded Cork as a trading port some eight hundred years ago. Through the centuries, they had lost their prestige and wealth to infighting, warring Gaelic chieftains, English invaders, and bad economic times. To escape the misery, Maureen had even considered indenture in the Province of Virginia, until Aristot's health began to fail. She stayed behind, feeling an obligation to take care of her schoolmaster.

"I fear he lies on his deathbed." Dressed poorly in a milkmaid's dress, Maureen shivered.

Ferret went back inside and found a thick cloak. He handed it to her.

"Please, I could not." Maureen held up her hands to stop him.

"Take it." Ferret draped the cloak over her shoulders, understanding well the pride of the impoverished. "You may return it later." He knew "later" never came. He also understood that he had to placate the too proud to get them to accept the slightest crumbs of charity.

"Come and see him. He called out your name."

"Your timing is poor. I must go to the dockyard." Without another word, Ferret departed.

Maureen hesitated at first, uncertain what she should do, looked around, and then ran after him, making every possible effort to catch up. Within moments they arrived at the gates of the dockyard and watched ale barrels being rolled from a warehouse, stood upright, and punctured with knives. With glee, men poured dark ale into tall wooden tankards and passed them around. All drank heartily from the same cups, each determined to get drunker than the next. One man, too gorged to swallow more, spat his ale back into the tankard as it moved down the line of thirsty drinkers.

"See what intoxicating drink has wrought," Maureen said. "They ride the wild mare." As she lodged more complaints to Ferret's ear, a mob of haggard men hooted and whistled at her. One drunkard came up and pinched her buttocks.

"You old dote!" Maureen shrieked, swung around and slapped the tosspot across his face so hard that he fell to the ground. The man sat up, shook himself, and then belched up a mouthful of bile. He wiped his face and pointed at Maureen. "Yaw frightens me like a hung scarecrow! That you do!"

Ferret grabbed Maureen's hand and dragged her away.

"Don't touch me!" Maureen resisted. "I'm very capable of taking care of myself."

"Fine!" Ferret released her and sprinted ahead. They quickly reached the epicenter of the disturbance, where there stood a larger crowd of intoxicated, jovial men. Perched on a crate, a fiddler screeched out long, whiny notes on his poorly tuned instrument, while others caterwauled in bliss. Meanwhile, a bearded man with silver earrings struck up a ballad on Irish bagpipes. He pumped and blew furiously, trying to compete with the fiddle. The men hollered in delight, jumping and stamping gleefully, arm in arm.

Suddenly, the pipes and fiddle ceased. A man climbed onto a shipping crate. His back was turned to Ferret at first, but when he twisted around, Ferret immediately recognized him. He should have known; it was his old rabble-rousing mate. Drawing in a deep breath, Strongbow began to speak. Waving his arms in the air, he warned of the misery of banned wool, and the heinous hunger that would darken the land. Ferret drew closer.

"*Eire* starves whilst England feasts!" Strongbow proclaimed. "Irish wool will be banned. Misery and death will overtake us all. What say you to that?"

Several firebrands shouted in unison, "Behead Cromwell!" The others cheered with voices loud and belligerent. The mood had changed from jovial to bloodthirsty. Men lifted their torches into the night air and shouted threats against England and Cromwell. Someone suggested attacking the vessel that brought the evil news. Chants of "Burn the *Sea Weaver*" grew louder.

"This is appalling," Maureen whispered into Ferret's ear. "They know not what they do."

The crowd was also tainted with infamous gangs of lawbreakers, including Arthur and his crew of armed ruffians. They were dodging behind a stack of crates, their hats pushed down, and collars turned up. Ferret struggled through a wall of emboldened revelers to reach Arthur's men. But when he reached the spot, they had all disappeared.

"What is it?" Maureen asked.

"Nothing. I thought I saw something." Ferret turned back and made his way to a spot just below Strongbow. He had to stop this nonsense before the drunken men rioted. He called out to his friend to stop. But his cries were drowned out.

"Dear brethren," Strongbow preached with his hands held high. "Are our chains not forged in blood? Are we not overwhelmed by crawling vermin? Do not our oppressors behave like arrogant locusts, infesting and plaguing our land—eating us out of house and farm? Have we not been lied to and betrayed with a Judas kiss? Have tyrants not prostrated us for years? I ask, is life so dear that slavery be so blessed?"

"No!" The mob roared in fury.

"But will our defiance make us free again?"

Silence. The crowd looked confused.

"Aye. That's the rub. Perhaps our destiny lies elsewhere? I know not what you may do, but I seek the sweet smell of liberty. I seek to govern with my own compass and to set sail in whichever direction I may choose. Who amongst us does not search for such heavenly delights? I know of none."

"But what shall we do?" someone bellowed.

"Seek out autonomy wherever it may be found."

"Won't be here, that's for sure," a dockworker sarcastically called out.

"Precisely," Strongbow shouted as he jumped down and pushed his way to the ale kegs. He picked up a tankard of suds and toasted everyone's good health. As Ferret approached the rabble-rousers, Strongbow plopped the tankard into his unsuspecting hands. "Cock-a-hoop, laddie. Nick the pin and swig one with us. 'Tis spruce beer from Prussia. Do it right, I always say. Let the other fellow drink rotgut."

"You stole this from my uncle's warehouse?" Ferret shook his head in disgust, but then thought better of it. His uncle was not the most virtuous saint in town and could spare a few petty kegs.

Strongbow laughed. "Are you accusing me of stealing? Me, a respected highwayman? What has this sad world come to? Besides, 'tis just a wee-bitty celebration to announce my departure. Nothing fancy."

Strongbow staggered closer to Ferret and finally confronted him face-to-face. He looped his arm around Ferret's shoulder and patted him on the back. "Want to see the real thieving magpies? Look over yonder." He pointed to the government's excise warehouses. "The English have perfected thievery. The only problem being, they abhor competition. That puts me at an unhealthy disadvantage. I believe you once chastised me over that very thing."

Maureen finally made her way through the unruly crowd of revelers and caught up with Ferret. She put her hands on her hips and tossed back her long hair. "This be your mate? I would have expected better."

"Listen," Strongbow said, slurring his words, "let's do something outstanding." He staggered back a few steps and leaned heavily against a crate. "After everyone's drowned with ale, let's storm Fort Elizabeth. Capture a few lobsterbacks, tie them up, and boil them alive. You and me. What do you say?"

"He's daffy!" Maureen almost shrieked.

"Daffy as the next mate I reckon, I wreck." Strongbow increasingly stumbled over his words. He swerved to Ferret. "Who's the flip-flap woman?"

"Who's the rum duke?" Maureen asked.

"Strongbow, me lady." He attempted to bow but almost fell over. "I plunder the high roads of Ireland for pleasure."

"And you'll burn in the low roads of Hell for certain."

Ferret took hold of Strongbow's arm. "You must halt this insurrection before it gets out of hand. Blood will flow."

"Stop it?" Strongbow howled. "Not a chance. I started it! And I aim to finish what I promised. Besides, there are those who wanted me to drum up a little merrymaking."

"Who?" Ferret asked, almost shouting. He had a feeling that a ragbag of conspirators was scheming behind the scenes. He was sure they would reap a big harvest. If only he knew what they planned to sow.

"I'm not one to tell. Real secret-peekward." Strongbow poured a tankard of ale into his mouth, but the beer mostly missed its target.

He slowly brushed off his vest. Suddenly, he pushed Ferret aside and staggered back into the crowd. "I'm afraid the Lord cannot help those who will not help themselves," he muttered with a sloppy grin on his face.

Ferret watched Strongbow retreat deeper into the crowd. He was not sure what to do. He glanced at Maureen. She wanted him to rush off to assist Aristot. That seemed pointless. He had little money to offer his old schoolmaster. There were many times when he wished he had wealth to bestow on benevolent causes. The shillings he had saved were set aside for his passage with Heather to the low-lying countries. Without money, his dreams amounted to a handful of sand. But it did sound heartless not to display sympathy to the unfortunate. He would do what had been done for him: show sorrow, offer pithy advice, and do nothing.

As he stood there, he watched the bonfires roared higher into the sky as more Irish thronged into the dockyard. He knew that this night was going to end poorly.

* * *

The noise from the revelers attracted the attention of a detachment of soldiers commanded by Lieutenant Holbrook. He stood still and surveyed the scene while hidden in the shadows of a two-story building.

"Perhaps they will stagger home soon, Sir," a young soldier offered lamely.

"They itch for a ruddy fight," Holbrook said grimly.

A horde of dockworkers carrying torches began to march toward the *Sea Weaver*. They were agitated and acted as if they intended to damage or burn the vessel. Holbrook looked worried and tightly gripped the handle of his holstered side-arms. He almost felt sick.

"I cannot allow this. Everyone into formation!" Holbrook ordered his men to come out of hiding. They rushed out into the open, stepped into a military formation, and began marching in a single line toward the edge of the mob. Fifty yards away, the redcoats stopped.

Holbrook walked out in front of his troops, halted, and eyed the situation. He knew he had to act fast or mindless violence might overtake the men's good sense. He had to nip trouble in the bud.

"Disperse now!" the lieutenant hollered at the crowd. His men fixed their bayonets and then reformed the line two-deep.

Many of the dockworkers turned around, stiffened their resolve and began jeering and shrieking at the soldiers. In a hand gesture, one dockworker imitated cutting a person's throat with a blade. He did it several times and then cried out "Death to the English!" Others showed their defiance by pelting the redcoats with rocks and spoiled food. The roar of the angry crowd became so loud that it drowned out further stern warnings to disperse.

Meanwhile, Madoc attempted to calm his dockworkers. He scurried from worker to worker and begged them to go home to their wives and children. Nobody would pay any heed. After screaming himself hoarse, he grabbed a half-bald man by the arm and whirled him around. He looked him in the eye and told him to stop.

The man pried off Madoc's tight grip. "Leave me be, you nick-ninny."

"Don't be a fool." Madoc's puffy face turned red as he slapped a rock out of the man's cupped hand. "You're all halfwits! Go home!"

"Mayhap. But you're not gonna starve like a mangy dog." The half-bald stomped away and vanished at the edge of the main crowd.

Madoc stood there perplexed and a bit frightened. He had lost control of the situation. He mumbled to himself that the ruffians were "ruddy dolts and may 'od rot their pitiful souls." At that moment, he caught sight of the column of armed soldiers. Without haste, he rushed to the redcoats, waving his hands wildly in the air, trying to get their attention. A frightened soldier aimed his flintlock at Madoc.

"Oaf! Put that thing down!" Madoc ordered, knocking the barrel away. "Where's your commander?" Another soldier pointed at Holbrook.

Madoc rushed up to Holbrook and gestured toward the harbor. "I own all of this, those vessels over yonder, those warehouses on the northern dockyard. What don't I own?"

"I don't care if you own every two-hole privy in Dublin," Holbrook said. "Disperse your dragsmen!"

"They're just making merry."

"Your dragsmen are breaking curfew. I'll be forced to shoot if they refuse to disband."

Madoc sneered. "I've seen them celebrate many a Holy Week out here more drunk than a mud-faced sow. Grant 'em an hour and they will go home to their wives and sleep like kittens."

Holbrook's fingers twitched. "Sir, ale and disorders are brethren. The sots itch for a fight. 'Tis my duty to enforce curfews."

Just then Ferret arrived, trailed by an annoyed-looking Maureen. He tried to get in front of Madoc, but his uncle kept moving back and forth, blocking him. As far as Ferret was concerned, the situation was at its tipping point. Things could get worse or die down. He could see that the presence of armed soldiers could ignite violence faster than a torch in a dry hayfield.

Holbrook caught sight of Ferret, appearing pleased to see him.

Madoc added more demands that Holbrook's soldiers withdraw back to the barracks.

"I wish I could avoid a conflict," Holbrook said. "Town streets make poor battlefields. But I believe the drunkards yearn for armed rebellion."

"Armed rebellion? That's ridiculous," Madoc said. "They're cowards! They haven't a stitch of gut to fight with. Why, they snivel and grovel at my presence. They want to make merry, rimble-ramble, and ride St. George in bed. Allow me, lieutenant, to dampen their merriment. I will scare the willy-wits out of them. Believe me, a stern warning will transform their legs to quicksilver." Madoc swaggered back into the crowd and disappeared.

"Your uncle is a fearless man," Holbrook said.

"He's only worried about his property."

"With me, it's my men. They're all greenhorns who have never faced the terror of battle."

"If you withdraw now, I'm sure these workers will disband. My uncle can throw more terror into the hearts of men than Satan."

"If I retreat, Cromwell will retire me."

"A riot would do it quicker," Ferret said. "Your presence puts spark to a powder keg."

Holbrook fingered his holstered pistol. "I cannot forsake my post. If I back down, they will see it as weakness. Respect is paramount to authority."

"Dead men command no respect. Besides, 'tis easier to prevent trouble than to repair it."

Holbrook glared at Ferret. "The royal family is not an enlightened entity. They are supposed to crush troublemakers, swiftly and forcefully. They must protect the kingdom's interest at all cost."

"You don't really believe that!"

Holbrook's shoulders slumped. "I'm not sure what I believe. Perhaps I should consult some tarot cards and call it a night."

"Believe me," Ferret said, "lead shot may kill the flesh, but not the cause. Men in authority instigated this trouble. They want you to put down those who starve under their misbegotten policy. There is a rabid dog loose, but you're out here tonight ready to punish those who have been bitten."

Holbrook looked over his shoulder. "You must take care how you speak. You have a bad case of the reason malady."

Ferret grinned as he replied. "I hope it will become contagious."

* * *

When Madoc reached his men, he whacked one with the back of his hand. "Get home or Martha will throttle your windpipe!" The man looked up and rushed home right away.

Madoc repeated his threat to another hothead and wrenched a torch out of the hand of a third. "Lay off the rotgut, or your eyes will go stone blind and your passion impotent!" He climbed onto an unstable crate and shouted, "Listen, men! If ye fear the pang of death, listen well. There be soldiery standing over yonder, armed with lead shot and vexed anger. They yearn for a bloody fight! So let's—"

"Let's give it to them!" A sailor jumped up and shouted. Immediately, war whoops erupted from the swarming mob, engulfing the air with blood-curdling screams.

"You heard Master O'Neill," a worker boomed. "Let's prod their pig-arses with cold steel!"

Throngs of rowdy men shrilled with excitement. Many pulled out daggers and pistols from underneath their garments and waved them overhead.

The moment Madoc realized his error, he lost his balance and fell headfirst into a pile of garbage.

* * *

Holbrook's face froze as he saw a rush of bodies and burning torches hurtling toward him. He barked to his men, "Formation! Stay in formation! Prepare to fire on my command!"

The soldiers stumbled into each other, desperately trying to get ready for combat. One soldier bayonetted another, almost causing a riot within his own ranks.

"You better depart," Holbrook warned Ferret.

Ferret stood there, determined not to desert his friend.

Holbrook pushed Ferret away. "Go! And take that woman with you!"

"I can't abandon you."

Holbrook aimed his pistol at Ferret. "You surely can!"

Ferret saw that the tipping point had arrived. He was in great need of a workable plan. He knew Holbrook was too proud to forsake his duty just to avoid the embarrassment of death. He had to prevent this travesty from happening. There must be something he could do.

"They'll kill him." Maureen punched Ferret in the shoulder. "The redcoats are completely outnumbered."

Ferret watched the fast-approaching rioters. There were always ways to alter a seemingly inevitable course of events. He could not let his friend die. In a flash, he had an idea that might possibly work.

Holbrook shouted a final warning to the rioters: "Disperse, or we'll fire!"

The mob swarmed closer.

"Raise firearms!"

The rioters were twenty-five yards away.

"Fire!"

The flintlocks clicked without a single shot fired. "They're unloaded," one private cried out after examining his gun closer. "Some thick-wit forgot to order us to load our weapons."

Holbrook cursed and stepped closer to the surging onslaught. Blame for leaving the weapons unloaded would fall squarely on his shoulders. He straightened his stance and cast a venomous glare at the surging mob. "Stand firm men! Prepare for combat!" He pulled out his pistol and fired a shot. An old man fell, shot in the forehead. Holbrook's men had no hope now. There was neither time to load their flintlocks nor time to organize an orderly retreat. They had to stand their ground.

Before Holbrook could draw his broadsword, Ferret approached and knocked his friend to the ground. Quickly he dragged him a short distance and slugged Holbrook ruthlessly, breaking his nose. Blood dripped down the lieutenant's chin.

Maureen ran to Ferret and pummeled him with fists and knees. "Stop it!" she shouted. "You're killing him!" She continued hammering until the mob of Irishmen surrounded them on all sides. She was caught in the mob's rising swell and carried away on its crest.

A bristly fisherman knelt beside Ferret to admire his handiwork. "Looky what we got here," the man uttered with a toothless grin. He pulled out a long, wicked dagger with serrated edges. "Let me gut him from head to fin. I'll chop off his head and fish out his entrails."

"I know how to gut a lobster." Ferret pulled out his own dagger.

"Have it yar way." The man took a swig from his flask and staggered off.

The mob chased the surviving redcoats down a narrow street, leaving a dozen bodies, mostly English soldiers, in their wake. A separate group of Irishmen torched shoreline dwellings. The fire spread across much of the waterfront warehouses and wharf structures. In one last act of defiance, the dockworkers heaved their torches onto the *Sea Weaver* and set it ablaze. Stragglers gathered next to the dying bonfires to toast the good health of Master Madoc O'Neill. As dawn approached, they went home, all agreeing a good time had been had.

Ferret worried that he might have killed Holbrook. His attack was supposed to be only for show. He only meant to injure him ever so slightly. After the rioters had dispersed, he lifted Holbrook up to his feet. After a few moments, Holbrook moaned a few unclear words. Ferret sighed with a great sense of relief. His friend was still among the living.

He felt terrible. His principles were tattered to shreds, far more bruised and injured than Holbrook. He had struck first blood and beaten up an innocent man. He surely deserved to be punished to the full extent of his own conscience, if not the King's law.

Maureen found her way back and began to clean off the lieutenant's bloody face with a scarf. "Now I understand why you have so few mates," she said with a lifted eyebrow.

Ferret could see that Maureen would make a wonderful millstone around some unlucky husband's neck. "At least he won't attempt to borrow money from me."

"'Tis not too surprising. Seems you are bereft of both principles and money."

Ferret was not going to debate with this shrew. All he knew was that he could not have allowed the revelers to slash Holbrook into fish bait. He had chosen the lesser of two evils. He recalled what Heather had said earlier and wondered if she was right after all. Perhaps people did abuse those they loved the most.

Chapter 20

"'Tis a demon sun," bemoaned an old woman as she squinted up to the heavens. She rolled rosary beads through her bony fingers. Trembling, she kissed one of the beads and hummed a short prayer. *"Daoraim!* Lord save us."

The reddish sun glared over a barren landscape of smoldering, gutted, black skeletons of buildings. Thin shafts of light pierced the dense smoke. Flecks of ash fell like black snowflakes. Tall clouds of soot mushroomed above Cork, shrouding the port in an eerie twilight.

Cork's streets lay deserted, buried under a deep silence that was only jarred by the occasional howl of distant dogs.

Many people feared it was the prelude to Armageddon.

* * *

Ferret found himself seated in the belly of the beast: the British fortress of Fort Elizabeth. Holbrook sat hunched in a chair to Ferret's right, lethargic, hands covering his face, resembling a grieving figure on an ancient stone sarcophagus. Cromwell draped a blanket over Holbrook's shoulders. "Do you feel better, Lieutenant? Our leech will have a look at you later."

Holbrook gave a reassuring nod.

Cromwell paced his office room until a young, white-wigged, and be-spectacled scribe arrived. The scribe, Richard T. Griffin, opened a leather carrying case and took out his inkwell, parchment, and feathered quill. He sat next to a two-hinged table that served as a board for backgammon. Cromwell swooped up the yellow dice and rattled them in his hand. He turned to Ferret. "Your uncle instigated this rebellion, and I think not by happenstance."

Ferret looked away and stared out the window. A waft of smoke was leaking in through some of the cracks in the window.

"I'm ready," the scribe declared.

"My uncle tried to prevent the riot," Ferret said. "He's no insurgent."

"Your uncle has an outlandish way of preventing mayhem," Cromwell said. Walking to the window, he swung it open, causing a blizzard of ash to rush inside.

Cromwell slipped the dice into his pocket. "This reminds me of the great London fire of '66. My father told the tale every year on its anniversary. Ash rained on London for an eternity. One superstitious Londoner even killed himself. Many feared a visit from the Four Horsemen and prayed to depart before the slaughter."

Holbrook slowly raised his head. He sat quietly gazing about the room, apparently detached from the proceedings. His lips were cracked and his left eye was bruised dark blue. His right eye was closed, surrounded with a white pocket of pus. His face was covered with welts and bruises. Ferret had indeed saved his life. A sense of gratitude combined with a desire to repay the favor weighed heavy upon his mind. Such friendship was a rare commodity.

Ferret approached the window. He was exhausted. He felt dreadful about what he had done to Holbrook.

As Cromwell and Ferret gazed at the freakish light together, Cromwell said, "At times like these, I wish I were back in England. Not a worry. Not a care. At peace with the world."

A sudden bout of tranquility engulfed Ferret. He was standing next to the man he had feared and loathed for so long, and yet he felt little hostility toward him. Cromwell seemed a different man. Could he have been wrong about him? Perhaps he had needed someone to hate to give purpose to his own existence. It was easy to despise and blame another for one's own misgivings. Had he fallen into that blind trap?

* * *

Cromwell questioned Ferret and Holbrook for hours. They rehashed every detail until Cromwell understood what had occurred. "Never before have I seen such a botched assignment." Cromwell sighed as he shook his head.

"'Twas my decision," Holbrook said. "My fault."

Cromwell picked up a silver box from which he sprinkled cinnamon into his tea. "It doesn't matter. I will be replaced. They will ship me overseas to perish in an unknown wilderness." Cromwell glared at the scribe and ordered him to strike his last statement from the record. Then he tapped his fingers on the arm of his chair and looked up at Ferret. "You saved my officer's life, but your uncle destroyed mine. Queer, to say the least."

Cromwell poured a cup of tea for Ferret, who was suddenly overcome by a strange feeling. He was being served by the most powerful figure in Cork. He felt privileged to be sipping tea with the major-general. Cromwell was a man of reputation. He commanded some importance with the Crown. Ferret wondered if this was how kings always felt. If it were, he could comprehend the delights of mastery over others. So tempting to sit among the powerful, and be worshiped and feared from afar as a man of importance, a man to be reckoned with! He had tasted the sweet power of privilege and found the flavor agreeable.

Cromwell returned to the window and opened it. Cupping his hand, he reached outside and allowed the floating ash to whirl into his palm. "You did what others would not. I call that notable." He turned back to Ferret. "I am curious. You struck Holbrook to prevent others from killing him. Why?"

"Holbrook's a good mate," Ferret said.

"I've found myself in a similar situation. There was this incident in Flintshire. Terrible Welsh uprising that led to years of turmoil. My detachment fired two volleys of lead. Sent the curs running, but not before I lost six good men. I still regret those losses. I should have done more to prevent their deaths. My remorse never abates."

Ferret eyed the playing pieces on the board. The game was only half completed.

"Do you play?"

"Sometimes," Ferret said.

Cromwell found the dice in his pocket and tossed them on the board. "The game fascinates me, but it is based too much on happenstance."

"It takes some skill."

"If I cannot have total control, I will not play."

"But to command," Ferret said, "requires rolling the devil's bones at every decision. And uncertainty has a way of cropping up when least expected."

"True," Cromwell said. "I do enjoy taking a risk. But I would never place myself in a bad situation."

"Few can control heaven and earth. Bad situations often get much worse before they get better."

Cromwell lifted an eyebrow. "I suppose so." He picked up the report and began to read. Before he got past a few lines he glared up. "But this incident is so... insufferable. I mean look at this." Cromwell stabbed his finger at the report and read out loud: "'Twenty-two men dead, over thirty buildings put to flame, and three vessels torched.' I suppose this is the usual Irish amusement after sunset."

With a sharp knock on the door, two soldiers entered the room and informed Cromwell that Madoc O'Neill was being detained outside.

"Splendid!" Cromwell said. "Bring him in."

"My old colleague," Cromwell mocked as Madoc entered the room, his hands in fetters. "And I thought that all rebellion had been eradicated with the demise of Black Fox. Apparently, I stand corrected, Master O'Neill, because in front of me stands the true firebrand of Irish insurgents."

Madoc frowned, looking away.

"My good man, you look ghastly," Cromwell brushed Madoc's shoulders and smeared ash across his fine coat.

"'Tis all a misunderstanding," Madoc said.

Cromwell nodded. "Yes, your nephew said as much. But I think we should discuss your plight in private."

"You'll incarcerate me and I'll never again see the bright of day," Madoc said. "I'm no rebel, and my nephew is no upstanding citizen."

"Rebel or not, we must—"

"My nephew be Black Fox's son."

Cromwell pivoted toward Ferret, his eyes blinking rapidly. "You are the urchin who slashed my face?"

"Did you not murder my father?"

Cromwell reflected for a moment. "I wanted to impale you with a fire-iron and tear off your arms like the wings of a gnat. Unfortunately,

202

my men could not locate you." Cromwell paused. When he started to speak, it seemed as if he were talking to himself. "I didn't shoot him."

"What?" Ferret's mouth hung open.

"I was attempting to uncover corruption. Some of my lower-ranked officers were selling our supplies to foreign powers and to your father. To keep their secret, they killed Black Fox."

"And hanging my father would not accomplish the same feat?"

Cromwell began to brush the ash off his uniform and realized that the ash would not sweep clean. "That was not my original plan. Still, I had to do what I had to do."

"You mean what's good for you." Ferret stepped closer.

"Your father was a rebel who flouted the law!"

"And you do not?"

"There is no reason to continue this hearing." Cromwell walked to the door and opened it. "I think it is time for you to leave."

Ferret blocked his path. "I know of your plans to murder an official from London."

With an alarmed expression, Cromwell turned to the scribe. "Did you get that? Did you!"

"Aye, Sir. Shall I repeat it back?"

Cromwell reached over and seized Griffin's sheets of parchment, ripped them up, and stuffed the pieces into his coat pocket.

The scribe stood up, looking befuddled. "Sir! What shall I write on?"

"Roll up your sleeves and write on your forearms." Cromwell snarled as he ran his finger inside his collar to loosen it. When that failed, he searched for his handkerchief to mop his clammy forehead.

"Sir," Holbrook said, "I cannot believe that you could be involved in any illicit activity."

"I appreciate your loyalty, Lieutenant." Cromwell sighed and laid his hand on Holbrook's shoulder. "But I'm no saint. Those positions have already been taken."

"I tried to prevent them from rioting," Madoc said. "You must believe me."

"I believe that you disliked our arrangement," Cromwell said.

"I don't like to be told how to conduct my business."

"So, you admit it!"

"I admit nothing," Madoc said. "But I am a merchant. I do not like to be forced to smuggle and murder."

"Sir," Griffin said, waving his arms in the air. "I'm running out of space!" He had indeed rolled up his sleeve and written across the length of his arm.

Cromwell shook his head. "Good Lord! I wish everyone obeyed me so precisely! Now, get out!"

Griffin sealed his ink bottle, stood, and prepared to leave. On his way out the door, he looked back and grumbled. "This ink will not wash off easily."

Cromwell watched the scribe scramble out the door and heard him swearing under his breath. He turned back to Ferret and Holbrook. "Why don't they follow common sense? Why?"

"Because they are too scared to think for themselves," Ferret said. "How can you expect more?"

"Force and fear are the only means of reshaping the world. However, those instruments must be applied delicately; commoners must understand that it's in their best interest to invade another land, banish the outspoken, and execute the traitorous. The collective will—that's what I call it. A glorious society, perfect and superior, with men willing to die not for money or territory, but for the greater cause of humanity."

Ferret sensed that Cromwell was the vanguard of a new breed of tyrants, a strain unknown in the world. Nobody talked about the purity of ideas and the intensity of devotion. This was something new and terrifying, a world willing to kill anyone in order to impose their one-sided notion of perfection. Fortunately, Cromwell had few devotees in Ireland.

Cromwell rubbed his blackened hands together. "Do you not understand? Superior men must rule the world. Ability, not birth, will determine their right to rule. The world must be reshaped carefully. Evil will be outlawed, the hungry fed and the homeless housed. Masterless men and troublemakers will be banished and replaced by a *new man*, godly in nature, stout of body, and sound of mind. And if we have to eliminate inferior people and races, so be it." He looked at the dice on the table. "Only fools take chances."

"But who chooses these superior men?" Ferret asked with a touch of cynicism. "Do you not see the paradox? Who authorizes the authorities? Who rules the rulers? Where is the limit? Or are these the questions most have been browbeaten not to ask?"

"Don't be silly. Men of superior minds must decide. They always have in the past." Cromwell laughed, permitting a sliver of a smile. "That is why we are the ones who exert mastery."

"Commoners are too fiddle-headed to understand what's best for them. Superior men must do that for them. In return, we will take what's rightly ours—their souls. They do not know what to do with them anyway."

"But they do," Ferret said. Cromwell was twisting everything around like a serpent. Those who benefited the most from the monarchy's largesse were always the king's strongest supporters. "Most people have a sense of purpose—just not yours. Most men desire to be left alone, to live their lives undisturbed, to see their children prosper. Why would they seek more edicts, rules, or wars? I know of none who seek suffering and misery. But you have no aversions to meddle in the affairs of others. You would trade their happiness for your ambition. A bargain so poor that even the devil would think it unworthy of Faust's attention."

"You sound like the Levellers." Cromwell cleared his throat. "I simply want wholehearted allegiance from my citizenry. Is that so much to ask?"

Ferret thought back to Aristot's warning that men of noble causes often ruled by ignoble means. Any method, any lie, any murder was justifiable for a good cause; evil consequences were ignored as if mankind had ascended to the role of the all-seeing, all-knowing God, able to predict every leaf falling from every tree—perfection trumping human deficiency. "How do you know you will do the right thing?"

"Because I know best," Cromwell said.

Ferret was surprised by the arrogance of Cromwell's answer. "I think you want commonfolk to sanction their own shackles. I once heard a story from a Spanish merchant. In a remote mountain village in the Americas, the crops had withered from a drought. The villagers were too poor to pay the annual tribute to their king. But the king was devious. If he seized all of the village's remaining food, the villagers would starve or revolt. So he commanded them to pay another type of tribute—one they could afford. The ruler demanded one basket of dead fleas as their tax. The villagers had plenty of fleas and were happy to comply. They remained loyal and the king remained in control."

"But the fleas were worthless," Madoc said with a dumb look on his face.

"No. They were not worthless." Cromwell snorted. "Their king wanted something worth more than gold. He wanted their loyalty. Good Lord! That's how to maintain an empire."

"But that's not the way I see the world," Ferret said. "Nature abhors people trying to change nature. The nature of man is his own, to choose his own ends and means. You overestimate your ability to mold the clay of mankind. He is not that malleable. It would be best to take the advice of Hippocrates of Cos and abide by his wisdom: 'First, do no harm.'"

Cromwell smiled. "I see we're at the opposite edges of day and night, connected only by the twilight of trying to better humanity. What a blooming shame. Nonetheless, I am the one with the final say. And my pleasure is to cast you out of my sight. I have ordered the *Green Sounder*'s departure in the morning. It is to be loaded with every flea-bitten rebel and rabble that has ever offended my command, including you. Don't disappoint me. Leave or suffer the fate of treacherous turncoats!"

"Why permit me to go?" Ferret had been sure Cromwell would never release him.

"You are too much like me," Cromwell said. "You're quick-witted and ambitious. You will command one of these days. 'Tis in your blood; I can smell it. You yearn to change history, and history only reshapes itself through coercion. One of these days you will do just that—but not in my Ireland."

Cromwell called several soldiers inside and pointed to Ferret. "Take this fellow away and make sure he boards the *Green Sounder* tomorrow."

Chapter 21

Walking through the cold halls of Fort Elizabeth and the streets of Cork to Madoc's house, Ferret decided that he had to make his own choices. If he were to abandon his homeland, he wanted it to be on his terms. Forget Cromwell's eviction orders. Nobody was going to tell him what to do. He refused to leave *Eire* until the appropriate time. Glancing at the soldiers escorting him, however, he knew his expulsion was near at hand.

Upon entering his uncle's house, Ferret saw a light emanating from Madoc's private room. Inside, Arthur was poring over his father's ledgers and muttering to himself about his "miserly father." It was not hard to see that the dockyard riot was advantageous to Arthur. That made Ferret wonder if his cousin had a guiding hand in this travesty. The only thing he knew for certain was that he would never find out. Conspiracies had a habit of pursuing policies that nobody wanted to publicly declare.

Seeing Ferret, Arthur slammed the ledger shut. "I have taken over the O'Neill estate and assets. Unlike my skinflint father, I'm not afraid to ride roughshod over kindred. I want you and that green tadpole out by tonight." Arthur strode past Ferret and disappeared down the long hallway.

Ferret slumped against the wall and closed his eyes. He would have to leave on the *Green Sounder* after all. But could Heather come along? He was sure she was far too ill to travel by sea.

Just then, Heather rushed up, barefoot and in pigtails, wearing a stained nightgown. She rose on her tiptoes and tried to push up his drooping chin. "I've been a burden. I know I have."

A burden? He mulled over the question. He had been responsible for her since she followed him from the cave that day. He felt a solemn duty to her that defied description. *Trouble* was a better word. "No. You've been a..." His voice trailed off. He stared at her soft lips and found it difficult to continue.

"I should be the one to go away," Heather said, "to some uncharted pagan land full of savages."

"I'm the one who must bid farewell. I've been banished from *Eire*."

"By whom?"

"Does it matter?"

"I suppose not. But I'm well enough to travel."

"Any journey could kill you."

"To stay here without you would be worse than death!" she cried. Then she ran to her small room, her nightgown sweeping the stone floor.

Ferret's world was collapsing. If he remained in Cork, Cromwell would order his imprisonment within hours. Two soldiers had been posted at his doorstep to escort him to the shipyard. If he fled with Heather, she would die from exposure to the harsh sea. If they escaped to the hinterland, winter would put her in a grave sooner than smallpox.

Suddenly, Ferret heard a familiar voice behind him. He turned around. It was Strongbow. His friend was a ghostly figure; he had never come to the O'Neill's doorstep, except once. He was a man of mystery who possessed many talents, but few traits of integrity. To get an audience with him, one had to search him out, carefully watch him like a hawk, and then grudgingly accept him for his self-indulgent weaknesses. Why was he here now? Ferret suspected the answer had to add up to something shady.

"I understand that you're taking a voyage," Strongbow spoke in an uncommonly serious tone.

Ferret's head drooped. "Not of my choosing."

"Come, come. I've had to change my locale abruptly before. It never bothered me."

Ferret inhaled deeply as the thought of leaving his homeland suddenly became more real. The likelihood of ever coming back was poor. Once uprooted, the migratory fate was to keep on moving until some other group stopped you. There was no looking back.

"I know farewells can be sorrowful," Strongbow said. "Nevertheless, *Green Sounder* will depart soon. She's ahead of schedule, I'm told. Let's just think of it as our date with destiny."

"My sister is too ill," Ferret said.

Heather stepped out from behind Strongbow and faced Ferret. "I'm fine as a farthing fiddle, dear brother." She was dressed in a heavy cloak and carrying a gray sackcloth bag. Weak and pale, she propped one hand against the wall to balance the weight of her heavy bag. "My decision. My life. Let's be gone."

Rachel was there, too. She joined Strongbow's choir of rose-colored singers. "*Chomh ceanndana le muc.* Don't be so stubborn. No choice. We've been... what you say, expelled. So we must go."

Ferret glared at Strongbow. He knew his dubious friend had something to do with Heather's sudden decision to depart. Strongbow's conspiracies knew no bounds. He could see now that she had been packed long before he had come home. And now here they were, acting like old chums.

"I will take passage on the *Green Sounder*," Heather said with a distinct air of finality, "whether you come or not, brother." She turned to Strongbow. "Please, assist me, sir."

Strongbow removed his hat, bowed, and picked up her overstuffed bag. "My pleasure, milady."

* * *

The late morning sun broke through the cloud cover sheltering Cork's harbor. At the pier, Strongbow, Rachel, Paco, and about twenty others studied the *Green Sounder* from bow to stern. The merchantman originally had been a Dutch warship, but she had been captured by the British. Madoc had bought the vessel and removed the cannon so she would hold more cargo. The previous night, the ship had been seized and handed over to Captain Jake Cajan, an associate of Cromwell's.

Corla had come to the dockyard to give her last farewells. Stricken with grief, she embraced Ferret and Heather before they crossed the gangplank. She knew that such voyages were not only dangerous, but that few ship wayfarers ever found their way back home.

"'Tis unlikely we will ever return," Ferret said in a low voice. He wanted to horsewhip himself for being too truthful.

"God hath forsaken me before," Corla said. "But I've become accustomed to it."

Heather shoulder's drooped as her heart sank. She thought back to the many years she had lived in her beloved *Eire*, knowing that she would never return. Her eyes were red and swollen from crying. Her only solace was that she would be with her brother. She turned to Ferret. "Sometimes I think God does not want me either."

Ferret simply nodded.

Corla stepped closer to Heather and clung tightly to her arm. "The Lord can be merciful. He will heed you wherever you may go."

"If only we knew our final destination." Ferret wished he could say something comforting, but good words of comfort eluded him.

"Only the Almighty knows what will happen." Tears coursed down Corla's wrinkled face. She released Heather's arm and hobbled away, disappearing into the fog.

Ferret assisted Heather over the gangplank. Although she looked weary, she stood up straight to show him her health had improved. As he followed her aboard the vessel, Ferret tugged on a rope. It was old and frayed. Other riggings were likewise worn and stiff, and some of the ship's planks were rotten. The vessel was barely seaworthy.

He noticed a man hiding behind several water barrels. His hat covered his face; still, Ferret had a feeling he knew the man. "Is that you, Lieutenant Holbrook?"

"Keep your voice low," Holbrook whispered.

"Have you been reassigned?"

"I've abandoned my post. If I stay ashore, I will be made the scapegoat."

Before Ferret could ask another question, a detachment of marines escorted dozens of chained prisoners aboard.

"Don't say a word," Holbrook said.

Ferret thought Holbrook should know that he would never betray an old mate, asked or unasked.

The chained men assembled on the top deck and waited for instructions. Captain Cajan appeared from below, counted the men, and signed some paperwork.

"This had better be the last." Cajan scratched his chin and ran his fingers down his long beard. "I've got no more blasted room."

"You take what we give you." The officer turned on his heel and left the ship with his men.

Ferret turned back to Holbrook, but he had disappeared.

"Who was that?" Heather asked.

"A good mate." Ferret grabbed ahold of the railing, and dug his fingernails into the rotting wood. He showed it to her. "You might have lived longer if you had stayed ashore."

"Strongbow assured me the vessel was seaworthy."

"*Eire's* in better health than this excuse for a ship."

"Well," Heather said, "if the ship were that damaged, she would not be afloat, would she?"

Ferret was not going to argue the point. Instead, he turned and watched a sailor throw the mooring ropes to several longboats. Oarsmen towed the *Green Sounder* to deeper water, inching the ship into an almost windless harbor.

Heather sighed, then spoke with the softness of an angel, "*Eire's* too... green." A tear trickled down her cheek.

Ferret reached for Heather's hand. She had become self-conscious about her missing thumb and wore sheepskin gloves in public. He could feel the space where her right thumb should have been.

"How can anyone leave their motherland?" Heather asked.

"I remember when you had to be dragged across the untamed countryside. Seems like it was only yesterday," Ferret said. "Your little face was so muddy." He wondered why he had rescued her. Now she was a full-bodied woman in a colorful dress, her bodice cut low to give an appearance of wealth, culture, and lasciviousness.

"Don't be silly." Heather cracked a thin smile.

"You kept running away. I had to tie a rope around your waist."

"Was I that naughty?"

Ferret bit his tongue. He had said too much. She believed that she had lived in Wexford as a girl and had never ventured far from the township. It always surprised him how she could have completely forgotten their arduous journey out of the interior.

"What was I doing outside of Wexford?"

Before Ferret could answer, the topmast sails unfurled with a loud snap and the ship lurched forward. The vessel sailed past the harbor's narrow opening to the Irish Sea. For a long time, they stood and watched the greenish-blue ocean churn and the foamy waves crash against the ship's hull. Ferret put his arm around Heather's shoulder as the chilly wind whistled against the rope rigging. He noticed that she seemed to enjoy his touch.

"Why were you dragging me across the countryside?" Heather asked.

"There's nothing to tell," Ferret said. "'Tis not important." Sometimes he thought that she knew they were unrelated. He understood the danger too well. If he allowed their fraternal affection to blossom into passionate love, she would torment him until he told her the truth. Like a woman, she would never trust or love him again. Her hate would stain his thin-skinned heart forever. It was better to keep silent.

* * *

After nightfall, the weather turned rough and the passengers moved below deck. The ship's hull quaked and creaked. At times it seemed as if the ocean would burst in at any moment. As the wind became more violent, sailors tried to repair torn rigging and plug holes with oakum and pitch, only to be pushed back by hammering waves and blinding spray. At one point, a rogue wave caught two sailors off guard and washed them across the deck and overboard. A sailor heaved some rope after them into the angry darkness, but the throw was symbolic. Nobody ever returned from the unbridled sea.

Assigned to the forecastle—the sailors' living quarters—Ferret lay in his hemp hammock, sleepless for most of the night. The hammock swung back and forth with each swell, causing his head to ache. His eyes were bloodshot from the salt spray. His clothes and blanket were soaked from tiny rivulets that trickled from the ceiling.

To add to the misery, the sailors were drinking tankards of *balderdash*, a mixture of beer and buttermilk. It made his stomach turn as much as the rolling of the waves.

"Here's to yaw gree health," a husky, one-armed sailor known as Harpoon Jack chuckled gleefully. He stripped off his soaking garments

212

and slipped into his wet hammock. He gulped his drink, whipped out a Jew's harp, and strummed it between his crooked teeth. Nobody was going to get any sleep.

"Bloody worst sea I've seen in ages," said Gubby, the jailer, a short, brawny Scotsman from Dundee. He spoke in a thick brogue. "That be the least of our putrid woes. Loaded to the gunwales with wool, we be. If we don't swamp and sink, we'll be hanged as smugglers. Dandy life, mateys."

"Don't piss yar tallow away." Harpoon Jack had stopped playing his harp. "Did ja hear about the heretic we cargo below? They say he's a viper of a sorcerer."

Gubby belched and scratched his stubby beard. "'Pshaw! Yaw cock-brains! If he be a true sorcerer, he would a have sprouted wings and flown off."

A third sailor disagreed violently. "Yaw stupid dotes. They don't sprout wings and flutter off! Sorcerers don't do any such thing. They disappear in a gust of flames and smoke. That's what sorcerers do."

Ferret jumped out of his hammock, irritated by the sailors' loud voices, poor hygiene, and superstitions. He had enough listening to the old seadog's barking. He left to search for Heather in the lower decks. He passed through dark gangways lit by scallop shell lamps encased in thick glass. He peered into cells of shackled prisoners, praying priests, skittish livestock, and a few seasick British marines. One cell contained several scantily dressed women who were fighting over the few remaining dry blankets.

Without warning, one of the women reached out from between the black bars and grabbed Ferret's arm. Ferret jumped back, startled; the woman's wispy hair hid her face.

"'Tis Maureen!"

"What?" Ferret drew closer. The other women were dressed in reveal-ing clothing, evidently prostitutes being deported. "You're with holers?"

"Sadly true," Maureen said. "Cromwell's men arrested me on charges of inciting the riot. They saw me with you."

There was nothing worse for a wholesome woman than to be impris-oned with whores. She would be marked for life. Feeling a need to comfort her, he laid his hand over hers. "'Tis all my fault. I should have never allowed you to follow me into the melee."

"Don't apologize," Maureen sighed, then pressed her pale face against the bars and spoke disjointedly. "I'm not one of them. I swear I'm not... I'm not wanton or unclean or..."

Ferret lunged at the jail cell, grabbed the rusty bars and pulled on them with all his strength. He wanted to break them or yank them out. But luck forsook him again. The bars were the only thing in the ship not falling apart.

"You must go. I have already been registered. I'm permitted only to whore. I'm worthless. Nobody can help me now."

Ferret applied his strength against the bars again. "I'll free you. So help me God. Even if I must scuttle this ship."

Maureen placed her hand over Ferret's to stop him. "Heed my plea for once. A force of redcoats dragged Aristot aboard. Please seek him out and comfort him. 'Tis my last request. You must honor it."

Ferret stepped back, stunned and speechless. Life was becoming more unjust with every second. Maureen had always been strong willed, endowed with confidence and purpose. She was enlightened soul who brimmed with a passion for greatness. Now she had fallen into the pit of hopelessness.

"Go to him." She pulled Ferret's hand closer, forcing him to touch her smooth, wet cheek. "The woman you knew no longer lives. Do not return."

Ferret stumbled backward, dazed. He had never realized how easy it was to destroy a virtuous woman. If only she had not followed him! Not long ago she was a studious young woman sitting beside Aristot, quill in hand, intensely engaged, listening to his every word. Beyond her schoolmaster, she ignored everyone. Now, the world reacted as if *she* did not exist. He hated this Old World of cruelty and pain. Someday he would destroy it, piece by piece until he had set things right.

Ferret moved down the dimly-lit passageways and stumbled upon a ladder that led down a companionway. He climbed down and found himself on a deck flooded with a mixture of sea and bilge water. The violent movement of the ship rocked him back and forth. The storm was intensifying.

Suddenly, the ship rolled to one side, knocking Ferret over. The floor was coated with black mold. The water was ankle high and getting deeper. He was wondering if he should explore farther when he peered into a barred cell and saw Aristot. His old schoolmaster was leaning against a bulkhead. He was covered with damp blankets, motionless and pale. Next to him sat a shivering fat man who appeared every bit as dejected and doomed as Aristot. A third man was dressed in black. He sneezed into his handkerchief and picked his nose hairs. It was the Dutchman, Heather's schoolmaster. A fourth man lay face down in the water, appearing dead.

"Aristot!" Ferret cried out through the iron bars.

The old man moaned. "Who beckons me back from my sleep?" His eyes remained closed.

"'Tis Ferret! I mean, Sean."

"Sean!" The old man's voice was distant and weak. "You be too late. I have already departed. I'm consulting with St. Peter, and he loathes being disturbed."

Ferret shook the gate violently. With a heavy clanking sound, the lock broke and the door squeaked open. As he moved inside, the Dutchman started to rattle his leg irons. "Come to join us? There's plenty of room for another troublemaker."

Ferret stepped into the cell and knelt beside Aristot. "I'm sorry."

"You ought to be," Aristot said. "'Tis the worst fate of mankind—getting old. The flesh rots while the mind brims with life. Isn't God magnificent!" Aristot opened his eyes. They were white. He was blind.

"Anything I can do?"

Aristot let out a mournful moan. His face was turning pale, his breath became short and shallow, exhaling with a wheezy noise. He struggled to talk but somehow found the energy to continue. "Flesh has this awful habit of decaying. It seems that the more we live, the more we die. I disapprove of the situation, of course. But does anyone listen to me? Mayhap we should get the Queen to outlaw death. That would do it." He forced a feeble grin from his bluish lips. "She has outlawed everything else."

Ferret said nothing.

"I'm the last of my breed—the last Leveller." Aristot's trembling hands tugged at the wet blanket. "I tried to teach you to be the sun in a fog of darkness, but you became nothing more than a short-wicked candle. You'll never rekindle the fire for the next generation."

"I tried."

"You didn't!" Aristot stirred, his leg irons clanking. Struggling to breathe, he paused. His lips were turning blue. "I have one last message, one last parable that you might remember. It concerns you directly." Aristot coughed, gulped for air, and then snorted. "Listen. Man came from the bowels of the earth, naked and primitive. So clever he thinks he has become. But I ask, if you put a naked savage in the same room with any lord of England in his finest silk breeches, what do you suppose is the difference?"

Ferret shook his head.

"Only the silk breeches."

"What has that to do with me?" Ferret asked.

"You befriend a beast. This man assisted in the death of your father and may have gotten most of us banished."

"Who?"

"That is unimportant. Man's nature, now that commands importance." Aristot's voice weakened. "Primitive men kill with wooden clubs. We have finely tempered steel and lead shot. No difference. Killing is killing, cruelty is cruelty, aggression is aggression. Man's weapons have improved, but not his disposition. This is the beast that we must all fight. No man must rule over another for any reason whatsoever."

"Who killed my father?" Ferret grew impatient.

"Beware of the beast—it is within all of us. It rages out of control. It will lie, cheat, and murder to rein over others. Do not let the beast dwell within the cockles of your heart. Renounce it."

Ferret shook Aristot. "Who was it?"

Aristot blinked. "Your beast runs amuck. Never underestimate the stupidity of mankind. Never!" He paused. "If you must know, it was the same man who saved your idle life."

"Saved my life?" Ferret thought. "Not Strongbow? Impossible!"

"Ever wonder why he happened upon you in the forest such a short distance from Macroom? Cromwell's spy, he was."

"No! Never!" Ferret refused to believe Aristot.

"'Tis true," came a raspy hoarse voice from underneath a nearby blanket.

Ferret pulled the blanket away from the man. It was Badger.

"Great snakes!" Badger cursed. "Gimme that back."

"Are you sure?" Ferret asked.

"'Twas in Cromwell's jail," Badger grunted. "I once overheard a blackguard jabber about Strongbow. See these bruises and scars." Badger showed his bare chest to Ferret. "They tortured me. Nearly sent Father Yeats to his maker."

Badger snuggled under his blanket. "Strongbow was paid to spy on Black Fox. Remember his lost poke of gold? That was his recompense. But Winchester's men stole it first."

"Forgive Strongbow," Aristot groaned, "as I have forgiven Lord Cromwell for condemning me to Ireland so many years ago."

Ferret drew closer to Aristot. His old master took one last breath and then his body turned lifeless. Ferret looked away. Everything around him was tumbling apart, and he was afraid to do another thing lest it kill another friend.

Ferret felt a profound loneliness that nobody else could ever understand. His world was dying, and he was becoming more isolated, remote and adrift. Cruel injustices surrounded him from every direction and waited to pounce again. Was it possible that Satan had created God in order to exploit the false hopes of men, to ransack their minds and consume their flesh? Had this fallible world been fashioned so the devil might never starve? It became all too clear. Evil fed on the good and leached out their substance, leaving only an empty shell behind.

He was not going to be left behind empty-handed or turn hollow. It was time to take action. He would have to take command of the situation, and then stay in control. But he knew full well that such courses of action might even lead to spilled blood.

Blood.

He had heard it repeated so many times—it's all in the blood. His royal blood entitled him to do things that others could not. Still, he believed that he could avoid being infected with the power-lust of kings. And if by chance he got off course and turned tyrannical, all he had to do was cut his wrist and let the bad blood bleed out.

Chapter 22

"Ahoy!" bellowed a British royal marine from a ship that emerged from a fog bank in the late afternoon. "Prepare to be boarded for inspection!"

The ship was a large British man-of-war bristling with forty cast-iron cannons. It drew alongside the *Green Sounder* and launched two boats of armed marines. The storm had abated, allowing the British marines to row up to the captured ship and clamber aboard unopposed. Shoving their way past gawking crewmen, they searched the hold for contraband wool. They were not disappointed.

With haste, Captain Cajan was fetched top-deck and flung in front of Rear Admiral Lyndsay.

"What do we have here?" Lyndsay asked in a Scottish lowlander's brogue.

"Not much, I reckon to reckon if I... could reckon," Cajan stammered, blinking his eyes repeatedly. He kept trying to focus his attention on the new arrivals. He reeked of Jamaican rum and stale chewing tobacco. His paunchy body was topped by a hairy neck, and a face circled by a wild, dapple-gray beard. A small ring hung from his left ear. Too drunk to stand up straight, he was propped up by his cabin boy. He continued, "I'll have ya know, I'm master of this thar vessel. Ya've got no authority here."

Lyndsay feigned surprise. "I guess I've been misinformed. After all these years, I thought *I* ruled the seas." The rear admiral had a slightly humped back. His face was chiseled with deep wrinkles that were partially filled in by a bushy mustache. He had dealt with ornery captains before, but this one's audacity was admirable. Took a real muck of an Irishman to do that. For once, he wished he could make one of these smugglers confess every convoluted detail without obvious lies, over-abundant distortions, or sudden loss of memory. That would make his old bones dance.

"I've done nothing much wrong."

"By Jove you have!" Lyndsay said.

"Get off me ship!" Cajan ordered.

Lyndsay faced the cool sea breeze and wondered how he had ever pulled such insufferable sea duty. He had commanded vessels in engagements that held England's fate in the balance, and now the Admiralty had put him in charge of inspecting drunken sea captains and smuggled merchandise. What was next? Inspecting privies in Dublin? Surely he had angered the gods somehow. "You think you're a hot shot in a mustard pot, Captain, but listen well: I have more than a wee bit of might. Wish to test my resolve?"

"I'm a fancy shot," Cajan said, slurring his words. "I'll shoot ya if ya don't get toff." He raised an imaginary gun and pretended to shoot. "Got ya all."

"You're a disgrace, Captain! I ought to strap you to a ducking-stool and drown you myself."

Cajan belched.

Lyndsay felt both nauseous and outraged. Trying to muzzle his anger, he slowly limped and toiled a few paces away. Pain was intruding fast and arresting his thoughts. His battered body kept screaming in agony. His aching hips were first to act up. Putting his full weight on the ship's blistered side railing, the rear admiral knew that his body was failing. Too often, he commanded it to do something and it flatly refused. Damned insubordinate. The body ought to obey; that was what it was for. Lyndsay gripped the railing harder as he prepared for another round of cramps. The leg spasms were now conspiring with his rheumatism. It was all one big mutiny.

"What do ya want anyway?" Cajan asked.

Lyndsay ignored the question and peeled a chunk of spongy wood off the side railing with his fingernails. Replacing it, he gave it a kindly pat and wondered what kept the *Green Sounder* afloat. He had to chuckle. His own vessel seemed even less seaworthy. It leaked like a sieve; so many ship planks were rotten to the core. He would have braced the hull and planks with oak timber, but could not requisition the needed material. Very troubling. Everything was wasting away.

"I have many wants!" Lyndsay finally said. "What I would give for

220

one last bout with the French or Turks. The Turks have a wonderful cannon. It fires stone balls weighing over a thousand pounds. I've seen a vessel hit and sunk in the blink of an eye. Mighty exciting. Makes the blood strong." Lyndsay's face soured. "Captain Cajan, I have revealed my desires. Now, I must skim the seaways of scum."

Cajan tucked his stained shirt into his baggy pants. "Sir, I take offense to that thar remark."

Lyndsay tottered a little closer to the Irish captain. "I don't have time to argue with barley-hood smugglers." A part of him always wondered if he would regret his actions. One never knew whom he had really incarcerated. A smuggler could turn out to be a relative of the royal family or a close companion of a powerful moneylender.

The rear admiral turned to face a young officer with a pockmarked face and asked him to prepare to read the report. As the young man stood silently, Lyndsay's mind wandered again to past engagements and glorious battles. If only he could fight one last battle to the death. Anything was preferable to this cursed assignment. There was no honor in dying a slow death.

The officer waited for Lyndsay to give the final order to read the report. But in a moment of distraction, the rear admiral instead waited for the officer to read the report aloud. Nothing was happening. Both motionless, each eyed the other in confusion. Finally, Lyndsay grew impatient. "Come to it!"

The officer shrugged and glanced around, not sure what to do.

"I said give the blasted report. How much contraband's aboard?"

"Sir!" The officer's muscles tightened. "The entire hold is stuffed with Irish wool." He reached over and plopped a handful of the wool into the rear admiral's hand.

"And the vessel's registration?"

"The ship's register lists one Madoc O'Neill of Cork."

Lyndsay looked at Cajan. "Captain, do you realize your hold carries contraband wool? And don't tell me you were unaware of the Queen's edict."

"Sir, 'tis a bloody revelation to me. Someone must have snuck it aboard without me permission. Why ya can't trust nobody nowadays."

Lyndsay rolled his eyes. "You're a truthful man, all right. And bulls sprout wings."

"Well," the captain began to sober up, "I never examine the hold. Cow dung could be piled to the foremast and I would be none the wiser."

Lyndsay grinned at Captain Cajan's remark. The Irish were such delightful liars. It was almost as if God had given them special permission to torture the truth. Some of his Scottish officers considered it pure entertainment, especially when everyone knew they were fibbing. But the Irish never lied with a serious face; that took the talent of a proper Englishman.

"Come, come, Captain. What commander could boast ignorance of his own cargo? If he did, he would be utterly mad. Willful smuggling be a hanging offense, and if you think insanity might save your thick neck, you're sorely wrong: Queen Anne understands insanity. Many can attest to that."

Some of the older officers displayed guarded smiles. Lyndsay was known to have differences of opinion with the Queen.

Lyndsay continued: "The Queen has established quarters for those who have fallen under insanity's spell. I believe they call it an *insanitum*. I call it a glorified prison. Ever behold one, Captain?"

"Naw."

"Pure rapture. The chambers are darker than a moonless night. 'Tis a blessing I daresay because the food crawls with maggots and roaches. Easy to eat what you cannot see, eh Captain? And then there are those muckworms. They fancy fresh flesh, consuming what has not already rotted away with leprosy. Why, they say if you weren't insane before going in, you would be on the way out. And looky here, all of this merriment for not one farthing. 'Tis a public service."

The captain cleared his throat. "I have nothing to say."

"I do. Throw the cabin boy overboard."

Cajan's eyes grew wide, his lips parted. "That's me nephew!"

"You mean he *was*."

Two marines picked up the cabin boy, dragged him to the railing, and tossed him overboard. He hit the water with a splash, surfaced for a moment gulping seawater, then sank out of sight.

Cajan zigzagged to the railing and threw up.

"Now!" Lyndsay demanded with more authority in his voice. "Do you recollect seeing some wool scattered about the deck?"

Cajan turned and shot an angry glare. "Ya killed him! Why?"

"The wool?"

Cajan glanced back at the black churning water. "I was at his birth..."

Lyndsay stomped his boot as hard as he could on the deck. "Who're the ringleaders? Do you hear me? Shall I throw another shipmate overboard?"

Finally, Cajan blurted out, "'Twas the Queen. She's behind it all."

"The Queen?"

"Ya. She ordered me to hide the wool."

"You expect me to believe that?" Lyndsay's forehead furrowed.

"Well, she's a bit fickle, I daresay."

"Aye! That she is." Lyndsay roared with a hearty laugh. He loved to hear Queen Anne bad-mouthed. He considered women soft-headed, confused, and weak. The thought of a woman telling fighting men what to do was unbearable. He wished King William III was still alive.

Cajan turned away from the railing and lowered his face. "I want to be hanged. I don't like the sound of that hellhole. No muckworms are goin' to gnaw on me edible parts."

"A most honorable choice," the rear admiral said. "Now don't you feel better telling the truth? Makes you feel honest again, ... at least for the moment."

"Remember, I want the gallows," Cajan said.

"Fear not. There's no such thing as an *insanitum*."

Cajan's eyes squinted with hate. "Yar a pawky fellow! Ya lie to me and then murder me nephew. Yar a crack-brain bastard!"

"To deal with lying Irish, you must fib back to them. You wouldn't know the truth if it bit you." He fingered the fleece he still held in his hand. "Mighty low-grade wool, I'm afraid."

"That thar wool be the finest this side of—"

With a hand motion, Lyndsay ordered two soldiers to drag Cajan away.

Lyndsay turned to a young officer. "The township of Cork—who commands it?"

"Major-General Winston Cromwell, Sir."

"Cromwell?" The rear admiral tried to picture a face to go with the name. "I believe I know the gentlemen. Would not surprise me one bit if he is behind this ruse."

The rear admiral turned to his fellow officers. "Put every able-bodied man in irons. I will parade these bad apples and ne'er-do-wells through the streets of London." He knew his actions would not persuade the Admiralty to award him another warship commission, but at least he would enjoy the spectacle of so many Irishmen hanging at Tyburn's tree.

Chapter 23

Aristot was dead. Maureen had been imprisoned as a whore. The ship was taking on water like a sponge. Ferret worried about Heather, wherever she was, amidst the dampness; her health was so fragile. He looked around the large brig and wondered if this were to be his last day on earth.

The Irish were taught to prepare for the worst and expected even worse things to happen. Despair was an ingrained trait. Ferret hated that sentiment. He decided he had to fight it with every resource he could muster. He was not going to be detoured by the self-defeating mood of the Irish. He needed solutions, not roadblocks. Forget whether they would work or not. Just get off one's duff and find something to do.

Ferret turned to the prisoners in the waterlogged cell. "Listen up! We must try to escape!"

"Odd's Bodkins! Who gives a bloody fig," Badger said. "And where would we go?"

Ferret nodded and forced an awkward frown. "We could seize the ship and change our course."

Badger laughed. "We can barely stand. We have no weapons. Just leave us be."

Father Yeats entered the quarrel. In a weak and feeble voice, he insisted that they had to break free, that God's work was still unfinished. He leaned against the bulkhead, nibbled on hard sea-biscuits while cradling his arm in his lap.

Before Ferret could propose another plan, a small group of people began to slosh down the flooded passageway. They were in a hurry. He squinted. It appeared that Strongbow was in the forefront leading them. *Damn*, he thought. He might have to spend time with a traitor.

Strongbow stepped into the cell, closely followed by Rachel, her baby nestled in her arms. Paco, lashed as always with gear, followed farther behind. Strongbow immediately leaped on a small crate and shouted. "An ugly tempest brews, with an appetite for blood! We've been captured! 'Tis a forty-gun man-of-war looms off the starboard. They plan to shackle every able-bodied passenger. We must hide!" He grabbed one of the wall-bolted chains and jingled it in Ferret's face. "Be a good fellow and clap these irons on us loosely so they'll think we're imprisoned. But take care not to lock them, laddie."

Without a word, Ferret locked the shackles around Strongbow's wrists. He snapped leg irons around Rachel where she sat. Nobody would care if Paco were chained or not. Then, Ferret slipped a pair of shackles on himself—these he left unlocked. He had just outsmarted the prince of treachery and captured his father's murderer without a struggle. It was as if a stout deer had run to the hunter and demanded to be shot.

"Don't forget!" Strongbow said. "When the jailer arrives, pretend to be chained."

Badger snorted from under his blanket. "Who's pretending?" He raised his face and fettered hands.

Strongbow beamed with a broad smile. "At least you're in good company now, mate."

"I'm not yar mate," Badger said. "I'd rather feast with the devil than the likes of ya. At least I may trust the devil to be devilish."

"What, another sermon? Jolly good! I always enjoyed your splendid sermons. I say, let's hear some of that haughty brimstone and fire. It just might warm this place up a bit."

"It be a sermon, to be sure." Badger grunted. "A splendid sermon fit for a funeral." Badger pulled the blanket from Aristot's body and laid his bronze crucifix on the dead man's chest. Kneeling, he prayed briefly. Then he fixed his eyes on Strongbow. "From death comes life everlasting. But ya better not stand too close to this poor fallen soul, me untrue Strongbow. The Lord might mistake ya for him."

"But he is no longer among us," Strongbow said, confused.

"There be many who breathe the Lord's air, yet stink of death." Badger stood and poked his finger in Strongbow's chest. "If only ya had died, yar reward would surely be everlasting pits of Hades!"

Voices were heard and a bright light was seen coming down the passageway. "They go in here," said a man's voice. The man swung open the cell door and entered. It was the jailer, Gubby. He raised his lantern and, with considerable concentration, counted the prisoners.

"Hoity-toity!" Gubby scratched his head.

"Come on, oaf!" a British marine standing behind him said. "What's the wait?"

"Somethin's wrong." The jailer started to count again. "Makes no bloody sense at all. I swear, thar wor only four an hour ago. I've lost prisoners before. Some died, some escaped. But they never multiplied on their own."

"What do you think criminals do? Bust inside and shackle themselves to the wall?" The marine stepped inside the cell to study the situation.

The clubfooted jailer moved aside and pointed at Strongbow. "That thar lanky one wasn't here before. I'm sure of that, I am."

The marine rushed over and shook Strongbow's irons. "See! Locked solid as a burial vault."

Strongbow gaped at his irons, trying to pull his hands free.

Meanwhile, the marine turned back to Gubby. "Next time, do a better job of counting."

Gubby nodded, then directed fifteen new prisoners, including Captain Cajan, into the large cell. The newcomers were all chained together in leg irons. After shutting the door, the jailer disappeared down the passageway, mumbling something unintelligible to himself as he counted the number of fingers on his hands.

Strongbow struggled with his shackles, twisting and tugging until his skin bled. Exasperated, he faced Ferret. "You accidentally locked them. Now free me!"

"I have no key."

"Laddie, I do. 'Tis hidden in my left boot."

Ferret gnashed his teeth. Strongbow was always cheating the system, dodging the rules, misleading his mates and anyone who had the half-brain of a haddock. Ferret found this intolerable. Lies clung to Strongbow like undersized breeches. He was the befriender of falsehoods and the backstabber of virtue. Nobody should allow such a creature to live. Ferret pulled the key from Strongbow's boot.

"Unshackle me," Strongbow said.

Ferret held the key up to Strongbow's nose. He turned and unlocked Badger's leg irons.

"You little puck!" Strongbow took a kick at Ferret, missed, and struck another prisoner. The man howled and leaped for Strongbow's throat like a rabid dog, but he was jerked back by the weight of the other prisoners he was chained to.

Ferret freed all the other prisoners, who appeared grateful, especially Harpoon Jack. The last to be unchained was a blackamoor with mulatto features, large-fisted, lofty—an oak of a man. His muscles bulged under a lacy white shirt, and he moved boldly like a nobleman. He was no timid slave. Ferret later discovered that the black man was the bastard son of the Sultan Ismail Ibn Sharif of Morocco. He had lived in Venice for much of life and was secretly engaged to an Italian woman, a great patron of the arts and theater. When the love affair was exposed, Othello fled Venice and a band of assassins was hired to kill him.

"Allah thanks thee," said the man. His baritone voice was a mixture of Norman and French accents. He lifted his leg irons up. "Chains cannot enslave a freeborn mind. Still, they do restrict the flesh from time to time." He hesitated a moment and then bowed to Ferret. "I am widely known as Othello."

Strongbow held out his chained hands. "Ferret! Why haven't you released me?"

"Because you conspired with Cromwell! You betrayed my father—Nay! You murdered my father!" Ferret drew his dagger and thrust the blade against Strongbow's throat. "Go on! Admit it!"

Rachel screamed. Badger covered her mouth with his hand to muffle her cries.

Strongbow tried to swallow, but his throat was too dry. "I'll admit anything under these circumstances."

"You must pay for your sins." Ferret said. His father had been a man of courage and kindness, risking his life to free *Eire* from English oppression. And how was he repaid? With treachery. *Eire* had lost its last royal chieftain. And he had lost his last parent. He had been orphaned by Strongbow. At least the thought of sweet revenge would keep him company on cold, lonely nights. "Did you conspire with Cromwell?—no more lies!"

Strongbow closed his eyes and then coughed. "There be nothing worse than betrayed comradeship. Gives a sickly aftertaste in the mouth. Do not think me a black-hearted man."

Ferret pressed the blade closer to Strongbow's flesh.

"You've forgotten, laddie," Strongbow choked, "your bones would be bleached if I had not happened upon you. Remember that witch?"

"Swear before the Lord Almighty. Did you, or did you not have a hand in my father's death?"

"I had dealings with Cromwell," Strongbow said.

"Did you spy against my father?"

"I did, but—"

"Aristot was right!" Ferret prepared to slash his dagger across Strongbow's throat.

Rachel wrestled free from Badger. "Please, let him live!" She lifted up her now-crying baby. "We named our chit after yaw! Ferret Tyrone! 'Twas in yar honor."

Ferret froze. He stared at the boy. No son should see his father killed in front of him. Still holding the blade close to Strongbow's throat, he eased up on it. What should he do? Revenge was so sticky, so repulsive. An eye for an eye, a father for a father. That way of thinking was barbaric. Drops of sweat ran down his forehead. Take revenge. Kill. The blade trembled as with a life of its own. Ferret wanted to swallow but could not. The ugliness within was controlling him. But his father was dead; no amount of revenge could change that.

Just then, a deep bellowing voice interrupted Ferret's internal struggle. "Release my mate or sea tigers will feast on your wretched bowels."

Ferret turned around to discover the large blackamoor standing behind him. The man slipped a dagger from his boot and threatened him. Did Strongbow have friends in every corner?

"Drop thy weapon," the blackamoor said.

"Nay!"

"Don't be pigheaded, Ferret," Rachel said.

"Lower your blade," the man repeated.

Ferret swung away from Strongbow and gripped his dagger tightly in his right hand. He stood up and faced the black Goliath, ready for combat. He would not be bullied.

"Shall I slay the lad, Master Strongbow?"

Strongbow shook his head. "No, Othello. He's an old mate."

Othello frowned. "A doubtful friend be worse than a certain enemy. This lad speaks his intentions with blunt honesty. Take heed. Better spend him quickly like spurious guineas."

"Ferret," Strongbow said, "I gave Cromwell information, but I believed it would lead him on a wild goose chase."

Ferret turned away, refusing to listen.

Othello inched closer to Ferret, displaying a malicious grin. In a flash, the thickly pressed crowd slowly moved backwards, clearing a small open circle. One onlooker tried to step in and stop the fight, but Othello's scowl stopped the man cold. As both blades flashed in the dim light, Ferret noticed that the black man's weapon was an exact copy of his own dagger. How could that be?

"Othello," Strongbow said, "do not dispatch him. Just seize his weapon and the key."

He bowed to Strongbow and glared at Ferret. "You ought to surrender whilst you can."

"Surrendering is not one of my more distinctive traits."

"I'm invincible," Othello said. "A dagger such as yours cannot injure me. It will pass through me like a soft morning breeze." His laugh thundered. He invited Ferret to step closer.

It was the first time Ferret had seen a black-skinned man up close. He wondered if the blackamoor would claim to be a god next.

Othello laughed again as he continued. "I can be what I wish. I can be a god, or a man, even a woman. Dead or alive."

Ferret gazed at the man, perplexed, uncertain about his next move. The man was so large. He was sure that this was not going to turn out well.

"You doubt my word? I shall prove it!" With the flick of his wrist, Othello twirled his dagger around and pointed it against his own chest, directly over his heart. "But if I'm wrong, you will be responsible for my demise. Guilt will stalk you to your grave."

Looking around, Ferret saw that even Strongbow was astonished. What Othello was about to do was utter nonsense. The blackamoor must be deranged; it would be an unfair fight to kill a frothing idiot.

"Mix steel with flesh and live thy life anew." Othello lifted the digger high overhead and thrust the knife into his own chest.

Ferret could see pain ripple across Othello's forehead.

Several gasps rippled through the air.

"What be death, but another stage?" Othello gasped as he embedded the blade further into his chest. He appeared tipsy at first, then weak-kneed. He did not fall. His eyelids flickered wildly. "See! No blood. No death!" Suddenly, he coughed violently and looked up in surprise. With glazed eyes he stared at Ferret, almost breathless. "What hast thou done to me? Murderer!" He toppled at Ferret's feet like a giant felled oak tree.

Ferret was shocked. He had never seen such a horrid spectacle—a man killing himself to prove his immortality. Someone had died, but not the man he wanted dead. He rushed over to the dead body, stared down and saw no blood. He cocked his head in disbelief and dropped his dagger. What had happened?

Suddenly, Othello's eyes blinked wide open; he stretched out his long arms and snatched Ferret's fallen dagger. As he stood up, he wiped mud and grime from his shirt and breeches. "Some have said death is my most impressive act."

A gasp erupted from Rachel's lips. A startled Harpoon Jack was left speechless. Captain Cajan threw his hand against his chest, trembling. Ferret leaned back with a sense of detachment.

"H-h-how?" Badger asked.

"'Tis a trick knife. The blade collapses into the handle. Very useful in *Macbeth*. We lost several thespians before I crafted this prop in Venice. Of course, some *should* have died. Terrible actors they were. More than once, temptation urged me to switch knives during acts."

Othello took a few bows, basking in the limelight after his bravura performance. Nobody applauded Othello's act; they were still in shock. He reached over and plucked the key chain from Ferret's listless hand.

With a short twist of his hand, Othello unlocked Strongbow's shackles.

He eyed his friend warily. "We may be as free as a lofty bird... but where do you plan to go, Master Strongbow?"

"When we retake this vessel, we may go to any shore we please."

Othello flashed his pearly white teeth and laughed.

Strongbow approached Ferret but kept some distance. "And what of you? Will you join us to fight the infernal English?"

Ferret knew any accord with Strongbow would merely be a short truce. After the crisis, all bets were off the table. "Sure." Ferret bristled with guarded caution. "Let's fight the bastards like brothers."

"'Tis better to kill your enemies than your mates. There're more of them. Holds true for me today!"

Ferret had wanted to kill Strongbow, but for now he would have to be satisfied with going after the British Empire.

Chapter 24

The night had grown late. Ferret was the first to take hold of the ladder and climb up. When he reached the top he cracked open a hatch and peeked out onto the stern quarterdeck near the helm wheel. A circle of armed marines, frostbitten and ruby-cheeked, huddled shoulder to shoulder in the frigid wind, appearing as if they longed for duty in the Caribbean. Ferret smiled. There was justice in watching the British suffer outside while the prisoners remained warmer inside.

"Do ya see the blackguards?" Captain Cajan asked from below.

"About twenty or so," Ferret whispered as he returned down the narrow companionway. The captain seemed perturbed and jumpy. His eyes were glassy, and his hair was slicked back like the ears of a riled tabby cat.

The captain closed one eye and opened the other. "Thar's a misfortune awaiting us above. What in tarnation can we do?"

"Take them down, sail away and never look back," Ferret said.

"Sail where?"

"Anywhere but England."

Cajan held his tricorn hat in his hand, looking more nervous than vexed, and faced both Ferret and Strongbow. "Looky here, I'm not a military gent. Nor am I good at dodging cannonballs, except when I'm down-on-the-floor croaked. So hear me out. I war only hired to scud the seas. Ya may have yar harum-scarum pranks, but there'll be no blood on me hands."

"We're over thirty strong," Harpoon Jack said as he squeezed into the companionway beside the captain. The tall man held a long spire-like harpoon tip. He had a distinctive tattoo—a two-headed serpent—on the left side of his face. Half Pequot Indian, Harpoon Jack had been a whaler in the Arctic Ocean and had lost his left arm in an accident off West

Spitzbergen. He stepped in front of the captain and stared coldly into his eyes. "I'll pin their livers to their toes."

"There still be too many," Cajan said. "We cannot take down the whole pod of lobsters."

Ferret could hardly believe that an Irish captain had no stomach to fight, whatever the odds. There was no question that they had to seize the ship or simply scuttle it. A dangling noose waited for every smuggler, firebrand, and Irish rebel in London. In either case, their prospects were none too promising. He turned to Harpoon Jack. "Do you think the crewmen will fight?"

Harpoon Jack took his time to think it through. He was one of the most imposing men in the crew, commanding the most respect. He rubbed his chin and frowned. After that, he ran his fingers through his thick matted hair. With wide-open eyes, he turned to Ferret. "To mock death is to mock life. There being none here, I believe the crew will hunt down and spear our beastly enemies." He paused for a moment. "'Tis better to perish than to live as condemned prisoners. That is the bare truth of it."

This was what Ferret had hoped to hear. If the captain refused to exercise his official authority, then somebody else had to step forward and take his place. He could see himself as such a leader, but he wondered whether the crew would follow a green sapling with no experience commanding men or ships. Somebody else had to take charge and move forward with a plan.

"We could jump 'em tonight." Harpoon Jack said. "Catch 'em by their flukes."

"It will escalate, by crikey," Cajan said. "I've seen it before. Besides, if we try to escape, that thar man-of-war will blow us asunder. We don't have a bugger of a prayer."

"We must take action if we wish to prevail!" Ferret said.

"'Tis hopeless."

Again, Ferret was dismayed by the captain's missing backbone. Here was an Irishman who would rather wait for the chopping block tomorrow than fight a battle today. He reached over and clamped his hand down hard on the captain's shoulder, drawing him closer. He had to make a better case for taking action. He had to get the captain aboard with a plan to resist and fight back. And in the meantime, he needed to reassure him that success was not a crazy notion. That was a tall order.

Ferret stared at Cajan with icy, unblinking eyes. "Will our fate be any better in London?"

"Lordy! No better, I wager," Cajan sighed. "Do what ya will. But I want no part of any cock-brained scheme." He pulled a flask of Scottish whiskey from his pocket and took a long swig. "I'm goin' to find an empty cabin." He walked down the passageway, vanishing in a curtain of black.

The others withdrew together, plotting intensely in private over how to break the tightening British chokehold. Ferret reflected on his predicament. He had more problems than the looming man-of-war. Ferret suspected that Strongbow, a man without a scrap of integrity, wanted to take command of the vessel. Ferret had a moral duty to prevent a travesty, but in doing so he would have to be ruthless. That was the rub. Was he willing to crush any opponent by any means? Would ambition make him as cold-blooded as those without moral scruples? Ferret believed he understood the lust for power in every man. He could see that virtuous intentions usually led to ignoble ends. With that knowledge, he believed he could avoid such pitfalls. Besides, it was his *duty* to cast the iron into the flame. He had to make sure a good man took charge, at least temporarily. Now that the captain had withdrawn, he could see no other alternative than himself.

Strongbow was working up his own lather of animosity and despair framed in shallow humor. "We'll surely hang if we're deposited in London. I daresay I'm not dressed for such a festive occasion."

"The hangman wouldn't care," Ferret said.

"I would," Strongbow said. "Maybe I should go top-deck and show the blackguards a thing or two. I've been in battle before. I have led men. Not hard. All you need is a loud voice and a big stick."

Ferret exploded, "You—the man who believes in unswerving duty to nobody, except Cromwell—is not worthy to command the stout-hearted!"

"Mistakes happen," Strongbow said.

"But some mistakes can't be changed!"

Othello interrupted them. "Gentlemen! Silence your deafening tongues."

They ignored Othello.

"I have more experience than you, laddie." Strongbow huffed as he crossed his arms and furrowed his brow.

"Aye, but traitors make poor commanders," Ferret said.

Othello grabbed Ferret's neck and lifted him off the floor. "Don't make me damage your nick-ninny skull."

Ferret clamped his hands over Othello's grasp in an effort to break free. The man's calloused hands were as dry and hard as pig leather. It seemed that nothing on earth could pry loose his meaty fingers. Ferret's lungs began to grasp for air.

"Aha! Lovely silence." Othello soon released Ferret, then lowered his face and placed his lips next to Ferret's ear. "Let's whisper like Cistercian monks. Agreed?"

Strongbow moved closer and placed a finger across his lips to signal Ferret to hush his loud outbursts. He leaned down until they were nose to nose. With his piercing eyes, Strongbow murmured, "Matey, let's agree to work together. Righto?"

Ferret stepped back with a look of shock across his face. He suddenly realized the real meaning behind that response. *Working together* was Strongbow's way of saying that he was going to take charge. He was now on the defensive. Without thinking clearly, Ferret quickly swung around, withdrew some distance, and retreated up the ladder to resume his watch. He felt far safer on the top deck with the British Marines. Up there, he knew who was a friend and who was an enemy.

He understood that he had lost the battle, but not the war. Still, he had learned a valuable lesson: if he wanted to gain authority, he had better assemble loyal men to do his bidding. What irked him the most was that a man of such poor character as Strongbow had the audacity to seek control. Who would follow an English spy and backstabber? That question was troubling. He worried that others besides Othello would turn a deaf ear to Strongbow's offenses and follow him as if he were a prophet. The thought hit a nerve. Rogues were often worshiped as heroic figures that could do no wrong. Such notions licensed men like Strongbow to justify any crime for any reason.

From the hatch, Ferret saw the moonlight dancing across the waves, shimmering like a cluster of stars. Thin clouds veiled the full moon, giving it a look of satin. Few ever noticed how beautiful nature was until there was a crisis. When life hung in the balance, most wanted a last glimpse of the world to see the beauty they would soon miss forever.

Ferret knew he had to come up with a plan. He looked around the top-deck for the enemy's weakness. There had to be some way to capture the sentries near the helm. Before long, he saw Gubby climb down from the aft quarterdeck to make his rounds. He was walking straight for the hatch. Ferret reached for his dagger, but Gubby changed course and drifted along the railing. The jailer stopped and peered out to sea. He slowly leaned over the railing as if to watch the water crashing against the hull. When the ship rocked lightly to one side, he jumped back in fear. It was a seaman's worst nightmare to fall overboard and sink into the bottomless black depths, especially at night. Ferret had once watched a half-drowned sailor pulled back to the living. He was ghostly pale and mute as a beached herring, lost in a trance. The man refused to walk after that, contending that a sea devil had bitten his legs off. Eventually, the sailor's legs withered to nothing, and he spent the rest of his life begging on his red, swollen knees. That was what fear of the unknown could do.

After less than an hour, all the sentries had put down their flintlocks, slumped near the mainmast, and begun to snooze. Besides Gubby, only the helmsman remained awake, guiding the ship along England's southern coastline on a direct course to London's harbor. Occasionally, Ferret could see the lights of the man-of-war trailing them two thousand yards behind. Seeing nobody else awake, he knew the time was ripe. This would be their best chance to rush the sentries, although the soldiers were practically sleeping with their weapons.

Before Ferret could do anything above, Gubby was on the move again. This time, he headed straight toward Ferret and the hatch. In rapid fashion, Ferret slid down the passageway and whistled an alarm to the others. They panicked at first, squeezing and contorting into every shadowy nook and corner. Unfortunately, there were too many men and too few hiding places.

"Pshaw. I do so know how to count." Gubby muttered to himself as he climbed down the ladder. At the base of the ladder, he stopped and held up five wiggling fingers. "They can't fool me. There were just four prisoners."

Harpoon Jack elbowed Ferret and dragged his finger across his own thick neck.

Ferret shook his head. There was no need to become cutthroats—at least not yet.

Still preoccupied with his fingers, Gubby limped away from the ladder, oblivious to the armed men around him. Then Othello obstructed his path. Startled, the jailer raised his lantern and examined the massive man.

"Who are ya?" the jailer asked.

"A prisoner has escaped," Othello said.

"Wasn't my fault," Gubby said nervously. He tried to pass Othello, who continued to block him. "Ah... what prisoner?"

"Why, it's me!" Othello flashed with childish glee. "You forgot to secure the gate. That calls for eight lashes with the cat-o'-nine-tails."

The jailer grunted and cocked his head in disbelief. "Ya mean ten lashes."

Othello leaned down, puckered his lips and gently blew air at the frightened man. "Who's counting?" Then, with a pearly smile, he brandished his dagger at the jailer's face and forced him down the passageway into another jail cell.

Gubby hesitated at the entrance of the jail cell, looking bewildered. He turned, glanced up and grumbled. "But I don't belong in here."

"Well, I daresay, 'tis improper to keep the jail keeper from his jail. 'Tis like keeping a mother from her child." Othello walked inside, gagged the jailer, and locked him in leg irons. He glanced down. "Why... look at you! Resting all comfy and content. Such a precious gem." He then exited the cell, locked the door, and rejoined Strongbow.

Fully animated with wild hand gestures, Strongbow devised his own plan to retake the ship. "Time to tickle the cockles of fate, mateys," he said. "We outnumber the bastards. We'll capture them by surprise."

"Blimey, yaw got to be crazy. We've got almost no weapons," one crewman said. "Why don't we just spit in their eyes?"

"Listen," Strongbow said, "we don't need too many weapons. Besides, the redcoats probably have their firearms stacked neatly in piles, ready for the snatching."

"What if they wake up before we can take them?" the Dutchman asked with a scowl almost tattooed on his face.

"We'll sing them back to sleep. I've got a potent lullaby in my back pocket." Strongbow pulled out a short club. "They'll sleep like babes."

"Clubs be no match for firearms," Harpoon Jack said. "We must take them down with keen blades."

The Dutchman grumbled. "We won't get two barleycorns before they shoot."

"Well, we'll just have to make do," Strongbow said.

It was obvious to Ferret that Strongbow had no plan except to run headfirst at the English and hope for the best. Strongbow was offering only outlandish humor and unrealistic optimism. There was no way to surprise the men on the top deck. Most carried pistols and were probably only half asleep. He could see that they were stuck in endless debate. Nothing was going to happen. They were going to blabber and whine until the sun came up. After that, it would be too late. In the morning, the guards would discover that they had broken out. Worst of all, they were not far from London's port.

Something had to be done immediately. Ferret climbed up the companionway, flipped back the hatch, and crept across the half-deck unobserved. He crouched next to a small jolly launch boat and watched. A plan was beginning to take shape. It involved sneaking up behind the helmsman and capturing him.

Before he could move, however, he discovered that Harpoon Jack and several others had followed him. He had hoped for some assistance but did not expect it. He never had led anyone to do anything. He was in uncharted waters and hoped he would not flounder.

"What can we do?" Harpoon Jack asked. They waited in silence for instructions.

"I'll get behind the helmsman and knock him out. He's the only one awake. After he's down, rush the lot of them. Tell the others to move their arses and get up here."

"Piping good," Harpoon Jack said. "How're ya goin' to sneak around the helmsman?"

"With a wee bit of luck." Ferret found a rag in a jolly launch boat and attached it to his belt. Then he snuck closer to the railing, crawled over it, and disappeared.

"That's the way." Harpoon Jack's eyes gleamed with excitement.

As Ferret swung over the edge, he wrapped the rag around one of his hands to absorb moisture. Immediately, he was hanging in midair, supported only by his fingertips and a keen sense of balance. Holding on took incredible strength and timing. One slip and he would be lost to the indifferent sea. He looked down at the ocean waves battering the hull. The ship swung him back and forth like a loose cannon. To make matters worse, the wet hull made it difficult to keep a steady hold; luckily, the outside hull was interwoven with patches of rigging, ledges, and boarding-netting. Ferret felt relieved that the storm had abated to calmer seas. Reaching the stern, Ferret pulled himself over the railing and maneuvered behind the unsuspecting helmsman. This was it. This was his chance to fight back and prove his fortitude. He did not need to be an assassin. He only needed to knock his opponent out and gag him.

Ferret jumped the helmsman, hooked his arm around his neck, and tried to choke him. The helmsman managed to bend over and pull a knife from his boot. He thrust it overhead erratically. But Ferret blocked the knife with his other arm. The man struggled for what seemed like forever. Ferret squeezed the helmsman's neck tighter and tighter, but the man pushed his blade close to Ferret's right eye. Suddenly, the helmsman gasped and dropped to the deck, unconscious.

Ferret had done it. He had taken the cursed enemy down. Just then, one of the British marines awoke, noticed him, pulled out his pistol and aimed at Ferret.

Before the marine could cock his weapon, however, a spear slammed through his chest. With a dull thud, the marine dropped dead. Harpoon Jack had plied his trade well, impaling a red beast.

Scores of Irishmen rushed out of hiding, seizing all the weapons they could, and aimed them at the awakening marines.

"Like me handy work?" Harpoon Jack asked as he yanked the harpoon from the Marine's body. He lifted the harpoon above his head and let out a war whoop of joy like a New World savage.

By this point, Strongbow had arrived at the helm.

Ferret untied the rag from his hand and threw it at the fallen helmsman. "Muffle him."

Strongbow leaned over the body and placed his hand over the man's face. "He has no air."

By this point, Harpoon Jack was at the helm, too, taking control of the rudder. He smiled with admiration. "Ya've become a true-blue kill-devil. That's the truth of it. Ya ought to be captain."

Ferret slouched against the mizzenmast and took several deep breaths. All he could hear was his pounding heart. He stared at his guilty hands, unable to believe what he had done. The plan had just been to overpower the helmsman, not to extinguish the precious flame of life. Kneeling next to the dead man's body, he felt an urge to strangle the dead man for dying prematurely.

Othello arrived; he leaned over the body of the dead man and shook his head. "Not good. Such a needless death pollutes the soul. It stains the purity of God's grace. I'm afraid you will fare poorly; bad luck will follow you to your dying days."

Ferret understood Othello's reference. He had come across this notion in several ancient Latin and Greek manuscripts. In the ancient world, to commit an impure act would condemn the violator to a lifetime of misfortune. He wanted to mark it up to superstition, but he had seen bad acts repaid with ungodly hardship. There might be something to fate.

Captain Cajan walked up behind everyone and belched. Barely able to walk, he cradled his half-empty bottle with loving tenderness as he gestured towards the crew. "Throw all the scurvy maggots overboard!"

The sailors prepared to hurl the British marines over the railing and into the coal-black sea.

"Wait!" Ferret shouted. "They're unarmed!"

"Fancy that." Cajan appeared amused. "They had thar jolly kill. By crikey, I'll have mine."

"They were just doing their duty," Ferret said.

"Doesn't matter one jig-jog bit to me. Let them swim with the sea-tigers and my nephew."

"There's a better way."

"Ya don't say?"

"We ought to hang them," Ferret said. "Let's see their foul faces before the noose. Let the fear of death linger like a malignant canker. I say that's the worst part of dying." Ferret paused. It seemed that he was getting the captain's attention. "Wouldn't you love to see the piss, dung, and vomit run down their boots as their necks stretch?"

"That's bloody wonderful!" Cajan shouted with excitement. "Let's rope 'em up now."

"Don't we want them first to agonize over a proper trial?" Ferret elbowed Cajan. "Of course, we know the verdict from the start. Don't we?"

"Agonize?" Cajan rubbed his beard, deep in thought. He did not know the word.

"We would ruffle some English feathers in London," Ferret said. "I can just hear the admirals squeal, 'What, some brassy Irishmen put my marines on trial for high crimes against *Eire*? How preposterous!' Indeed, the sweetest words that any Irishman could ever hear."

"By crikey," Cajan glowed with delight, "take 'em below. We'll have a hanging trial with all the trimmings."

Ferret felt relieved to have prevented Cajan from killing the captured men, but it seemed a hollow victory. He had done exactly what Cajan had been tricked out of doing. He had killed another living soul, maybe a family man with wife and children. He could rationalize that the slaying was in self-defense, but that gave him little comfort.

"Mighty dauntless," the Dutchman interrupted, his eyes narrowed with a disapproving glare. "Our savior and murderer all in one. But it will do you no good." He stomped his foot and pointed to the man-of-war trailing behind the *Green Sounder*. "Two gun decks and a full battery of firepower. We're still not free to drift with the wind. 'Twas God's design from the start, I tell yaw." Within moments, other crewmen echoed the same pessimism, drooped their bodies over the ship's railing, faces stripped of expression, and moaned about their short ration of luck.

Ferret scowled at the Dutchman. The real curse of mankind, Ferret mused, was not hangings from the yardarm, or warships to the rear, but sharing the planet with the old bastards of malcontent and gloom. But the Dutchman was sadly correct. An overloaded and rickety merchantman was no match for a warship.

"We must surrender!" The Dutchman smirked.

"Liberty's a harsh mistress," Ferret said. "Nobody ever won without a fight, no matter how low the chance of success." He suspected his attempt to rally the men was destined to fail, considering the ingrained hopelessness so prevalent with the Irish. They had lost too many battles and wars throughout the centuries to believe in the possibility of victory.

"We might as well couch a hogshead," Cajan said with fear growing in his eyes. "Let's scuttle her and be done with it. Better to drown with Neptune than to feed the chopping block." The captain brushed his hand through his beard and downed another shot of Jamaican rum from a larger flask. "I once saw a man under the iron axe. The bloody executioner missed. Cracked the man's head wide open. The poor devil. His body flopped about like a freshly caught cod." Taking more swigs of rum, the captain tried to remain upright by holding onto some rigging above him. The rope drooped where his two hands gripped it.

Noticing the sagging rope, Ferret recalled an old fisherman's yarn which told of an unarmed vessel that destroyed a man-of-war. It was surely a liar's tale to entertain children at bedtime, but the ruse always seemed theoretically possible.

"Do we have any gunpowder aboard?" Ferret bellowed to a number of crewmen and officers.

"Aye. A goodly number of hogsheads," Cajan stated matter-of-fact. "But it won't do you any good."

Strongbow huffed. "Gunpowder? We carry no cannon."

"Let fate take its course," the Dutchman said. "The Lord wishes us to die. Learn to accept your fate. You taunt these here wretched souls."

A number of crewmen clustered around Ferret as he climbed down from the stern quarterdeck. They appeared curious, even amused over any plan, sane or insane.

"Tell us: what ya scheming?" Harpoon Jack asked with a hopeful glow in his eyes. He listened as Ferret revealed most of the details. Afterward, Harpoon Jack stepped back, face drooping, clenching his chest. He looked around, not sure if he had heard it right.

Holbrook, who had been hiding in the ship's hold, was also nearby and keenly listened to Ferret. His face first brightened, then soured as Ferret disclosed more details. Holbrook began to slowly realize its implications and danger. He tapped Ferret on the shoulder. "It could work. But who would undertake such an outright act of suicide?"

Ferret ignored Holbrook's question.

Cajan disregarded the danger and cheered the men on, shouting that Ferret's plan was a godsend and their only hope.

More men huddled around Ferret, and he began barking out orders, instructing them to fetch kegs of gunpowder, powder fuses, two pots of hot coals, hemp rope, and one of the marines' red coats.

Meanwhile, Strongbow sat, alone, his arms crossed, drumming his fingers impatiently and muttering, "Impossible! Sink a man-of-war without cannon fire..." He sounded like the Dutchman.

Two small jolly launch boats were loaded with kegs of gunpowder concealed under saddlecloth. They were lowered into the water and the bows connected by a rope. The crewmen were excited over the prospect of escaping from the man-of-war that shadowed their every move. None wanted to talk about who would command the two boats. That would be a sorry story.

"You do realize the danger?" Holbrook elbowed Ferret.

Ferret nodded and lowered his voice. "Aye. Someone must aim the boats and spark the fuses. Someone must remain aboard until... well, until he dramatically enters Kingdom Come."

"'Tis a one-way voyage, to be sure." Harpoon Jack squeezed through the crowd that had encircled Ferret. "Nobody ever comes back from a watery grave. Nobody!"

This realization struck a silent chord among the most lionhearted. The crewmen stood around in a daze, mouths hung open, realizing that whoever stepped forward would never return. Everyone looked at each other and frowned. It was awkward. They felt an uneasiness that soon provoked a sense of fear and anxiety that almost descended into terror. It was not the explosion that scared the men most. It was the deep endless ocean. Its depths were worse than being blown apart. The crewmen glared at each other, positive that nobody would volunteer except a madman.

"'Tis my plan," Ferret declared. "I will take the risk."

Holbrook shoved Ferret against the topside cabin wall. "No! Have you gone utterly mad?"

Ferret broke free of Holbrook's grip. "Someone must starve the chopping block. 'Tis my chore, my task. I will not allow anyone to take my place."

Only stunned faces and sunken eyes disturbed the peaceful flapping of the mainsail as Ferret walked to the ship's railing. He stopped, turned and took one last glance at the wall of sagging faces and eyes. He swallowed with visible apprehension. He knew he had to leave immediately before common sense regained its hold. With a bouncy leap, he flew over the railing and began to climb down a rope ladder. He jumped into one of the boats. He had to get moving, the light of dawn waited for no man.

Everyone made a mad dash to the railing and peered down at the blackish water. All eyes were fixated on Ferret, then they turned their attention to Captain Cajan, who jutted out his lower lip and shrugged his shoulders. "Well, he's not the first man who entered Davy Jones's Locker without permission."

"Sir," Othello faced Cajan, "'tis far worse than suicide. Don't you Christians take a dim view of self-inflicted ruin?"

"He does what he wills. And I do what I must." Cajan threw his empty flask overboard. "Better him than me. Release the lines."

With an oar, Ferret pushed his boats away from the stern of the *Green Sounder*. He rowed silently toward the warship as he mentally ran through the key points of his plan. He found it difficult to concentrate. The thought of death kept haunting him with images of bodies eaten by sharks and sea monsters. His thoughts drifted back to the man he had killed. A sense of justice became clearer. His own death would offset the life he had taken. He was guilty and he had to be punished.

The two small boats began to rock back and forth wildly. Ferret cleared his mind and focused what he had to do in precise timing. He came up with a crude calculation of when to light the fuses and aim both boats at the oncoming man-of-war's bow. He was not sure whether the explosions would sink the warship. At least his plan might damage the vessel enough to buy his countrymen time to escape.

Ferret took one last glimpse at the *Green Sounder* in the brilliant moonlight, watching the vessel grow smaller and smaller on the horizon. He was running out of time. The dawn was beginning to outshine the waning moon. If only he had had time to say his last farewell to Heather. But at least she was far safer aboard the *Green Sounder*.

As the warship's tall bow approached, Ferret lit the fuses and positioned the two boats perfectly in front of the oncoming ship. A trail of blue smoke curled from the burning fuse. As he watched the flame burn closer to the kegs of black powder, he wondered if it was too short. What if it blew too soon? He would die for nothing.

After slipping on a British redcoat, Ferret noticed a sentry peering down at his boat. Instead of sounding the alarm, the marine pressed his flabby face on the railing and yawned. Finally, the warship's bow caught the unseen, underwater rope, causing both boats to veer closer and closer to each side of the warship's hull.

Aboard the ship, another sentry spotted one of the boats. He rang the ship's bell, alarming the marines and sailors below. Men, drowsy and half-clothed, stumbled above decks, flintlocks in hand. They searched the horizon for an attacking warship. Seeing none, they groaned, grumbled, and threatened the sentry with a dunking.

"Looky!" The lookout guard pointed to Ferret's boats.

Ferret glanced at the fuse, then looked up at the marine's gun aimed at him. Gripping a small empty barrel with both hands, he dove overboard just as several redcoats fired. Only a stream of air bubbles and the barrel floated above the surface.

"What's going on?" Rear-Admiral Lyndsay demanded immediate answers. He leaned over the railing. Before anyone could reply or even react, one of the boats exploded, violently rocking the warship. Within seconds, the second boat detonated, ripping open the hull above and below the water line. The warship began to roll to one side, forcing the sailors and marines to lower their deck launches and jump inside. The more impatient ones leaped overboard.

Rear-Admiral Lyndsay stood alone in the center of the warship as the bow sank below the water line. He remained steadfast on the deck as though he were nailed to the floor. Within minutes, his face and his ship disappeared beneath the turbulent water.

The *Green Sounder* conducted a search for Ferret until a dense fog blanketed the area. All they found was a few pieces of flotsam and bodies. After a few hours, Captain Cajan called off the search.

The *Green Sounder* lay motionless in the sea for most of the day. Cajan was unable to decide what to do next. Late that afternoon, Harpoon Jack spotted an English launch crammed with shivering men. At first, Cajan ordered the crew to ignore their pleas. But then he had a change of heart.

"Bring 'em aboard, by crikey. We'll have more fish to fillet. That will avenge our losses."

As the redcoats were brought aboard, Badger delivered a eulogy for Ferret. Most of the crew and passengers gathered around a small makeshift coffin that represented the hero's remains.

"He was a man of gallant deeds," Badger said as the last redcoats arrived on deck, shivering and looking dejected. "A lionhearted soul who gave his life so others may live. Never again shall we see such stalwart bravery."

Just then, a voice from behind the mourners shouted, "I hope you're wrong, Father!"

Everyone turned around, indignant that one of the captured marines would dare interrupt their funeral service. They were surprised when one of the redcoats removed his coat and climbed up on the railing. "I hope I'm not too late for my own funeral."

The crowd swamped Ferret from all sides and cheered wildly. As Ferret jumped down from the railing, everyone felt a need to slap him on the back as if he were a warrior king returning from a victorious battle.

Heather tackled Ferret with a hug. "You thick-headed fool. You do that again and I'll bash your head against a stone baluster. And I mean it."

Holbrook put his hands on Ferret's shoulders. "Back from the dead! Truly biblical and noteworthy."

This was his moment in the sun. Only a few such times ever came during a lifetime, if ever. He wanted to bask in the praise and adulation as long as possible.

* * *

Ferret's basking was short lived. Within several days, sharp divisions arose along racial, religious, and political lines. The infighting became fierce, and it was hard to tell who stood on which side and for what reason. Nobody aboard the *Green Sounder* was shot or killed, however. There were a few isolated fistfights, mostly shouting matches that started with someone impugning someone else's ancestry. A pistol had been drawn and fired, but the bullet missed its intended target. Most sat and listened to various options, fearful that another British warship would capture them before they could reach a safe port. To prevent violence, the Irish crew only permitted Irishmen to carry arms; English passengers were searched and relieved of their weapons. Only Holbrook was allowed to keep his gun, since he was an army deserter.

The first matter to be decided concerned the location of a friendly seaport. Strongbow urged Dunkirk, a haven for privateers. Ferret was the first to object, arguing that Dunkirk's ill reputation far exceeded its benefits. Although the port had a large fleet of French privateers and hostile brigadiers unfriendly to the British, the privateers were also indiscriminate. They would attack any nation's vessels, sometimes their own. He suggested Rotterdam instead, even though he knew some would oppose landing in the Netherlands. The United Provinces of the Netherlands had recently allied with England against France. But it *was* an uneasy alliance. The Dutch still fumed from the last war with England. Most of the crew appeared to agree with Ferret, which perturbed Strongbow.

The final decision fell upon the shoulders of Captain Cajan; he was still the man wearing the captain's hat.

Cajan searched for something to drink. "Lordy be gored! Thar be far too many blasted currents in this here pond. I'm not up to it. I'm forsaking my command."

248

"Then we must choose a new captain," Strongbow declared.

The Dutchman snorted angrily into his stained handkerchief and glared at them with condescension. "Democracy! 'Tis a flam! You fools. You can't vote until you create your little democracy. But you can't create it without first taking a vote. It can't be done."

"Delightful. The perfect dilemma." Strongbow yawned. "Now, who shall vote?"

The cries were chaotic; all should vote, only the Irish should vote, only those who could read and write. A shouting match decided that all should vote except women and Englishmen.

Only Strongbow and William O'Leary, a half-Welsh barrister from Waterford, voiced a desire to be captain. Ferret flatly refused many pleas to become a nominee, arguing that he was too young. Besides, he already knew that O'Leary could not lose. He was well-known and respected and once had an audience with the Queen. The vote was not even close.

Captain O'Leary shocked everyone when he announced, "We sail to London Harbor and plead our case. I'm sure the Queen will understand and pardon us."

In quick order, O'Leary was deposed and chained below deck.

Strongbow stepped forward. "Again, I offer my leadership. Be there any loyal opposition?"

"I will challenge him." Ferret finally had had enough. His father's murderer was not going to overlord him—not now, not ever.

Strongbow grumbled, "He's too young!"

Nevertheless, the vote was almost unanimous for Ferret, hands rising high overhead with ecstatic cheers, hoots, and whistles.

Holbrook was given the honor to declare Ferret the new commander, the rightful master of the ship. He presented the captain's telescope and tricorn hat to Ferret. The hat represented more than a mere article of clothing. To wear such a hat meant that Ferret was from a class of men who make their own destinies, who command respect without the need to demand it. He was now recognized as a man who stood a cut above everyone else.

Hearty cheers rang out across the crowded deck.

As soon as Ferret plopped the captain's hat on his head, he issued a warning. "I'll arrest anyone who attempts to undermine my authority!"

To prove his word, Ferret pointed to Strongbow and ordered him clapped in irons.

"I thought you respected everyone's rights!" Strongbow balked at being singled out and arrested.

"Take him below!"

"You may have your moment in the sun," Strongbow said as Holbrook and Harpoon Jack dragged him away, "but don't forget, even a bright sun has its eclipse!"

Someone in the crowd shouted, "Where to, Cap'n?"

"Rotterdam!" Ferret said without hesitation. He enjoyed getting others to do his bidding. There seemed to be no greater pleasure in life.

Even so, the taste of victory was bittersweet. His sudden arrest of Strongbow was evidence he could become exactly the kind of tyrant he had opposed for so long. Yet he felt almost powerless to stop it. He believed he had to protect his position of authority. He also felt he could stop his abuses any time; after all, he now had the power to do that and more.

Ferret began to realize why nobody ever surrendered power gracefully. Its appeal was too strong to resist.

Chapter 25

With the Union Jack fluttering high overhead, the *Green Sounder* sailed up the Nieuwe Maas River. She encountered four large British men-of-war at the entrance of the river. Ferret quickly slipped on a British officer's uniform and nonchalantly tipped his hat to the passing British crewmen. He almost felt obligated to pay homage to the English. After all, it was their unbecoming actions that had led to his position of captain. Besides, it would take weeks or months before the British Admiralty put all the pieces together. It would take them even longer to decide what to do. But when they did figure it out, they would not rest until the *Green Sounder* was captured. By that time, his vessel would be well beyond known civilization, wherever that was.

Although the crew protested against his actions, Ferret decided to put the captured English marines ashore along the French coast. He argued that they were just poor conscripts forced to do the bidding of the British Crown. He also dropped off a number of English passengers who had nothing but ill-will for the Irish.

The harshest complaints came from the Dutchman who was relentless in opposing anything that Ferret proposed or carried out. Always on the warpath, he glowed with unending criticism and charges of conspiracy. Threats of jail only caused the Dutchman to smile maliciously, as if his detention would prove an imminent conspiracy was afoot. Ferret had flirted with the idea of arresting the malcontent just for intruding on his authority, but he reasoned that the old grouch would enjoy imprisonment far more than freedom of movement. Besides, nobody took the Dutchman seriously, except for a few belly-aching hotheads, the sort who would grumble if a roasted pig were too fat. Ferret avoided these malcontents as much as possible; they loved to feast on the woes of others.

As agreed by most of the crew and passengers, the seaport of Rotterdam was their preferred destination. However, the Low Countries had been allied with England for decades. Ferret worried that could cause a problem, but Holbrook advised Ferret that the Dutch-English concord merited little concern. The Dutch were practical people, mostly interested in commerce, and cared little whether a merchantman slipped into their harbor from a hostile nation. They knew the difference between politics and trade, and would not let one influence the other.

But Ferret realized that the Dutch authorities would someday discover their presence and report them to the Admiralty in London. They could not stay forever in the Dutch Republic. They had to find a permanent homeland. That argument became a touchy subject, and Ferret wanted to take it slowly and see what others had to say. Despite a great variety of opinions, it appeared that only Ferret was aware of the dangers that lay beyond the territorial waters of England. Many foreign kingdoms were either allied or bowed to England's powerful military fleet. The British could easily demand the return of their ship from most seafaring nations. Even if they settled in lands hostile to England, a new treaty could change that situation overnight. They had to settle in mostly unclaimed and unexplored territory to escape the meddling of royal entanglements.

The most important crisis currently facing them was what to do after landing in the Netherlands. Everyone seemed to have his own take on the next course of action. Ferret had never watched so many agitated souls tormented over what the future might bring. Back in *Eire*, most commoners lived for the moment and would just let the day happen on its own without much reflection or anxiety. They had to eat today and purge their bowels tomorrow—a condition he called "short-term thinking." A full belly at the moment seemed to be life's ambition.

That listless feeling had fallen entirely by the wayside. A sense of excitement and self-worth filled the air as groups joined together to discuss future objectives. These discussions climaxed almost within sight of Rotterdam. Almost a hundred men and women gathered around Ferret on the midships deck, eager to discuss how to proceed. They wanted to hear Ferret's opinions on what to do. He had been mostly silent on the matter; he was unsure and decided to listen to what others were saying before he would openly speak.

After listening to everyone with a cogent opinion, he had gained a sense of what most people wanted and what dilemmas they were trying to avoid. He felt it was time to give them a meaty bone to chew on, something ample to keep their spark of hope alive and their spirits afloat. It was time to test his insights and see if he had accurately gauged the people's sentiment. He was not sure what a democratic republic was, but this might come closest in letting the people consent to how they would be governed. That had to be the linchpin and bedrock of his power. No more accidents of royal birth that ushered in tyrannical kings. The Old World had to be left behind.

Harpoon Jack was first to put a question up for debate. He almost seemed afraid to bring up the question that was on everyone's mind. "Be thar a safe harbor on our horizon?"

"Aye, but it lies far beyond the horizon." Ferret felt as if he had prepared for this moment his entire life. The hour had come to prove his mettle, move mountains and give hope for a brighter future. That meant that he had to reach for the stars, arouse excitement and inspire a dream of a better life in a land without conflict and bullies. He had to create a vision that inspired and rallied his troops.

"And those horizons include knowing our true dangers," Ferret said, trying to be as open and frank as possible. "The British are not the only ones who will pursue us. Every monarch will take unkindly to what we have done. We did take over a ship, not for the pleasure of a kingdom in their pursuit of legal plunder, but for ourselves. For that, we'll be decried by the world as pirates, marauders who thieve on the high seas for our daily fare. And that claim can be made in earnest. For we're a people without a patron nation, estranged from everything we had once known."

Ferret climbed up on a crate. He stretched out his arms. "The solution begs the question: where does our destiny lie? Shall we surrender to those who had imprisoned us?"

"Nay!" came the thundering reply.

"Or shall we seek more than a hangman's noose or a cold blade to the neck?"

"Aye!" the crowd roared back.

"Amen to that! For we have a vessel with which we can sail to faraway lands. A large merchantman that can take us to places we may rightfully call our own. Where the water is sweet, the land is fertile, and the game is a'plenty. Where nobody can stop us from worshiping in peace and speaking without fear of reprisals. What say ye?"

The Dutchman shoved his way up front and pointed an accusing finger at Ferret, appearing gloomier than usual. "You speak of the New World! That be too far and too close. We will never withstand the voyage or escape from their iron bilboes."

"We can and we will!" Ferret felt a sudden urge to have the Dutchman thrown overboard. Too bad he had already assumed the right of free speech. Big mistake. He was sure that error would haunt him long after he met his maker.

Before Ferret could continue, Father Yeats came forward and spoke about resettling in Spain. He was shouted down by the Dutch crewmen. The Dutch hated Spain. The Spanish monarchy had once attempted to force the citizens of the Netherlands to become Catholics, which plunged the nation into a bitter war that lasted almost a century.

"Listen!" Ferret shouted, trying to regain everyone's attention. "Much of the land to the south of England's North American colonies remains unclaimed and unexplored. 'Tis ours for the taking! A new land, no, a new country just waiting for us to come and colonize it. Can we afford to refuse such a grand offer?"

"Nay!"

The approval was loud and resounding. The crew, led by Holbrook and Harpoon Jack, began to cheer Ferret. They were all eager to leave behind the Old World and forge a new Irish nation.

* * *

Just before nightfall, the *Green Sounder* dropped anchor two hundred yards offshore in Rotterdam's harbor. The men lit lanterns, huddled together for warmth, and watched the sun's last rays strike the square dwellings along the quay. Red shadows sprayed the buildings as the sun fell, a dazzling sight that gave the Irish a feeling of warmth and peace even though the North Sea wind iced their skin.

The harbor was jammed with hoys and bilanders. Dockworkers unloaded cargo and stacked casks in the streets. Hardworking men rolled pushcarts full of slab cheese home to the countryside. Closer to shore, shopkeepers tossed cabbages and strings of onions inside from under sidewalk canopies. Carts pulled by dogs rolled down tightly knitted cobbled streets. Men on ladders lit street lamps that transformed Rotterdam into a sparkling city of glamour and enchantment. Its tree-lined avenues were alive with carriages that gave it charm and sophistication unparalleled in Europe. Many of his crew drooped their faces on the railing and gawked at the remarkable sight. To them, it seemed that they had reached the highest rung of civilization.

Maureen drifted over to Ferret to watch the city lights. She spoke with a soft voice. "You were very uplifting and heroic. Few dare to tease valor without the possibility of salvation."

"Luck often favors the foolhardy."

"I don't believe in luck." Strands of hair blew across her face like thin ribbons of smoke. "Luck only comes to the skillful." She slid her hand next to Ferret's.

"Call it what you will." Ferret shrugged, feeling uneasy. She was almost touching him, and he blushed. He looked down and caught a glimpse of her smooth face and bright eyes. "I just happened to be at the right spot at the right moment. Nothing special about that."

"You're being too modest," Maureen cooed. She placed her hand on top of his. "I also appreciated being exonerated."

Ferret looked surprised. "I'm not a magistrate. I only released you from the jail quarters. The British will still have you recorded as a harlot."

"Nonetheless, you've proven your valor." Maureen stretched up on her tiptoes and planted a kiss on his cheek.

Ferret had always been timid around women, never sure how to handle himself. But her closeness was exhilarating. He felt as though he could relax and share his most bizarre, half-cocked thoughts with her, and she would neither laugh out loud nor ridicule him. Ferret rubbed his neck, aware of the growing tension. He was interested in her, but she was usually so stiff-necked, aloof, and unpredictable. For now, however, he moved closer to her, gazing into her large and beautiful eyes. He realized he had to say something to affirm his interest.

Holbrook interrupted the moment. "You might want this back." He handed the ship's maritime spyglass to Ferret. "It might help you prove your claim of captaining a large vessel." The ship's name and other official wording were engraved on its brass casing. Next, Holbrook said a few words about releasing Strongbow.

Ferret glared at Holbrook with disappointment. *"Et tu, Brute?"*

"You cannot keep him imprisoned indefinitely," Maureen said.

Ferret moved away from the railing. He was being boxed in by his closest allies. He disliked the feeling immensely. He felt they should be showing their gratitude instead of smothering him with grievances. He knew where his enemies stood; but friends were cudgeling him with seditious prattle.

"He knows Rotterdam," Holbrook said.

"So do others."

"I hear he knows it better," Maureen said.

"I'm in command, and I make those decisions."

"You're wrong!" Maureen said. "Your command depends on those who put you there."

"Why are you protecting Strongbow?"

"Because he protected others," Maureen said. "He's known for easing the plight of the needy and suffering. In the hinterland, he is seen as the Robin Hood of *Eire*. Generous to a fault, some say. He helped many of my friends."

Ferret had to turn his head aside to prevent himself from laughing. He too could be generous when spending other people's money. "So why didn't you knock on his door for the offerings?"

Maureen crinkled her nose. The question annoyed her. "The money wasn't for me. Heaven forbid. I asked only for a few sixpence for Aristot. I never knew the whereabouts of Strongbow. Nobody does."

"So, then why—?"

"Because you need to know," Maureen said.

"Know what?"

"That Strongbow has the ear of the crew. You should tread lightly. There are grumblings."

"Against me!"

"No, not in particular, but I felt obligated to warn you. He is a man of many talents and rapport with many people."

Ferret nodded his head, striking a more conciliatory tone. "Then I am indeed grateful for the advice. I'm not infallible, nor do I have all the answers." He gently placed his hand over hers. It was not planned; it just happened, like the rustling of fallen leaves. This whole episode seemed foreign to him. He had won the ship and the vote. What more could the crew expect of him? He began to see why it took heartless men to captain a ship or lord it over people. Maybe he should have let someone else take command of the helm. There would surely be less heartburn in the long run.

"You should release him at once," Maureen said. "If you wish to be a leader, you'll need devoted followers. Without them, you're alone."

"I have little need of rogues like Strongbow."

"Strongbow is innocent of any wrongdoing, at least any I've witnessed. Either put him on trial or release him. Otherwise, you risk acting like a despot." She pried off Ferret's hand and snatched the telescope away from him. "You do not need a spyglass to see where you go." She stomped off, her long dress fluttering in the wind.

Her words punctured him. He was anything but a tyrant. He had been fairly lenient and understanding.

He shook his head and gazed at the sparkling city. After what he had just gone through, he thought captaining a ship might be easier than navigating around women.

* * *

A small landing party, which included Ferret, Holbrook, Strongbow, and Othello, assembled on the deck of the *Green Sounder* the next morning and climbed down a jack-ladder into a jolly launch boat. Before the boat pushed off, Maureen arrived at the railing clenching the telescope she had taken from Ferret the day before. She tossed it to him.

Ferret reached up, but the telescope was thrown past him. Strongbow caught it with ease.

"I believe this be yours, your captainship." Grinning impishly, Strongbow handed him the telescope.

"Keep it for now. I believe your eyesight is worse than mine."

"I have a few blind spots, I admit," Strongbow said. "But what of yours?"

"Mine are less pronounced." Ferret moved toward the front of the boat, clambering over a dozen men to get to the bow. He sat next to Holbrook and remained quiet. He had had no intention of releasing his former friend. Before yesterday, nothing in this world could have made him do that. But he had to admit that Maureen was right. Strongbow probably had been to the Dutch Republic in the past. He was well-traveled, but if Strongbow had even a shred of knowledge about Rotterdam, he could help the mission. That was paramount. He had to put his personal differences aside for the success of their mission. That was what a good leader would do.

It seemed incredible how people were prone to ignore the lying traits of others, acting if they were immune to the chicanery of others, until the nettles of deception had stung them repeatedly. Strongbow was like that. His charm could melt a block of ice in the dead of winter until something went wrong. People who did not take into account the possible bad consequences of doubtful actions were destined to relive unhappy experiences. That was an eye-opener that he wished he could suppress. But it did explain one mystery. He now knew why the wrong people often ended up in charge. Maybe this was why he decided to let Strongbow roam the city with them; he would bring some merriment and buffoonery, but also encounter bad consequence that might be a lesson to others.

Just as Ferret ordered the boat launched, Holbrook informed him that one of the rowers, a short, barrel-shaped man, had been a native of nearby Haarlem. Known as Rutten the Storyteller, he swore that he knew every tradesman and merchant in Rotterdam since Charlemagne was crowned Roman Emperor by the Pope.

Ferret eyed the man and noted his features. Rutten had rough, leathery skin and a face that was tanned and blistered. His few front teeth were cracked and pointed, resembling sharks' teeth. He stank of seaweed and dead fish, causing Ferret and the others to move as far away from him as possible.

Rutten would scrape his whiskered face with his broken fingernail and talk about his travels. As the boat moved toward shore, he boasted that he had sailed to the far corners of the world. "Thar Japanners take water baths every day. Seen nothing like it before. Washes away ya very soul, ya ask me. Turns the skin puker yellow. No Christian I ever knew took to boiling. Never catch me in 'em hot pots." He guffawed as the others nodded in agreement.

Rutten was just warming up. He rambled on with tales of sea serpents and narrow escapes in wild, unexplored lands. He was fluent in English and Dutch and occasionally forgot which language he was using. His tales were mostly incoherent and disjointed. He would switch back and forth between stories. He would try to make the stories parallel, but upon reaching the climax of one story, he would forget the moral of the other.

After they reached the shoreline piers and docks, Rutten and Strongbow were able to engage with several merchants in the market square near the waterfront, but they found the trading arduous. The Dutch were suspicious of the Irish wool, knowing well that the English had banned it.

"There's a glut of wool," one merchant mumbled indifferently.

Rutten closed his left eye and stared at the merchant. "Even with the war goin' on?"

The merchant doffed his red hat, sucked on his lower lip and changed his story. "We might have some need..."

Ferret listened to Rutten and the merchant haggle, first in English, then in Dutch. His first impression was not flattering to the Dutch. He could see a mixture of distrust and pride. He overheard another merchant bragging that he was always right and therefore everyone else must be wrong. Ferret wondered if all the Dutch were this brassy. They seemed to be an extremely conservative lot, unyielding, frugal, methodical, and industrious.

"Our wool is high grade," Ferret interjected, interrupting the merchant in mid-sentence. He felt that he had to say something or he would be considered a useless bystander.

"So?" the merchant cleared his throat and continued his conversation with Rutten and Strongbow.

When some sort of agreement was reached, Rutten's face sagged. He was not particularly pleased and growled in an outburst of anger. "It wasn't a caterwaul, by no means. The Jew leeched us white. Took only a few bundles. Not enough to buy a thimble-full of buttermilk."

Everyone knew that provisions were plentiful in Rotterdam, but they were also expensive. They had to continue to search the seaport for bargains. As they did, street urchins attacked them at every street corner, hurling mud and insults reserved for strangers of foreign lands. One child even threw a hunk of hard cheese at Ferret. Incredibly, it was still edible. *Eire* starved while the Dutch heaved food at outlanders for sport. He slipped the cheese into his pocket.

As the urchins' attacks grew bolder, Ferret noticed that the children's parents were watching from windows and doorways, but did nothing to restrain them. The Dutch were stoic, unemotional, and rigid in their own behavior, but allowed their children free run of the streets.

"Why do they fail to punish their children?" Ferret asked Rutten.

"Cutting the nose spoils the face," Rutten said with a shrug.

Ferret pulled the cheese from his pocket. "We starve and these wags throw food away."

"Lowlanders have so much."

"And *Eire* so little."

"That's our reward." Rutten grinned. "We fought dearly for our rights. Beat those horse-leeching Spaniards. And all the others. Galled them good. That's why."

Ferret was momentarily ashamed of his Irish heritage. Then he looked at the dirty children again. So this was what freedom meant—uncontrollable children, food to waste, and frigid hostility toward strangers. Mayhap the Irish had not lost after all.

* * *

It was on the third day of their search for supplies that Strongbow heard a rumor of a colony of disgruntled Irish and Swedes who were preparing an expedition to the New World.

At first, Ferret paid no heed to the rumor, considering its source was Strongbow. But then he reconsidered. If there were such a colony, they might forge some type of alliance to merge resources. It was better than staying in the Netherlands and waiting for the British to raid their ship.

A search for the mysterious colony was begun in earnest. Unfortunately, everyone was either tight-lipped or said that they knew nothing. Even Strongbow's charm could not break through the wall of apprehension. Finally, Othello convinced Rutten to pose as a Dutch official from Rotterdam's Office of Burgomaster. The ruse worked. A merchant told them to see a man named Erik van Noord who worked with a coppersmith near the waterfront.

They found van Noord working outside in a blanket of fog. They heard the blows and echoes of his hammer before they saw him. He was a large, muscular man garbed in black broadcloth. He was hammering barrel lids intensely and hastily.

"What you want?" van Noord asked without lifting his head. "I have no stivers to lend. Go away!" He continued swinging his hammer.

Ferret frowned. This man was obviously no leader. Leaders led, laborers labored. Even Strongbow and Othello looked discouraged.

"Erik van Noord?" Ferret asked.

No answer.

"Sir! I understand that you lead a colonial expedition to the New World."

"I can hear," van Noord quickly said, "but you cannot make me listen."

Ferret wondered if van Noord was capable of doing anything besides hammering barrels. "We're new arrivals from *Eire*! We seek to escape to the New World."

Van Noord spat on the ground. "Oh, you do!"

Ferret looked across the foggy marshlands. He turned and spoke to his companions in a dispirited tone. "There is no colony or expedition here. Let's return to the ship."

Van Noord's hammer froze in midair. "You have a vessel?"

"We indeed do." Ferret pulled out his telescope and presented it to van Noord. "We command the *Green Sounder*. See the inscription?"

"I can see." Van Noord huffed and pushed the telescope away. "Anybody can engrave anything on a spyglass."

"We have more than a few trinkets to show." Strongbow attempted to display a pleasant demeanor. "'Tis out in the bay. Want to inspect our vessel, matey?"

Van Noord craned his neck to look beyond them, as if he were being watched. "Come with me!"

They followed van Noord into an adjacent warehouse that appeared to be abandoned. He closed and bolted the door behind them. Only a sliver of sunlight shone through a small, broken windowpane. "I desire secrecy above all," he said. "I do not want rumors to fly like wild geese. Geese squawk like old women. Do we have any old women here?"

No one spoke.

"Then who sent you?"

"No one," Ferret said.

Van Noord swore. "Criost! No letter of introduction, no references. I do not listen to street beggars. Good day, gentlemen."

"Beggars we're not," Ferret said. "Do beggars command a five-hundred-ton, three-mast merchantman?"

"Larger than a brigantine," van Noord muttered. "Good vessel?"

"'Tis seaworthy." Ferret lowered his voice. He felt ashamed to call the rotting *Green Sounder* seaworthy.

Van Noord's mood changed. "We have much need of good ship." He paused. "But who told you of us? Was it Winchester?"

"Street rumors," Strongbow blurted out. "It appears hard to keep old women from squawking."

"Not good," van Noord said, scowling with annoyance. "Rotterdam reeks with spies."

"Spies you say," Strongbow gleefully joked. "Fancy that."

"Don't jape. They flitter about like angels of death," van Noord said. "There are those who keep a close eye on us."

Ferret felt the Netherlands becoming less inviting with each passing minute. Now he had to worry about spies. And who was this Winchester? And why did van Noord's group not have a vessel of their own? At every step, there were more questions than answers.

Van Noord unbolted the door. "My daughter will fetch you in the market square tomorrow at noonday. We will talk then, but with my council." With a slight bow, Van Noord stepped outside and vanished into the ground fog.

Chapter 26

Ferret and his crewmen had been waiting for over an hour in the market square. Van Noord's daughter was nowhere to be found. As they waited, an angry, obese woman began to shout, "Swinger!" Immediately, she confronted Paco and shook her agitated finger at him. "*Je bent een vreselijke man!*" Next, she doubled her fist and took a swing at Paco. She missed. Then she lunged for Paco's throat but missed again.

Paco dropped his silly grin and hid behind Ferret and Holbrook, afraid for his very life.

"Better to tease the devil himself," Ferret chuckled. Paco had mocked the Dutch woman's plumpness by looping his hands over his own over-sized belly and walking around with his stomach pushed out, while following closely behind the portly woman. His mockery had set the woman on a warpath. At first, Ferret was puzzled over why anybody would take offense to Paco's prank. Most people throughout the world prized fatness as a laudable sign of wealth, health, and happiness. Fatness was a blessing in a world under constant threat of starvation and disease. But not here. This was when Ferret realized that the Dutch were different. They had been apparently cursed with bodies of whales and the thin skin of frogs.

"Foreign curs!" The Dutch woman continued to bellow out a string of curses. Frowning, she raised her nose and sniffed the air as if she had smelled a basket of rotten eggs.

"Perhaps we do smell, Madame," Ferret grinned, "but we don't resemble windmills."

Holbrook laughed with an air of great amusement. "Indeed, she could crush Othello's bones on impact."

Almost breaking into tears of laughter, Ferret reflected that *Eire* never had such debilitating handicaps. Fat was a stranger to a foodless land.

Glaring with a cross-eyed scowl, the fat woman turned and plodded back into the crowded marketplace.

Scanning the marketplace, Ferret observed that the young Dutch women were entirely different. They were blessed with ample bosoms and wasp waists and endowed with boundless energy and contagious smiles. Ferret suspected that age was the determining factor. Like caterpillars coming out of their cocoons, older Dutch women spread their wings and transformed into bulging balls of fat. He discovered that foreigners had a term for the oversized Dutch—"butterballs."

* * *

Van Noord's daughter arrived as the sun rose straight overhead. She greeted them warmly, kissing Ferret and the others on the cheek in accordance with traditional Dutch hospitality. Paco blushed. Strongbow applied for a second kiss. Othello was too tall to reach. Holbrook offered his hand instead.

Van Noord's daughter motioned them to follow her to a two-story wood-frame house near the center of the seaport. It was a lovely house surrounded by a green garden that overlooked a wide canal. There was a sitting bench outside to watch the passing vessels or to enjoy the flowers. Ferret noticed that all the houses had fancy gardens, wooden benches, and streetlights. They radiated wealth and serenity.

Inside, Ferret was greeted by six somber men. Each was garbed in a black suit with a wide white collar draped over his shoulders. Each man's hair tumbled from underneath his black, wide-brim hat. They had clean faces. They were the councilmen.

Ferret and the others were ushered down a long corridor decorated with wall clocks, painted dishes, and long curtains. Ferret wondered why these people wanted to flee to the New World. They were affluent—they had food and homes. What more could they want?

In a large back room, an oak table stood next to several levels of boxes built into the wall. The long drawers occasionally rattled on their own. Curious, Ferret opened one. He saw a sleeping child, perhaps six months old, bundled in a coarse red-and-blue striped Dutch blanket. The child opened its green eyes and reached up with its small, chubby arms. Ferret

264

felt an impulse to pick up the baby and cradle it in his arms. He had never thought much of children before. He regarded them as nonentities that usually caused trouble or died before reaching adulthood. Gurgling, the child waved its arms, impatient to be held. Ferret made a face, and the child became excited. The child's smile was contagious. He reached down to touch the child.

A woman glided past Ferret and lifted the child into her spindly arms. She glanced at Ferret, appearing distrustful of him. "She's a good girl. Never fusses. You have children?"

"No," Ferret said. "Could I hold her?"

The young woman hesitated, but she placed the child in his arms. "You must be careful."

The child reached up to touch Ferret's face. Warmth swept over him. He wondered what it would be like to be a father. The act itself did not take much effort. He only had to hoe a woman's garden and the seed would germinate—all in a night's work. But to teach a child important values so he would not die in vain when the Lord recalled him, that was the difficult task.

When van Noord entered the room, the young woman reclaimed the child and whisked away. The other councilmen sat and lit clay pipes. They called van Noord "*stadholder*."

After a recital of the Lord's Prayer, a man named Johan van Perk turned an hourglass over. He proclaimed that the meeting was to disperse in one hour. "When sand ends, we end."

Van Noord spoke first. He was a broad man and strong, but he had the haggard look of an old man, with baggy eyes, dark wrinkles, and thick white eyebrows. His skin was coarse and large-pored, making his cheeks resemble strawberries. He spoke in English with a Swedish accent. His speech was passionate: he thundered one moment, then whispered the next. He appeared impatient as if he feared he would die before he had accomplished his life's goals. Yet he also indulged in speeches so long they would surely have stopped death itself.

"We've been oppressed," van Noord said. "That's the crux of our problem and what brought us to the nethermost of Europe. We seek only to be left alone in peace. But there be no peace. The Netherlands surround us like an angry sea." After his short introduction, van Noord recited a detailed history of their struggle. Brevity was clearly not one of his strengths. He explained that they were a mixture of Irish, Swedes, and Norsemen who had fled to Holland to escape war and religious persecution. Their long-range plan had been to construct a fleet and establish a colony in the New World, free from any European influences. Through the years, van Noord's colony had married into several wealthy Dutch families, but many in Rotterdam opposed them. The Netherlands' alliance with England left the province of Friesland as their only refuge. They had spent most of their resources on reclaiming sea bottom land there. Now almost penniless, they had no means to take their remaining colonists and equipment seventy miles north to their new home, a ship-building town where they were to construct two or three ships for the Atlantic crossing.

Van Noord slammed his hands on the table. "Our children are in danger of losing their faith. Scarcely few Catholics amongst the Dutch—before long, our offspring will be Dutch. Sooner or later, the Britons will again impose war against our shores. And worst of all, the Dutch squeeze more levies from us each year. They have forsaken liberty. We have no choice but to flee."

Pragg Nattle, one of the younger councilmen, stood up. He had a scar-like cut over his upper lip that gave him a sinister look, yet his face glowed with friendliness. A milliner, he stitched ribbon-like cockades on a half-dozen hats strewn across the table when he wasn't speaking. "How can we leave?" he said. "We have no vessel to sail to Friesland."

"The sand grows thin and weary," van Perk said, tapping his fingers on the hourglass to let everyone know that the meeting was taking too long. His face permanently sagged, even when he tried to smile, which was seldom.

"We're fettered and bound," van Noord said, resuming his speech. His eyes were trained on Strongbow. "We suffer harsh persecution here. 'Tis even forbidden for Catholics to celebrate mass."

Pragg Nattle spat out a threading needle to correct van Noord. "That's not entirely true. The Sabbath day is observed. Priests perform the mass unobstructed. Have you forgotten? Your pew is beside mine."

Van Noord smiled childishly. "I mean, we must pay the burgomaster twenty guilders for the privilege. 'Tis against the law. We bribe to circumvent the law."

"'Tis the price we pay for our liberty and—" Pragg stopped. He had pricked his thumb with a needle and begun to suck on it.

"We're treated as outlaws," van Noord said. *"Inget bättre än avskum! What law next must we pay to circumvent?"*

Pragg gripped his thumb tightly to stop the bleeding. "Laws are enacted to be circumvented. Only takes a few guilders. How else would the burgomaster feed his children? 'Tis his privilege. He profits; we worship. 'Tis something to live with. Nothing be free."

"Not even blood?" Van Noord grinned with a slight smirk.

Pragg wrapped a handkerchief around his bloody thumb and sat down.

Van Noord continued, "The burgomasters may curtail our liberties at any moment. If they have such power now, they will one day employ more. We must settle in Friesland and finish our ship carpentry. Calvinists gather more strength each passing day. They seek harsher laws and harsher punishment. I've warned this council before. Principles cannot be circumvented or bribed."

Johan stood up holding the hourglass, looking displeased. "Sand is gone. We go now!"

"Sit down!" van Noord thundered. Turning to Strongbow and Holbrook, he said, "We have need of seaworthy ships."

Ferret stepped forward. "I'm Captain Ferret O'Neill and—"

Van Noord glanced at Strongbow and Holbrook, but neither man spoke up to contradict Ferret's claim. His eyes switched back to Ferret. "But you're so... young."

"I nevertheless command a five-hundred-ton merchantman." Ferret stood his ground, head up, making direct eye contact with van Noord and the council. "We, too, seek the New World. It would be a far safer journey if we sailed with a fleet of ships."

The councilmen grumbled among themselves for a brief moment, but looked generally pleased.

"I propose we work together for our mutual advantage," van Noord said.

"Only if we depart soon," Ferret said. "We have made powerful enemies."

"Enemies?" van Noord asked.

"We sank an English warship," Ferret said with a touch of pride. Some of the councilmen began to whisper to van Noord.

Van Noord asked, "In self-defense?"

"Aye."

"How many cannons do you have?" Pragg asked.

"None."

"How—" van Noord said with a little grimace. "How is that possible?"

"We set two boats adrift, attached to each other by rope. They were full of powder. By the grace of God, they hit the warship and sank her. Lady Fate honored us that day."

The councilmen looked suspicious.

"'Tis the truth," Holbrook said. "It was a miracle of rare deliverance."

"Make an inquiry with the English authorities, if you must," Ferret said. "Luck shined her grace upon us that day. But now we seek her goodwill again. We wish to escape the Old World. My shipmates and I will not live unfree. We would rather drown in the cold Atlantic."

Van Noord cleared his throat. "Our luck has been less impressive. We are behind schedule. Our shipyard and village lie only half-completed. 'Od knows when we shall depart. I pray it will take less than two years to construct the ships."

"Two years!" Ferret understood the perils of crossing the harsh Atlantic alone, yet there was danger in staying too long in the Netherlands. The British would be searching for the *Green Sounder* in every port.

"Not longer than two years," van Noord said. "'Tis better than crossing the Atlantic alone."

Everyone nodded in agreement. The meeting ended and several young women brought in trays with blackjack mugs of dark ale. Toasting their new alliance, the councilmen lost no time in setting up chairs and tables to play cards. They gambled with tulip bulbs. Several women joined the men, playing cards and puffing tobacco like professionals.

Ferret and his crew returned to the ship. It appeared they had found a temporary home in a strange land.

Chapter 27

Ferret felt like a prophet as he prepared to address the assembled men and women of the *Green Sounder*. He searched for words to encourage his people to settle down with the Dutch until a fleet was constructed. It would not be easy. The Irish always suspected treachery. They neither trusted their leaders nor followed their instructions. And yet, if by some trick he managed to pull it off, he knew the bards and poets would sing of his deeds until the end of time.

As his people gathered topside, an uncanny sense of history over-shadowed him. Like Moses, he had delivered a subjected people out of bondage and been assigned to lead them through to a Promised Land. But Moses had God's direct intervention and two stone tablets written by the Lord's imposing hand. Ferret had far less to work with.

"With divine guidance, we shall escape the English blackguards," Ferret proclaimed. "But where will our sails blow us? Shall we disband and roam the continent, without country or home?"

The crowd roared, "No!"

"Shall we become Phoenicians and live our lives on the seas?"

"No!"

"Shall we take our chances with the fearsome Atlantic, alone and defenseless? A journey of unspeakable dangers to untamed lands?"

The crowd was unsure how to respond to such a frightful question. They glanced at each other, shrugged, and argued in whispers.

"Do not be disheartened. Hope is nigh," Ferret promised. He spread his arms like Moses parting the Red Sea. "The crestfallen need not leap overboard, for I bring good tidings. We have discovered men of like passion here in Rotterdam. Men yearning to flee the Old World for the new. Men desperate to live in a better world."

The crowd grew silent, not sure what to expect. Everyone moved closer and squeezed tighter to hear the announcement. Those of shorter stature had to stand on their tiptoes to see over another person's head.

"I propose we merge with our brethren, to construct a stout new life for us all." Ferret lifted his arms higher. "There's no need to drift aimlessly or risk the ruthless Atlantic alone. We can sail toward the setting sun in a magnificent fleet. We can establish a permanent colony of free men on our own land. 'Tis true liberty for the taking. What say ye to that?"

The crowd roared its approval.

Ferret was both delighted and disturbed by the ease with which his appeal had swayed everyone. The crowd could have been whipped into a frenzy with the snap of his finger, and led off to Lord knows where. He was not sure whether his success was due to his oratory or because he had hit a popular chord.

Scanning the crowd, his eyes fixed on the reclusive Maureen. In a sea of swirling cheers and compressed bodies, she was like a rock, unemotional, unable to be swept away by his speech. She was probably the only one who understood how he had manipulated the crowd like a power-hungry king with little remorse in embellishing the truth.

"We shall rekindle a new beginning in the New World," Ferret said as he was nearing the end of his speech. "Hope has been replenished. Rapture imbued and life renewed. We shall no longer hunger for bread or yearn for liberty. We have reached our destiny!"

The crowd cheered. They patted each other on the back as though they had already crossed the Atlantic and were ready to celebrate. Within a short time, the crowd dispersed, most heading below for warmth. Only Maureen remained topside. She glared at Ferret as if he had committed a horrendous crime. Frowning, she approached him and said, "You think you can do what you want."

"I've been trying my utmost."

"You indeed have a royal tongue. Only it's forked like a repulsive snake."

"I'm simply looking after my people. I told no falsehoods." Ferret lightly bit down on his tongue. He knew he had stretched the truth and committed sins of omission. He had no idea if van Noord could live up to his agreement. In fact, he suspected that van Noord could not build a fleet in two years even if they found financial backing. But he had to go along with the impossible. He had to avoid the question of how long it would take. His people could barely wait for their next meal without throwing a fit or threatening rebellion. He worried it might be half a lifetime before they would set sail for the New World. But he would never disclose that worry. He stared at Maureen. "I will do what I must," he blurted out, and then briefly closed his eyes.

"I feel so honored, Sire," Maureen snickered, curtseying. "But when has a Philistine leader ever truly cared about his people?"

Ferret grabbed Maureen's shoulder. He could feel her thin collarbone under her dress. "Must you be so, ... so high-principled?"

"It's all I have left! That and a wee bit of honor. But I'm sure many will testify that I have already sold that virtue to the highest bidder." Maureen's face flashed red with agitation. "This world stinks of a spumy chamber pot. And to think you were once a disciple of Aristot! You've been seduced by the morass of statecraft. Aristot warned of this day. Sirens always entice their victims with sweet songs of deceit."

"I'm responsible for the lives of my shipmates. *Lives*. Not an inkpot of high ideals. My decisions are scripted in blood. Men live or die depending on what I do." Ferret released Maureen. "But despite it all, I am merely leading these men. I do not wish to rule them."

"You lead them where you want them to go. Do they have a choice?"

"Did they ever?"

Maureen's jaw tightened. "And what will you do if they fail to follow?"

"Hang them from the nearest yardarm, of course."

"Surely, a king could do no less." Her voice dripped with sarcasm. She grabbed Ferret's hand and dug in her sharp fingernails. "I don't need a despot to manage my life. I have enough trouble doing it myself." She turned and rushed off.

Ferret glanced down at his hand. Blood was oozing from the tiny pinhole wounds. Something told him to follow Maureen below deck, but another encounter with her might require an armful of bandages. Mayhap all women were hard-hearted, hot-tempered, and distraught. He convinced himself to stay away from her for the time being. It was too painful to orbit too close to her world.

* * *

Maureen was the least of Ferret's problems. Each week brought new problems. The first developed after the colony moved to the newly-created island and township of New Friesland. His people and the Dutch refused to work together, each accusing the other of favoritism. Dissent grew, tempers flared, and Ferret feared that the alliance would crumble. Like many such predicaments, however, it resolved itself on its own. The groups began to tolerate each other by ignoring each other.

The next crisis revolved around the war with France, which delayed the construction of the dockyard and fleet. Claiming the Netherlands for Louis XIV, France's armies overran Southern Zealand, threatening all of the republics. The Dutch did what they had done to prior invaders: they broke open several dikes and drowned the advancing French army. The Netherlands lost a little land and France lost a large army. However, New Friesland was required to contribute men to the Dutch military, which took the most able-bodied men away from their shipbuilding duties.

The war with France had other effects. Dutch merchants grew unwilling to invest in New World colonies during wartime, and van Noord's main investor, an Englishman, had lost two vessels to storms and privateers. His last ship had been captured, looted, and set on fire adrift. Without the Englishman's money, the colony became insolvent, forcing men to work in Rotterdam to buy timber from Norway.

As more warships sailed past the island to fight the French, Ferret worried that they might discover the *Green Sounder*. So he ordered the ship refitted, re-tarred the seams with pine pitch, built a small mast near the stern, and registered the ship with the Dutch as a new vessel christened *Triumph*.

While Ferret's deception seemed to have worked, the Irishmen under his command did not work well at all. They were often drunk, argumentative, and dogged by low morale. It was common for the more imbibed Irishmen to tie themselves to poles near the construction site to give the appearance of labor, though they were in fact passed out.

In short order, the Dutch came face-to-face with the crude behavior of the Irish. They already had a deep-rooted contempt for any "inferior" people, and the Irish perfectly fit their image of backward bumpkins. They began to describe Ireland as the sinkhole of Europe, and the Irish as odious "bogtrotters," complaining that they were unshaven, unschooled, underfed, and under-clothed. Ferret freely admitted to his people's shortcomings, but told his Dutch companions that the Irish were simply ignorant, like newborn babes. The Dutch disagreed and pointed to ingrained defeatism in the Irish, saying that the bogtrotters appeared to go out of their way to degrade themselves.

Ferret knew that what the Dutch reported was true. The Irish would boast of how much misery they could endure. They enjoyed bathing in self-pity in an effort to blame everyone else for their wretchedness. Ferret had always ignored this self-defeatist behavior until he had arrived in the Dutch Republic. Living in another nation made him much more observant of his own countrymen's drawbacks.

Most of the Irish lived aboard the *Triumph* or along New Friesland's shoreline in huts of canvas and wood. That would have been Ferret's fate except that Van Noord had observed Ferret's lack of defeatist traits.

When van Noord learned of Ferret's heroism in sinking the English warship, he deemed the young man to be a leader courageous beyond exception. And because he believed in the capabilities of royalty, van Noord's impressions were strengthened when he discovered Ferret's royal bloodline. He chose Ferret to be his second-in-command and made arrangements for Ferret and Heather to stay in a two-story wood frame house on the island.

The council had less confidence in Ferret's royal blood. The Dutch had rebelled against Spain's monarchy in the sixteenth century and declared themselves a republic, a measure that shocked and appalled the rest of the world. It was such a radical act that every monarchy of Europe warred with the Netherlands from time to time and publicly warned that they would do so again until it surrendered to a royal sovereign.

Van Noord's insistence, however, wore the council down, and they approved Ferret's seat on the board, along with the Englishman who had financed the colony. Ferret thought he recognized the man, and he knew why as soon as they met in person.

The Englishman bowed as he introduced himself as Colonel Winchester. Then he pulled a scented handkerchief from his pocket and touched his lips with it daintily. He was lumpy and wore bulky clothes that made his pockets protrude as if he were carrying onions. His wig was powdered and his clothes richly fashioned. He carried a fragile, ornate cane. He had an aristocratic air, effeminate bearing, and dainty walk.

"I was at the battle near Macroom," Winchester said. "What happened to Black Fox was shameful. Cromwell is a most hang-dog fellow. He meddled in everyone's affairs. A sly-boot he was. A terrible liar on top of that. He pretended to be puritanical, pious, and godly. Never trust a godly man. So help me God, I never will again! He framed his own officers with charges of treason and smuggling. The bastard even accused me of selling army supplies to the Irish rebels!"

"Did you?" Ferret asked.

Winchester guffawed. "Me, a smuggler? Selling British military goods to Irish rapparees? Preposterous!" Motioning Ferret closer, he waved his pinky and whispered, "The profits were shameful!"

Ferret thought Winchester an ugly sort at first, but within weeks, the ugliness melted away, and the two became close friends. Loathing Major-General Cromwell, they had much in common; they would drink together and fire off insults at Cromwell's name. When Ferret mentioned his uncle Madoc's plots with Cromwell, Winchester tapped the ground with his cane in rapture and offered to have his friends in the Admiralty investigate the major general.

"That will bring down Cromwell and the O'Neill clan," Winchester laughed. "They will lose their power and influence, tossed out of Ireland like river rats."

* * *

Meanwhile, Maureen was suffering. She had tried to manage her own affairs and failed. She was slowly starving in a hut along the seashore. Although she had a distant uncle in Zealand, he gave her little food or money. Even Maureen's age allied against her. In her early twenties, she was considered almost unmarriageable.

She refused to become a whore, despite having few other means to secure a livelihood. Nevertheless, men would pinch her buttocks, run a short distance, bend over while wiggling their rumps and ask for a friendly "pump" in the back room of a nearby coffeehouse. Women were appalled by the men's antics, but they too would ostracize her at social events.

Ferret badgered his people to give Maureen odd jobs or handouts until she discovered he was her secret benefactor. She confronted Ferret and demanded he let her handle her own affairs. Avoiding her fingernails at all costs, Ferret said that he could not let her die needlessly.

"I neither beg nor accept alms." Maureen's thin fingers were swollen at the joints. Like many proud people, she would rather starve than accept charity.

She would not compromise, and Ferret would not relinquish. One day, he took her hand and dropped several coins into her palm.

"You do this for the colony?" she asked, wide-eyed.

"I do it for me. I need your expertise."

"Me?"

Ferret nodded. "You might be able to help us run the colony."

Maureen glanced at the coins, then back at Ferret.

To his way of thinking, Ferret's action was what a good shepherd does when a sheep is lost. And yet, he knew that his kindness would be his own undoing.

* * *

For the next few weeks, Maureen heaped compliments on Ferret in public, calling him a man whose heroism reached biblical proportions. Men would snicker and women would frown. "Lordy knows, she's fishing for a husband," Badger muttered at every opportunity. He believed Maureen was a woman whose rose had been plucked and that women's only mission in life was to wedlock and grow fat with child. When it came to capturing a bedroom partner, they schemed like warring generals, using offensive tactics to pursue goals that would put battle-hard Celtic warriors to shame. Ferret saw it differently, reckoning that if women's skills were ever applied to other areas, men would someday find themselves demoted.

Maureen's assault began by presenting Ferret with food. First, it was sugar-brown biscuits. Another week, he was besieged with steaming hot hutsepot stews. Later, it was cheese pies. After that, she offered to sew Ferret's frayed shirts and wash his breeches. Finally, she gossiped about recently wedded couples.

However, instead of alluring Ferret, she repelled him. Ferret half agreed with Badger's assessment of women. He also hated the thought of marriage. He could not recall one marriage that had remained happy. He saw marriage as living torture—a screaming, pot-throwing melee, a combative match that made the bloodiest cockfight appear benign. Matrimonial "bliss" was not for him.

He considered Maureen as a beautiful rose that languished on a thorny stem. A single prick could cause considerable pain. She had what most men did not—a formal education. She had studied long and hard under Aristot's tutelage. Her knowledge of the classics was breathtaking, her skill with language impeccable. She flaunted her flawless use of the Queen's English and often corrected people's grammar in public, including his own. He considered that a terrible liability for any man. Her greater skills gnawed at Ferret's self-worth and undermined his authority. He found it humiliating and threatening.

* * *

One day, Ferret visited Maureen and found her forlornly sipping tea from a chipped cup in her small, cold hut. She shivered on a floor of wicker, leaves, and hay. Her few belongings were scattered about.

He crawled into the low canvas tent and found her withdrawn, talking to herself in a confused, rambling manner. Ferret tried to get her attention. "Miss O'Hall?"

She ignored him.

"I did enjoy your hutsepot stew."

"I've been a muddle-headed fool." Her eyes remained downcast and she clenched her teeth. "Please leave me be."

Ferret felt a need to convince her otherwise. "You're not a fool."

"And you make for a most terrible liar, Captain Ferret O'Neill." Maureen lifted her face. He noticed her larger than normal eyes again. They were lustrous and very round. She studied him for a moment, turned away, and closed her eyes.

A gust of cold wind swirled inside, causing Ferret to shiver. "I must find you better lodging. 'Tis the least I can do."

She looked up again and gripped Ferret's wrist tightly. "Why?"

"I'm responsible for your plight. You followed me into the dockyard. You were arrested and imprisoned aboard the *Green Sounder*. It haunts me like a witch's curse."

"You have it all wrong." Maureen raised her voice. "Everyone affixed to Aristot was arrested and jailed. 'Twas Cromwell's fault. Pity him."

"I still wish to help you."

"I'm beyond help. I'm dead." She turned away and rearranged the hay on the floor.

Ferret knew there was a woman hiding somewhere inside Maureen's harsh exterior. He was convinced that only circumstance hid her true, luminous beauty. He knelt in front of her and gripped her shoulders. "You're alive and ill—I mean well."

"You had it right first," Maureen said. "I make poor company. I have striven so diligently to shove you away." She poured some cold tea into a cup, stirred it with a stick, and handed it to him.

Ferret took her hand instead. His strong fingers entangled her spidery ones. He kissed her hand. Maureen stared at Ferret with her big, seductive eyes. They sat for what seemed like hours, gazing at each other, hand in hand, happy to know that each cared for the other. They realized that they had a future together, one that could bring happiness and companionship.

As darkness approached, Maureen lit a small candle which was protected by a wooden box. The little flame glittered across the small tent, illuminating one side of her soft face. "Come closer, my dear," she said, reaching for Ferret and pulling him to her lips.

Ferret's hands inched around her soft buttocks. He pressed. His skin had turned hot and sticky. He wished he could squeeze her tighter. Reaching for her loose-fitted outer garment, he lowered it on one side. With one slight tug, it tumbled down, revealing one of her white breasts. He kissed it just above the nipple. He felt he could do almost anything with Maureen. But she was not some harlot in a bawdy-house. He didn't want to cheapen the moment. With effortless grace, he rehung her dress above the shoulder, covering up her breast.

277

Maureen began to cry and rubbed her eyes with the palm of her hand.

He watched several tears escape down her thin cheek and wondered if it came from sorrow or happiness.

"I've always been a strong woman. Nobody ever rode roughshod over me. I thought I could control anything within my reach. I was mistaken. Now behold me. I'm an invalid!" She lowered her head. "I wish not to die alone."

Ferret replied, "You will not die alone. I'll be with you."

Maureen's crying grew louder, but Ferret knew now that they came from joy. Bidding her farewell, he wiped one of the tears from her cheek and kissed her one last time. "I shall return in the morning and take you away from here."

She beamed with a radiant smile. "I'll make you very happy. That I promise."

Walking near the shoreline, Ferret noticed the stars' light dancing in the heavens above—warm, enchanting, and full of life. A lean crescent moon hung alone in the heavens, so small and insignificant in the immense black sky. He felt sorry for it, but not for himself. In his new world, he lived under a two-moon sky.

* * *

The next day, Ferret ordered a room for Maureen, and within a week, he had found her work in van Noord's kitchen. She put her full energy into the task, but her cooking was truly uninspired. It might have resulted in her dismissal except for van Noord, who learned that Maureen was educated. He put her in charge of New Friesland's financial ledgers. Her knowledge of other languages gave her work writing correspondence with merchants. The longer she worked for van Noord, the more invaluable she became.

Ferret would often watch her work at van Noord's desk. Maureen had a natural beauty. Her round, delicate face was enhanced by her large, round eyes. She would speak in French, occasionally claiming that only the French could express deep feelings. Her long arms would glide gracefully. She avoided talking about her Stoicism and principles of independence and autonomy. Now, it seemed she loved to love.

The Dutch were loose in sexual matters. They shocked even the jaded French. Men would visit girls in their bedrooms. Groups of young people on holiday would ride into the countryside together, without chaperones, to play sinful games in the sand dunes by the beach. Trial marriages were not uncommon either. A girl would try out several potential husbands until one got her pregnant. She would marry the father of her child.

The engagement to Maureen had its consequences. Heather was dismayed by the wedding, saying that her brother could have done better. Maureen's alleged crimes ran the gamut. Nothing was left out. She was accused of being a spiteful shrew, sinful adulterer, cheap whore, frostbitten woman, and an ungodly freethinker. The gossip left little to the imagination.

As the marriage date moved closer, Heather's moods swung wildly. Acting like a scorned woman, she would refuse to cooperate with Ferret and nitpick at the most trivial of things. At other times, she attempted to become indispensable, fetching him hot food, mending his clothes, cleaning his boots, anything that Ferret might desire. When that failed, she would revert to odious ways, scolding him for neglecting her or failing to do something right. The contrast was dramatic, almost comical. One night she tried to kiss Ferret fully on the lips, instead of her usual sisterly peck on the cheek. Ferret had to gently push her away and remind her that he was betrothed to another woman.

Ferret followed the traditional Dutch custom and placed a green wreath on Maureen's door. She pinned a white sprig of wildflowers on her dress, the symbol of true love. Their official courtship was short, and they were officially married at the betrothal, when they exchanged vows, cut their fingers, and drank each other's blood. They had a public wedding ceremony a week later.

The wedding was long and cumbersome, and revolved around a somewhat secretive mass. Since masses were officially prohibited, Rotterdam's burgomaster required a hefty sum to circumvent the law. Van Noord offered a loan, which Ferret refused. Holbrook insisted he could afford the fee, and did so as a gift. Secretly, Holbrook had borrowed the money from Othello who, in turn, had borrowed it from van Noord.

After the ceremony, the new couple and their guests plunged into a lively feast, which quickly became an orgy of shouting, drinking spiced wine and ale, and eating. Rutten and Badger spun lewd stories, while others sang songs of sensual love and blissful happiness. Everyone—even Heather, though still frail—danced country jigs. An old woman recited Germanic poetry that spoke of the delights awaiting the couple in bed.

As the celebration heightened, Strongbow and Rachel arrived. Although Ferret had prohibited Strongbow's appearance, Heather had begged him to come. Strongbow watched the half-drunk Ferret from a distance. Finally, he found Maureen and offered her a gift—a silver spoon. She cried and hugged him. Silver spoons were rare and expensive.

Late into the celebration, several young guests captured Maureen and compelled her to dance to the upstairs bedroom. She stumbled and twirled her way up the stairs. The guests followed her. In the bedroom chamber, they began to undress her. Maureen struggled, but they pulled off more of her garments, and she fell onto the bed, giggling. The guests continued to undress her. The Dutch wore layer upon layer to keep warm from the cold, but Maureen was scantily dressed, in the Irish fashion. When the Dutch ripped off her inner clothing, they were surprised to find her bare-breasted. Everyone laughed, including Maureen.

Ferret, who was unaware of what had just transpired, staggered into the room propped up by van Noord and Holbrook. He was told that he had to buy back Maureen and her clothing with the promise of another feast at some later date.

"I'm not a wealthy... f-fellow man of goody means," Ferret slurred. Then his eyes fell upon Maureen. The guests were beginning to pull off her last garment. He looked on with amusement until he realized she would soon be completely naked. Ferret stopped the stripping-of-clothes custom with a promise of "more feasts fit for a kingly or queenly gala!" That satisfied the wedding onlookers. In a frenzy of laughter, the guests returned downstairs, some dancing in a drunken stupor as they descended.

One last rite remained before the newlyweds were considered properly married. Maureen's uncle had demanded proof that the marriage was consummated properly before he would pay a small dowry. Both Maureen and Ferret protested until a compromise was reached. They agreed to allow Paco to witness their coupling. Paco was told to climb up a ladder and pretend to peek through a small window. The whole affair was supposed to be a farce. But Paco disobeyed, and instead gawked through the window, hoping to catch a generous show of flesh. He was disappointed. The newlyweds had collapsed on the bed, too drunk to perform. Paco climbed down the ladder and was immediately accosted by nosy revelers. He had to invent the details, complete with graphics and obscene hand gestures that delighted giggling women and snickering men, and satisfied Maureen's uncle.

Not long after Paco lowered the ladder, Maureen stepped down from the high bedstead and peered out the window, relieved to see the street deserted. She crawled back into bed and faced Ferret.

As Maureen hovered over him, Ferret touched her naked skin, his fingers creeping up her belly to a nipple. Softly he pinched one, feeling delightfully nasty. To his surprise, his actions caused it to rise.

With an impish smile, Maureen slapped his roving hand. Groping for a candle on a nightstand, she lit the wick and lay next to Ferret, pulling off the last of her clothes.

Ferret wondered why she needed candlelight.

"I want to see."

"See what?" Ferret pulled the quilt and bed sheets back over his naked body.

"Don't be silly." Maureen threw the covers off. "I've never seen a man's pump handle. At least not up close."

Ferret rolled on his belly, his mind still muddled from the strong wine. The lure of sleep had more appeal than plowing her garden.

"Fiddle-faddle! You act like a wretchock." Maureen slid closer to Ferret, stroking his back with tender care.

It did not take long for Ferret to rise to the occasion. He turned on his side and embraced her, his body quivering slightly as they pressed closer together.

"You're shaking," Maureen said.

"I'm nervous."

"So am I, husband."

Ferret felt clumsy and awkward. He wondered why anyone would go to such effort just to propagate the human species. He found his first foray almost as hard as threading the eye of a sewing needle. He was sure he would find the right place, but the whole undertaking seemed crude and overdrawn.

A few moments later, Ferret discovered that the ordeal was worth the trouble. He had a fleshy and moist sensation that was both exciting and exhausting. He closed his eyes to enjoy it. Unfortunately, he was interrupted by Maureen's sudden urge to nip him on the neck, leaving a little red bite mark.

Mildly shocked, Ferret's eyes opened wide. He worried briefly about what pain she might inflict next. Then Ferret shot his arms under her back, wishing he could press her body closer to his, even for one brief moment. As they thrashed back and forth, the bed began to shake and vibrate until one of the bedstead legs cracked and collapsed, slanting the bed to one side.

Maureen laughed as they slid to the edge. "You make the earth dodder."

When the sun rose the next morning, they found themselves in a pile of quilts and wool blankets on the floor, embracing as if they had always been that way.

Part III

Chapter 28

By 1713, the colony at New Friesland had been in the Netherlands for what seemed like endless cycles of seasons.

Ferret spat over the railing of the *Triumph*. He watched the ball of spittle strike the dark water below, hardly making a ripple. The crew was carrying the last provisions below deck. Though they were finally leaving the Old World behind, he had a nagging premonition that it would pursue them wherever they wandered.

Gazing across the shipyard at the cemetery, Ferret thought about the decade that had passed. Maureen had borne him three sons, and two daughters who had died. One was stillborn, the other smothered in a featherbed, accidentally crushed by her mother. Maureen had wept for weeks and vowed never to bear another child. He secretly thought it had been a good vow; they couldn't have squeezed another person in their house. Many others had died, too. Rachel had succumbed to smallpox and been buried in a flowery shrine. Strongbow's gaiety and humor had died with her. With help and guidance from Maureen, he concealed his misery from some, but he lived a weary-hearted life of seclusion. At times he suffered from melancholia. He was unable to care for his only child, renamed Hendrick, and had to rely on the kindness of Heather and Maureen. Heather had received proposals of marriage but had never wed.

Strongbow's misery worried Ferret. Did Strongbow have the stamina to live without Rachel? Could he survive the cold nights? Would memories haunt his dreams? Would he wither away to nothing, like so many other heartbroken souls? The tragedy of Strongbow's life was heart-wrenching. Here was a man who had been gleeful and carefree as a bird, now caged in a prison of his own making. Life was too short to abandon the pursuit of happiness. Seeing Strongbow's misery, Ferret was inclined to forgive his former friend and let their past live in the past, though he had never spoken about it to Strongbow.

As he distressed over Strongbow's plight, the memory of a dog intruded on his thoughts. The dog, which he had named Lobo, had been fiercely independent, scavenging the garbage-littered streets of Cork. For years, the mongrel had hung around Ferret until the dog became decrepit. Lobo would howl in pain as he sat and licked the festering tumors under his hind leg. He was slowly starving but would take no handouts. The sound of his suffering was too much to bear. One day, Ferret took the dog to a knoll overlooking Lee River and with one of Madoc's pistols put an end to his misery. He dug a small burrow there and buried Lobo under a bed of white gillyflowers. Ferret thought that suffering could bring about similar fates in humans.

And now, after ten years, the Irish-Dutch colony was moving to the New World. Hundreds of sobbing people waved from the dike's crest. Many had decided to remain behind in the Old World. Their red faces were covered with white handkerchiefs and tears.

Heather approached Ferret as he stared at the sky. She slipped her dainty, pale arms around his waist. "We must find fault with something."

"The trees dress in too much green." Ferret moaned, pointing to a cluster of horse chestnuts on a small nearby island.

She pointed to the sky. "The sky shines with too much blue."

Ferret reached for Heather's hand and rubbed it. He loved his wife, but he had never lost his affection for Heather. If only conditions were different. He could see Heather as his loving wife, loyal and true, a woman with the capacity to give love and be loved. He still had not told her the truth about her unknown heritage. He realized he probably never would.

"We stayed too long," Heather said. "And you're thinking of Arthur again. You should think of something more pleasant. A nipperkin of ale, mayhap. Thick and syrupy. Just the way you fancy it."

Ferret turned away and faced the placid bay. He could not help but train his thoughts on one particular problem in his big litany of worries—his troublesome cousin. Arthur had arrived in New Friesland three years prior to his banishment from Ireland by the British authorities. Upon his arrival from Cork, he used his wealth to buy a position on the council. At first, Arthur's attempts to control the council failed, but as time passed, his persistence paid off. The council gave in to Arthur's many demands. Ferret thought Arthur was trying to cozy up, ingratiate himself, and test the council's resolve. That was easy to see because Arthur had hired a band of rough men whose only allegiance was to Arthur. One day, he knew, the council would regret the day they had ever partnered up with his cousin.

Ferret turned his eyes on Heather, touching her slender neckline and long curly hair. "You're so lovely this morn."

Heather blushed. "Now, now, brother. You're a taken man. 'Tis a shame too..." She frowned as she spotted Maureen strolling across the deck, followed by her two youngest children. "I mean, you could have done better. But of course, nobody pays any mind to her trollop past!"

"She was never one of them."

"I suppose she wasn't a wanton blowzy. But you might have become infected with the pox or lost your sight or a leg or—"

"Or a half-sister." Ferret turned away from her. He wondered if a man truly could love two women at the same moment. He didn't feel quite right about having such strong feelings for both. It did not seem proper or wise.

Van Noord approached and wished Heather a good day, as he pointed to a passing forest of tall whirling windmills that rotated in the distant horizon. He pointed off into the distance and spoke: "'Twas built over two hundred years ago. The Hagg Dike be far older." He attempted to say more, but he shuddered with a hacking cough. Holding the railing, he tried to catch his breath.

Darbee, Ferret's seven-year-old son, poked his head between van Noord and Heather. "Why must we go?" he asked.

"The Lord," van Noord said after clearing his throat, "has sent us forth on a great mission."

"Could he not let us stay home?"

With difficulty, van Noord lowered himself to Darbee's eye level. "See those dikes?"

Darbee nodded.

"They've been here since the twelfth century. Someone had to build them, someone from distant lands. They came to drain the swamps, build earthen dikes, and bring forth a new nation."

Darbee peeked over the railing to see the dikes better. "But they're just mounts of dirt."

Ferret noticed how much van Noord was shaking. He felt he had to say something. "You ought to go below. Your health—"

"And you ought to keep a watchful eye on Arthur." Van Noord then turned and walked away, coughing.

Ferret felt powerless. A foreboding chill of doom was threatening to engulf him. Van Noord's health weakened daily along with his ability to control Arthur O'Neill. Without the influence of van Noord, the colony was almost defenseless against his cousin.

A strong gust billowed *Triumph's* white sails like pillows, pushing the flagship ahead of the other two vessels. Ferret sniffed the cold, humid wind and sensed a change in the weather. He felt positive that stormy clouds lay ahead.

* * *

With all of the political infighting whirling around Arthur, sometimes Ferret thought his only loyal friend was his large Irish setter. Ferret had wanted to name the large dog Lobo, but it had already been named Zeph by its original master, a courageous sailor on a Dutch warship. As the story was told, the sailor had rescued many of his shipmates after an engagement with the French, but he was unable to save himself. Zeph had escaped and had even managed to pull a drowning Dutch officer ashore. The dog was pronounced lucky and given free run of Netherlands' wartime fleet. Sailors would compete to brush the dog in hopes that some luck would rub off.

The rescued Dutch officer had assumed full custody of Zeph after the war. Upon his return to New Friesland, he was put in charge of requisitioning needed supplies for the colony. During one fateful resupply trip to a nearby province, the officer was caught in a smallpox outbreak and died. A fierce battle brewed over the dog's new ownership. Although

Zeph had been left in van Noord's custody while the officer was away, the strongest bids for the dog came from the three ship captains who understood the danger of superstition and the benefits of perceived luck. The fear of sinking into the Atlantic could paralyze a crew, or worse, inspire mutiny. Zeph's presence could instill the belief that safe passage had been guaranteed. All three captains knew this, and they would do almost anything to keep the dog.

Custody over Zeph was resolved not long after Captain John O'Marr of the *Lady Pegasus* unsheathed his sword and threatened to gut Captain Abe McCloud of the *New Hope*. They circled each other, face-to-face, each waiting for the other to strike first. Eventually, van Noord intervened by suggesting they use playing cards to decide the dog's ownership. Captain Ferret drew the king of hearts and won Zeph.

Not everyone held a favored spot in their heart for the hefty dog, so large that a child could ride him. Othello regularly shook his angry fist at Zeph and besieged Ferret to cast off the flea-bitten mongrel. "You should not touch the cur. They be 'the rankest compound of villainous smell that ever offended the nostril.' And that be from Shakespeare." Like most Moors, Othello believed that dogs were filthy, unfit companions. Once, however, when pressured, Othello scratched Zeph's shaggy fur cautiously. Examining his fingers afterward, he felt grease under his fingernails. He cursed the dog at the top of his lungs, and everyone backed away, afraid that Othello would be struck by lightning at any moment. Othello lost several friends because of that incident. They were afraid to stand next to a marked man.

Othello had lost other friends, mostly over his discriminating way of identifying men's good and bad traits. In his mind, the greatest gift to mankind was the appreciation of truth and beauty. He had made it his lifelong quest to become an ardent truth-seeker. But this devotion to truth compelled him to drift away from Strongbow. His old friend had fallen in with the wrong crowd—those who sought to prosper at the expense of others. As Othello saw it, Strongbow was associating with bad actors who sought goals and not necessarily the truth. Othello often warned Strongbow that to ignore the truth in exchange for gains was a poor man's bargain. Such comments only provoked Strongbow's temper.

* * *

Seven days into the voyage, van Noord took ill with jaundice and fever. As the sea turned gloomier, so did van Noord's health. His lips turned blue, and his face shriveled up. He was incapable of command.

As van Noord tossed and turned in his bunk, the *Triumph* rolled in a rough sea. Whirling black clouds exploded from the south as thunder crackled overhead. The ships listed, buffeted by high waves that reared nearly over the topmast. They had entered a world of piercing rain and slashing wind that no one aboard had witnessed before. Ferret attempted to keep the other ships in sight but lost them between troughs of wind-tossed waves.

Arthur and his men had watched van Noord's waning health with the interest of circling vultures. During the height of the storm, Arthur made his first move. With his gang in tow, he swarmed over the stern, grabbed the helmsman, and overwhelmed him with punches and kicks to the groin. When Ferret saw the commotion he came running. One of Arthur's men pushed him aside, pinning him against a mast pole. Ferret broke free, twisted around, and floored the man with a single blow.

"I'm the captain," Ferret shouted, trying to compete with the ear-shattering wind and ocean spray. "You have no right!"

"I do!" Arthur defiantly sneered. "Ask van Noord. I've just been chosen leader." He snapped his finger and a half-dozen men, including Strongbow, surrounded Ferret. He was outnumbered. One man pulled out a turnip knife and toyed with its sharp blade.

Suddenly, a massive wall of water crashed onto the top deck, washing everyone to the starboard side of the ship. Picking himself up, Ferret scrambled below deck and tried to figure out what to do next. Despite his escape, an air of hopelessness hung over him. It suddenly struck him how devious Arthur could be at playing political games. It was suicidal to yank his crewmen away from their duties during a tempest. If he did, the ship might topple over and sink. At the same time, if he didn't round up his loyal sailors and arm them, the ship might fall into the hands of his cousin.

He knew the crew would put the safety of the ship first and a power struggle second. This was the weakness of dutiful men. Even if the meek did inherit the earth someday, who would want it? The strong would have already achieved their ruthless ends.

As he hurried to van Noord's cabin, Ferret began to map out a course of action. At first, he thought about gathering all the councilmen together. At that point, he could pressure them to condemn Arthur as a mutineer. But that was probably a waste of time. Without muscle and grit to back up their decision, the council's actions were empty gestures.

Entering the cabin, Ferret first bumped into Pragg Nattle. He had been keeping a nightly vigil by his friend's bed. Only he would know if Arthur had actually talked to the leader of the colony.

"Did van Noord converse with Arthur?" Ferret quickly asked.

"Arthur came here," Pragg said nervously. "In a hurry-scurry, he was."

"Did they talk?"

"I heard nothing."

"Just as I suspected," Ferret roared, pounding his fist on the table. "He wishes to seize my position."

"So?"

"I'm in command!"

"Apparently not for long."

Pragg had always been an astute observer and could be brutally honest when he spoke his mind. Ferret realized he had to be quick, decisive, and brutal to his adversaries. To take any other road would permit both enemies and fellow travelers to seize his rightful power.

Ferret went back to the top deck and searched for crewmen who could be pulled from less vital jobs.

The first men he came upon were Holbrook, Othello, Rutten and Harpoon Jack, who were huddled together. Holbrook was talking about the damage to the ship. He saw Ferret and made his report: "The ship's taking on water, and our bilge pump has been damaged. The mizzenmast has cracked—might topple at any moment. The foretop and rigging—"

Ferret interrupted him. "Assemble some men now and issue them arms, Mr. Holbrook!"

"They work on repairs," Othello said, raising his eyebrows.

"Arthur has instigated a mutiny." Ferret pointed to his cousin standing at the helm amidst his small army on the other end of the ship. "We must rouse those who are not on duty."

"Most are up," Othello said. "They're needed here. Otherwise, we might as well scuttle her. We'll sink if we fail to make repairs."

"Then, by God, let her sink! I'm not giving up command without a fight."

"Begging your pardon, Sir, but the sea be far more unmerciful! It gives no quarter."

As Othello spoke, an ocean swell slammed into the ship, flooding the half-deck completely. Losing their grip, Ferret and Harpoon Jack were swept across the deck, barely catching a loose rope at the railing. Othello reached out, wrapped his massive hands around Ferret's waist, and pulled him from below the washboard. Harpoon Jack had stayed aboard by plunging his harpoon into the wood decking. Othello smiled at them both. "I say we parley with the swagger."

Ferret nodded and hurried to the helm to face Arthur. He knew he had to take his nemesis by the throat and knock him senseless. When he arrived, he pointed his finger at the traitor and shouted, "I take unkindly to ill-sop mutinies. You're under arrest!"

Arthur chuckled with barely any humor in his voice. "You're the one disobeying van Noord's order!" Arthur motioned for his men to seize Ferret.

Othello intervened. He towered over Arthur and the others, forcing them to move away from the helm. He spoke with a deep, commanding voice. "Sir, Captain Ferret has been designated the successor upon van Noord's death. Do you dispute this?"

"I do!" Arthur snorted and narrowed his eyes. He turned to Strongbow and ordered, "Kill them. Kill them all!"

Strongbow raised his broadsword.

Othello reached down and slipped a blade from his high boot. Harpoon Jack raised his harpoon.

"Come nigh, old mate." Othello motioned his knife towards Strongbow.

Strongbow slapped his forehead. "What am I doing? Why should I spar with you? I have a splendid array of expendable cutthroats." He waved for his men to attack Othello and Harpoon Jack.

Three scruffy-looking men gaped at Othello's height and girth. "Lordy," one let out a loud gasp, "he's as big as a Bartholomew pig."

Strongbow repeated his order.

The three men raised their clubs and surrounded Othello like a vicious dog pack preparing to attack a large bear, unsure how exactly to topple their prey. They finally leaped at him, one at a time. Othello threw one of the swag-belly men overboard; he sank beneath the surface of the raging water. The other two were flung senseless against the outer cabin wall. "I would be pleased to entertain more auditions," Othello said, cracking his knuckles and bowing.

Harpoon Jack fared just as well. The two men assigned to attack him were armed with wet pistols and small cutlasses; they were no match for the dead-eye accuracy of the harpooner. The men lifted up their hands and surrendered.

Ferret strolled up to Arthur and poked his finger into his chest. "I will not press charges if you abandon your mutiny."

"We'll see," Arthur said, smiling feebly. Suddenly, he rushed past Othello and down the companionway. In like fashion, the other men scattered. They all disappeared below.

"Get to the armory!" Ferret said. "Round up some of the colonists and capture Arthur!" Time was running out. Ferret knew Arthur would strike again, but with more force and men for the second round. Putting Rutten in charge of the helm, Ferret hurried off the bridge, in search of other loyal crewmen and colonists.

Arthur found the council first. He had sent his men to each councilman's cabin and demanded an emergency meeting. The councilmen objected vigorously, but were told that "no" was not an option. They were forced out and herded toward the captain's cabin. Arthur escorted the councilmen inside, startling Maureen, Heather, and the children.

Maureen blocked Arthur's path. "What do you think you're doing?"

"Cleaning out the rat's nest." Arthur pushed Maureen aside and motioned his henchmen inside.

"Captain Ferret will have you under the headman's axe," Maureen said.

"I think not." Arthur snickered, then ordered the children taken to an adjacent room. Maureen tried to follow them, but she was blocked.

Arthur sauntered up to Heather and attempted to steal a kiss. She turned her face away in disgust. Arthur grinned with a gleeful smirk on his face. "You would do better with me."

"I think not," Heather said, scowling.

Arthur turned and gestured for his nervous guests to sit down. "I gathered you here for important matters. Captain Ferret has disobeyed van Noord's final orders. He is an insurgent, a pretender. I am here to rescue you from his misdeeds."

Maureen had refused to sit. She moved closer to Arthur. "What final orders?"

"Ferret's in command," Johan van Perk whimpered sheepishly. "Be he not?" He tried to stand but fell backward with the rolling ship. Wrapped in damp blankets, the other councilmen sat silently.

"Van Noord has honored me with command," Arthur said.

"Be you sure?" Pragg asked, looking befuddled.

"Rightly so," Arthur said. "There's more. Van Noord has accused Captain Ferret of incompetence. As do I. He pulled men off the line to challenge my good intentions. Blatant disregard for the safety of our vessel, I daresay."

"But I heard nothing from van Noord," Pragg said.

Several large men hovered above Pragg, flexing their muscles aggressively. One of Arthur's men took off his shirt and strutted around the cabin, threatening to do bodily harm to anyone who got in his way.

"Can you be so sure?" Arthur glared down at Pragg.

Pragg looked at the menacing men and then back at Arthur. "Nothing's certain, I suppose."

"See!" Arthur moved away. "I'm the legitimate heir. Now, reaffirm my command before Ferret sinks this vessel."

Just then, Ferret entered the room. He was followed by Badger, Holbrook, and Zeph. Two of Arthur's men attempted to block them.

"I'm the Lord's watchman," Badger said, shoving a silver cross in front of the men's faces. "Do you wish to challenge my authority too?" The men stepped back and not a word was spoken.

When Zeph trotted into the cabin, he tried to leap into his favorite hardwood chair. One of Arthur's henchmen, Murray Higgins, was occupying it. Higgins was a portly man with no neck, a flat nose, and clung to a strong belief in superstition. Confronted by Zeph, he trembled slightly, but he remained seated. It was a stalemate until Zeph gave an impatient growl and Higgins crawled onto the floor. No one laughed for fear of offending the dog.

"You have no authority here," Ferret told Arthur. "Mutineers only have rights in Hell."

"I was merely exercising my new power," Arthur said.

"Van Noord's too ill to give orders," Ferret said. "And you would be his last choice."

Arthur turned to the councilmen. "I want Captain Ferret removed from this council. He's the usurper of van Noord's final wishes."

"This be an outrage!" clamored Bax Fendly, a councilman whose face was turning green as a squall of thunderstorm tossed the ship sideways. The others mumbled their dissatisfaction, folding their arms across their stomachs.

"I suggest a council vote," Ferret said, convinced that Arthur would lose.

Arthur strolled to the head of the table and plopped into a chair. He grinned as he propped his shoes on the edge of a footstool. He drew his knife and fingered its sharp edge. "My point is, gentlemen, we don't need a vote." Arthur paused and looked at Ferret. "Van Noord lies on his deathbed, and we have a faint-hearted leader over thither. He's a weak-livered milksop and pigeon-hearted knave. He allowed our honorable councilmen to be abducted from their bedchambers at an ungodly hour. He has no stomach for protecting his people."

Naturally, his cousin was lying. But Ferret knew the truth was the first casualty in battles over power. Men like Arthur came out ahead because they could lie so easily, twisting around the facts faster than a spinning waterspout. With those talents, fool-mongers could easily trick anyone into believing anything. How could an honest soul battle such treachery?

"You never had van Noord's ear," Ferret said.

"We have desperate need of capable leadership," Arthur said. "Without it, our colony will succumb to the barbarism of the wilderness. Believe me, I have beheld the savagery of the New World."

"The colony will not follow you," Ferret said.

"But it will." Arthur stabbed the table with his knife to emphasize his point. "I only need tell them that without me, they are lost. The rest follows naturally."

Ferret understood Arthur's candid statement. The colonists would follow whoever controlled the council because most of the colonists were settlers, not conquerors. They were fleeing the Old World because of power struggles, war, and oppression. They were not fighters; they were withdrawers.

Arthur got up and walked up to Ferret. His eyes flared, and his lips split into a crooked, artificial smile. "The New World savages have customs to deal with two aspiring chieftains." Arthur set down his dagger and unsheathed his sword. He pointed the tip at Ferret's chest.

Undaunted, Ferret stepped forward, touching the tip of the sword.

"Strongbow," Arthur said, "throw him your sword."

Just before the sword reached Ferret's hand, Arthur slashed at his young cousin, hoping to behead him in one fell swoop.

Ferret ducked just in time, then confronted Arthur with ferocious swordplay. Arthur jabbed at Ferret. Ferret blocked the move and twisted around, ramming his elbow into Arthur's stomach. That took the stuffing out of Arthur, giving Ferret time to pin his cousin against the cabin wall. Just then, Higgins threw a chair at Ferret to distract him.

In a flash, Arthur took the advantage and attacked. The blade gashed Ferret's forearm, forcing him to drop his weapon. Ferret dropped to his knees, blood running down his elbow. He knew his time had come. He had reacted too slowly to Arthur's challenge and believed he deserved to die.

Arthur prepared to strike the final blow when, in a blur, Zeph leaped at Arthur's throat, knocking him against the wall. Arthur struggled with the now savage dog. Arthur's men were awestruck, too terrified to interfere with an animal blessed by the hand of God.

Ferret struggled up and pulled Zeph away, allowing Arthur to rise and wipe streaks of blood from his face. Arthur did not give up. He doubled up his fist and took a swing at Ferret. Despite his injured arm, Ferret blocked the punch, seized Arthur's hand and slowly forced Arthur to the floor. "Now, who is the pigeon-hearted one?" he asked.

Arthur broke free and the two tumbled to the floor. Ferret finally immobilized Arthur with a choke hold. With his good hand, he pulled out his ancient dagger and thrust it against Arthur's throat. He demanded that Arthur's men surrender their weapons.

"Kill him, you fools!" Arthur coughed in a last-ditch attempt to elude defeat.

Higgins drew his pistol, aimed it at Ferret's head, and cocked its hammer.

Strongbow saw Higgins raise his pistol and, with all his might, slammed Higgins against the wall, wrestling for control of the weapon. In the brief scuffle, the gun fired. The bullet barely missed Ferret's head and lodged in Maureen's abdomen. The force of the impact threw her against the cabin wall. As she slid to the floor, a trail of blood was left on the wall.

"No!" Strongbow raced to Maureen's side and lifted her head; there was no response. He was holding the smoking pistol in his hand.

Ferret felt dizzy and sick. He closed his eyes. He desperately wanted to reach Maureen, but everything began to spin. He could see blood stains on her dress, but he tried to block out the image. He cried her name. He had to get to her. He had to give her one last kiss before she passed away, but Arthur kept struggling to break free. Exhaustion was beginning to overpower Ferret. He could not keep this up for long. He wanted to be with Maureen, but could not. He wanted to get rid of Arthur, but could not. Life had become incredibly dreadful. He felt trapped. All he could do was look at Maureen's pale body. He was caught between two purgatories.

Ferret finally regained his senses and ordered Arthur's men to drop their weapons. "Go on!" he shouted. "Drop them or I'll slash Arthur's belly like soft cheese, so help me." The men looked to Strongbow for instructions, but he ignored them. He was still crouched over Maureen. Without leadership, half of Arthur's men threw down their weapons. The others scrambled out the cabin door.

Holbrook and Johan collected the surrendered weapons. Johan armed himself from head to toe, carrying four flintlocks like a load of firewood.

He crammed three pistols under his belt, swung two thin swords from his hands and clenched a scimitar in his teeth.

Within minutes, Othello and Harpoon Jack arrived with a dozen men, armed and ready to fight. They grasped Arthur and his mutineers, paraded the prisoner below deck, and clapped them in irons. The rest were captured or killed after a long hunt and pitched battle below deck.

Ferret finally reached Maureen. He tried to hold back the tears. He stroked her face and watched her blood pool on the floor.

Badger made the sign of the cross, gently knelt, and prayed.

Ferret stared at the gun that Maureen's murderer had shot her with. He felt numb, and as cold as the steel of its barrel. One shot had ended the joy of his life. It had been meant for him. He was the one most deserving to die. His greed and lust for power had exacted this toll.

In a far corner of the room, Heather leaned against a wall, gazing at empty space. She was slumped forward, humming to herself the same phrase over and over again: "Hoddy-doddy, all arse and no body." Johan offered her tea, but she ignored him.

Eventually, the room emptied. Ferret remained. He tightly embraced Maureen's cold body, refusing to let go.

* * *

The next few days were chaotic. The council overreacted to the mutiny. A dedicated group of guards brandished swords and guns, positioning themselves at all companionways, doors, and hatches. No one knew for sure if every mutineer had been captured. The council questioned everyone's loyalty and imprisoned several outspoken colonists who were summarily jailed on sedition charges. Ferret realized the council's actions were close to what Arthur would have done, building up an armed state and oppressing its citizens. It reminded Ferret of what Aristot had once observed: "Rulers don't protect people; people protect rulers."

As time passed, so did much of the hysteria. Van Noord and Maureen were buried at sea in a formal ceremony. The council confirmed Ferret's leadership. Even though he felt uncomfortable taking power, he reasoned he had no choice. If he did not accept the position, someone like Arthur or Strongbow would.

* * *

It took six weeks before they spotted small sandy islands dotted with slender trees that spiraled upward toward green fronds that waved gracefully in a warm breeze. One of the better-traveled colonists referred to them as "palms."

A week later, they sighted the main coastline and kept a mile offshore. Beyond the white beaches were dark jungles of thick brush and trees. The weather was hot and muggy, and there were no signs of human life, no dwellings or vessels. It was as if they were the only humans left on earth. It gave Ferret a sense of peace and tranquility. Fewer people meant fewer problems.

They discovered a small village on the southern tip of the Carolinas. After rowing ashore, Ferret learned that they were Scottish-born settlers, and were occupying the southernmost British outpost. Otherwise, the territory was uninhabited, though it had been attacked by savages and Spaniards three years earlier. Both Spain to the south and England to the north claimed it.

Ferret decided to sail south, away from any English-controlled settlement. He believed he could better deal with the Spanish and their Indian allies. The Spanish had been friends of the Irish for centuries, once even offering to make any Irishman a citizen of Spain.

They soon discovered a wide, protected bay sheltered by offshore islands, with plenty of timber and a sizeable river. It looked promising.

Chapter 29

Jumping overboard into shallow water, Ferret began pulling the jolly launch boats toward shore. From what he could see, they had landed in what could be described as paradise. He wondered if they had reached the biblical Promised Land. It was more than what he had expected. Dense green foliage echoed to the trill songs of colorful birds. Lazy waves lapped at the white beach. Warm breezes scented the air with sweet smells of flowers and overripe fruit. A musky, steamy perfume from the jungle defied description. The land was primitive and tranquil, as if time had no meaning. It invigorated his blood and excited his imagination. They had found an uninhabited land begging to be molded by men of intellect and conviction. They had surely discovered the Garden of Eden.

From a distance, it seemed as though the shoreline was blanketed with round, spiny objects. They littered the beach so completely that he could barely see sand in some areas. A cocky Scotsman from Glasgow had warned him of just such things. He said the objects came from strange creatures of the deep. The old seaman warned him about other hazards of the New World. He spoke of endless wild lands, savage cannibals, and ferocious beasts. He also spoke of the settlers; he suggested that they would bring along bad seeds. Ferret wondered why any farmer worth his salt would sow land with defective seeds. Later, he realized the Scotsman was bemoaning the bad traits of men, who, like hermit crabs, carried their hates, fears, and prejudices along with them.

Upon reaching the beach, Ferret saw that the objects were large seashells, glistening a rainbow of colors and an oddity of shapes. He picked one up and shook it. The object was beautiful but wondered what use could be made of them.

Ferret scanned his surroundings and the horizon beyond. The trees were draped in green moss that fingered its way to the moist ground. He breathed deeply, but the air was so heavy that it bordered on being solid rather than vapor. His clothes felt clammy and sticky. There was stillness to the air, only disturbed by timid breezes that could barely be called a wind. And yet it was so green, it almost resembled *Eire*—a sweltering *Eire*, but *Eire* nonetheless.

When Heather got out of the boat, she tiptoed a short distance, listening to the shells crunch underfoot. "They crackle like stale biscuits," she said. She picked up a spiky, horn-shaped shell of pink and yellow and smiled. "Where did they all come from?"

Meanwhile, Othello looked on with indifference. One reason he had left Morocco was to escape the heat. He rubbed the back of his neck and kicked one of the larger shells. Harpoon Jack gazed at a hawk soaring north and arched his arm as if he were going to throw a spear at it. Father Yeats was preoccupied with some religious text and murmured to himself, insensitive to the alien landscape. Holbrook was commanding a small contingent of armed men in the jungle, searching for unfriendly inhabitants. With a spyglass, Winchester surveyed the sea; he appeared uneasy as if he feared something was watching. Badger was still squirming and toiling to get out of the launch.

Ferret wanted to take in the entire splendor and forget about directing the gathering crowds of colonists landing on the beach. He had to admit that he never did like being around groups. He would rather be alone with his thoughts and not have to worry about petty squabbles.

He strolled down the beach and muttered to himself, "Are we truly free now?" Although he had agreed to take charge, that fact alone bothered him. Someday a person like Arthur would rule with an iron fist and control the populace with fear and threats, real and imaginary. On that day, the people would gladly exchange liberty for security. It would come like the summer rains. Liberty was passive and shallow. Only took one bully to ring the death knell of freedom.

Trying to ignore what the future might bring, he reached down to pet Zeph, but his dog's interest soon waned. Distracted by a dray of squirrels, Zeph took off in pursuit and was soon running after every little creature that scampered out of the jungle.

Reaching a stretch of white sandy beach, Ferret dropped to his knees and closed his eyes. He scooped up a handful of warm sand and let it trickle through his fingers, charmed by its fine, squeaky-clean texture. He savored solitude and peace, but soon he was surrounded by sailors and colonists milling about in expectation of a brief ceremony.

He got up, brushed the sand off his pants and faced the crowd. "In the year of the Lord 1713, I, Ferret O'Neill, commander of the colony *New Eire*, hereby claim these vast lands as ours. We proclaim ourselves independent and free, beholden to nobody but the Lord Himself. Never again shall we be enslaved or bonded by outlanders, be they English or whomever. Fight and fight we will if any nation affronts our independence."

The crowd cheered. Ferret smiled and waved his hand. That was it. He was in no mood to pontificate further. Leave that distinct rudeness to other men. He wanted no more obligations to these colonists. He had done his job, almost dying to give birth to a new land. The voyage was completed. Let them pick another leader if unsatisfied. He knew that one day they would all forget that a Captain Ferret had ever existed. That would be fine if he could leave and explore the unknown interior. Nothing was impossible now.

Still, Ferret worried about the pitfalls the colony would face. There were almost four hundred colonists in an unexplored land without any supply line or hope of rescue if the colony floundered. They had to fend for themselves. There would be no royal colonial handouts; no serfs, slaves, foot-lickers or peasants; no buildings to huddle under, and no cellars filled with food. They would be truly sovereign and vulnerable. Even if they wanted to go back, it was too late. There were not enough supplies for a return voyage.

Running like a spooked rabbit, Darbee took a big leap and landed next to his father. Ferret's youngest son sat and started to dig, pat, and sculpture a large sand castle. He glanced up at his father. "Papa! Is this our land?"

"I hope so. I wish not to trespass. I believe it to be uninhabited."

"But how do we know?" Darbee brushed back his long, stringy hair.

"Someone will tell us."

"When?"

"When we become a nuisance."

"Ya have become a nuisance already," said Badger, who had extricated himself from the launch and made his way over to Ferret and Darbee. "We must not be idle. Our supplies be almost spent and ya sit like a sluggard." He pulled at the moss hanging from a nearby tree, and then he hobbled over and struggled to sit on a large piece of driftwood. With both hands behind him, he tried to feel the wood in order to break his fall. Finally, he let go and collapsed onto the log, panting and exhausted. He gave a short blessing.

Ferret helped his son stack shells and handfuls of sand. Before long, a wall of slouching black-robed priests approached. They were led by the oldest, Father Yeats.

"Building castles of sand?" Yeats asked.

"Nothing lasts forever," Ferret said.

"But it does, my dear captain." Yeats's humor fell flat.

Ferret believed that Father Yeats was a good-hearted man whose energies were directed toward getting people to do things that they did not want to do. He was righteous and desired everyone else to be the same.

"I have been chosen archbishop of this new land," Yeats notified those around him. He cradled his lifeless right arm as he spoke. "As archbishop, I'm empowered to perform certain duties. Captain O'Neill, 'tis now the perfect opportunity to offer thanks to the Lord Almighty."

The priests bowed their heads as Father Yeats spoke a few words in Latin. Ferret looked beyond them to the jungle, wishing again that he could explore it and forget his obligations to priests and commonfolk.

"Captain," Yeats said, "God has brought us here to answer his calling. He has appointed us caretakers of this virgin land. We must make good with the Lord's wonderful gift. I offer my most humble services, God willing. I recommend that you allow me the privilege of bestowing a royal title upon you. The coronation will be simple and brief."

Ferret was stunned by the suddenness of the request.

"You being of the O'Neill clan, the title is rightfully yours. All the lands in the New World are claimed by kings."

"I'm no king," Ferret said. "That's the Old World."

"But you must! We have need of a royal sovereign—a new country, a new king."

By now a small crowd had gathered. An Irish woman surrounded by children approached. "We beseech you," she said with a blissful smile. "Be our lord and master."

"Every nation has a king," Yeats said a confident tone.

"Not the Dutch," said Pragg. "*New Eire* remains a republic, with a ruling council of ordinary men. We live under the rule of law, not the whim of kings!"

"Then, we will vote the ordinary men out," Yeats said with a glibness that dared anyone to confront his authority. "Forget not, we Irish outnumber you Dutch lowlanders."

A young man stepped up and bowed his head in respect to Ferret. He almost sang his praise. "It would be an honor to serve you, Your Lordship."

Ferret knew no leader could ask for more devotion than such an accolade. He could almost feel a golden crown already resting on his head. And what if he refused the honor? Would they crown another, less enlightened man, someone who would no doubt become a tyrant? Ferret might have to become a good king to prevent a bad king from ever ruling. And yet he was taught that all kings were nefarious—every single one since the dawn of time. He must not get trapped into thinking that kings and queens were noble in heart and action. But could the allurement to abuse power be resisted? Ferret rubbed the back of his neck. Lord Cromwell of England thought he could resist it and was overthrown by power's potency. Despite his promises to free England from the monarchy, Cromwell beheaded friend and foe alike, and ruled like any other tyrant. Ferret and his shipmates had sailed thousands of miles to escape the old ways, yet many wanted to plant bad seeds in good soil.

Then he began to see Yeats's ploy for what it was. The priests wanted a king to rule the peasants so that the Church could rule him. They would want to build a cathedral and levy a *land-scot* on everyone to pay for it. He would not take part in that shame. Ferret shook his head with a sense of foreboding. "I need time to think about it."

The crowd of people cheered wildly as though he had said yes. The woman with the children knelt and kissed Ferret's hand.

As the crowd dispersed, Badger, who was still sitting on the log, muttered, "King... *Ha!*"

The woman scowled at Badger. "May the Lord pity your draffsack soul. They shoot traitors to the crown, I'll have you know."

Surprised by the woman's intensity, Badger tried to stand but instead fell over.

Heather had watched from a short distance, delighted to see that her brother was getting the respect he deserved. Her eyes shined with pride as she approached. "My, my, King Ferret O'Neill. There's such a nice ring to it."

"Papa's not a king," Darbee said.

"He and I are highborn, Darbee. You, too. That makes us different from commonfolk."

"I don't feel different," he replied.

Heather reached for Ferret's hand and squeezed it. "Talk some sense to your son."

Ferret grinned and turned to Darbee. "There are no real kings. There are only silly men who have become accustomed to the term."

"Tilly-vally," Heather snapped, appalled. "Where do you dig up such wild nonsense?"

"I suppose I inherited it. Nobility has its quirks."

"And I have mine." She wet her lips. "I know this might offend your delicate ears, but what will you do about Maureen's death?"

Ferret looked away and watched a wave crash on the beach. Maureen had loved the water, and they had strolled together along the shore of New Friesland for hours. She would tell him the naughty things his children had done that day. At night she would invent stories for the children. She would sit in an old chair and make up tales of elves, pixies, and Greek gods. If she were alive, she would have pinned Father Yeats's ears to his armpits for suggesting a royal title. Her absence left him empty and hollow.

"The guilty will pay," Ferret said.

"Strongbow tried to stop it," Heather said. "He's not guilty."

"I saw the smoking pistol in his hand!"

"He had no reason to kill Maureen."

"He missed! He was aiming for me."

"That's not true."

"Does it matter? Winchester will hang the lot of them for mutiny and treason."

"You cannot just hang him. He saved your life more than once. You must learn to forgive, Brother. There's a purpose to everything the Lord does. There's a reason for Maureen's death."

Ferret knew there was no reason for Maureen's death, no reason for anything. The universe was running amuck, spiraling out of control, without any shred of order or decency, and everyone was holding onto life by a bare thread.

"As king you could stop the trial or pardon Strongbow."

"I wouldn't know how to act like a king."

"Pretend. Most kings do."

"Aye, that they do, and with gusto. Of course, the council might find a king too poor a servant."

"As king you would have no need of the council."

Ferret squinted at the sun, then at Heather. A king could dissolve a council, arrest his critics, and put anyone on trial—most anything in the world—except bring back the dead.

* * *

As the colonists cleared land with bow saws and fire, they also unloaded the supplies from the ship. They had brought along pieces of a seventy-foot-high windmill that could power a sawmill or be refitted as a grinding mill. A large area of land had to be cleared of pines and underbrush to accommodate the windmill first, since it provided the lumber for all the other buildings. Next, a primitive foundry and blacksmith shop were constructed.

It had already been agreed that each family would receive five acres in the New World. Numbers were drawn out of Pragg's tricorn hat to determine who would receive what particular acreage. After that, everyone could trade, sell, or give away their land. Larger stretches of land beyond the settlement were sold by the council to anyone in any reasonable acreage, to fund public works.

New Eire was laid out as a surveyed township. The streets were designed with a square, gridiron pattern that hearkens back to the Roman days of civic planning. As it turned out, the five-acre lots were too large for merchants at the center of town. The long distance between buildings made neighborly visits time-consuming. Many property owners chopped up the parcels to under half an acre and sold the rest.

Most homesteads were built near the front of the streets. There were frame structures with clapboard siding, window shutters, and shingles on the roofs. A few were stately two-story homes with crude plaster daubed on the inside and leaded glass window panes. The poorer houses were slapped together with fallen logs, swamp reeds for thatched roofs, and windows made of cloth coated with linseed oil. Floors were covered with blankets, woven palm fronds or baked earthen bricks.

To augment their food supply, kitchen gardens sprung up in everyone's backyard. Vegetables were grown for food, and herbs for medicinal purposes. The gardens were planted alongside sizeable tobacco barns, chicken houses, smokehouses, and privies. Some had extensive workshops. A number of owners built small cottages in the expectation that more people would arrive by passing schooners.

From the start, the council had planned a colony that resembled a medieval fiefdom, weighed down with a long list of social and economic controls. That's why, even before the first structures had been completed, the colony's council began to restrict Ferret's authority. They were afraid he would transform *New Eire* into his exclusive kingdom. The council voted to strengthen the rights of its citizens, prohibiting Ferret from making any decision without the council's approval. In retaliation, Ferret prohibited the council from making any decision without first getting his approval. It became a stalemate, cordial at first, but soon polarized the settlement between supporters of Ferret's still unofficial monarchy and of Dutch republicanism. In effect, the deadlock prevented *New Eire's* government from acting. There were neither taxes nor controls by government officials eager to dictate every aspect of the people's lives. As a result, the community prospered beyond anyone's wildest expectations. There was no state-sanctioned religion to impose its particular faith. There wasn't even a military to scare or imprison outspoken citizens, although Winchester and Holbrook were in charge of setting up a citizens' militia for the general defense. Ferret soon realized that *New Eire's* citizens had what he had wanted all along—more freedom than anyone could imagine.

* * *

The first contact with outsiders occurred six months after the colony was established. Two Spanish warships anchored offshore and landed with a small detachment of soldiers and Muskhogean Indians. The Irish colonists waved and cheered the Spanish troops as they marched into the center of town. Both nationalities were deeply Catholic and hated the English with such frenzy that to fight them seemed like an official duty ordained by God. Others espoused the old adage that the enemy of my enemy is my friend. The Dutch and other nationalities were not as excited.

Ferret greeted the Spanish leader, Captain Cordez, who was overjoyed to see an Irish colony so far north into British-claimed territory. Spain laid claim to all land north of the Carolinas. Its long-term military objective was to push the English back to England. As yet they had been unsuccessful, but Cordez thought an Irish colony just might keep the English from advancing further south.

"*Señor!* Many greetings from the King of Spain." Captain Cordez's voice was high-pitched. He was short and dark-skinned; his teeth were almost black. His gums bled, and he would occasionally slap his own face to disrupt the pain.

Ferret hesitated. He watched the Muskhogean Indians hide like shy children behind the Spanish soldiers and thought they resembled wood-cuts of ancient Irish warriors in old manuscripts: long-haired, naked, and barefoot. It struck Ferret that his Irish colonists might be seen by these savages as foreigners, invaders, and trespassers. The English had been the same in *Eire* centuries before. Would he seize the land and massacre the native people, as the English had done? He felt it was important to ask Cordez about the status of the land. "Do you know who owns this land?"

Cordez cocked his head and blinked. "Who owns land? Those who take it. You do."

"I mean, which clan of warriors?"

"Oh! Si. Which *indios* claim land." Cordez took a moment to think. "I believe the Cherokee or Shawnee. But do not worry. I will send word. They will give the land to you, I promise."

"You do not understand," Ferret said. "I wish to purchase the bay and surrounding acreage."

Cordez nodded and smiled. "Noble intentions! I will see that the rightful owners are compensated. It will only take few cheap beads and gewgaws."

"I would appreciate that," Ferret said.

As they walked through the settlement, Cordez's eyes searched for something. Eventually, he blurted out his concerns. "I see no soldiers. They hide?"

"No."

"None?" Cordez rubbed his chin. "If you need men for protection, I can—"

Ferret was quick to refuse; he knew that Spanish soldiers would attract the English to *New Eire* faster than flies to fresh horse dung.

"I will leave some Muskhogees, at least. They are gentle heathens." With that, Cordez ordered six of the braves forward. Some of the younger braves were naked except for ribbons around their necks, tattoos, and body paint. The older ones wore deerskin breechcloths that barely covered their private parts. Many women blushed and turned their faces away. Heather and two other ladies gathered clothing, and, without looking at the Indians, tied garments around the savages' waists and draped wool blankets across their chests.

Cordez laughed as he glanced up at the hot sun. "Will do you no good, Señoritas. No good at all. They think us the fools for wearing heavy garments."

The Indians frowned at each other. They pulled off the clothing and blankets and threw them on the ground.

"I cannot accept these men," Ferret said.

Cordez winced at a sudden jolt of pain from an infected tooth. "Believe me, *Señor*, you'll be in need of my slaves. They will assist you to plant the land and fish the sea. They have knowledge of medicines to cure swamp fever. Listen to them. They will keep the belly from shrinking thin and the skin from turning yellow. They make good slaves. 'Tis my tribute to your admirable settlement."

Ferret gazed at the Muskhogeans. To permit slavery meant that anyone could be chained to it. Anyone could be taken and made to follow the wishes of another. Slavery cheapened all men, even the slave-traders. Yet, free men treated slavery as natural. Ferret lowered his head. It would always be so. Who could stop it?

"They will obey faithfully," Cordez said. "And they will remain until you release them."

Ferret decided to send them back within a fortnight.

Before Cordez departed, he proposed a joint venture to attack the southern tip of Carolinas. "We could strike at the English curs together at Charles Town. I have a larger fleet to the south. I could rig cannon on your ships."

"We wish to remain at peace," Ferret said adamantly.

"Do you think the English will permit you to stay here unchallenged?" Cordez spoke of the horrors of the English persecution of Catholics. "*Señor*, the English Colonies be infested with Protestants, Dissenters, and Calvinists. 'Tis our God-given duty to put these heretics asunder."

Father Yeats arrived and greeted Cordez warmly.

Ferret looked at Cordez straight in the eye. "Captain, over a quarter of my colony are Dutch Protestants. Another eighth worship in a dozen-odd sects that I don't even understand."

Cordez's face dropped. "Protestants fornicate with devil, *Señor*. They will come to naught. You should scour your colony free of them."

Father Yeats assured Cordez that the colony would remain a Catholic stronghold. "We will cast out the heretics, Captain! But all in good time."

After a few more friendly words, Yeats stretched his good arm over Cordez's shoulder. Without excusing themselves, they walked a few yards away.

Ferret was uneasy with the priest's promise. He wondered what they were saying and whether the priest was merely pacifying the Spanish captain.

As the two returned, Cordez grinned. He flashed his blackened teeth, then turned abruptly and walked back to his launch, his soldiers following. As the boat was pushed into the water, Cordez shouted, "We will destroy the English curs together!"

Within a half hour, the warships had set sail and disappeared to the south.

"They will be back," Father Yeats said. "The Lord will protect us from the unholy."

Ferret had his doubts. He felt he had given approval to Cordez and the Spanish. He was sure the alliance would lead directly to something worse than unholy.

Chapter 30

Father Yeats was agitated again. Today, the priest was bound and determined to interrupt Ferret before he could escape out the door of his two-story house. Yeats waved his arms in the air and cried out hoarsely, "The Lord shall weep oceans of tears!"

Ferret knew why Father Yeats was so vexed. The Quakers had completed their friendship hall and the Lutherans had framed the foundation of their church. Yeats's church was half-completed and unadorned, a modest structure, bleak as a horse barn. The priest envisioned something far grander. Nevertheless, Ferret felt compelled to react. "You know this for a fact?"

"You do not understand," Yeats said. "You must submit to His will. God is omnipotent."

"Have I ever submitted to anyone's will?" Ferret asked.

"You shall when death knocks."

"Perhaps I will simply not open the door."

"But you have the means," Yeats said. "You can bestow much good under your kingship. You be a decent man, principled and forthright. Why do you refuse to be crowned? The crown is just a trifle symbol that carries little weight."

Ferret chuckled to himself. He knew kingship would carry burdens, responsibility, and danger. The crown was a giant magnet that would draw in every haggard man with a self-serving scheme or a poison-dipped dagger. He would have to defend his scepter with every possible measure at his disposal. Ferret realized that a position of power would alter his sense of reality. He wouldn't even notice the change in himself; it would be almost too faint to detect. His old schoolmaster once warned that the seduction of power was so potent that ambitious men would confuse malicious demons with peaceful doves.

That was what he had seen in Europe. Kings would grow complacent and content with the arrogance of infallibility. With a republic, the people determined their own fate. They chose who would oversee them. Even the bottom rungs of society could partake in self-governance—"consent of the governed," as John Locke had put it so brilliantly.

Ferret grew impatient. For months this belligerent papist had been snipping at his authority, making little cuts and digs at every opportunity. Sometimes, Yeats would switch tactics and bait his hook with flattery and sweet talk. The biggest plum presented so far was an offer to name the three-story cathedral he planned after the O'Neill clan.

"Its height will rupture the sky," Yeats said with a devilish grin.

"You mean it will shatter our purse," Ferret said. Yeats's offer was a bribe, not dissimilar from what the devil offered Christ in the wilderness. Neither Christ nor he was dimwitted enough to take the bait.

"But society demands a proper church," the priest said. "We do it for the people's sake."

"You speak eloquently of Society's needs. How may I talk to Society? Is he among us?"

Yeats fumbled for a definition, then pleaded that it was trivial. "'Tis merely a figure of speech!"

"I know. But you want me to do so much for something that might not exist."

Yeats then appealed to Ferret's religious sympathies. "You must concur that the Lord demands someone to oversee his faithful followers."

Ferret was sick of hearing about what God wanted. Why couldn't He just do what He wanted and be done with it? Why did man always have to do it for Him?

At this point, Ferret wanted to taunt the priest. "What if there were no God?"

"Without God," Yeats said, "there would be nothing in this universe."

To Ferret, that nothingness resembled man's blindness. It seemed to him that men blinded by faith saw nothing possible unless God was involved. He had always taken a contrarian's outlook. It seemed to him that man could do wondrous works with his own two hands if given half a chance. To Ferret it seemed that any God worth his salt would want it that way. He could still remember an old religious adage that spoke of a God who would help those who helped themselves.

When he was a young child, he had the utmost respect for the clergymen at his local parish in Cork. The men of God walked on hallowed ground, and their words were sacred; they were completely above reproach. If he had a disagreement with a priest, he blamed his own ignorance or impertinence. Here, however, he understood that the church was more interested in herding society than in serving the Lord. Priests were dubious do-gooders who hid behind crucifixes and monarchies. If anyone should weep, it should be Christ.

Such was the pattern of their arguments. Father Yeats eventually made a plea for understanding, bowed quickly, and retreated.

That was fine with Ferret. He had scheduled a meeting with Othello. He had to get moving—the trial would start in an hour.

* * *

Othello had built a small cabin near the beach. Originally it was to house his tools and firearms, but it had become one of a growing number of blacksmith shops. When people discovered Othello's ironsmith skills, they went to him to get their knives sharpened, farming tools forged, and guns repaired. Othello would rather have starred in a Shakespearean tragedy, but most of the colonists were too busy building homes and tending to their tobacco to bother with play-acting.

Ferret was still vexed over Yeats's untimely visit when he entered the back area of Othello's shop, passed a hedgerow of trees and bushes, and greeted Othello. He now considered the man one of his most loyal friends. He had come to let Othello sharpen his dagger and dull his frustrations.

Before he could hand Othello his dagger, a burst of rain, brief and loud, showered down on them. Othello looked up and grinned. A display of lightning flashed to the west as faint rumbles of thunder echoed in the distance.

"My word," Othello said, "something wicked this way comes. We are in need of cover." They hurried inside the airy workshop. Wearing a black apron, Othello reached for Ferret's dagger. "'Tis a mighty tempest that brews on the horizon. Many will be battered by its gale."

"Hopefully it will be short-lived."

"It will grow worse," Othello said as he put Ferret's dagger to the grindstone and pumped the foot pedal. "When troubles come, nobody knows which way the wind will blow."

"It must end someday. Who can endure such pelting day after day?"

"Some manage."

"But it benumbs the heart and drowns the spirit."

Othello stopped. "What are we yammering about?"

"The trial for treason and mutiny."

Othello returned the blade to Ferret. "Aye, I thought so. But I had to know for sure." Othello bit down on his lip. "I'm ready. I'm too ready. But will the jury be ready?"

Ferret found it painful to think about the trial, which would begin within the hour. Doubt was intruding on his sense of fair play. Could he allow so many men to be hanged? And what of those who had played almost no role in the mutiny? It seemed like a cruel hoax to kill so many men in a land almost devoid of anything that looked human. He had come to favor banishment for all but the ringleaders. It seemed more equitable. He would propose the idea when he testified. He wasn't entirely sure how the jury would take that notion. He wondered what he would do if the jury delivered a death verdict for every prisoner.

* * *

Winchester arrived on the beach with the prisoners. Most of them had been imprisoned aboard the *Triumph* because the colony lacked an adequate jailhouse.

Winchester led the captives down the main street of *New Eire*. They were nearly two dozen men. They stirred up the dust as they dragged their irons on the newly created road that was routed through the center of town. A few colonists had gathered alongside the street to jeer. One teenage boy threw a rock that nicked Arthur's chin and bloodied Strongbow's nose. Only Paco, watching from behind a water barrel, looked downhearted.

The leaders of the mutiny—Arthur, Strongbow, and Higgins—were fettered to a bench inside Judge van Doyle's half-completed barn, which

316

would serve as the temporary courtroom. The room was stacked with van Doyle's collection of books and papers. Because the judge worried about his books getting wet from the rain, he demanded that construction of the roof continue during the court session. The workmen on the roof showered judge and jury with wood chips and drops of sweat.

"Everyone settle down!" demanded van Doyle as people filed inside. Bespectacled and draped in black, the elderly judge shuffled papers on an unstable lectern as he gazed up at the men hammering on the roof.

When Ferret concluded his testimony, he faced the judge and jury and spoke in a dry, measured voice. "'Tis true that reckless men challenged my authority at a precarious moment on our voyage. They planted the kiss of death on my cheek and plotted to betray and murder whoever stood in their way. But Arthur's conspiracy engrossed only a few traitors. Many more have been indicted for crimes of association and by hearsay. Men whose only vices were the lack of good sense and an abundance of bad choices. We must embrace forgiveness for the blind and foolhardy. We must reckon with the wide chasm between malice and stupidity. Only Arthur, Strongbow, and Higgins struck a deal with the devil. Only a few conspired against the virtues of justice and truth. And only a few should share their bloody deathbed. I say to you, slaughter not the sheep just because the shepherd has been found in the company of wolves."

The cramped room exploded in wild applause, catcalls, and hisses. It seemed that only the Dutchman, who always sought the harshest punishment for the smallest infraction, wanted all of the men hanged.

The trial appeared fair, at least to Ferret's sense of justice. Both Arthur and Higgins had an official court hearing. But the proceedings resembled a poorly-run circus. The accused took every opportunity to bad-mouth everyone and anyone, freely perjuring their testimony while ridiculing the court's authority. Without a shred of shame, they accused the council of many misdeeds including lying, cheating, and the abuse of power. Arthur maintained his innocence, claiming that he was given full control of the colony by a dying van Noord. He charged Ferret and the council with treason and sedition, swearing before God that he was doing his civic duty. Higgins confessed that he had drawn the pistol, but that Strongbow had aimed and pulled the trigger. Strongbow offered no defense. He sat in a chair, lethargic, hands pressed together, bowing his head as if in prayer.

A few minutes later, the judge instructed the jury to render a quick verdict. Ferret took the opportunity to leave the court. He did not want to hear the outcome.

Outside, Ferret met Heather and Darbee. Heather was angry.

"They will hang an innocent man," Heather said. "You didn't see what happened; I saw everything, and yet you discount my memory. Everyone ignores what I witnessed."

Darbee looked up at Heather. "But he murdered my mama."

"'Twas an accident. I know it was." Heather lowered her face to Darbee's level. "But sweetie, Strongbow is innocent, as God be my witness."

There was nothing worse than a clan in turmoil, especially when the trouble was between family members. Ferret tried to make his case without sounding critical.

"Did he not plot with mutineers?" Ferret asked.

Heather grabbed Ferret's shoulders. "You're the criminal! Will death bring back the living? Will it?"

Ferret pushed her away. "No. But evil must be punished. Someone must pay the price for murder."

"You're the murderer!" Heather slapped Ferret hard. "You're the one who should be hanged!"

Ferret was stunned as he watched Heather disappear around a corner. He felt he had lost her for good.

As he rubbed his stinging cheek, several men approached and informed Ferret that the verdict was near at hand. He was unsure of what to do. His first thought was to go after Heather and seek forgiveness. But he had no idea how severe her suffering was and how long it would be before she would calm down. He understood Heather's loyalty to Strongbow. She had promised Strongbow's dying wife in New Friesland to take care of her husband and son, which she did religiously. Both women were close and often in each other's company.

But Heather was correct about one important detail. Nobody in court had testified against Strongbow. Not one person claimed to have actually witnessed him firing the fatal shot that killed Maureen. Heather maintained that Higgins was the shooter, but few paid her any heed. Ferret could not shake the possibility that Strongbow was innocent.

* * *

Judge van Doyle tried to sip his rum-spiced tea, but he found bits of wood and sawdust bobbing up and down in his teacup. Perturbed, he glared up at the workmen, but he was only showered with another cloud of sawdust. Then he tapped his cane on the lectern and addressed the court. "Let it be recorded that every witness has spoken testimony. I call upon the jury to render an impartial verdict forthwith. You may take a little time to deliberate."

The jury showed little interest in giving a speedy verdict. The jurists joked and guffawed and chatted of the impending thunderstorm, rumored Indian uprisings to the north, and who had stolen Mary Williams's hot meat pies. The jury foreman, Rutten, spun a lewd tale about a bevy of scantily dressed maidens shipwrecked on an island. The whole jury listened with delight.

Impatient, van Doyle slapped his cane across the lectern. Unable to get the jury's attention, he stomped his feet. "Gentlemen!" They all looked up. "Sorry to disturb your merrymaking, but I require a verdict!"

Rutten stood. "Aye, ya honorable. A wee bit more time be needed. 'Tis a delicate situation here. Hanging mutineers and all." Rutten sat back down, turned to the jury and continued his storytelling. His new tale wove together memories of his first wife, a quarrelsome vixen of a woman who had murdered a midshipman with a broken draw knife.

Growing more impatient, van Doyle found his gavel and pounded it hard. "I said forthwith! No more gossiping!"

Standing again, Rutten stepped towards the judge. "What if I said 'not guilty'?"

"I would have the jury penalized and incarcerated!"

"On what charge?" Rutten asked.

"Obstruction of justice! I'll have you flogged with a cat-o'-nine-tails and then hanged in irons."

"All right, all right!" Rutten lifted his arms in a surrendering gesture. "I know a good threat when I sees one." Rutten paused to spit out a dark wad of tobacco. "Ya honorable, we come to a decision. Hard-fought verdict I tell ya. 'Twas a decision of profound implications. I mean to say—"

"Get on with it!" Van Doyle said.

Rutten strolled up to the lectern with a handwritten note. Without looking at the paper, he said, "In the year of our Lord, seventeen hundred and thirteen, this jury, under the jurisdiction of *New Eire* and—"

"Your paper is upside down," van Doyle whispered.

"Of course it's upside down," Rutten said. "I can't read. Who can? But I tell ya, it looks mighty formal this here way." The crowd roared with laughter.

* * *

Meanwhile, Ferret was wandering the center of town. He felt terribly alone. Heather—the starving girl he had saved from death—hated him. And he was about to see Strongbow—the man who had saved his life from an old witch and from the flood in Cork—convicted and sentenced to the gallows. It made little sense.

From somewhere behind him Heather yelled, "Wait!"

Ferret twisted around and spotted her. Was she shouting at him? He could see her fiery eyes glaring at him. She looked like she was ready to sink her teeth into the nearest human body.

"You owe your miserable, crack-brain life to Strongbow!" Her voice grew hard and cold.

Ferret picked up his pace and ignored her rant. He was in no mood to be assaulted again.

Heather caught up with Ferret. She grabbed him and twirled him around. "Strongbow saved your worthless skin! Does that mean anything?"

Ferret fired back with his own secrets. "And I saved your skin! Does that mean anything to you?"

"What?"

320

"I rescued you from the hinterland. You were wandering like a lost, half-starved fawn. I fastened a rope around your waist and dragged you halfway across *Eire*. Strongbow refused to lift one finger to help. He's no Saint Patrick by any measure."

Heather's face went blank. She lowered her voice. "You... found me? But I'm not an orphan. I'm your sister!"

Ferret had revealed too much. He swallowed hard and shifted his weight to one side. "'Twas near Raca."

"Then... who am I?"

Ferret refused to answer and walked on. He decided to shut out everything: the trial, the hangings, anything that caused pain. He had experienced enough unpleasantness to last a lifetime.

As suddenly as he began, Ferret stopped. Too often he had seen miserable, empty-hearted men shut out everyone. They breathed air, pumped blood, and broke wind, but they had no reason to walk the earth with another soul. They lied to themselves each day and pretended that nothing had changed. The lucky ones found truth and peace with a steady pistol. If he had kept walking, he might have suffered the same fate.

He turned around to discover Heather had disappeared again. It was Winchester's turn to trespass on his fragile, unsettled mind.

"Did you hear the verdict?" Winchester asked as he approached. "Hard to believe, but the muddle-headed fools voted for decimation. Miscarriage of justice, I daresay. They should all be hanged, not just the bloody conspirators. Bad weeds sprout in any soil. To kill the ringleaders does not kill the struggle."

"How many will be hanged?"

"Arthur, Strongbow, and Higgins. All the rest will be banished. I daresay these miscreants will bring the English wrath upon us sooner or later."

* * *

The banished prisoners were taken aboard the *Triumph*, transported two hundred miles south of *New Eire*, and set ashore, abandoned to the wilderness. Such practices were common. The English monarchy routinely dumped criminals and debtors along the coastline. It was a way to save costs. Nobody was expected to last more than a few months.

The three condemned men remained in the stockade. A gallows was built hastily, next to the windmill. Gangs of children mocked the prisoners and threw hard dirt clods at them. Arthur threw them back until Gubby stopped him.

The day before the prisoners were to be hanged, Heather volunteered to serve them their last meal. She scooped stew into a small wooden bowl and pushed it through a barred window.

When Higgins seized the bowl to inspect it, the stew spilled onto Heather's gloved hands. Removing her soiled glove, she scooped a new bowl and offered it to Strongbow. When she pushed the bowl through the bars, she begged for a favor. "I am in need of assistance."

"I wish I had something to offer."

"But you do. Can you tell me who I am?"

Strongbow squinted his eyes and opened his mouth. He touched his lips. Finally, in a low voice, he asked, "You're Ferret's sister, right?"

"I'm not and you know it."

"I don't know what you mean."

"I was the girlchild whom Ferret lugged across the hinterland. The one you wished to have no part of." Heather paused. "Please, what do you know about me?"

"More than most... less than some."

Heather sighed and drooped her chin. "If I'm not an O'Neill, then who am I? I must know!"

Strongbow remained silent and gave no reply. Then he noticed that Heather's right hand was thumbless. "Your thumb. What happened?"

Heather immediately jerked her hand away, very self-conscious about her hand. She had always been careful to keep her hands gloved so as to hide her deformity from the public. "'Twas so since birth, I've been told."

"I... I was once told that I begot a daughter with a deformed hand." Strongbow's voice lowered to a whisper.

Heather's voice quavered. "Near Raca?"

"Aye. Near Raca..." Strongbow stepped back, astonished. His mouth was agape.

"What became of her?"

"She... she died." Strongbow moved closer to her, reached for her hand, and caressed it. "'Tis impossible... She died so long ago."

"What of her age?"

"It would be the same as yours."

"Could I be her?"

He turned away, trying to hide his tears.

"I've always had this silly notion," Heather's voice trembled, "that I was not of the O'Neill clan, that I belonged to someone else."

Strongbow's face sagged. He squeezed her hand and kissed it. "This cannot be. No good can come from it. 'Tis better to be a sister of a king than the daughter of a murderer. Don't torment yourself. Please leave." He walked away, dragging his leg irons, to a dim corner of the stockade.

"No," Heather murmured to herself. She shook her head. Tears rolled down her cheeks. "I wish I had a true father, even if he is a convicted murderer!"

* * *

At home that night, Heather pulled out the silver spoon that Strongbow had given to Maureen. She examined it wistfully then tapped it against her warm cheek, feeling its smooth surface. Feeling utterly bereft, she looked for something to do with her hands. She pulled out a pot and threw everything at hand into it. Potatoes, lard, and a handful of pepper. She appeared to care little what she cooked or how it would turn out. It was something to do, something to keep her hands and mind busy. Cooking made her feel better.

This was how Ferret found her. He thought there must be something he could do for her. He placed his hand on her right shoulder.

Heather whirled around. Glassy-eyed, she jabbed a ladle at him, as if it were a sword. "How dare you!" She jabbed again. "Go on, say something! Anything! Henceforth, I will not believe you,... you liar!"

"You know then?"

"I know of your little bemired secret. I'm not an O'Neill, and Strongbow is my father! You knew all along!"

Ferret stepped back, puzzled, trying to remember what he had seen at Raca. "That's not possible. I saw his daughter's remains. She had been consumed by fire."

"'Tis so indecent of you to say that to me now." Heather's face seared red. Droplets of sweat beaded on her forehead.

"Must I repeat? His daughter died in Raca! Strongbow's wife and her children died in that village, burned beyond recognition. I hope never to see such a horrid sight again in my life."

"You saw them?"

Ferret nodded.

Heather's body slumped, her eyes downcast. "Then who am I? Beelzebub's bastard?"

"An abandoned orphan with nowhere else to go. A child whom Uncle Madoc would have booted out unless I came up with a convincing lie. That lie saved your life!" Ferret reached for Heather's thumbless right hand, pulling off her glove. It was then that Ferret recalled Strongbow's description of his daughter, once mentioning that she had a similar deformity. Was it a coincidence?

Heather jerked her hand away and clamped it across her low-cut bodice. "I beg for mercy. I must know if Strongbow fathered me. You must delay the execution. I need more time." She paused as tears welled up in her eyes. "You said Strongbow's wife and daughter were burned beyond recognition. How do you know this to be true?"

"I don't." Ferret bit his tongue, knowing he was now in an awful situation. He was powerless to release Strongbow, but he could not wrong Heather. Life was becoming more unlivable with each passing moment. "The jury has made its decision! I can't overturn a judicial ruling."

"You must release him!"

Ferret slumped into a chair and stared at Heather. He knew something about hanged fathers—knew it all too well.

Chapter 31

"God-a-mercy!" Heather exclaimed. "Must I beg on my knees? You must free him!"

"I cannot interfere with the court's ruling! 'Tis the law of the land. I'm helpless."

Heather's eyes started watering again. Rage had sapped her energy completely. Her knees buckled. She collapsed and landed cross-legged on the floor, her face gripped by profound sadness. Her breaths were shallow, bordering on another bout of sobbing.

Ferret stooped low and laid his hand on her shoulder. She remained motionless, oblivious to the comfort he was offering. His fondness for Heather had never ceased, even after he had married Maureen. He remembered the day—it seemed like centuries ago—when they were young and Heather had played the part of a bride. She convinced him to play the groom and they both engaged in a lively and complicated Rigadoon dance. Clumsily, he tripped and they both tumbled to the floor laughing. She hugged him, thanking him for a most wonderful marriage. Heather was pure of heart, almost impervious to anger and vengeance. She forgave others, never complained, and radiated the innocence of an affectionate child. Now she had sunk to the dregs of despair. He hated to see her brought down this way. He understood the weight of hopelessness. But he needed time to digest what he could do. If he did do something and got caught, it could bring him down, swallowing him whole like Jonah's monster.

Ferret touched her wet cheeks. She was a full-bodied woman, yet she was also petite and graceful, with a glowing softness that Maureen could never possess. She was a white dove in a black-hearted world. He had offended her deeply. He felt her love escaping like a feather that had been blown to the four corners of the earth, never to be retrieved or cherished again. He had become her enemy, and unless he did something soon, she would blame him for Strongbow's death. That loss would signal the end of almost everything remaining that he held dearly.

"Maybe... I could do something," Ferret said with reluctance.

"You could?" Her voice barely rose above a murmur.

"'Tis a possibility. Nothing is completely hopeless."

She stared at him for a moment, eyes still watering, and then she tackled him with a tight hug. They landed on the floor. She peppered him with kisses on his cheek.

"I cannot promise much."

"Beggars cannot be picky," Heather said. "We ate the same bread and slept naked in the same bed, but we were unrelated. Were we wicked? Some might say sinful? Contrary to God's will?"

"No!" Ferret said. He had never done anything improper. She had taunted him with her body. But that type of teasing came naturally to women; they had to deal with a constant shortage of men due to heavy drinking and war.

Ferret sat up and rested his hands on Heather's waist. She did not resist and even drew closer. He put his mouth close to Heather's ear. "I've always had a heartfelt warmth for you, far more than a brother ought to feel. I told no one. I was duty bound. It was my secret obligation. I swore to keep you and my secret alive, out of harm's way. I prayed that you would wed early so that all my temptations would die." He paused. He was afraid that he had been too truthful. "We must not be together."

Heather wrapped her slender arms around his chest and pressed herself against Ferret's body. "An affinity would indeed appear sinful."

Ferret's fingers combed her fine, silky red hair.

"I often asked the Lord to be unrelated to you," Heather said, her voice quavering. "Lord knows how I prayed. If only we were strangers of blood and lovers of heart."

Ferret embraced her like an affectionate brother, unsure what to do. Then he kissed her, lightly on the lips, wishing he could kiss her until the end of time.

She reciprocated, awkwardly at first, but their kiss soon became passionate. Her eyes blossomed with joy. It was beautiful; it was dangerous.

"Do you remember, dear Brother, when I showed myself to you? I was so proud of becoming a woman." She began to undress, unhooking her ruffled bodice in the front. She unlaced her corset and slipped it down, exposing small round breasts.

Ferret rose to his feet and helped Heather up. Taking her hand in his, Ferret escorted his beloved down the short hallway to his bedroom. He shut the door as Heather sat on the bed's edge.

With nimble fingers, Heather removed her corset. "I've waited so long." She purred, almost like a cat. "I would not have been happy with any man except one. But he was taken."

Naked now, they lay down next to each other. Ferret stroked her smooth skin and studied the deep curves of her body. Her beauty was illuminated as a shaft of moonlight highlighted her creamy-white body and dark triangle of pubic hair. He saw that she had a thin ring of black hairs encircling her nipples. He pulled at one until he had wrapped it around his finger.

Heather gently slapped him.

Ferret then moved over Heather and entered her, causing some pain and much delight. He bit her neck, leaving a purple mark as the bed creaked and swayed.

"You're good at the featherbed jig." Heather giggled, then she became quiet, suddenly overpowered by pleasure and happiness.

Rolling his hips, Ferret pressed down and sank deeper into Heather's soft flesh.

He gasped for breath as intense waves of pleasure surged over him. After peaking, he felt relaxed and spent. He took her face in his hands and kissed her lips. Their bodies were dripping with sweat.

"A child of my own, that's all I ask," Heather said in a hushed voice. "I hope the Lord is listening." She stopped talking as if deep in thought and mulled over what just happened. She stared at Ferret. "We must tell no one. You have so many enemies."

Ferret nodded. If Father Yeats found out, the church would wage war on him as if he were Satan's right-hand man. But he did not think on such things long. For now, he was content to lie next to someone he had loved in secret for so long. He had never thought he would become involved with another woman. His wounds were deep, his scars still freshly crusted with scabs. He realized that time could apparently heal them—especially when somebody else helped.

"I've always wanted to make stockings for children's feet," Heather said as she shifted to allow him more room.

"We have children."

"None belong to me. I want to feel the mystery of life swell inside me."

"The pain is unbearable." Ferret had seen Maureen in labor and never wished such agony on anyone.

"Children are God's grace, my dearest." Heather suddenly felt a sticky substance on her thigh. She rolled over to one side, fingered the gooey paste, and examined it. "From you?"

Ferret grinned. Heather had no carnal knowledge of the flesh, except what the old crones had gossiped during tea time.

"'Tis all over me!" Heather found a handkerchief and tried to wipe off her body.

Ferret laughed out loud.

"'Tis not funny."

"You desire children. 'Tis the milk of motherhood."

"But it's so messy." Heather found a wet spot on the quilted bedspread and scrubbed it furiously. "This took me two years to sew. Will it stain?"

Ferret watched her scrub the quilt, enjoying the sight of her jiggling breasts.

"Men be such dirty creatures," Heather sighed as she cuddled next to Ferret.

"We're beasties, to be sure." Ferret smiled as he began to tickle her, but she did not show any pleasure from his playful antics. Her demeanor had changed to a quiet sadness.

"What of Strongbow?" Heather asked with a tremor in her voice, fear intruding upon her glossy eyes.

That's when Ferret understood the scope of what had just happened. Women were the foremost manipulators of the world, better than any shrewd camel trader of ancient Egypt. Had Heather done this to save her alleged father? He decided he did not want to know. The point was moot; nothing mattered now except his undying love for Heather. They were now part of each other and Strongbow had been the reason for his newly found happiness. He would honor Heather's claim and clan, even if he had to rescue a bottom-of-the-pit rogue.

Ferret rolled out of bed and began to dress, slipping on his breeches and shirt.

"What's wrong?" Heather asked.

"Nothing," Ferret said as he pulled on his boots. "If anyone asks, I never left the house." Pulling open a drawer, he lifted out a box and pulled out a loaded pistol.

"What are you going to do?"

"I cannot tell you." He wrapped the pistol in one of Heather's hand-kerchiefs and headed for the doorway. "Remember," he said, "I never left."

Chapter 32

"No slaves. *Nihil*," Ferret said adamantly to Captain John O'Marr.

"Some merchants won't listen," replied the captain. The half-Scotsman had worked his way up from midshipman to a commanding position on several war brigantines. Now middle-aged, his pug nose made him appear fierce as a bulldog, yet he was kind to most people. Ferret had invited him to the house for lunch. O'Marr had recently returned from a voyage up north in his search for supplies. He had parleyed with a merchant on the high seas who was eager to hawk wares and Negro slaves.

O'Marr took a sip of tea. "Aye, he was a slave trader, but most of his cargo died en route. Said he got the chattel from the Arabs near the Bight of Benin. Still, he had a few stragglers, mostly sick. Offered a good price. I told him our colony had abolished slavery."

"How did he take it?" Ferret asked.

"He cursed like a madman. Spat and bellowed that he could sell his slaves anywhere he damn well pleased."

Ferret sighed and leaned back in his chair. "If we cannot stop slavery here, then I might as well plow with dogs." He thought back to his childhood days in Cork when shackled Irishmen were marched to the market square and sold to the highest bidder at auction. They were usually feral men from the interior, or debt-ridden farmers. He had once witnessed an impoverished Irish mother and her young daughter sold separately. The child screamed and cried, clawing at the bailiff's arm until her mother was chained and carried away. Too weary to cry, the child continued to reach out for her mother hours after she had been snatched away. To this very day, in his nightmares, Ferret could see the child's face pressed against the metal bars of her cell. No one comforted the girl in her hour of desperation. Only Aristot had dared to speak out against such cruelty. He understood that "every man has a property in his own person," as John Locke had so elegantly penned.

Ferret was disturbed by what he was seeing. The institution of slavery was trespassing on his small colony and its inhabitants. A sense of fairness and justice was being violated. He addressed O'Marr: "Do you think people should be bought and sold like chattel?" Ferret sliced a loaf of sweet black bread. Heather was churning butter beside the hearth.

O'Marr watched an infant coo in a basket next to the hearth. He looked at Ferret. "What's to think? Slavery flourishes in every land, like weeds. Whatever we do, it spreads like unyielding hunger."

Ferret nodded his head. "And that was one reason why we abandoned the Old World to escape such cruelty."

"I beg your pardon, but I never felt it was cruel or inhuman," O'Marr said with an aloof tone.

"So, it's not piracy to buy or steal others?"

"They're just savage Africans. They know no better."

Ferret turned away, feeling a sickness in the pit of his stomach. It was as if God had forsaken humanity. He tried to reason with O'Marr. "For centuries the English authorities have treated the Irish like chained workhorses. We suffered under the yoke of servitude. They burdened our lives with every affliction. They extract heavy tillage, confiscate our land, and murder those who dare speak out. Do you not see? The Irish have been treated just as poorly as the most primitive Africans! The Irish be the Negroes of England."

"Nobody ever locked me up in irons," O'Marr muttered.

Ferret reflected back to Aristot's teachings. His schoolmaster kept reminding his pupils that the best slaves were those who thought they were free. He eyed O'Marr with a slight frown. "'Tis true. Most men have no physical irons to restrain them. They do the king's bidding in order to survive another day of misery. But they nevertheless cower to authority. Hate to disparage, but our bodies are not our own."

O'Marr yawned. "I say, slavery is perfectly good as long as it's done correctly. Just needs to be managed better. Anyway, I came here to converse over more urgent matters. Father Yeats says he found a mono-grammed handkerchief with your sister's initials. He says it proves that she helped the mutineers escape."

"Where was it found?"

"Don't rightly know, but if I were you, I'd keep an eye glued to your back and a gun hidden inside your belt."

"She could have dropped her handkerchief anywhere." Ferret thought back to that night, more than a year ago. He shouldn't have wrapped the pistol in Heather's handkerchief. But Strongbow begged to keep the kerchief. He said it would remind him of Heather. Letting him keep it was a mistake, too.

"Father Yeats came into possession of it recently. He will make public accusations soon, along with... other allegations." Captain O'Marr stared at the child. "Pardon me, but in particular, there's only one Virgin Mary."

"That there is." Ferret grinned, knowing exactly what O'Marr was implying. He motioned for Heather to come closer. "Captain O'Marr wishes to know where your child came from."

"The same place they all come from," Heather said, smiling sweetly. "If you had married you would understand. 'Tis not forbidden knowledge."

"Aye, I can see that, Ma'am."

Ferret enjoyed watching Captain O'Marr squirm, just like all the others who had asked the same question. The entire colony had been trying to guess the father of the child. He knew that Heather wanted to keep it secret. She feared what the colony would think and do. It was why she urged Ferret to become king. Few would dare accuse a monarch of seducing his half-sister in a night of lust. And yet to many that was almost a qualification for being imbued with blue blood.

"Some," Captain O'Marr whispered, "even believe the child to be Strongbow's. Fancy that."

Ferret locked his eyes on O'Marr and just stared. "I would worry more about finishing the rampart walls. That's more important than half-baked rumors."

* * *

A few weeks later O'Marr's words of warning about slave merchants looking for buyers came true. A ship entered the harbor, anchored, and launched six boats stuffed with pricey wares, armed crewmen, and a train of timid slaves.

Captain Jay Yankson, a chunky merchant from Boston, led eight white men to the center of town. They came to trade hogsheads of Barbados rum, crates of pewter dishes, painted chintz, taffeta dresses, and a coffle of thirty chained Negroes. The larger male slaves were joined in pairs by forked poles, which were lashed to their necks with leather thongs. The others were fettered with ankle irons bolted directly through the flesh near the back of the ankle. They stepped gingerly and with considerable pain.

The colonists soon gathered to stare at the sight of the Negro slaves. Some of the settlers dragged bundles of tobacco to the market square— since few had any coin, tobacco had become the preferred medium of exchange.

Othello showed up, too. He had been the only black man in *New Eire* since they had arrived. But because of his lighter skin, *savoir-faire* ways, and mulatto features, few in the colony considered him either a savage or a Negro. He strolled down the line of slaves, their eyes downcast, hands bound by ropes. "They're mighty black," he said casually.

Captain Yankson was a blend of pirate rogue, New England merchant, and naval officer. He wore a moth-eaten admiral's hat and two broad bandoliers across his chest. A pistol on each lumpy hip was secured only by his tight leather belt. Unshaven, his greasy black hair was braided into tails and tied off with ribbon as yellow as his teeth. He dropped a crate in the middle of the street, climbed on top, and began to peddle his wares.

"I've got stout Negroes from Guinea. Who will make me a fair offer?"

Judge van Doyle raised his trembling hand, holding two doubloons.

"They'll cost more than that, me good fellow," Captain Yankson said with a sly smile.

Van Doyle reached into his waistcoat pocket and pulled out three more coins. "I got some guilders too."

"You still need more." Yankson jumped off the crate and grabbed the neck of a tall Negro with wavy dark hair. "This here one was a prince in Sierra Leone."

"I'm buying labor, not blue blood." Van Doyle scoffed sharply.

"Sooth!" The captain nodded, then grinned. "Throw in nine large bundles of Indian weed and we've got a dandy deal."

Badger elbowed van Doyle. "You betray God's laws. Captain Ferret will not permit this travesty!"

"Why? They're not human."

Ferret had been watching the auction and was mesmerized by the swarthy men and women who were deemed subhuman, on par with pigs and horses. It seemed everyone thought the Negroes were incapable of any intelligent thought or human virtues. He could *almost* understand why. At times, their dark skin gave an ominous look of evil, as if they had been broiled in the torrid ovens of Hell and dumped on earth as blackened rubbish. Still, the English had treated the Irish with the same disrespect as Yankson showed his Negroes, and he vowed never to make the same mistake in his land. Ferret pushed through the auction crowd and prepared to interrupt the proceedings. He first approached van Doyle, and slid next to him. "Well, they appear quite human to me. Mayhap we should put you up for auction?"

Van Doyle faced Ferret. "Ah, well... I mean, mankind has always held slaves. Nothing odd about that."

"'Tis true," Ferret said as Heather joined him. "But did not the English seek to enslave the Irish and other folks? Did they not regard *us* as mere livestock? Shall we repeat those offenses here? You dwelled in *Eire*. You witnessed the abuse."

Most of the colonists looked on in silence.

"I no longer stand with the strength of an oak," van Doyle said. "And yet I require labor to tend my crops. You see, my legs sting with gout. I need slaves. They have no capacity for civilization and in that, I can take consolation. I can feed them, clothe them, and instill in them respect for the Lord Almighty. I will care for them since they be unfit to look after themselves. I mean, what more may savages expect of life?"

"Again, the English made the same claim against the Irish," Ferret said. He secretly reached for Heather's right hand and held it, caressing the tops of her fingers with his thumb.

Van Doyle continued to protest. "Is it not legal to own animals? Besides, by what measure may we declare ourselves to be free? I know of none. We all serve masters, whether God, the landlord of an estate, or a surly wife."

Heather shook her finger at van Doyle. "You can't enslave those who dance the jig of ignorance. They merely play like innocents. Who amongst you would fetter the feet of children? Captain Ferret will not allow slavery in New *Eire*. I know his temperament too well."

"Very few harbor that opinion." Othello smiled at Heather, his deep voice resonating with wryness. "In Morocco every man of wealth owned slaves. White, black, half-breed, it did not matter. I once possessed three slaves. One was white. I had them released upon my father's death. The ridicule I received was unmatched and unbefitting. I had no use for them, but slavery might be good for some people."

"'Tis not Christian." Heather leaned back and let out a sharp gasp. "Slavery is inhuman."

"Quaint notion." Othello's eyes strayed upon a bare-breasted female slave, turbaned with black hair. With fear etched across her face, the Negro spoke softly to Othello in a strange African tongue, her voice quivering with emotion.

"What did she say?" Heather asked.

"I believe she asked if we are going to eat her."

"Eat her?" Heather pressed her infant closer to her breast.

"'Tis a common question. They do not understand why else we would want them." Othello grinned. "Maybe I should say we hunger."

"Why, that's the meanest thing I've ever heard!" Heather said shrilly. "You're acting like a printle-prick. Tell her 'No!'"

Othello laughed. "I'll be a plucked goose! You *do* have the hot blood of your brother. And something else, too, I'll wager."

Heather stared at Othello, confused about what he meant.

Othello bid good day to Heather and sauntered over to the female slave. He fingered a shell and bone necklace that hung gracefully from her long neck. The woman followed the movement of Othello's hand without moving her head. She looked like a spooked horse preparing to bolt at any moment.

Captain Yankson noticed Othello's interest in the woman and walked over to him. "Jar a freeholder, Blackie?"

Othello nodded.

"Sir, let it be known that all of my wares grace the selling block. To anyone. I do not discriminate."

"But I do," Ferret said with a commanding voice.

Yankson frowned at Ferret, treating him with as much contempt as he could muster. "Ja must be one of those soft-headed Quakers! I don't cotton to radical skeptics."

"I'm Captain Ferret."

"I'm Captain Yankson, but me mates call me Yankee." The captain motioned for the Negroes to gather together, forcing them into a narrow circle. "I have many wares to hawk."

"Our colony will not sanction anyone owning another!"

"Have ja explained this quaint gibberish to jar authorities?"

"I *am* the authority."

Yankson blinked his eyes and looked around, not sure what he had gotten himself into. "Don't give me that thar cock and bull!"

He turned back to Othello. "She's a fine specimen of womanhood. A good bargain too. Would ja want to see her stripped down?"

Ferret clasped Yankson's shoulder and twirled him around. As he did, he snatched Yankson's pistols and pointed them at his obtrusive belly. "Take your slaves to some other port."

In a flash, Yankson's crewmen drew their own weapons and pointed them at Ferret.

"Now see here, Cap'n Ferret!" Yankson's eyes flared. "I have every right to sell my wares in any English port."

"What makes you think you're in an English port? We're Irish and Dutch!"

"Ja jest!" Yankson studied the other settlers with a wary eye. Nobody disputed Ferret's claim. "There're English warships up North. They won't sanction such nonsense."

Two dozen colonists, including Winchester, Holbrook, Harpoon Jack, and Badger, gathered behind Ferret and cocked their flintlocks and pistols. They far outnumbered Yankson's men.

Harpoon Jack brandished his harpoon in Yankson's face.

Captain Yankson reached out and touched the sharp spear tip. "A mighty sharp toothpick ja got thar."

"Aye," Harpoon Jack mocked. "I always keep it by me side. Never know when jar gonna spot an angry white whale of a man."

Ferret stabbed Yankson in the chest with his finger. "Don't rile me. I have the power to remove you without delay."

Yankson stepped back, wiped his brow and appeared to be counting the colonists. "I have other wares to peddle. Ja'll have much need of gunpowder, no doubt. Savages have assaulted the southern Carolinas."

"Did they kill many settlers?" Holbrook asked.

"That they did, indeed." Yankson picked at bits of tobacco in his teeth. His speech turned vulgar and he spoke quickly, spraying his audience with tobacco juice. "Heathens attacked below Port Charles. The bloody Yamasees massacred every last white freeman in the territory. Murdered women and children too. Tomahawked the lot of 'em. Worse, they cut away the men's cocks and balls and slit thar heads from front to back to scalp 'em. Bloodiest thing I ever beheld."

Yankson noticed that women had begun to back away. "Forgot my civil tongue, ladies. I say 'em horse-leeching Spaniards be behind this here war. I hear 'em Yamasees be stirring south. 'Tis trouble heading this way. I'd scatter, I would. 'Tis not like pissing in the quill. Yamasees scalp first and parley later. No gewgaws will save ja. Better escape with full heads of hair. I warn ja, they be a'coming."

"We have a well-armed militia," Ferret lied. "We can take care of our own."

Yankson glared at Ferret and scanned the unfinished wooden palisaded walls that half-circled the township. "Sure—and the fox will feast in the henhouse." Swearing once more, he grabbed his pistols from Ferret, and his men gathered up their wares. He snatched a silk dress from one woman's hand and tipped his hat. He stomped back to the beach with bundles of clothing under one arm.

Within an hour, his ship had sailed north.

* * *

Captain Yankson's remarks about Indian uprisings upset the settlers. Everyone had heard rumors about massacres in the Carolinas, ever since they had landed. Most believed that their alliance with the Spanish spared them.

Two months later the uneasiness flared up again when four badly damaged Spanish galleons sailed into the bay—Captain Cordez had returned. He asked Ferret's assistance in repairing his crippled vessels. All four of Cordez's warships had been splintered and raked, their hulls riddled with cannonballs. *New Eire* had little equipment to repair the damaged ships, but Ferret put men and materials at the Spaniard's disposal.

Cordez soon asked Ferret to join him at the church to pray for their mutual salvation. As they entered Father Yeats's still unfinished house of worship, Cordez confided that the King of Spain had taken some interest in the Irish colony.

Ferret was apprehensive. He was sure Cordez's visit had more to do with the Spanish fleet's less-than-victorious naval battle to the north. He doubted whether King Philip V of Spain had any inkling of an Irish colony in the Americas. From what he could gather, the Spanish were likely retreating south with heavy casualties. He suspected that they wanted to secure a friendly seaport from which to launch military raids against the British. He had only one searing question for the captain. "Can you defeat the English?"

"Not sure. They grow strong. They multiply like flocks of botflies." Cordez paced in front of Father Yeats's unadorned altar. He placed his heavy, two-sided *espadon* on a table, turned and fingered the unpretentious pinewood altar. "No statues. No gilding. Nothing to adorn our most holy Lord."

Overhearing Cordez, Yeats appeared and said, "We're a paltry nation. I beg you to understand. Our government has not seen fit to provide for our needs."

Cordez placed a gold crucifix on the altar.

Father Yeats bowed in gratitude.

Cordez turned to Ferret. "Señor, I see you need our protection."

"Captain Cordez speaks the truth," Father Yeats said. "We require Spain's most gracious assistance."

"It appears as if you need ours more," Ferret said, ignoring Yeats.

Cordez tried to smile, but an aching tooth made his face ripple with pain. "English curs fight like spiteful devils. They be, what do you say... unrelenting. I beg. Become a colony of *España*. We will protect you strong."

"We're a free Irish nation. We bow to nobody."

"But *Señor*, you have no ruling king. Our king will only recognize you if you have one."

Ferret understood too well that the Spanish would persecute any and all religious faiths other than Catholicism. They had done that in the Netherlands and the freethinking Dutch had revolted.

"*Mi amigo*, take kingship of *New Eire*," Cordez said. "I'm told you be high born."

"Aye. But I refuse to rule as a king. I don't believe in ruling others."

Cordez glanced at Father Yeats. "No one does. But it be most necessary."

"'Tis unnecessary," Ferret said.

"*Señor*, what of *New Eire*? The English curs will come and lay waste. They will rule instead."

Cordez had given voice to Ferret's greatest fear, that the English would indeed arrive one day and seize control of his colony by force or intimidation. They had done the same to the Dutch colony to the north, invading New Amsterdam on the Hudson River and reclaiming it as the township of New York.

Yeats drew close to Ferret and spoke softly into his ear. "I know who freed Arthur, Strongbow, and Higgins. Either you accept title gracefully, or I will request that the council have Heather O'Neill arrested and put on trial. Many are eager to see her reputation and authority soiled further."

"Arrest Heather?" Ferret jumped back. "Why?"

"We found her handkerchief in the stockade."

"She could have lost it anywhere!"

"She was also the last one seen at the stockade," Yeats said. "Besides, we have a witness."

"Who?"

Yeats ignored the question. "Why not take the high road?" he paused and cast a cold glare at Ferret. "You can oversee your kingdom alongside your beautiful queen. That would solve a host of ticklish woes."

Ferret was not sure what Yeats had meant.

"Let's be aboveboard," Yeats said icily. "I know Heather is not your half-sister. Many know of this deception. I say, let her rise to the dignity of a queen. The prestige will restore her besmirched past. Otherwise, a court hearing might be most damaging to her position, especially if convicted of high treason."

"I will accept the title if I'm under no obligation to... to act like a king," Ferret said.

"So you wish to be a king without being one?"

Ferret nodded. "That's my condition."

Cordez laid his hand on Ferret's shoulder. "Hear, Hear. That is good enough!" He reached for his *espadon* and hat, then he bowed to Ferret. "King Ferret, my most honorable *amigo*, I will tell King Philip V that America has Irish kingdom to hold and protect. He will be joyful." Cordez bowed again and then hurried out of the church.

Yeats was still angry. "What of my church? I must possess a cathedral to rival those of New Spain. I cannot do this without official tillage! Others have promised me that I may levy a tithe!"

"Who?" Ferret asked.

"Perhaps a devoted friend of the church—someone like Arthur."

"I heard that he succumbed in the swamp."

"Did he now?"

Chapter 33

Father Yeats opened a leather-bound, gold-leafed book and addressed the church's congregants. He wore a white, ankle-length tunic topped with a silver and red chasuble—his finest vestments. Looking up to the rafters, he proclaimed, "By the power of grace Divine, let us rejoice! The Lord, in his infinite wisdom, has anointed Sean O'Neill as the rightful king of *New Eire*. A king of kings, a ruler amongst rulers, a man to praise and be praised—the first Irish king of the Americas."

The congregation broke out in wild cheers.

"May God save the king," Yeats said as he lowered a silver crown onto Ferret's head. He turned around and faced the crowd. "May his reign be cherished by all."

Ferret turned around, faced the audience, and bowed to his people reverently, but he struggled to keep his tongue. What he would give to speak about the horrors of royalty, about the treachery of kings and high court officials; that they were all evil hang-dogs who oppressed, robbed, and cheated the people. They would be shocked with disbelief and squirming in the aisles. But such a diatribe was not appropriate for the moment. Let them have a king if they wanted one. Let them see what power does to those who wield it. Within a year they would be snarling under their breaths, "May God kill the king."

In like fashion, a smaller crown made of tin and semi-precious stones was lowered onto Heather's head, proclaiming her queen. Beaming, she kissed Ferret with the sweetness of an angel. Minutes before the coronation, Ferret and Heather had been officially married in the church, although in Ferret's mind, it was just a formality.

Near the end of the coronation, Yeats continued, "Hear ye, all of gentle ears! From this day forth, we sit with the Lord's grace, a nation under the blessed stewardship of King Sean O'Neill and his devoted Queen. Obey them as you would the Lord." Father Yeats lifted his hands upwards and prayed. "Righteous art Thou, O Lord. May *New Eire* prosper under Thy reign forevermore." He faced Ferret and Heather, knelt, and made a sign of the cross. "Your Majesties... I am your most sincere and humble servant."

As Ferret waved to the crowd, he thought Yeats's words anything but sincere.

When the ceremony was finally over, Ferret and Heather strolled arm in arm down the church's aisle. They were set upon by waving, stomping, and cheering colonists. Outside, the entire militia—five dozen men in blue waistcoats, brown breeches, long stockings, and black tricorn hats, commanded by General Winchester and Colonel Holbrook—stood at attention. They held their swords high. Six cannons on the beach fired in salutation as the king and queen were escorted away. Upon arriving home, they discovered two armed soldiers standing guard next to their front door. They were permanently stationed there, giving the colony all the trappings of an official European monarchy—everything he had tried to avoid for so long.

That night, Ferret pondered his fate and fortune. What had he done? How was it all possible? He loathed kings and their power. Yet, he also felt honored to be consecrated as something that rivaled divinity. He now had the power to do almost anything he wanted. It was a seductive sensation to be revered and worshiped above all. Even the councilmen had attended the coronation, fearful of his reprisal if they did not attend. They understood all too well that kings often dissolve parliaments and behead or banish outspoken malcontents.

Ferret thumbed through the pages of his Bible until he came to the eighth chapter of the first book of Samuel. He read aloud sections of God's warning to the people of Israel who demanded a king:

> This will be the manner of the king that shall reign over you:
> He will take your sons, and appoint them for himself, for
> his chariots, and to be his horsemen; and some shall run
> before his chariots... And he will take your daughters to be

confectionaries, and to be cooks, and to be bakers. And he will take your fields, and your vineyards, and your oliveyards, even the best of them, and give them to his servants. And he will take a tenth of your seeds, and of your vineyards, and give to his officers, and to his servants. And he will take your menservants, and your maidservants, and your goodliest young men, and your asses, and put them to his work. He will take the tenth of your sheep: and ye shall be his servants. And ye shall cry out in that day because of your king which ye shall have chosen you; and the LORD will not hear you in that day.

Heather frowned and spoke in a soft, innocent voice. "That won't happen here. You are a good man," she cooed, appearing delighted with her new position. She turned and repositioned her crown, gazing happily at herself in a small looking glass that had been gifted to her by some neighbors whom she now referred to as "peasant women."

"You don't understand. The Lord didn't just condemn kings as evil, but the concept of governance itself."

"'Tis a paltry concern," Heather said. "You will be a fine king. I know you will. You have noble blood. That means you can only do noble deeds."

"But there is more," Ferret said and reached for Heather's hand. "We will both be targets of faultfinders, firebrands, and assassins. Adversaries are never far. I feel my actions today will lead to our early demise."

"If we die, we die together."

Ferret looked into Heather's beautiful eyes and realized how much she loved him. He could murder every single colonist in *New Eire*, torture and horsewhip them on a rack or shuck their skin like corn down to the bloody bone, and she would still stand by his side, loyal and unfailing. He pulled out his father's *Brehon* ring and slipped it on her finger. He had never had much need for it; he was sure she would appreciate the ring far more.

"One last ritual," Ferret said. He slipped out his dagger and snatched Heather's hand. He slid the blade across her index finger, drawing blood.

Ferret then slit his own finger. "Forever. Sworn lovers till eternity." He put her finger to his lips and sucked the blood.

Heather reached for his finger and did the same. "We shall never part. Coupled for life."

"If you die," Ferret said, "I die. For I wish not to draw breath alone in this world."

"Nor I," Heather said. Her eyes sparkled.

* * *

Four months later, word of another Indian massacre to the north arrived, prompting an urgent meeting between King Ferret, his militia leaders, and his advisers. Colonel Holbrook reported the rumor, which had come from a pilot aboard the Jamaica-bound *Sea Bounty*: "Hundreds, maybe thousands, cut a deadly swath across the land below Port Charles. The pilot swore it was the Yamasee, Creek, and Apalachee tribes."

General Winchester wiped sweat from his face with a handkerchief as he lifted his eyes. "My God, not a single survivor was ever found."

Holbrook nodded. "The terror will rush our way. We must fortify our defenses."

Ferret unrolled a map marking the coast and the territories to the north. He was about to propose the construction of military outposts to the north, but before he could begin, his hot-tempered six-year-old son Darbee interrupted the meeting to accuse his older brother of stealing his marbles.

Winchester coughed. "Sire, we must continue."

Ferret ignored Winchester, excused himself, and took his son outside.

Darbee burst into tears. "Travis stole almost them all! Except these"—he placed two roughly cut balls of glass in Ferret's hand—"guard them, please!" Darbee often gave Ferret his marbles to safeguard.

As he pocketed the marbles, Ferret noticed a ragtag parade of men, women, and children entering the village from the beach. They carried little more than the clothing on their backs. They were wispy and coarse, like the wandering and starving nomads of Ireland. They were immigrants from the *Sea Bounty*. More and more such immigrants came each month with each passing ship, seeking their own land and a life worth living. More than fifty had disembarked the month before. Many settled to the southern section of the colony.

Ferret called Holbrook outside to talk about the immigrants.

Holbrook watched the new settlers with worry. "Our problems seem to breed like mosquitoes," he said with a nervous tremor in his voice. "How can we protect them? They're fresh from Europe and unaccustomed to any type of hand weaponry."

"We're no longer a lonely outpost in unexplored territory," Ferret said dryly. "The British must be aware of us by now."

"Probably drawing lots to decide who shall attack first," Holbrook agreed.

"I would if I were they."

Just then, latecomers arrived—Captain O'Marr, Father Yeats, and Othello, all arguing with each other.

O'Marr bowed his head slightly. "Sire, if we are to defend our nation, we have need of more armed men."

"The Yamasees have allied with the Spanish," Ferret said. "We should be reasonably safe."

"We don't have a formal treaty with them," O'Marr said.

"That's not the worst of it," Holbrook said with a cautious look. He motioned everyone to go indoors and sit down. Once inside, Holbrook closed the door and searched adjoining rooms to make sure nobody was listening to their conversation. He walked to the front of the table and revealed something more disturbing. "Rumor is that a throng of cutthroats and sharpers from north of Port Charles are plotting to invade *New Eire* with the English. They intend to lay waste to our colony as if the Lord had mistaken it for Sodom."

O'Marr held up the flat palm of his hand. "'Tis no tomfoolery. I heard the same rumor. I was told that one of the cutthroats was Irish. Loony as they come. He boasted that he would have revenge on those who did him wrong."

Ferret mouthed the word "Arthur" to himself.

"They must be the escapees," Othello said slowly and clearly. "Men of such character will retaliate with utmost cunning and ferocity. The stage has been set and fate is waiting to play its role. Gentlemen, we must strengthen our defenses." He turned to Ferret. "Or he will seize our sovereign's birthright."

Even though he could justify seeking more power by saying he was defending his nation, Ferret was sickened by the thought of seeking it simply to protect his position. Ferret considered the fact that the British would take control of the colony if he abdicated and fled. They had more resources with which to defeat any potential enemy. Ferret knew that in the long term, his people would do better without him. The fact hung around his neck like the chain of a ship's anchor.

Within an hour after the meeting, and without council approval, Ferret put the colony on full military alert. He ordered more cannon, flintlocks, and black powder; he imposed stiff tariffs on incoming merchandise to pay for the new weaponry. Committees and agencies were set up to improve roads, and to build jailhouses and barracks, but he also enlisted spies to keep a watchful eye on disloyal citizens. One of his agencies had instituted licensing of every profession. Those who were unlicensed were flogged in public. He created a civil force to keep outspoken critics in line. His power seemed to grow independently of him, like some thorny vine that spreads into new territory of its own volition. It was only a matter of time before its destructive influence would wreak havoc upon the whole colony, and yet he felt powerless to stop it. He had to protect what he had.

Every one of his advisers applauded his actions, especially Yeats. He was elated to revive the same power structure that had dominated the Old World since the Roman Empire.

"Tis a good deed, Sire," Yeats said with a fleeting smile. "England rose to greatness because of its ability to wage war and amass high levies. 'Tis your destiny, too."

Ferret thought destiny had nothing to do with it. He was filling the slot of leadership, a position someone would take, no matter the circumstances. It didn't matter who the leader was, so long as he occupied the position long enough to appoint his friends to official positions and grace them with generous pay.

After the first hour, the meeting veered out of control: Winchester expressed fears of English and Indian invasions, Yeats complained of insufficient church funding, Holbrook warned of undisciplined recruits, and Othello fumed over the incomplete rampart. Yeats appeared to be the eye of the storm, opposed to anything new to solve problems, and maligning anyone who had positions contrary to his own. Yeats had fossilized into a crusty old man who neither permitted a kind word to escape his lips nor tolerated others' shortcomings. Old age seemed to be the culprit, to put it politely. To his way of thinking, the young were foolhardy, addicted to hard liquor, playful women, and endless gambling. But Ferret thought the very old were overbearing, overwrought, overblown killjoys, who squeezed all joy out of those who found life worth living. Only those of wisdom and strong constitution could overlook the poison spewed by such men.

After three hours of infighting with little accomplished, Ferret walked out of the meeting without a word. Kings could do that, he supposed. Outside, he found himself in the company of his young son Darbee and his loyal dog Zeph. His son had always been more sensitive than most. He could see that his father was troubled.

"What's wrong, Papa?"

"The enemy slithers closer every day," Ferret said.

"What enemy?"

"Those who love conflict and war more than life."

"You mean the Yama-zee-zee-zee?"

"The Yamasees," Ferret enunciated, correcting him.

"Will they attack?"

"I think not." Ferret paused and thought about it for a moment. "You see, we're Irish, and the Spanish favor us over the English."

"But how do the Yama-zee-zee know the Irish betwixt the English? Don't we look the same?"

That was a good question. Ferret hoped the Spanish would explain the difference. However, he also knew that if he stopped cooperating with the Spanish, they would tell the savages that *New Eire* had gone to the English and was therefore the enemy. He could see that the ten-foot rampart was vital to their survival. For a number of reasons—farmers had chores in the fields, militiamen had marches to attend, and the regular townsfolk had their own excuses—its construction had dragged along at a snail's pace, facing setback after setback.

Rutten had agreed to supervise the wall's construction, and he was usually accompanied by a mug of syrupy ale that had to be refilled on a minute-to-minute basis. The workmen took little pride in their work and ended up half-drunk or trying to drift into that stage of blissful delight before midday. When Winchester inspected the rampart's daily progress, he usually found either no workmen on the site or poor workmanship. Ferret mourned the slow pace of work, and he predicted that Armageddon would befall the world before the walls were raised.

* * *

A week later, Ferret was the first to hear a faint howl that chilled the air and quaked his heart. The forest that surrounded the settlement had gone silent—no birds singing, no crickets chirping, no hawks soaring overhead. He heard the eerie sound of a dog howling in the distance, then it stopped with a sudden cry.

He ran into Othello first. They both agreed that something was not right. Othello was almost poetic in stating his concerns, saying that the air was too still, the forest too tame. Ferret ordered him to the unfinished wall with all the men he could muster.

Ferret hurried to the center of town and ordered the church bell rung to sound the alarm. After locating his sons Darbee, William, and Travis, he forced them inside their home and slammed the window shutters. He grabbed his flintlock from above the fireplace.

"Oh, God!" Heather wiped her hand on her apron, then picked up Rosemary, her only child. She grabbed Ferret's hand tightly. "Is our fate at hand?"

Ferret peered into her eyes. "It may be nothing at all."

"But what if it's them?"

"We all knew this day might come."

"I'm not prepared for that day. I'll never be."

He hugged her tightly, kissed her forehead and said that he loved her.

"I too." Heather began to sob. "But I cannot live without you. You hear me. I'm not strong enough."

Ferret held her tighter, never wanting to let her go. But he felt the weight of obligation upon his shoulders. He had to carry out his duties. He broke away and headed for the door. At the doorway, he stopped, turned around and instructed her to bolt the door behind him.

As her lips trembled, she let out a tearful cry of anguish. She was now sobbing uncontrollably. A flood of tears began trickling down her cheekbones. "I cannot lose you." She struggled to gasp for air. "You're not coming back! All I see is dark emptiness."

Ferret stared at her. She was shaking with fear, too scared to utter another word. He went back and hugged her again. "Stay inside. I will return. I promise." Without another word, he rushed outside.

Within minutes, war-whoops pierced the air, and a swarm of brown-skinned warriors had reached the unfinished northern section of the rampart. Seeing that his men were outnumbered, Othello ordered the retreat of his detachment. Only Othello remained behind; he was determined to confront the hordes with one flintlock and an axe. Steadfast, he stood his ground and waited for the Indian onslaught to approach. He dropped his weapons and beamed. The Indian front line ground to a halt.

"A fine day for carnage, gents," Othello chortled, doffing his hat. "I greet thy love, not with vain thanks, but with acceptance bounteous." Kneeling, he lifted his hands high above him in as if performing some type of ritual. "Oh Lord, go with me apart," Othello prayed, concentrating on his words, "for swift life means swift death... or something to that general condition." Othello shook his head. "Damn, forgot the proper line."

"*Nonta moonta*," one of the Indians shouted out, looking spooked. He wore medicine beads and war paint. He tiptoed ahead of the others apprehensively, often glancing back at his men.

"I must bid you adieu," Othello said loudly. He bowed, turned, and walked away with a carefree, gentle stroll as if he were the only man alive in the world.

It took the Yamasees several minutes to regain order and resume their advance to the township's center. Othello had bought the colony enough time for the men to lay hands on their flintlocks and congregate at the market square behind a barricade of barrels, wagons, and tobacco bundles. The women had remained inside their buildings. Their faces were glued to the windows; they were too frightened to move. The Indians stopped twenty feet in front of the barricade. As Ferret's men raised their weapons, the redskins raised their bows and tomahawks. The earth stood still, like the brief silence after a lightning flash—everyone waited for thunder to crack and the battle to begin.

There were more than five hundred Yamasees and Indians from related tribes. Their rough faces were painted black and red. Most sported long black hair; others had it braided and adorned with tufts of feathers and shells. Their bodies rippled with rock-hard muscles. A few wore pieces of shell in their ears or bracelets around their wrists. Most had elaborate tattoos of totems representing exploits in war, mostly on necks and arms. Apron-like breechcloths made of deerskin hung from their belts, hiding their nakedness. Scalps covered with flies hung from their belts. Most carried tomahawks, bows, and arrows, and a few brandished Spanish muskets.

Ferret crawled over the barricade, unarmed, and walked a short distance, his hands in plain sight. At first it did not seem so courageous, but as he neared them, it seemed that he had made one of the more monumental mistakes of his life. However, the Indians remained aloof. They seemed uneasy over his appearance, but they did nothing. They seemed to be waiting for something.

An infant's cry from a nearby cabin interrupted the silence. The Indians frowned, gazing around with confusion. A few of the younger braves moved closer to the building. When they pressed their face against the glass, they saw a tow-headed child lying in a basket, howling. They tapped the strange material, trying to reach inside, but instead streaked the glass with their fingers. Inside, a distressed woman clutched the child and hid behind a bed.

Thinking fast, Ferret reached into his pocket for the two crudely made glass marbles he had taken from Darbee earlier. He clicked them together. Inquisitive, the closest Yamasee warrior motioned to see what was in Ferret's hand. The Indian reached down and poked at the gleaming objects. Soon, a crowd had gathered around Ferret, all eager to touch and nudge the rainbow-colored glass. One Indian with a necklace of bear claws picked the marbles up and squinted at them. He held them high like a prized bird captured in a snare. Ferret grinned. Who said savages could not be tamed with beauty?

A panting, breathless voice came from deep within the Yamasees' ranks and said in Spanish, *"Debo hablar con el rey Ferret!"* Then a short-necked, bronze-faced Spaniard, armored in rusted mail, pushed his way through the Indians. *"Queridos amigos!"* The dwarf-sized Spaniard looked exhausted. He bowed slightly. "They run much too fast for my short legs."

"You command these Yamasees?" asked Ferret.

"I was with Captain Cordez."

For once Ferret was excited to hear English. But Ferret's English also excited the Indians. One raised his bow and stretched his bowstring, pointing his arrow straight at Ferret's chest. The Indian's eyes narrowed and he barely controlled his urge to release his arrow. "Speaks Englaise. They must all die!"

The Spaniard turned and confronted the Indian, treating him like a mindless child. "No! These be good men. *Amigos!* Irish! Hate English too! They will not sell you into slavery like the English traders."

The Indian grunted but lowered his weapon. "Irish good?"

"Si! True believers in the Lord Almighty."

Hearing this, the Indians relaxed, broke ranks, and began to roam freely around the unbarricaded portion of the town. The colonists lowered their weapons too, although they remained alert.

The Spaniard introduced himself. "I'm Manuel Sanchez, from the *Queen of Antilles.*"

Hearing Spanish, Paco came running. He longed to hear one of his own countrymen, but could only moan and slur his words when he attempted to speak. Sanchez pushed the halfwit aside, almost knocking him over.

Ferret was horrified. "The poor man had part of his tongue pulled out."

"He must have stolen something," Sanchez said coldly. "He probably deserved it. I hate thieves."

"English did it," Ferret said in a gruff voice.

Sanchez lifted his shaggy black hair above the ear. "Look here, *amigo!* I also! See my cropped ears. English *perros* done this to me! Murdered whole *familia*. We all have many crosses to bear." Sanchez paused. "I have another cross to carry. Our lack of supplies has limited our success. We're desperate. I beg generosity. Can you spare some supplies for our most noble cause?"

Ferret bit his lip. It was dangerous to give supplies to unruly outsiders who could turn against his colonists at any moment. Ferret glanced at the Yamasees. They roamed the colony with few restraints. The Indians poked at the settlers' white skin and made funny faces at the frightened children. Two well-armed Indians kicked open a barred cabin door, rifled through the room and took what they wanted. They gaped at a quivering woman hiding in a dark nook. One Indian grasped a white man's flintlock. The man refused to surrender it. The agitated Indian tried to wrestle the gun from the colonist, eventually succeeding. After examining it, the scowling Indian shoved it back into the white man's arms.

"We're low on powder and shot," Ferret said to Sanchez. "However, our summer harvest proved plentiful."

"Then you will share."

"We are not so prosperous as to dispense our supplies freely to anyone."

Sanchez looked surprised. "I ask not for charity. What I take, I will return."

"How?"

"You haggle like a Jew, King Ferret."

"And artful dodgery be no stranger to you."

"I promise to keep many watchful eyes on your kingdom. You shout and we come with Godspeed."

Ferret glanced back at the savages. Was the Spaniard trustworthy? He doubted it. Still, it was better to pretend an alliance of friendship than to stir up a cloud of distrust. He nodded. "Agreed. We shall honor our allies. Take what you require."

Sanchez gestured to his men. The redskins attacked the storehouse, hacking the door with their tomahawks until they had smashed through it. Rushing inside, they leaped at the goods and carried away bags of grain, baskets of corn, and slabs of venison. Sanchez then told his warrior army to head south. Like a herd of deer, the redskins ran down the main street of *New Eire*, out beyond the houses and through the gaps in the rampart, melting back into the woods from which they had sprung.

"The door was unbolted," Ferret said.

"*Señor*, they don't understand how to use it." Sanchez shrugged. "These *indios* are from interior, more primitive. Anyway, much better this way. Only Englishmen need doors. Before I leave, I must warn you. The English curs bark louder each day. I say clot their black-hearted souls. They're not far to the north. Have powder and lead shot when we return. We all will have much need of it." Sanchez rubbed his neck and began to follow his army. Before he disappeared into the woods, he yelled back, "I will give a most favorable report to Captain Cordez in St. Augustine."

Most of the colonists were speechless.

Winchester was first to grasp the obvious. "Why hasn't the rampart wall been completed yet?"

Yeats had harsher words: "Are we so wealthy to hand food to any sponger?"

"'Tis the Christian way." Othello grinned. "Alms to the poor." His joke fell flat.

"They are heathens!" Yeats said.

"No!" Ferret said. "They're not our enemies."

Yeats cornered Ferret. "Do you believe they will assist us someday?"

"I believe they will follow their commander, a representative of the King of Spain and the true Church." For the moment, that seemed to shut Yeats up. However, Ferret had not planned to shower the savages with supplies. Such generosity only begged for repeat visits for more unearned handouts.

There was at least one good to come out of the Yamasees' unexpected visit. Work on the rampart roared at an unparalleled pace, precipitating some of the more terrified men to labor under torchlight late into the night. Within three weeks, the fortification around the township had been completed and the populace felt safe from outside invaders.

But Ferret knew that no wall ever built could keep out a determined foe.

355

Chapter 34

Rutten raised his telescope and scanned a fleet of ships two miles to the north. "Must be sea-dogs from Barbados! I hope we haven't tweaked the devil by the tail."

Winchester snatched the telescope and rubbed the dirty glass with his sleeve. "I doubt they would attack a backwater port like us."

"'Em freebooters traffic in greed," Rutten snorted with a disdainful curl of the lip. "They'd steal a ruddy lame dog too crippled to walk."

Winchester glared at Rutten with an air of superiority, and then he looked through the telescope himself. "I see no skull and crossed bones... I only see..." He stopped in mid-sentence, and his face went blank. He gulped. "Great snakes! 'Tis a Union Jack!"

Rutten retrieved the telescope and looked again. "By hickory, you be right! Those are mighty tall ships." He seemed more amused than alarmed.

"Our days are numbered," Winchester mumbled as he stared at the approaching warships. "We must warn the others."

Within minutes, the militia, including Othello and Holbrook, ran to the ramparts. Everyone struggled to get a look at the approaching fleet. Only King Ferret was offered the luxury of an unobstructed pathway to the rampart. After gazing through the telescope, Ferret confirmed that the ships were indeed British. There were four three-mast, double-decked ships of the line—likely the entire southern fleet. By European standards, it was a small flotilla; a local French fishing village could defeat it with hooks, harpoons, and a bad case of garlic breath. But in the Americas, it was an armada.

New Eire's only saving grace to date had been England's inability to wage war so far from its northern colonies. The English were even now stretched to their limits, Ferret thought. Wars with Spain and France had forced them to station relatively few troops in the New World. He believed they were too weak to launch a full attack anytime soon. Even so, he knew his defenses could not hold up to a full assault. He had only three sixteen-pound cannons on the wall. They would be a mere nuisance to any sea bombardment.

On the other hand, though *New Eire's* three ships had been lightly armed during the Atlantic voyage, each ship now carried a full battery of immense guns. Othello had a more skeptical phrase for them: *extraordinary fakes*. The idea had come from an old seafarer's book that told the story of an unarmed merchant vessel in the South Pacific. The ship's captain had discovered a cheap, unique way to deter Chinese pirates by hollowing out old log stumps and coating them with tar. Their own cannons had been constructed with similar artistry.

From a distance, it appeared that *New Eire's* vessels each carried forty-six thirty-five-pound cannon, enough to scare potential freebooters. Already, two pirate ships—rumored to be Black Caesar's fleet, which had ravaged many Spanish coastline towns—had been discouraged from attacking *New Eire*. This was why Ferret turned to his men and shouted, "No cause for alarm! We're too well defended!"

They all knew, however, that the English had a stubborn habit of attacking—and winning—against impossible odds.

* * *

Despite the conspicuous windmill to draw them in, the British continued south past *New Eire* and disappeared over the horizon. For hours Ferret paced the ramparts. He was fatigued, nauseated, and nervous. He was trying to figure out what the English were up to. As he paced, he watched Othello and Hendrick clean their weapons. Hendrick was Strongbow's twelve-year-old son who had a sizeable chip on his shoulder. He was quick to blame others for his problems and most people tried to avoid him.

"There's something afoot out there," Othello said as he whetted his knife. "Those flap-eared Britons know a thing or two. You know how I know?"

Hendrick shook his head. "How?"

"Ever see a pesky crow? I mean the big, black ones?"

Hendrick nodded.

"Well, you shoo them away and they clack and yak, fly to a branch, and scold you. They hide up there in the tree until you leave. Then they come right back. That's how I know."

"Why not just shoot the fowl and be done with it?" Hendrick asked.

Before he could reply, the sound of drums and fifes drifted through the air. For a split second, Ferret imagined he was back in Ireland. Othello stood up and shouted, "I believe it's the sound of Jericho a'calling." Then, speaking almost to himself, he added, "I hope our walls do not come tumbling down."

Ferret ordered the alarm. Church bells began to ring. A shockwave of panic rippled across the township. Everyone threw down their iron-shod hoes, two-eared spades, and forked branches. They scrambled like chickens. Women gathered bandages and ointments and men loaded their weapons and ran to the wall.

The Englishmen were on the beach marching toward the ramparts. They were handsomely dressed in bright red overcoats and white knee-high stockings. Brown pouches swung from bandoliers across their shoulders. They appeared more Hessian than English with their high, pointed hats and rigorous marching formation. They resembled an army of hustling red ants, one behind the other, never wavering, never looking back. A dreadful sense of weakness struck Ferret's mind. To witness an invading army at your doorstep could unnerve the most battle-hardened soul. Bigger issues than death were at stake. He and his people were defending their new homeland, the center of their small world. To lose was to lose everything—their land, their livelihoods, and his nation.

* * *

Major-General Winston Cromwell stopped the column fifty feet in front of the gate. His men followed his orders like clockwork. He watched the armed men on the wall watching his every movement.

Lieutenant Mountjoy approached the commanding officer with a per-functory, casual tone. "Sir, rumor has it that they're Irish or Dutch." Young for his rank, Mountjoy was a recent arrival from Hastings who had had little contact with the settlers of the New World.

Cromwell walked briskly to the gate, stopped and shouted, "Are you Dutch, Irish, or English?"

"We're English-speaking colonists," Ferret said in his best King's English.

"Sound like proper Englishmen to me, Sir," Mountjoy said.

"Most perplexing. I wonder if Captain Yankson rows with all his oars," Cromwell said as he turned to Mountjoy. "Christ! How the blazing devil did they escape the Yamasees' wrath?"

Mountjoy shrugged. "Mayhap it's too large a settlement?"

"I seriously doubt that." Cromwell turned toward the wall again and shouted, "Are you in any immediate danger?"

"We're fine as a fippence!" Ferret said. He began to examine the commanding officer closely. The Briton seemed familiar—his rigid stance and reedy voice. But the officer's large hat obstructed his view. If only he could get a better look! He caught a glimpse of something—was it a scar?—on the man's cheek.

"I am pleased," Cromwell said, "but I have no official records of any English colony this far south of the Carolinas."

"We were blown off course," Ferret said.

"You will have to resettle further north! The crown's resources are limited here. I'm sure you're aware that the Spaniards and savages run amuck. The danger is most grave!"

"They must be crackers, smugglers, or sea-dogs," Mountjoy said.

"I'm not so sure." Cromwell rubbed his chin. "Yankson insisted that they were Irish. Irish! How preposterous. The Irish cannot even hold their balance when searching for the next tavern, much less maintain a colony."

As Cromwell and Mountjoy conversed, Winchester approached Ferret. He leaned over the wall to survey the British troops.

"Unbar the gate!" Cromwell demanded, losing patience.

"I'm not at liberty to do that," Ferret said.

Cromwell looked up. "Come, come. Open up so we may chat over some fine bohea tea." He paused. "Before I get a sore neck."

There was silence.

"Funny." Cromwell let out a low chuckle. "They act as if we were the enemy."

Mountjoy began to speculate. "Mayhap they are wary of the rivalry betwixt royalists and the parliament. Gets rather murky. Out here, you can't know the happenings of London. They might suspect another civil war brewing and wish not to take sides."

Cromwell chewed over that thought for a few moments.

"Under those conditions, I might bar my gate too," Mountjoy said.

"That's not it," Cromwell said. "You have got a lot to discern about colonists. They're barely proper Englishmen. Try to think of them as bastard chits, untamed and untrustworthy."

As Cromwell argued with Mountjoy, Winchester finally got a glimpse of the general's face. He gasped in disbelief, turned, and rushed for the ladder.

He was intercepted by Ferret. "What is it?"

Breathing rapidly, Winchester snarled. "It's him. The bastard."

"Who?"

"The devil himself, Winston Cromwell. 'Od rot his bedeviled soul!"

Ferret's face went numb. His old nemesis Cromwell in the New World? How was that possible? It was becoming evident that something far more sinister was afoot. He was only seeing the tip of the spear, the first glimmer of what lay ahead.

Ferret went back to his position and peered down at Cromwell. There was no reason to hide the truth. Nothing was going to change. The conflict was unavoidable since both sides would be unwilling to compromise.

"General," Ferret yelled, "we are an Irish and Dutch colony!"

Without orders, the English soldiers slung their flintlocks to a firing position.

"Hold the line! Hold it now!" Cromwell walked back to his troops and knocked one man's weapon to the ground. "Get back into formation!"

Mountjoy followed Cromwell. "Sir, this cannot be. I have no papers for any chartered Dutch, Irish, or hell-born colony this far south. None."

Standing in deep sand, Cromwell turned and trudged back to the wall. "I want to see your royal charter!"

Ferret knew that nothing he could do now would prevent bloodshed. He would not surrender to English authority. And they would not give up. As they had done in *Eire*, the English would brawl and scheme for every inch of land, no matter if it were worthless swampland or Lucifer's fire pits of Hell. The English were relentless. There was no way to tame their lust for conquest.

"We have none!" Ferret bellowed defiantly. This was his domain, and he was willing to protect it with the lives of every armed colonist. Let the women grieve over their freshly dug graves. Life was bitter and hard. A man was fortunate to live beyond his thirties and if he did, some ailment, affliction, or disfigurement haunted him until the earth had digested another crippled body. He was convinced that he was doing what he must. And his subjects would do as they were told.

"We can make arrangements!" Cromwell said. "The Carolinas need as many able-bodied men as can be mustered. Savages are many and the Spaniards swell with more forces. What say ye?"

"We have little need of protection," Ferret said. "The savages have not molested us. I would expect no less from you, General."

"They spared your colony?" Cromwell asked. "They've slaughtered every other settlement in their path!" Then he saw Winchester crouching next to a large Negro. "God-a-mercy! 'Tis Winchester, my most beloved assassin!"

Ferret found Cromwell's choice of words eccentric.

"Assassin?" Winchester said with hands on his hips. "How absurd." There was a note of panic in his voice.

"Is that not one of your most cherished pastimes?" Cromwell asked with a mocking laugh. "Shooting your mates in the back."

Winchester glanced nervously at Ferret. "The man speaks nonsense. I have no idea what he means."

"Back to my point," Cromwell said. "'Tis my duty to evacuate all British subjects from dangerous territories. And I declare this territory dangerous."

"You should," Winchester said. "I know of your corrupted activities in Cork!"

"And," Ferret said, "I know of the secret arrangement you had with Madoc!"

Cromwell stuttered. "Madoc... Madoc O'Neill? Who... who are you?"

"I'm Ferret O'Neill!"

Cromwell ran a hand over his scarred face. He glanced at Mountjoy. "I thought I had escaped the stench of Ireland forever. Instead, it has pursued me like scarlet fever."

"Sir?" Mountjoy's eyes widened.

Cromwell began to pace, deep in thought. He stopped to kick a piece of driftwood out of his way. He shifted his weight uncomfortably. He peered up and locked eyes with Ferret. "Are you in league with the Spaniards?"

"We're independent," Ferret said.

"Independent?" Cromwell coughed, almost doubling over. When he regained his composure, he clenched his fist and let out a slight groan. "This territory is claimed by the King of England. The King's subjects are expected to follow his laws. That makes you trespassers or traitors. Which is it?"

Holbrook took his turn. He leaned over the wall and did his share of yelling, "King Ferret is beholden to nobody! Nobody!"

Cromwell shook his head in disbelief. "Holbrook, too," he mumbled to himself. He glanced at Mountjoy and said with a hint of sarcasm, "How bloody droll. They have their own kingdom!"

Rutten slipped next to Ferret, lifted his pistol and prepared to fire a round. "Let me take a pop at the general. Take him down like a treed opossum."

Ferret knocked away the barrel. "Good God, have you no honor? He's unarmed."

Mountjoy trudged forward a few feet in the soft sand, stopped and glared up at Ferret. "We cannot permit an Irish sovereign to take root here. This is not your land."

"Then come and get it!" Ferret said.

Mountjoy turned and stared at Cromwell. "Well, that was rather a definite reply. They seem to fit the profile of the thick-headed Irish."

Cromwell nodded. "Aye, headstrong and obstinate. We'll have to lay waste to this settlement."

"But they are distant countrymen," Mountjoy said in a low, guarded voice. "That might be difficult to arrange."

"Who gives a bloody farthing how it's done!" Cromwell said. "Maybe the savages will take them down first. But one by one, down they will fall. I can assure you. Besides, they're just Irishmen."

Returning to his men, Cromwell ordered an assault, on his command. He directed his lieutenants to make quick work of the colony—scale the ramparts and capture the enemy. Then he called to Ferret again: "I demand your surrender!"

Ferret glanced at his own army. His hand began to shake. His men looked frightened, but they held their flintlocks high and glared with stiff, unbridled determination. He could see the resolution in their eyes. They would risk all, not just for him, but for what his kingdom stood for. He had given them the sweet taste of freedom, more than they could have expected. And he had promised to restore much of it once the war had ended. They would return the favor with every breath in their bodies and every resource at hand. He would have their undying gratitude. It was the greatest honor any man could bestow to another. He looked back at the army of redcoats and gave no reply to Cromwell.

Cromwell turned to his men and shouted, "Ready!" He motioned for the assault to begin. Marching formally, the soldiers fanned out, creating three rows of men. The first row knelt and aimed their flintlocks at the wall.

Ferret shouted to his men, "Do not return fire until I give the order!" He knew that the English probably possessed most of the ammunition in the world, and his kingdom's own supply was limited.

"Fire!" Cromwell ordered.

The colonists ducked as the lead balls whistled overhead or hit the rampart. Miraculously, no one was hit. Only Rutten returned fire, felling one English soldier.

"God-a-mercy!" Cromwell halted the battle. Waving his sword fanatically, he swaggered to the wall. "Now you have done it! Blood has been spilled. The King has no sympathy for murderers." Hastily, Cromwell began to count the number of barrels pointed at his troops; there were more of them than there had been on his original count. He conferred with Mountjoy and came to a rather humbling conclusion. "We cannot win. Not today. Just too many of them."

"We're in need of reinforcements," Mountjoy said.

"That will take months."

"Sir," Mountjoy said, "they are not going anywhere."

Cromwell nodded. In short order, the English packed their gear and, with drums rolling and fifes playing, retreated to their ships.

The colonists gave three cheers and praised their king with toasts of corn liquor and gun salutes.

Ferret knew, however, that Cromwell would return with more troops and a better plan.

Chapter 35

War was coming. Ferret could not block the coming bloodbath from his thoughts. Sleep evaded him. He had developed dark circles under his eyes. When the night grew old, he would pinch himself or kick a rock to feel the arousing sense of excruciating life. He would endure anything to protect his kingdom: sleepless nights, aching back, throbbing head—everything it took to prepare for war. The thought of failure was unthinkable.

It had been decided to construct a three-foot-high stone parapet above the shoreline, directly in front of the wooden rampart. The council complained bitterly, especially Pragg, who argued it was unnecessary. But Ferret considered a full frontal assault the most likely invasion route of the British. The council said it would provide little protection. Ferret overruled them. The council retaliated by condemning his disregard for their authority. They threatened to find a way to block his funds and manpower. Without further discussion, Ferret dissolved the council permanently, imprisoned Pragg, and advised that those who disagreed would face arrest. Nobody would tell him how to run his kingdom or fight a war! The wall was built within a few weeks.

Ferret wanted to emulate the English mode of building a well-trained, professional army. Yet their warfare was so foreign to the warriors of *Eire*! Irish men fought for honor and justice for their clan, for private revenge. They fought each other with few men and no organized armies. Their conflicts resembled local cattle raids and not military adventures. The clashes rarely spilled over into the general countryside, and those not involved in the fray were left alone. But the English had crafted a standing army to fight for territory, power, and plunder.

The British were also indiscriminate. They attacked neutral towns and clans, and killed any who stood in the way. War was waged for the sake of war. It was self-perpetuating and all-consuming. There was no honest effort to determine who was right, only to fight until only the British remained.

New Eire roared into wartime preparation on a grand scale. The militia marched back and forth in the town square with more spring to their step. Women sewed bandages and made crutches. An assemblage of blacksmiths forged swords, sharpened scythes, and mass-produced lead balls. Each cabin roof was fortified with earth and sand as protection from cannon fire. Food was stockpiled underground, beneath homes. An armory was built and stocked with gunpowder, flintlocks, and swords. The colony's weapons were plentiful and powerful. If the British wanted war, Ferret would give it to them.

* * *

There was another simmering battle to worry about. The strife was domestic. Strongbow's son Hendrick kept bullying Ferret's children, especially taking out his frustrations on Travis, Ferret's ten-year-old son with his first wife, Maureen. The last time Ferret had entered the boys' room, Travis sported a black eye while Hendrick wore a bandage on his injured arm. A stiff tongue-lashing and threats of corporal punishment had little effect. No discipline seemed to work.

Ferret recalled an affray with his big brother. Brian would call him "monkey-face" and then punch him in the arm or shoulder. When Corla saw the bruises, she told him to smack Brian right back. Ferret had taken that advice to heart. With a rock in his hand, he leveled it against Brian's nose. His brother never hit him again. He wondered if Travis would have to do the same.

Ferret hesitated to advise Travis to fight back with hard objects because of what Heather might do. She repeatedly ignored Hendrick's physical attacks against Travis. She openly displayed her bias, rationalizing that her younger half-brother's actions were somehow justified. She had completely swept impartiality under the rug. Heather saw Hendrick as her last blood relative, besides her fugitive father.

On one of her more brooding days, Heather demanded that Ferret do something about Travis's ill-behavior, without blaming Hendrick for his.

When Ferret explained that it would be unfair to punish one without the other, Heather blurted out that they should forsake *New Eire*.

"We must leave," Heather cried out, turning her face away to hide her tearing eyes.

Ferret reeled backward with one hand clutching at his chest. "But why?"

"'Tis too dangerous to stay." Heather turned back and faced him with tears on her cheeks.

"You mean flee the colony? Just leave everything behind?"

"Soon there won't be anything left to leave behind."

"There is something here more important than just fighting."

Hearing faint cries, Heather rushed over to her infant daughter and picked up her up, cradling the child in her arms. She gently nudged its mouth to her nipple. "Don't bite, hinny," she said gently.

"I will not abandon my nation."

"But what about the children?"

"What makes life so precious?" Ferret asked with a hint of desperation in his voice. "'Tis the air we breathe, the ones we treasure, the life we live unto ourselves. What if they took that all away? Would life be worth the pain of birth? To the north, in the Virginias, they live under blistering tyranny. If tradesmen and commoners refuse to be licensed by the royal governor, they are scourged so vigorously that their ribs are visible. Some have died. In other townships, if men fail to attend Sunday church the English have the authority to put them to death. They have preachers of different faiths rotting in jails. Where would you have us go?"

"You do the same! Look at yourself. You stride like a peacock in English boots. You've imprisoned those who cry for their rights to speak freely in peaceful gatherings. Many fear your wrath. You have lost much of their goodwill."

"They had to be restrained."

"Listen to yourself, sweetkin. You say we must fight to be free. Free of what?"

"I will restore their rights after the war."

"But what if the war never ends?"

"We must not perish!"

"What's so special about our land? 'Tis just a little swath of sand and swamps. Often hot and inhospitable at that."

"Forget about the land. We represent the ideals of heartfelt liberty. A guiding light in the dark madness of mankind. If we succeed, our beliefs may spread to the northern colonies and beyond."

"Bosh. The English will never change. They're heartless through and through. Loyal subjects of their precious king, purebred, stubborn, and bloated." Heather, still feeding their infant, leaned over and kissed Ferret on the cheek. "I give life. I wish not to be part of those who take it."

"What is life without the right to breathe without permission?"

Heather returned her attention to her baby.

Ferret watched a bead of milk drip from Heather's breast, some trickling down her pale skin. He wondered if he was too adamant. Still, he believed he had to draw a line in the sand and challenge the tyrants of the world, even if it meant becoming a tyrant himself.

Suddenly, a loud thud echoed from the other end of the house. Both Ferret and Heather ran to the boys' room. Hendrick and Travis were on the floor fighting, their bodies locked together and their thin white night clothes torn.

Ferret pried the boys apart. "Who started this fray?"

They pointed at each other.

"The truth!" Ferret was convinced that Hendrick was the culprit, but unwilling to accuse anyone. He would let them talk until Heather could see for herself who was the aggressor.

"The fob attacked me!" Travis said.

Hendrick pointed at Travis. "He called me a prigman. I had to defend my honor!"

Ferret grasped Hendrick's arm. "So you struck the first blow! I see I must instill some respect in you!"

Heather interceded. "Just parley with him. No whipping."

* * *

Ferret and Hendrick walked down the dark, deserted main street, passed McGee's trading post and tavern, a clothier of some note, two cobblers, and a cooper's workshop stacked with half-finished barrels, all boarded up. Neither of them said a word. Ferret glanced at Hendrick and noticed how tall Strongbow's son had grown. When they neared the rampart he demanded that the brawling cease.

At first, Hendrick hemmed and hawed, but finally admitted that he felt worthless. "Nobody likes me," he said. "I don't belong here. I must leave. Everyone only sees my father in me."

Ferret looked up and gazed at the endless sea of stars shining brightly above. One particular star shimmered in the north. It stood out so prominently in the immense black sky. Without the light of the stars, there would be no illumination in the darkness, no substance to hold onto, and no soul to call their own. Mankind would be lost. He thought about the fact that all he wanted to do was sleep and forget the wretchedness of life. If Hendrick decided to leave the colony, would Heather follow? Blood kinship was more important to the Irish than life itself.

"Sons often pay for the crimes of their fathers." Ferret spoke in a gentle, compassionate voice. "Not exactly fair."

They climbed up the ladder to the rampart's platform where Ferret looked for a spot to better see the bright stars and tranquil beach.

Hendrick asked, "Am I to be flogged?"

Rubbing his neck, Ferret felt a chill. He realized that if Strongbow and Arthur attacked with Cromwell, his forces would be obligated to kill Strongbow. It was a disturbing, nauseating thought.

"Well?"

"I seem to have lost my whipcord."

Hendrick pulled a long thin branch from his pocket. "Will this do?"

Ferret instead gazed at the moon rising over the ocean, so round and bright that he could see gray continents on its surface. The sight made him feel small and insignificant.

"Will you punish me or not?"

A surge of rage broke into Ferret's reverie. Ferret snatched the branch from Hendrick. "Fine! Take off your shirt." He reasoned that if the boy wanted to be whipped senseless, so be it. It did not matter if Strongbow's son had been at fault or if he deserved punishment. Someone had to be punished for *everything* that had gone wrong, and Hendrick made a good whipping boy.

Hendrick obeyed, turned around to expose his bare back, and braced for impact, but the sting of the whip never came. "What do you wait for?"

Ferret tossed the green switch away. "Go home. I have better things to do."

Hendrick slipped his shirt on. "You know what they call me? The boy who dwells amongst the dragons of Hell."

Ferret understood Hendrick's meaning. He recalled the story of a shepherd from Wexford who had lost his entire flock to blackleg and sheep-pox. Reduced to wretched poverty, he became despondent, saying that he had no reason to live. Within a year, he had fulfilled his own prophecy, dying in the middle of the night. Self-hatred was like that. Anyone with stout legs could dart away from foes or flee wicked noblemen, but nobody could outrun themselves. For these people, there was neither a distant land nor a wide ocean far enough in which to escape.

Just then, someone called to them from outside the settlement. Ferret searched but saw nobody. He leaned over the wall and shouted, "Who goes there?"

"Down here," the voice whispered again. "I have an important message."

"For whom?"

"Hush," the voice murmured. "You'll wake the dead."

"You'll be dead if you fail to identify yourself." Ferret slipped out his pistol and let it dangle next to his thigh.

A shadowy figure crept up to the base of the wall. "Stand back, laddie," the voice commanded.

A grappling hook flew up and over, dragged along the floor and finally anchored itself to the rampart wall. A few moments later, Strongbow clambered over the wall's top and pulled out a pistol. "I have come to warn you."

"Why in God's name should I believe you?" Ferret asked with a crinkled brow.

"Because I wish not to see my kin murdered by Arthur O'Neill. Come, Hendrick, we must flee."

"No!" the boy answered in a firm tone.

"We must make haste, son. Tomorrow will be a world of hurt."

"I want no part of you."

"You heard your son." Ferret moved closer to Strongbow. "We're all staying."

"My dear King Ferret, believe it or not, but I came to rescue you, too."

"So that is what you call this?"

Strongbow stepped forward so close that the barrel of his pistol almost touched Ferret's chest. "Must I shoot you to save you? I've had to do that before."

"Isn't that what you do best? Treachery for hire." Then, with a quick snap, Ferret knocked the pistol out of Strongbow's hand. The gun tumbled over the wall.

"You don't understand!" Strongbow pleaded. "Arthur will draw and quarter you alive. I tried to dissuade him, but he remains resolute and peevish. Don't be a stubborn arse. You must abdicate. We can escape through the swamp and back to *Eire*. 'Tis where we belong, laddie."

It seemed that everyone wanted him to relinquish his crown and scamper away like a frightened rabbit. Ferret shook his head. "So, you're in league with Arthur, and you want me to abdicate so that Arthur may plunder my throne."

Strongbow choked. "Your throne? Heaven forbid I get betwixt you and your scepter!"

"I could have you hanged!"

"What? Kill your father-in-law?"

"No, a traitor to the crown."

"Listen to me," Strongbow said. "You must take Heather and the children away forthwith. Arthur plans to invade tomorrow morn. The puckfist will pick your bones clean. And Cromwell will scavenge what's left."

"I cannot abandon my kingdom. The people depend on me."

"Well!" Strongbow said. "Folly has clotted your brain. You are lion-drunk with power. Look at you, so eager for others to defend you from clan rivalry. You once talked so piously of liberty! Now, how many must be slaughtered to satisfy your pride?"

"Do you think Arthur will rule with leniency?" Ferret asked. "Or that he's a man of honor and enlightenment? I say he will poison the well of decency, and force everyone to drink from its tainted waters!"

"That is the custom, laddie. They all taste the bad water of political power and always find the poisonous flavor appealing. You can't change that."

"Someone must challenge that."

"Why not ask Father Yeats about your quaint daydreams?" Strongbow scoffed. "He's the one who beckoned us with open arms and siren songs."

Before Ferret could reply, a shadow moved behind Strongbow. From the breadth and girth of the man, it had to be Othello, who lifted his flintlock and pointed the barrel at Strongbow's back. "Shall I take him to the stockade?"

Strongbow turned, and his face lit up. "Othello, my old mate."

"Old mate, nothing," Othello said.

"Othello is one of my most loyal subjects," Ferret said. "He will do anything for me."

Othello nodded slightly. "What shall we do with this troublemaker, Your Majesty?"

"Take the traitor to the cathedral. Arrest everyone there, line them up against the wall, and shoot them," Ferret ordered. He had had enough of Father Yeats and his treacherous company. The only way to deal with betrayers was to shoot them and let dogs gnaw on their disloyal bones.

Othello lowered his flintlock.

"That's a direct command, Othello."

"Sire, what if General Winchester and the whole colony occupy the church?"

"Then kill every single traitor!"

Othello set down his flintlock gingerly, stroked his chin, and sighed. He glanced at Ferret, then back at Strongbow. He pondered for the longest of time, taking care in choosing his words. Then he spoke in a humble, almost reserved, manner. "I stand here before a bloody traitor to the crown who rightly deserves to see St. Peter's gate firsthand in all its splendor. But I must bespeak my mind with brevity, for I wish not to be long-winded or verbose." Without warning, Othello slugged Strongbow across the face, knocking him over the wall and into the sand below. Then he grinned at Ferret. "Pardon, Sire. My actions are shorter than my words."

Strongbow slowly staggered to his feet, rubbed his scraped jaw and poked his finger into his ear, dislodging some sand. He glanced up, took a few steps backward, and then stumbled away into the underbrush.

"You wanted him to get away!" Ferret shouted as he watched Strongbow disappear into the darkness.

Ferret faced Othello and looked him dead in the eyes. "Why?"

"I escaped to the New World to flee men of life-taking ways. You don't want to execute everyone, do you?"

"They're rebels!"

"Weren't you once?" Othello asked with the innocence of a child.

Ferret didn't reply.

"Plum craziness. You've been sickened with moon blindness. If this malady is left unchecked, it will impair your sight. Make you blind to the things that really matter and to everyone you love." Othello paused. "Do you want casks of blood on your conscience?"

Ferret just stood there and stared up at the sky. What had happened to him? Had he gone too far? Why was he acting like the kings of Europe? *It must be the effects of moon-sickness*, he thought. Ferret approached Othello and placed his hand on his arm. "I'm in your debt."

"For what?"

"For opposing me. Lesser men would have defied their own conscience. You're a man who puts principles before ill-behaving kings."

Othello bowed. "I'm here to disobey on command, Sire. Is there something else I might have the honor of not doing?"

"Call General Winchester and several dozen militiamen to the armory. I will meet you there in an hour. And arrest Father Yeats."

"I daresay, that is an order I won't disobey."

* * *

In the armory later that night, Ferret and his most loyal supporters, almost two dozen men, prepared to repel any attempts to capture their weapons and ammunition. Working fast, they reinforced the armory's walls with wood and bundles of tobacco. They also poked holes between the logs for their gun barrels.

Ferret's strategy relied on the element of deception. He would let Arthur surround the armory under the illusion that he had captured the militia's weapons. Just as Arthur's men encircled the armory, he would have someone ring the church bell. The alarm would alert the rest of the militia, which would then surround Arthur's cutthroats and mow them down in their tracks.

The only hitch in the plan so far had been the disappearance of Father Yeats. He was nowhere to be found. Othello suspected that Yeats was conspiring with Arthur. That was worrisome. Ferret wondered if he had misjudged the priest's role in Arthur's ploy. Strongbow might have been right all along. Yeats might be actively involved in bringing about a regime change.

From his lookout atop the armory, Harpoon Jack waved to Ferret. "I see a'something moving to the south and west."

Immediately, Ferret dispatched Captain O'Marr and Johan to the churchyard to get ready to ring the bell and organize the counterattack against Arthur. O'Marr had been selected because of his wartime experiences in the Dutch navy. Johan had been sent because he was clumsy and poor of sight, and there was a good chance that he would injure more friends than foes in the armory.

Not long after he sent the men, Ferret saw sixty to seventy men prowling from building to building with the cunning of thieves. It also became clear that Ferret had guessed right that his cousin would be attracted to the armory. Men of might could never resist the aroma of gunpowder.

Othello cautiously peered outside and appeared befuddled. "How did they get past our sentries? We should have been warned."

"Slit their throats, I wager," Winchester said.

At the last minute, Rutten and Harpoon Jack piled crates and beams across the doorway. *This is it*, Ferret thought as he watched Arthur's men creep closer.

* * *

Arthur was first to reach the armory. He stopped next to a two-horse wagon and noticed a row of gun barrels poking out from the log cabin's walls. He turned to his men and frowned. "Fancy that. Someone has alerted them." He looked back and glared at Strongbow.

In quick order, Arthur gestured his men to surround the armory on all sides. After they were in place, he strolled into the middle of the street, standing right in plain sight.

"I'm in control of the township," Arthur said. "Surrender!"

Ferret replied instantly. He fired a shot in the air with his pistol—the signal—to ring the church bell. Everything hinged on the militia's ability to surround Arthur. He waited.

The church bells did not ring.

"Perhaps Johan's wife killed him for staying up too late," Othello joked.

As the seconds ticked away, Ferret began to realize the extent of the potential damage the priest might have caused. Yeats could have told Arthur everything about *New Eire*: the number of armed men, who were loyal and who were not, and that the church bell alerted the militia. Captain O'Marr and Johan may have been captured or dead.

Ferret finally shouted, "Surrender to us! Our militia is over three hundred strong."

Arthur laughed. "Where are your loyal subjects? Methinks they have no stomach for battle. Do you see any resistance? You're despised as much as any overlord. And, as for O'Marr, he... has been delayed."

Ferret still believed he was not a tyrant; he ruled with good intentions and tolerance. He recalled what Cromwell had confided about loyal citizenry rising up to protect their leader, but realized no sane Irishmen would rush into a battle between rival clan members.

Ferret continued to wait, hoping for a last-minute miracle, but nobody came out of their houses. It had to be true. His own people were forsaking him in his hour of need. He knew that the only thing that mattered during clan strife was picking the winning side. He guessed that his people had already made that choice. As for the Dutch, most of them were still fuming over his decree to dissolve the council. They were going to sit it out and hope that the feud would not be too disruptive.

"Come out!" Arthur demanded.

Ferret shouted more refusals and both armed sides traded a few volleys of gunfire. But then Higgins and several other men arrived with Heather and Darbee in tow. They were followed by Paco, who poked and kicked at Arthur's men until he saw Strongbow. Happily, he ran to Strongbow and hugged him. Strongbow pushed him aside.

"Where are his other chits?" Arthur asked. "Ferret has three or four of 'em!"

Higgins shrugged. "They got away. One of the tykes bit me finger. Want to see it?" He lifted up his bloody finger and shoved it up to Arthur's disgusted face.

Arthur knocked Higgin's hand away.

"It really hurts."

"Just bring me the runty bitch," Arthur said with a deep guttural snarl.

Within a few minutes, a man almost threw Heather into Arthur's arms. With ease, Arthur locked his arm around her neck and dragged her into the street for all to see. Paco, unsure what to do, followed them.

Heather squirmed violently. "King Ferret will behead you all!"

Arthur started to laugh as he approached the armory. Near its entrance, he strolled with a feeling of sweet victory as he promenaded his captive like a prized trophy. He enjoyed parading Ferret's wife, boldly displaying his hostage as if they were romantic lovers, stealing every chance to kiss her on the lips.

Ferret turned away and collapsed to his knees on the armory floor. Heather was right; he had favored his rulership over everyone else. He was the monster.

"King Ferret, set your eyes on my prize!" Arthur shouted with glee. "I have something of yours."

Hearing Arthur, Ferret got up and watched the travesty, knowing that he had to make a fast decision. His face went white as he watched Arthur pull out a long cutlass and hold its blade against Heather's neck. He could see that Arthur was serious, inflamed with the unblinking glare of a killer.

"Need I say more, me royal cousin?"

Just then, Strongbow confronted Arthur, reminding him that he had promised not to harm anyone.

"That I did—and I might keep my word." Arthur chuckled, then pointed at Paco. "Bring me that mooncalf."

Two men pounced on Paco and dragged him to Arthur.

"Must I illustrate, King Ferret?" In one quick stroke, Arthur jabbed his blade into Paco's chest. Paco's mouth bloated with one last breath, and he fell, dead.

Strongbow sprinted to Paco, knelt next to him and embraced his lifeless body. He glared up at Arthur as anger seethed up from deep inside.

Othello groaned. "God-a-mercy! They've murdered Paco. That will henceforth stain Arthur with eternal misfortune."

Ferret rushed to the barred door and began to rip away the barricade.

Othello pinned Ferret to the wall. "You cannot go outside! 'Tis a hell-fire suicide."

Ferret struggled against Othello, finally breaking free only to be held back again by Winchester, Rutten, and Holbrook. Ferret cried, "What would you have me do?" He ordered them to step aside.

"No!" Othello said. "You think you can trust Arthur? He is the sort who would murder you in your sleep."

"Heather is as good as dead!" Holbrook said. "Why add your name to his murderous roster?"

Ferret could feel the terrible burden crushing him from all sides, squeezing and compressing until nothing remained. His meager empire meant nothing without Heather. Life without love was mere existence, like a cold rock sitting in a stream or a lone tree blowing in the wind. He turned to his men. "I must surrender. If I do it now, he may let you all live to a ripe old age."

Slowly, most of his men relented. Only Holbrook and Othello refused to have anything to do with hoisting the white flag, saying they would rather be taken prisoner and hung. Ferret attempted to convince them that surrender was the only possible course. Holbrook turned away and refused to listen to talk of submission. After a while, he moved to a window, stared out and rocked back and forth on his heels. Othello hid behind a storage shelf stacked with flintlocks, and fiddled with the guns, acting as if nothing had happened. They both refused to pay attention. Ferret turned to Rutten and handed him his pistol, who in turn, let the gun drop to the floor.

As Ferret trudged towards the door, an idea came to him. He remembered that his cousin had always been enamored with dueling. Considered a good shot, Arthur had boasted of mortally wounding several challengers in Cork. Ferret saw this as his only hope.

Ferret shouted to his cousin, "I will surrender under one condition!"

"No conditions!" Arthur chuckled sardonically. His men followed suit, laughing heartily.

"I ask for a fair fight. Victor takes all!"

"A duel?"

"Aye, and you have the choice of weapons."

"Why should I accept?" Arthur asked. "I have what I want!"

The doorway was finally cleared, and Ferret stepped outside. He hoped Arthur had some speck of honor left, or at least a hot temper that would get the better of him. "Because only a white-livered coward would refuse. Neither my colony nor any true Irishman would stomach a coward for a king."

"Coward? I—"

One of Arthur's men, Big Bill McSheen, whispered something to him.

Arthur nodded with a sly smile. He released Heather and shouted, "I accept your offer, dear cousin."

* * *

Ferret and Arthur faced each other in a grassy meadow on the western edge of *New Eire*. The heat of the midmorning sun was almost unbearable. Three men from each side were permitted to witness the duel. Othello, Winchester, and Holbrook watched, as did Arthur's seconds, Strongbow, Higgins, and Big Bill McSheen. A dozen more of Arthur's armed men stood nearby, just in case.

Father Yeats presented a pine and leather box. Inside the case were two smooth-bore dueling pistols, sitting side by side. In accordance with the agreement, Arthur was awarded the first pick. When Arthur's hand hovered over one, Yeats nudged his arm, prodding Arthur to select the other pistol. Immediately, Ferret objected, but his protest went unheeded. When Ferret's seconds hastened over to inspect the weapons, they were blocked.

Arthur lifted up his weapon and examined it. "Men of righteousness will win the day."

Ferret looked down on the remaining pistol. It was rusty and old. *Might misfire*, he thought. Still, this was his only chance. He had never dueled to the death before, but he had to kill his cousin. Then he would have to deal with Strongbow and the other cutthroats. He was sure the day would be either short or never-ending.

Yeats explained the rules. "Walk fifty paces, turn, then fire. May God be with you." Then he started to count. "One pace, two paces..."

Ferret's hand remained steady.

"Twenty-two, twenty-three..."

Sweat poured down Ferret's face. Seemed all wrong. One shot to determine everything.

"Thirty-one, thirty-two..."

Should have listened to Strongbow, Ferret thought. *Should have abdicated. Who wants to be king?*

"Forty-five..."

Any time now. Must turn quickly. Must fire first.

"Fifty paces!"

Arthur turned around as Ferret aimed carefully and squeezed the trigger. Nothing happened. Something wasn't right. Arthur's pistol was in his hand, but its barrel was pointed skyward. His cousin grinned and began to stroll toward Ferret as if he were taking a Sunday morning walk to church. He bowed to his men. What was he doing?

Ferret aimed at Arthur again and pulled the trigger. Iron clanked against iron. There was no spark of life. Ferret examined the pistol. It was empty—no powder, no ball. An empty pistol and a dirty trick.

Ferret knew how to play the same game. He reached into his pocket and pretended to load pinches of black powder into the barrel. Next, he took one of Darbee's marbles, dropped it down the barrel and with a stick from the ground, rammed the ball down the barrel. To anyone with a keen sense of foreboding, he had a loaded pistol at his command.

"I'm waiting, dear cousin," Ferret said, swinging the barrel up and pointing it at Arthur. His finger poised on the trigger. "Let's try it again."

Arthur stopped. A sickening frown rippled across his face.

"Well?" Ferret aimed at Arthur's chest and cocked the flintlock's hammer back, the engaging tumbler making an audible click. He was ready to pull the trigger.

Arthur called Strongbow to his side. "Shoot the tomfool! I don't want to get caught up in a clan dispute. They are so messy."

"The last I heard," Strongbow droned, mocking his boss, "you're supposed to do your own dueling. I believe I saw it in a rule book somewhere."

Ferret stepped forward. "What's the matter? Are you afraid they might not take orders from a cowardly milksop?"

Arthur smiled with a manic gleam in his eye. "My tadpole of a cousin finally grows a backbone. What a blissful moment."

"I know not what awaits me. But if I must, I will die here. What about you?"

"What about *me*?" Arthur groused with a scowl. "I ought to spare your life and put you on trial, just as you did to me. But I shan't. You might escape. Someone might drop a pistol inside your cell and unlock the door. Still, I could arrange safe passage out of here. Just surrender your weapon."

"A dishonorable man pledging his honor," Ferret chuckled. "Should I cry or should I laugh? You promised never to return. What is a promise worth these days?"

"Father Yeats's offer was very convincing," Arthur said. "The gist of it was that I have more suitable abilities. Could I refuse him?"

"My people will not follow you."

"On the contrary, the commonfolk will never notice the difference."

"You're wrong."

Arthur leveled his pistol at Ferret's abdomen. "Come on. We both know that commoners are born victims, willing to sanction almost any god-awful overlord. Your demise means nothing to them. 'Tis only a changing of the guard, the lighting of a new candlewick. I do not speak of pious philosophy or hide my intentions. I am open-handed. You sit and wait and scheme. I grasp for power so that all may see my intentions. We are much alike. I'm just a bit clumsier. I seized power too quickly. But we both understand it. We know that brute strength is what matters, that it sustains our authority. People desire to be ruled, mistreated, and tortured. They expect it. They pray for it. 'Tis their very nature. They beg for the whip, and I am all too willing to provide the welts. And so are you."

Ferret shook his head. In some ways, he could not blame Arthur. Depravity was contagious. Ferret's claim to sainthood was weak. Given more time, he might have also wallowed in the same wickedness. Maybe he was akin to Arthur. But his cousin had gotten one thing dead right: not even the most innocent child could play God without getting his hands dirty.

"Even if your pistol is loaded," Arthur said, "I doubt it will fire. I requested an unloaded and damaged one. Chances are, it will misfire."

"It all comes down to trust, doesn't it?"

"Not trust—fear."

"Well, then what do you wait for? My blessing?"

"Farewell, me dear cousin," Arthur said as he squeezed the trigger.

A shot rang out.

Arthur's face drooped with a look of surprise and bewilderment. He glanced at his weapon. It had not fired. He soon staggered backward, his knees buckling, gasping for air. His pistol tumbled from his loose fingers as he fell. Blood bubbled from his mouth.

Strongbow dropped his smoking pistol and took a running kick at Arthur's lifeless body. "That's for Paco!" Tossing a sword to Ferret, he whipped out another pistol and prepared to shoot Big Bill McSheen and the others.

But, before anyone could discharge their weapons, gunshots and cannon fire thundered from the beach. A colonist ran up and shouted, "The British regulars are attacking!"

Chapter 36

Wave after wave of British launches, brimming with soldiers, firearms, and small cannon, assaulted the shoreline. On the beach, the redcoats struggled to get out of their boats, weighed down as they were by gear, ammunition pouches, and their cumbersome coats. When they finally extricated themselves, they trudged across the deep sand, panting and cursing the difficult terrain, until they reached the front line, where they began to fire. With the British were over fifty Indians who leaped out of the boats like graceful deer, uninhibited by heavy equipment or explicit orders.

In the bay, *New Eire's* three ships had been torched. Six English men-of-war sailed past the burning ships and fired into the colony, shattering many of *New Eire's* houses into tinder. The colony had already lost a quarter of its men and the advancing onslaught had barely begun. Half of the militia that remained was assembled behind *New Eire's* first defensive line, the three-foot-high stone parapet, and was firing indiscriminately at the advancing enemy. Behind them, women and older children frantically stuffed gunpowder and lead balls into the flintlocks. They then passed the loaded weapons down a chaotic supply line.

Ferret, Strongbow, Colonel Holbrook, and Harpoon Jack took shelter behind the wall, too. Holbrook could see that Cromwell had the means to achieve victory. The tactics were by the book. First and foremost, distract the enemy with a frontal assault. Then launch a second attack along the flank and slaughter them with crossfire. Holbrook explained this to Ferret. Their only hope was that Cromwell had failed to muster enough troops to overrun the seaside wall.

As Holbrook watched the redcoats assemble, Big Bill McSheen flopped down beside Strongbow. McSheen was a half-breed of Scottish and Cherokee blood, rumored to have pirated with Black Caesar as a powder

385

monkey. He took off his hat, spat a stream of tobacco juice, and threw up his hands. "This is barmy. I'm taking my men out."

Strongbow growled. "*Your* men?"

"I didn't come to battle the whole British army," McSheen muttered as he looked over the wall at the approaching tempest. "Something's amiss here. *Cromwell* is attacking." He slapped his hand on his head and leaned toward Strongbow. "Did you hear me?"

"You're bloody observant," Strongbow said as he took a potshot at the British line.

"You don't understand," McSheen snarled, showing his yellow teeth. "We sit amidst a trap. We've been double-crossed! Cromwell wasn't supposed to come until we summoned him!"

Ferret, who had overheard the conversation, interjected, "You were conspiring with Cromwell? Have out with it."

McSheen rolled his eyes. Nobody else volunteered a word. The answer was painfully obvious.

The coincidences were piling up faster than palm fronds during a hurricane. Ferret closed his eyes. The truth was sickening. Cromwell's assault at this moment had been meticulously arranged. The major general was gambling on Arthur to plunge *New Eire* into civil war. In the ensuing confusion, Cromwell would pluck the overripe plum and then squelch it under his heel. The victor of the infighting would be deposed and the township wiped off the map. Ferret detested when history repeated itself, especially at his expense. He swore that the backstabber would not succeed this time, but he had a feeling he was no position to reprimand Cromwell.

"'Tis true," Strongbow said. "Cromwell encouraged us to attack *New Eire*. We divulged every detail about your township and operations—your plans, your weaknesses, and your timing. He said it was his chance to rid the world of a menace."

Ferret remembered that the major general had once boasted that he played to win or he would not play at all. Ferret worried that this game was practically over. He figured that Cromwell believed he had set a strategy in motion that could only end in *New Eire's* defeat—the same opinion reached earlier by Holbrook.

Before Ferret could come up with a plan of his own, the vanguard of the British regulars reached the stone wall and, with bayonets fixed, jabbed and fired at the thinning line of defenders.

Ferret vaulted up and swung his flintlock's butt at a soldier's head, knocking him down. A second soldier drew a pistol and fired, but the pistol misfired, sending sparks and iron in every direction. Ignoring his burned hands, the Englishman pulled out a long knife and leaped at Ferret.

Ferret drew his own pistol and fired. The bullet lunged into the redcoat's chest, knocking the man over.

Just as they were running low on ammunition, Hendrick arrived and passed out loaded flintlocks and pistols. He looked scared and confused, but also determined. He knelt beside Holbrook, the man who had taught him marksmanship, and fired at the advancing redcoats. He shoved two pistols into the colonel's hands. Holbrook smiled gratefully. Before he could use either, a shot struck him in the head. He fell backward. Blood streamed down his forehead.

Ferret was first to kneel next to his injured friend, but the colonel was already dead. Ferret jumped to his feet and prepared to lead a charge against the redcoats and kill every last one with his bare hands.

Harpoon Jack pulled Ferret down. "Don't be daffy. We can't lose you, too."

The English continued to advance, a powerful red wave about to crash against their feet. But the volley of gunfire from the rampart wall also began to take its toll. The British line had thinned to a few stragglers. Those left standing retreated back to the launch boats. Some of the Irishmen stood, weapons in hand, and let out a war cry. Ferret knew that the battle had just begun.

However, the lull in fighting gave Ferret and the others the time to withdraw from their rocky defensive line. They retreated to the main rampart. They had lost too many defenders—too many dear friends. They dragged the dead and wounded though the small chokehold of a gate.

Now commanding from the rampart, Ferret had a bird's eye view of the British reassembling their forces. They were dragging twelve-pound cannons closer to the front line. That seemed unnecessary. The wall had already been breached by cannon fire in several locations. Ferret watched more troops come ashore. There were hundreds of reinforcements landing on the beach.

Heather bumped into him, flustered and worried. She was not sure what to do. Two of the children clung to her feet, scared. Heather had been loading flintlocks and pistols with the other women but had made so many mistakes that she was relieved of her duties.

"Go home," Ferret said. "Hide under the floorboards with the children. There's nothing you can do here."

"I can't leave you," Heather said.

Ferret took hold of Heather's shoulders and pulled her close. Ferret had a sinking feeling that this would be the last time he would see her again. "I'll be fine. We'll meet again."

Heather had the same premonition as he. She kissed him softly on the cheek and said her farewells. "On the other side, my love." A tear trickled down her thin cheek as she reached for her children's hands and hurried away. She stopped at the edge of the rampart, looked at her husband, and tried to imprint his image on her mind.

When Ferret turned to his right side, he saw Hendrick. The boy had his weapon vaguely pointed at Ferret. "I'm staying with my father. And there's nothin' you can do about it."

Ferret did not have time to argue with him. The siege from the beach had renewed in earnest. To his right an explosion rocked the colony's southern wall. As the smoke cleared, Ferret saw a gaping hole in their fortifications. Redcoats poured through it with ease. *More English to kill,* Ferret thought. *Let them come. The more the merrier. If we kill enough of them, someone might investigate the massacre.* Otherwise, *New Eire's* struggle would die not only in vain, but also in obscurity.

Strongbow grabbed two loaded pistols from a woman and tucked them under his belt. Scanning the battlefield, he spoke in a sorrowful tone. "We're caught in a vise. I'm afraid they have us by the windpipe."

Ferret nodded. He had a sick feeling in his stomach. He ordered his last remaining detachments to the southern wall to stop the advancing English. It was a senseless order and a useless rear-guard action that only delayed the inevitable. Within minutes, half of his remaining militiamen were mowed down.

Meanwhile, colonists were retreating to the northern wall, still under the illusion that they might escape the wrath of Cromwell. Ferret knew better. The major general typified a new breed of man, ruthless and cunning; the quintessential millstone that crushed everything within reach, leaving nothing but chaff in its wake. Personally led by Cromwell, the English pursued the colonists to the northern gate. But the soldiers took their time, exploring the razed cabins and firing at small pockets of resistance. Others smashed cabin windows and tossed torches inside.

"General Winchester has become a turncoat," Othello reported to Ferret. He had seen Winchester hurrying toward a small English regiment wearing the old, ill-fitting military uniform from his military service in Ireland. "Allah will punish him."

Ferret knew that Winchester was attempting to trick the English regiment, pretending to be one of Cromwell's men in order to live another day. He hoped he succeeded—someone must live to expose the treachery that befell his hapless nation. Ferret wondered if the ploy would work. Winchester's uniform was out of date, tatty, and lacked any accolades he would have earned during enlistment.

"He's disloyal," Othello said. "In Morocco we would slice his belly like an overripe melon."

"At least he has a chance," Ferret sighed.

In a desperate move, Ferret divided up his remaining men and took half of them to the northern wall. Three dozen men followed him down the rampart and through the center of town. That seemed to be his best chance to escape. Reports had come back that Cromwell's forces were lightest to the north. On the way, he ran into Rutten with a small squad of men. They were fleeing from British forces to the south.

"We don't gotta chance, by crikey," Rutten said. "We're ensnared like a school of netted codfish."

Panicking, the remaining colonists condensed around their king. They were surrounded. The colony had been checkmated, and Cromwell was in a good position to take the king.

The fighting intensified. The English gunfire became more deadly, cutting down the colonists like stalks of wheat under a sickle. Rutten fell with a bullet through his chest. He swore bitterly, then he asked for a drink. But the small bottle in his coat pocket had broken; he cut his fingers as he desperately fingered for it.

"Don't let them get me," Rutten said.

"I won't," Ferret whispered.

Ferret watched the slaughter unfold. Big Bill McSheen, who had not managed to escape, was seriously wounded. Before he succumbed to his injury, he managed to stab his assailant to death. Strongbow helped McSheen up and the two limped away. Ferret thought *Strongbow will survive. People like him always do. They know about the changing tides of war, when to stand up and when to abandon a lost cause.*

The circle around Ferret grew tighter. Ferret tripped over the Dutchman's body, the head nearly blown off. Ferret thought to himself: at least he would never again have to listen to the man complain about the world going to Hell. It was indeed rushing to Hell in a handbasket, but neither he nor anyone else wanted to hear about it.

He saw Judge Van Doyle's lifeless body, as well as Higgins's. The judge's spectacles were broken; he had been shot in the face. Bits of burnt gunpowder blackened his face.

Harpoon Jack was wounded but still slashing at the redcoats with his spear. Ferret crawled over other dead men, Captain Abe McCloud... so many others. Everyone was dying. He could feel his blood draining, his heart sinking.

General Winchester broke through a line of fighting colonists to fight by Ferret's side. "There's no escape! My uniform was too old to dupe the bastards."

Othello grabbed hold of Ferret's arm. "We must surrender! The battle goes badly."

"Cromwell will not accept it," Ferret said. "He wants to bury the truth. Dead men can't tell secrets."

* * *

Major Mountjoy, who was at Major-General Cromwell's side, was enthralled. "We've got these pocky wits by the neck."

"Almost," Cromwell said, "but the deed is not done until the hellcat is strung."

"They are defeated, Sir. We should allow them to surrender."

"No surrendering this time, Lieutenant," Cromwell said. "This will forever serve as a lesson for all to remember. This is English territory—my territory. This is not Ireland. When we are done with them we'll be welcomed as war heroes back home. And nobody will ever dare accuse me of misdoings again."

Mountjoy looked confused. "What misdoings?"

"Never mind! They were all lies," Cromwell said with so much intensity that his neck veins popped out. "I wish to strangle Winchester with my own hands. He's the true traitor here."

Mountjoy looked surprised. "He was one of your men?"

Cromwell squinted through the smoke and haze and pointed. "Look at the bastard—the fat one. He fights alongside their king. I shall grind his bones to dust, I—" Cromwell stopped. He began to scan the battlefield nervously. "What was *that*?"

"What was what?" Mountjoy fired his pistol, killing a woman holding an infant.

"That cry."

"Must be our savages," Mountjoy said.

"No, this was too far away. Much too far."

Mountjoy lowered his pistol and listened closely. "I hear something, too. It comes from behind us."

At that moment, Cromwell saw his own Indians struck by a bout of fear and panic. They chattered frantically among themselves, waved accusing fingers at each other, and then scurried back to the boats.

Cromwell was perplexed. He wondered aloud, "What's going on here?" Then an arrow struck one of his corporals in the neck, and Cromwell watched in horror as a large army of Yamasees spilled over the southern wall. Parts of the wall caved in as the Indians hacked at the wall's lashings.

"Retreat! Retreat!" Cromwell shouted. "Return to the longboats or we'll be cut off!"

* * *

391

Ferret watched the Indians plow into the retreating British. They leaped at the soldiers, hair flying wildly, war-axes arched overhead. The British blocked the axes with their sabers and slashed in defense, iron sparking against iron. But the once-invincible English soon fled like cowards. It was magnificent. The Yamasees advanced from all fronts, and the battle soon deteriorated into small pockets of savage fighting.

As the English line thinned, Othello found himself cornered by a burly, short-haired Englishman with a square jaw. He charged the redcoat and drew his dagger. Grasping the soldier's arm, Othello twirled the man around and plunged the knife at the man's chest.

The soldier screamed until he looked down at his chest and saw neither blood nor a wound. "What the hell-fire?" he cried out.

Othello examined his dagger. There was no projecting blade of steel. He grinned. He had pulled his trick blade by accident. Othello shrugged. "Wrong knife."

"Not on my account." The redcoat snorted and whipped out his own dagger, much larger in size, and took a wide swing.

Othello deflected the blade with his mighty arm and rammed the soldier's head with his own.

"Why you flat-headed Neger!" the soldier yelled, more irate than before.

Othello slammed his head harder this time, knocking the Englishman unconscious.

There was another pocket of heavy fighting near the center of town. Cromwell, Mountjoy, and several young officers had been cut off from the main English column. Ferret arrived to confront them, shadowed by a party of Indians. Cromwell thrust his sword at the Indians, stabbing one man in the belly. Enraged, the Yamasees fought back with tomahawks.

When Sanchez arrived at the scene, he ordered his men to withdraw. He pulled out his sword, bowed slightly, and beamed with delight for a chance to engage in swordplay. His face soured, however, when he discovered that everyone but Cromwell had retreated.

Finding himself alone did not seem to bother Cromwell. He towered over the short-legged Spaniard and prepared to impale the little man.

Ferret pushed Sanchez to the side and prepared to fight. "Your move, my dear major general," Ferret said, with a sword in hand and a revengeful glaze in his eyes.

Cromwell bowed with grace. "My pleasure, indeed. I've been looking forward to this reunion."

Ferret returned the pleasantries. "It will be an honor to watch you meet your maker sooner than expected."

With sudden dispatch, Cromwell leaped at Ferret, twirling his sword expertly, though it did not hit its mark. Springing back, Ferret fought with equal skill and artfulness, soon gaining the upper hand. But then Winchester arrived with a cutlass in hand, determined to join the fray. The moment was ruined. Winchester was not up to any standards. He was overweight and outmatched, and his uniform fit so poorly that it hampered his ability to fight.

Cromwell's eyes flared with a sense of irony. "I daresay, I must be a most popular fellow."

"Popular as scum in the Thames." Winchester grabbed his sword like a spear and threw it at Cromwell, but he missed.

Cromwell pointed his sword at General Winchester. He glanced at Ferret. "If you want to find the man who murdered your father—look no further."

Ferret coughed, almost choking on the words. General Winchester was a gentleman of good taste, but also a man with a murky background. Ferret did not want to believe the accusation. And yet there was a slight ring of truth to the charges. A nagging voice reminded him that Winchester had been at Macroom and freely confessed to selling arms to the Irish rebels—an important bit of information for which many would kill. He decided to wait to hear Winchester's side of the story. It could all be a load of twaddle. "You're just trying to displace the blame."

"If so," Cromwell said, "then why does he run like a scared possum? You're surrounded by cowards, traitors, and spies."

Strongbow shoved his way through a half-circle of Indians. He bowed to Cromwell. "Are you referring to me? I'm the only spy here, and an exemplary one at that."

"You were my best informant," Cromwell grinned, "until that wench turned you into mush."

"I was never paid well," Strongbow said.

"You got what was coming to you," Cromwell sneered.

Ferret glanced at Strongbow. "Sorry, but I was here first." He took a running leap and struck at Cromwell with full force, hacking, slashing, and gashing. The fight propelled them into a field of crossfire. Ferret could hear bullets buzzing overhead like angry wasps. One nicked his forehead, but he continued to fight. Another bullet lodged deep into his shoulder. He fell, and Cromwell moved in for the kill.

In a flash, Strongbow slammed into Cromwell, preventing him from impaling Ferret. They both tumbled to the ground and rolled several times before coming to a stop.

Cromwell regained his feet with grace and faced Strongbow. He stiffened his lips and twirled his sword with a flick of his wrist. "My trusted spy turns against me! Rejoin my ranks and I will forgive your sins."

Strongbow smiled and pointed his sword at Cromwell. "And for my penance?"

"You're no more Catholic or Irish than I am," Cromwell said. "You were born not far from my estate." He paused. "I have never understood why any good Englishman would protect such scum of a race."

"I'm not sure either. But when I find out, you'll be the first to know." Strongbow plunged his blade at Cromwell, nicking him in the forearm.

Ferret felt deeply betrayed. *Not Irish.* Was there nothing that Strongbow could say without lying? Was truth itself a hoax? Should all men be considered liars until proven truthful?

As Ferret watched the fight, someone began to bandage his shoulder. Turning, he saw a worried Othello hovering over him. A tingling sense of numbness had set in, which was a good thing since Othello's manhandling could have killed the hardiest of men.

Despite Strongbow's fine swordplay, he grew weary.

Cromwell advanced, whirling and thrusting his sword, barely missing Strongbow. "You should have remained in Ireland. You were a better highwayman than you are a swordsman."

Leaping back, Strongbow tripped and fell backward. Cromwell saw an opening and pierced Strongbow through the chest. Pain rippling across his face, Strongbow refused to surrender. He grabbed hold of the blade and clawed at Cromwell's red coat, pulling and dragging him down. Teetering, Cromwell began to topple over. He struggled to pull loose of Strongbow's grip.

Ferret pushed Othello aside. He was not going to let Cromwell kill everyone he had ever known. He stood and somehow found a sword and attacked his old nemesis, slashing in a blind frenzy until his blade sliced through Cromwell's arm, severing it above the elbow. Cromwell fell in a spasm of pain.

In quick response, a stronger contingency of British led by Mountjoy rushed to Cromwell's rescue, driving off most of the Indians and colonists. They dragged Cromwell back to the beach and lowered him into a launch, his armless stub spurting blood profusely.

"Me laddie," Strongbow murmured between shallow gasps.

Ferret dropped his sword and sank to his knees beside Strongbow.

Strongbow clenched Ferret's collar. "You should have abdicated, you fool-hearted lout. When will you listen to me? Was for your own good."

Ferret reached for Strongbow's shoulder. It felt cold. "I don't listen well."

"Protect... them." Strongbow coughed up blood and went silent.

"I promise." Ferret slowly stood up. Strongbow had again saved his worthless life. He had been more of a father to him than Black Fox. Why the concern? Why take in a lost orphan? Made little sense. If only he had something to give in return, something to show his renewed affection. But he had nothing to give back. Even if he did, it would never be good enough for his old friend.

"Let's go," Othello said. When Ferret did not respond, he grabbed hold of Ferret's arm and shook him. "Everything's a'burning! We must go now!"

Ferret finally snapped out of his trance. The whole township was engulfed in flames. The Yamasees were in a killing frenzy, torching cabins and killing anyone whom they suspected of being English, including the colonists. The first word that rushed to his mind was *Heather*. He had ordered her home with the children.

When he arrived back to his house, the structure was engulfed in flames so bright that they obscured even the door frame. *There must be a way to get them out*, Ferret thought. He assumed they were hiding under the house, in the cellar, but it had not been built to withstand fire.

Othello pulled Ferret back. "Your Majesty. They're all dead. Nothing escapes the inferno." He turned Ferret around. "Look at 'em. The redskins have gone crack-brained."

Ferret looked over at the burning windmill and saw Winchester in peril. The Yamasees had surrounded him near the cooper's shop. One Indian jabbed Winchester's belly with the handle of his axe.

"I'm not with the English!" General Winchester cried out.

Hearing the word *English*, two savages buried their tomahawks in Winchester's skull. His head resembled a bowl of pink sludge.

Othello yanked at Ferret again. "'Tis getting out of hand. We must retire."

"How can I leave Heather?" Ferret trembled as he spoke. Pain over-powered his rational thoughts. He had to take charge and lead his people to safety and away from danger. He couldn't find the words to bark out any commands. It seemed as if his feet were stuck in the mud, and no matter how hard he struggled, he could not get free. His wound was still bleeding and his legs were becoming numb. He could see his blood pouring out of his wounded shoulder. Othello tried to bandage the wound again, with little success. He put his hand across Ferret's bandage and applied pressure, but it did not stanch the flow. Dying. That was what life was—blood to dust.

Ferret fought against Othello and tried to break free. He had to get Heather and the children. He had to rescue his family. If only he had the strength, the energy, to do something. Instead, his body was shutting down, his vision blurring, his concentration waning. Everyone moved in slow motion. He thought of Heather and her cries of help. His thoughts were breaking up. Just could not remember what he wanted to do, could not remember what her face looked like. Darkness gathered around him.

Othello carried his motionless king away. The Yamasees raised their tomahawks in respect, believing that the big black man had killed a white man and wanted to continue his mutilation in the serenity of the forest. Othello escaped the wrath of the Yamasees safely. The other colonists were not as fortunate.

Chapter 37

There was a stark emptiness, an absence of substance and warmth. Ferret felt as if he were floating above the earth, upside down and swinging, without body or form. Was he dead or just near death's doorstep? An elderly monk had once said that newly departed souls floated above the earth until the warm and gentle hand of God lifted them to heaven's gate, accompanied by the songs of children. But something was wrong. Neither warmth nor sweet sounds met his senses. Instead, he smelled wild jasmine and heard a baritone voice sing, "Your Majesty?"

Ferret attempted to respond, but his voice was uncooperative. He tried to move his head toward the man's voice. He tried moving an eyelid, a fingertip, anything to prove to himself that the stubbornness of life still dwelt within his battered body. Finally, with great effort, he managed to twitch his finger ever so slightly. The realization that he was still on Earth gave him a distinct feeling of disappointment.

Soon Ferret heard other things. Muffled cracks of gunfire wafted through the dark, stationary air. For a moment it had resembled the popping and cracking of a dying campfire. Ferret lifted his head. He saw the drab and gloomy face of Othello.

"I thought you were amongst the dead," Othello said. He cupped his hand and drew water from a creek which he dripped on Ferret's hot face. "You've been on the road of hard luck, Allah knows."

Ferret licked the water that spilled on his lips. "We escaped? Where are the others?"

"There are no others."

He turned away from Othello. He saw a dull flickering light reflecting off the low clouds. It radiated like the stars on a clear, cold night. Ferret realized it was the dying coals of *New Eire*. He remembered the night he had cut Heather's finger. They had trothed their death pact, neither to live without the other. Now it seemed like a hollow promise.

Othello laid his shirt across Ferret's chest. "Your body's cold, but your head burns hot with fever. I've bandaged your wounds, but I can do no more."

Ferret understood Othello's meaning. Death stalked him like a lean wolf in winter. Even a physician could do little except bleed him. He would take his chances with a merciful God.

* * *

The next morning brought an Indian woman who had stopped at the creek to drink and rest. Behind her, a horse dragged a ladder-like structure made of lashed branches. It held the body of a dead child adorned with beads, white plumes, and a headdress. Although a cloud of profound sadness hung over the young, dog-faced squaw, she hovered over Ferret and worried about his condition. She tugged at Othello's arm, suggesting with sign language that she could help the injured white man.

With a knife, she cut roots and moss. Examining Ferret's hot forehead, the Indian woman rubbed his swollen shoulder. Angrily, she turned around and scolded Othello, poking him with her finger. Grasping the knife tightly in her right hand, she ripped open Ferret's bandages, causing him to bleed. Ferret struggled feebly and pushed the woman back to defend himself.

Othello shoved her away, too.

She threatened Othello with her knife.

"You will not get past me," Othello said, standing in front of Ferret with the fortitude of stone.

Suddenly, three Yamasee warriors appeared from the underbrush. Othello reached for his dagger and prepared to lunge at the intruders. However, the Indians were faster, and they brandished their bows and arrows at him, halting his advance.

The squaw proceeded. She slit open Ferret's inflamed wound and pushed the roots and moss into his shoulder.

After retying the bandages, the woman went to her dead child and wiped her bloody hands on the child's colorless face. Kneeling, she prayed, moaned, and howled, then she placed a blue glass bead into the child's hand. The bead rolled out and disappeared on the ground. She embraced her child and wept. She was escorted away by one of the Yamasee warriors; the other two led the horse down a narrow path.

"I'm sorry." Othello lowered his head in shame. "Shall I scrape off the concoction, Sire?"

"No," Ferret said. "Let it be. A little magic may still remain in this grim world."

* * *

One week later, Ferret felt strong enough to travel and decided, against Othello's advice, to backtrack and see the charred remains of *New Eire*.

There, he found large black carrion crows hopping from body to body, eating the decaying flesh of his countrymen. He wanted to bury all of his companions before they were consumed, but he did not know where to start.

He made his way to his former home. A haunting silence hung over him as he hobbled through the crumbling frame of his doorway. Most of the floor planks had collapsed over the large hole under the flooring. He leaned on one of the remaining posts. A slick coat of black soot covered his hand and fingers. He tried to rub it off, but it only smeared. In the rubble, half buried in the pit under the house, Ferret saw skeletons burned beyond recognition. There were at least five contorted and disfigured small bodies, maybe more. Poor Heather. Poor Darbee. Poor everybody. He could have prevented this tragedy. It was his fault. He had been a bullheaded lout, unwilling to release the reins of power. His stubbornness had cost him everything. No one should try to rule the world—no man can be trusted with power. And if they try, they had better be willing to lose everything in the deal, even their soul.

When Ferret saw Zeph, he gasped. The dog was lying on his side near the fallen stone chimney, flies buzzing around his body. Ferret looked away, so as to remember Zeph as he had been, not what he had become. He saw a hawk sailing across the blue sky. Nobody could hurt a hawk up there; was just too high, too far removed. He remembered the burnt remains of Strongbow's first wife in Raca. She had also been incinerated by English injustice. He could see that he and Strongbow were more alike than he had ever wanted to admit. He should have taken his friend's advice more seriously. Looking back, he could see his own idiocy in the making. Hindsight was a harsh mistress, a punishment more ruthless than the tongue-lashing of a nagging wife.

A cloud of ash surrounded Othello as he approached. "There's nothing to be done here. We must withdraw. 'Tis unlucky. We do not want to disturb the spirits."

"'Twas our home," Ferret murmured. He scraped at the soot baked into the chimney. "Two months. Took me two long months to finish. William and Hendrick helped me lay the stones." Ferret stopped. He did not want to speak about the dead as if they were alive. The past was past, and it would never live again. He leaned gently on a window frame, but it crumbled under his weight. He fingered the blackened wood framing of the window. "Never did keep out the wind."

"Heed my words," Othello said. "The spirits won't sleep much longer."

"I should bury them all."

"It will collapse. Let them rest."

Ferret scanned the sky again, searching for the free-soaring hawk, but it had flown away, apparently to get away from a land devoid of life. Who could blame it?

"I will at least bury Strongbow," Ferret said, and he went to search for his friend. He found instead a robed man kneeling in the churchyard next to a freshly dug grave. The man was consumed in prayer and oblivious to everything else. The church was the only building that had escaped destruction.

Walking close to the mysterious griever, Ferret saw an inscription etched crudely onto the wooden cross. It read, "Massacred by evildoers, 1715. Have pity on his soul." There was no mention of the colony or the battle with the English. It was as though his nation had never existed.

Ferret spoke to the hooded man. "Whose grave is this?"

The man did not reply. His body remained rigid like the white cross.

Finally, the hooded man whispered, "I must confess to the Lord my God, I'm responsible for this depravity." Ferret knew it had to be Father Yeats.

Ferret was unwilling to hear others blame themselves for his misdeeds. He reached out and gently touched the priest's shoulder to comfort him. "You're wrong."

Yeats's face was covered with deep cuts and black bruises. He had a broken nose. "I summoned the demons. I begged Arthur to return. 'Twas my meddling that brought such wrath upon our land."

Ferret felt a tinge of empathy for the priest. There was plenty of guilt for all. He inquired again about the victim buried in the grave.

"'Tis Badger's resting mound," Yeats said.

Ferret jerked his hand away. He knew that everyone had died, but to hear the name spoken aloud made it all the more shocking.

Yeats lowered his head and recited a few sentences in Latin. Then he stopped, lifted up his head and spoke in a soft, calm voice. "Who amongst us can predict what others may do? I'll have Lucifer to pay, I will. I will make my last bedding here. I warned you to heed my concerns. You had a kingdom without a king, a ruler without rules, and a man without a destiny. And look what it has wrought." He closed his eyes and spoke softly. "'Twas a New World, and I, being from the old, could not fathom it. I brought the plague from the old to sicken the new."

Ferret realized he and Yeats were victims of unrelenting guilt, a power just as fatal as a musket ball. He could testify to it readily; he had an immense one lodged in his own heart, the blood still spurting freely, the gash widening by the day, the shame still infesting his tarry soul like leprosy.

Ferret left to find Othello. As he departed, Yeats muttered, "I will never leave these hallowed grounds."

When he found Othello, Ferret told him about finding Yeats.

"I could hog tie him and force him to come with us," Othello said.

Ferret shook his head. "I already have enough anguish to carry by myself." He paused. "And find myself just as lost as before."

Othello smiled. "Maybe, but a mysterious continent begs to be explored. Surely we can lose ourselves there."

* * *

The massacre at *New Eire* affected Ferret profoundly. He no longer found time to talk of philosophy or the great possibilities of mankind. He became pessimistic and despondent. He withdrew. He believed that hope was for the hopeless, and the future for the foolhardy.

Ferret and Othello wandered together for two decades, trapping in nameless rivers and valleys, braving cold winters and hot swampland, and making contact with other humans only occasionally, to trade furs for supplies. Their roaming lasted so long that Ferret compared it to the nomadic Jews who had followed Moses into the desert in punishment for their crimes.

Journeying deep into the interior, they reached the shores of the great river—the Mississippi. They bartered with Indian tribes, dined in splendor with Spanish generals in Florida, and floated down the Mississippi to trade with the French in New Orleans. But somewhere in the Ohio Valley, they were separated when they were captured by hostile Indians. Only Ferret managed to escape. He followed the savages north for weeks hoping to rescue his friend, but he lost the trail at the shore of a great freshwater ocean.

Ferret spent several more years trapping alone, avoiding people and towns as much as possible. When he had to sell his beaver and fox pelts, he would go to a frontier outpost, trade, drink a blackjack of ale, and return to the wilderness. Sometimes when he was there, he would hear stories told of an Irish king who lived in the southern colonies and stood up to the British army in the name of freedom. Although the stories were about him, they didn't sound like anything from his memory. But he remained silent; let the stories be what they were.

As the years passed, it became harder to live as he had. His body slowed down. His long auburn hair faded to white, his hands cracked, and his face tanned with the look of rawhide. He had grown old.

* * *

It was in the colony of Virginia that Ferret once again confronted civilization. In the valley of the Shenandoah River, he entered an alehouse. He longed to taste hot-buttered rum again and ordered a large tankard. As his spirits lifted, his tongue grew young and loose, and he boasted of his royalty and lost Irish kingdom to any friendly ear. The half-drunk patrons laughed uproariously and patted the old man on the back, toasting his regal health. Ferret's unrelenting guilt and unhappy memories melted away with each tankard.

The patrons' stories soon turned to the English king, their language becoming sharp-tongued and fiery. One backwoodsman cursed him, and others roared with approval. Another said they all should be ashamed. Lifting up his tankard, he made a toast: "May the King live long... but somewhere else."

Enthralled, Ferret joined the merriment in earnest and damned the King in vinegary language the likes of which no man had heard before. A long round of cheers roared throughout the tavern, the patrons banging their ale mugs on the tables, hooting, laughing, and guffawing until a dozen British soldiers arrived. They arrested Ferret and charged him with defaming the King.

Ferret was imprisoned at a nearby military stockade, locked inside a cramped, murky cell, alone and forlorn. He found the confinement belittling and restricting. He was not accustomed to living under ceilings. He found it difficult to sleep without the immense sky of bright stars overhead and gray moonlight. Sometimes even that was confining.

Within days of Ferret's incarceration, a thin man trembling with age visited. "That's him," the man said in a high-pitched voice, tapping his cane on the ground. "That's the ruffian."

Twenty days later Ferret entered a primitive courthouse and discovered he was on trial for treason. Three judges—black-robed and white-wigged—entered the empty courtroom, sat on a crudely built bench, and studied the written charges. The chief magistrate was George Locke, the youngest of the three. He was of medium height and uncommonly handsome. When Ferret approached the bench, Locke spoke first. "I understand that you had an altercation with some officers."

Ferret thought the man seemed sincerely concerned, though he had no reason to be. Ferret looked him in the eye. "I did not. I merely spoke freely in the alehouse."

"Did you not defame the king?"

"Aye! And I would have resumed if not so rudely escorted away. Do you wish to hear more?"

Judge Stonewall, an old and stodgy man, broke in. "Why should we listen to this malcontent?"

"Because," Locke said, "we have a duty to dispense justice."

When Judge Locke stood and read the official charges, Ferret found something familiar about the man. He felt positive that he had seen the man before, but he could not remember when. Locke pointed out to the other magistrates that Ferret's alleged crimes occurred a long time ago.

"A crime is a crime," Judge Warminster said.

Stonewall nodded. His puffy face, round eyes, and pug nose gave him the look of an old, fat hog. He spoke in a strident tone. "I agree. 'Tis a crime, whether now or in 1715."

Ferret mouthed the year 1715. Was such a long time ago. He could barely remember the assault by Cromwell, the frenzied Yamasees, the resulting massacre. Who else would remember all that and still demand revenge? Ferret searched the courtroom. His eyes fell on a thin, one-armed man in a corner. His good hand quaked like rustled tree leaves in stormy weather. It was the same stranger who had identified him in the stockade. It had to be Cromwell!

Locke cleared his throat. "Ferret O'Neill, a native of Ireland, is charged with treason and supplying arms to the Yamasee tribes." He paused and looked at the other judges. "The Yamasees, to refresh your memories, allegedly attacked and destroyed a settlement south of the perimeter of South Carolina."

"Allegedly?" Cromwell shouted. "They murdered everyone!"

"Hear, hear!" Judge Warminster said. "We are not here to dispute what happened to that colony. We are here to determine whether this Ferret O'Neill has committed a crime against the king."

Judge Locke ignored Warminster and continued. "Ferret O'Neill has been accused of attacking, with the assistance of Spaniards, British troops under the command of Major-General Winston Cromwell. The Yamasees and Ferret O'Neill were engaged in an attack upon a shipwrecked colony. Cromwell, as the report states, arrived at the settlement after the massacre of several hundred colonists. All had perished at the hands of the savages. Cromwell did engage in battle with the Yamasees. At this point,

Cromwell captured Ferret O'Neill and other conspirators. However, the battle proved to be indecisive and turned against Cromwell's forces. A retreat was called and the accused escaped imprisonment and ran into the hinterland. Cromwell was able, at a later date, to muster more men and counterattack. Cromwell was decorated with honors for his courage. He lost his right arm in the battle."

Ferret was silent.

"I do not believe we need delve any further," Stonewall said.

"The evidence is insurmountable," Warminster said. "I say we find him guilty."

"What do you plead?" Judge Locke asked.

Ferret studied Locke's face and thought, *What is it about this judge?* He was sure he knew the man.

"Your plea?"

Ferret hesitated. His face grew hot. Nobody had the right to judge his conduct over *New Eire* except himself, and he had already come to a verdict long ago: he was guilty as sin.

"I'm innocent," Ferret declared.

"Must we continue with this?" Warminster asked. "He's just going to lie like a flatfish. The Irish are good at that."

"May I speak?" Ferret asked.

"No, you may not," Warminster said. "We ask the questions."

"The report says that you referred to yourself as King Ferret in the tavern," Locke said, "King of what?"

"King of *New Eire*. 'Twas a colony of Irishmen and Dutch."

Stonewall huffed. "And who, pray tell, gave you the right to rule as king?"

"Who gives the King of England the right to rule?"

Locke interrupted, "We are not here to question the authority of the King of England or, for that matter, any king."

"Then do not question my title," Ferret said.

Locke looked amused. "May any rogue call himself king?"

"A rogue by any other name may rule with as much deceit."

Locke grew serious. "Why did you assist the Yamasees? Were you unaware of their murderous misdeeds in South Carolina? They murdered over two hundred colonists, traders, and slaves."

"Get on with it!" Cromwell stood, slapped his cane against a chair, and approached the three magistrates. "You're charging this man with treason, not as some spectator in an Indian war."

"Aye," Judge Stonewall said.

"I wish to answer the question," Ferret said.

"I revoke the question," Locke said. "Brevity is important here."

"What of justice?" Ferret asked. "I wish to answer for justice's sake. I did not assist the Yamasees. They assisted us."

Surprised, Locke asked, "Can this be true?"

"I ruled over a colony of free Irishmen and Dutch," Ferret said. "We were sovereign, independent, a country proper. It was Major-General Cromwell who attacked our settlement. The Yamasees came to our assistance."

"Sheer madness!" Stonewall said.

"Nonsense!" Warminster said. "Bloody tripe! The man has lost his mind."

Locke leaned back and disregarded his colleagues' outcries. "Why did the Yamasees assist you?"

"We had befriended the heathens. We had given them food and—"

"See!" Cromwell grew shrill. "See, he freely admits it! They gave supplies to the enemy!"

Ferret did not care if he was to be hanged, but he wanted the truth known. "Weeks earlier, the Yamasees had broken through our fortifications, and we were in no position to deny them anything."

Locke asked, "Why did they spare your lives?"

"There was a Spaniard with the Yamasees. He was under the impression that we had an alliance with the Spaniards. And since we were Irish and Catholic, we were considered foes of the British."

Stonewall pushed the question. "Did you sign a treaty with the Spaniards?"

Ferret shook his head. "We did not. However, we did meet with a Spanish general and talk of a mutual defensive alliance. Nothing came of the talks."

"Are you sure?" Judge Locke asked.

"Quite sure. We hesitated to sign any treaty. We did not want to alarm the British Navy."

Cromwell inched forward and began to shout. "Your settlement was illegal. Could I allow it to remain independent? Nay! The Irish are subjects of England. I did my duty."

"You did more!" Ferret stood and shouted back. His chains rattled as he moved. "'Twas personal revenge. Cromwell wished to silence me and others because of his secrets. He had corrupt dealings in Cork and conspired to murder an official from England who would investigate his administration. If anyone should be on trial, it ought to be Cromwell."

Cromwell slapped his cane against a chair. "You lying, horse-pissing prig!"

"Order! Order!" Judge Stonewall stood up and blared with a voice so forceful that spittle rolled down his chin. "I will have order." The magistrate remained standing until the courtroom had calmed down. "See here. The distinguished war hero Major-General Cromwell is not on trial here! As for you, Ferret O'Neill, by your own admission, you colonized a settlement without charter or authority. You resisted the King's army in battle, and as such must be labeled a rebel. Furthermore, you freely admit to treasonous acts. We have no recourse but to pronounce you guilty of treason."

"Aye," Warminster said.

"Cannot a man disagree without being treasonous?" Ferret stared at the judges. "We wished not to level or destroy authority, but to withdraw from it. We wanted sovereignty for each man to rule himself with a conscience. To allow him to choose his own values and destiny. I was a king, but I led others without a whip." Ferret paused and looked down, almost sheepishly. He *had* used the whip. In a fit of anger, he had almost had Father Yeats and his cohorts shot. He had been caught up in the pomp and pride of his kingdom, just like every other king. It was only a matter of time before he would have become just like Cromwell. However, the court was not judging him on that. That fact gave him a certain repose. "We only wanted to withdraw from authority. If in doing so we became rebels, then so be it. We wanted liberty. Without it, we welcomed death."

"That's surely what you shall receive," Stonewall said.

Ferret rolled his eyes as he sighed. "So, may the King or Parliament aggress without recourse? Must we tolerate any abuse, any violation? What true Englishman would allow his home to be entered without his consent? I know of none."

"The penalty is death. Death by hanging. Court dismissed." Judge Locke banged his gavel, then peered at Ferret. "Only the Almighty Lord can save you now."

Chapter 38

Ferret shook his head. No point reliving the past. What he had already gone through was nothing but a relic of ancient history. It should simply be forgotten. There was nothing left for him in this world. Ferret rearranged the blade he was pressing against Major Mountjoy's throat. He knew there was no reason to harm the man. He had lost again, and prolonging the inevitable was causing undue pain. Just when Ferret decided to surrender and drop the blade, someone in the crowd shouted out, "The dagger bestows life after death—use it!"

Coming out of his trance, Ferret examined the old dagger closer. It looked like the Irish dagger he had unearthed as a child. But he had given that to Othello long ago, during a forage down the Mississippi River. The man who shouted had the general stature and demeanor of Othello, but Ferret's eyesight had become too poor to distinguish features at any long distance. It did not matter anyway. He was not going to kill himself under any circumstance, not for the lively entertainment of depraved colonists and not for the indulgence of the English. Still, he had to do something. He was growing weak. Cold numbness swelled through his strained arm. He could not hold this English bully-rook forever.

"'Tis life after death!" the black man yelled again.

Mountjoy squeaked, "Listen. I promise to release you if you release me."

For a moment Ferret relaxed. It seemed like a decent offer. Then again, the promise was coming from an English officer. It was no doubt a lie. Everything was a lie.

The Negro fought his way through the crowd to the scaffold's edge. He was followed by the same red-haired woman that Ferret had noticed earlier. Something about her made his spirits lift up to proclaim to the world that hope and love had not been totally uprooted and thrown away. That was an odd thought, since he was never going to escape from this sea of armed redcoats and English settlers.

"Release me," Mountjoy stammered, "or... fear the wrath of..."

"I've had a bellyful of promises." Ferret tightened his grip on Mountjoy, squeezing the officer until he could barely breathe. He found his control over the major exhilarating, as if he controlled the fate of the world.

"You're only making matters worse." General Williams spoke sternly and ordered more men to the scaffold. However, before the men could climb the ladder, the magistrate, Judge Locke, had appeared beside the general. The judge briefly exchanged words with General Williams. Then, with a quick turn, he faced the line of soldiers and ordered them to lower their weapons. The men complied once the general nodded in agreement.

"Calm down," the judge said as he approached Ferret. Locke lifted his hands up high, palms open, to show him that he was unarmed. "Take me if you must. I'm the one who sentenced you to death."

Ferret sneered and then laughed. "What do you want?"

"To do justice," Locke said in a soothing, calm tone. "Kay thee, kay me. I wish to see nobody harmed."

Ferret had no reason to believe that an English judge would assist him. He let out an animal-like growl. "I will kill before I'm killed. Be sure of that, magistrate."

"Mighty cock-sure of yourself," Judge Locke said. "You did not believe in such brutality in *New Eire*."

"How would *you* know?"

"I know you better than you think."

Ferret still could not recall the Judge's face. He had never been very good at remembering faces.

"Your fate is not sealed. Life is balanced on a scale. You must jump off before the scale swings back. Take me captive and release the major."

Ferret shoved his hostage away and grabbed Judge Locke, slipping the blade under his chin. Mountjoy fell to the floor, breathless and stunned. He glared up at the restrained judge, rubbed his sore neck, and began to crawl backward, like a rock crab. Reaching the stairs, he rose to his feet and quickly scurried down. Before he reached bottom he tumbled into the row of soldiers.

"You have nowhere to escape, Ferret," Locke said.

"Some believe I do. I could escape where few men wish to go."

"You are not alone," Locke said. "Believe me, you still have some old mates."

Ferret eased up on the knife. "Impossible! You're a bald-faced liar."

Locke pulled an emerald ring from his robes and placed it in Ferret's free hand. "This is from a dear friend. Do you not recognize it?"

Ferret stared at the ancient ring. "Who are you?"

"My father went by the name of Strongbow."

Ferret's mouth gaped as he slightly lowered the blade. Everything was moving far too fast to comprehend. It *had* to be a trick. Yet... the ring was his father's, the same ring he had given Heather. *Heather.* Images of her overpowered him. Could she have duped death?

"There is a way out of this hot soup," Locke said. "No man is immortal, but some men know how to cheat death—at least for a moment." The judge leaned over and whispered into Ferret's ear.

Ferret listened, but he soon balked at the suggestion. "God-almighty, I'm not Christ! You ask too much!"

"'Tis the only way."

"Are you sure?"

"You must if you want to see the others," Locke said, lowering his voice.

"The others?" Ferret's eyes blinked rapidly. He was sure the judge was toying with him. "Who? Name the names."

"The bereaved ones. Those who had been left behind."

"Not possible! No one escaped. I saw their graves."

"Not everyone from *New Eire* sleeps soundly in their final resting place," Locke said. "Some have been waiting long to catch sight of you."

"Why do you mock me?"

"Why would I lie? What would I gain?"

Ferret stepped back and crooked his head to the side. He began to feverishly think about what the judge had said. He had to agree. There was nothing the judge would get, except a freshly hanged corpse in a pine box—a rather worthless commodity. "But is one of those others named Heather?"

With difficulty, Locke pointed to a red-haired woman in the crowd.

Ferret stared down. The old woman beamed with a warm smile and lingering eye contact. In a flash, he pushed the judge out of his way and stormed near the edge of the platform. He faced the unruly crowd. He felt an urge to spit on the spectators below. Instead, he glared down at the colonist's gawking eyes and gaping mouths. He took in a deep breath and raised both hands, preparing to plunge the knife into his chest. These onlookers had come to see someone die a gruesome death. He did not want to disappoint. He would give them the performance of a lifetime. He would show them what they deserved, something they would not soon forget.

"I was once a noble king in a noble land." Ferret spoke with the conviction of a fire and brimstone preacher. "But like most kings, I ruled like a heartless rogue. I compelled others to languish and die needlessly. Soon after, I was a ghost, a soulless vagabond, a king without a kingdom, in a nation without humanity, and a world without substance. Only shame lived lavishly. And I, a man of means, stand all alone to pay the piper. For I deserve only to lie under a mound of lilies. I deserve to rot under the blame. I stand here without any reason to live."

Ferret paused to see how the crowd was responding. He could see that they were captivated by his message.

"I must be punished for my crimes. Woe to those who fail to see the beast, the evil that lies dormant within us all, ready to lash out at anything or anybody for any reason. Only liberty chains the beast, but liberty's links are thin and brittle and often falter. I know of such neglect. 'Twas I who broke the demon's cage. 'Twas I who set the darkness free. I say to all henceforth: seek not to rule or be ruled. Seek not to control or be controlled. Defend the sovereignty of conscience and not the whims of potentates. Liberty must be for all or for none. I know not what course others may take. But for me, give me liberty or grant me death."

Ferret looked to the sky. Arching the blade higher overhead, he jabbed the dagger deep into his chest. Some of the women gasped in horror. Others cringed and let out cries of grief and shock. Ferret's knees buckled.

He fell over with a thud, rolled to the edge of the platform, and slid off, hitting the ground in a cloud of dust. The colonists leaped back, stunned.

Locke rushed down the stairs to Ferret's lifeless body, pushing aside the tightening circle of gawking colonists and baffled soldiers. Breaking through the circle, he placed his hand over Ferret's face and felt for his breath. He looked up at the horrified faces and announced that Ferret was dead. As soon as he said it, the blackamoor lifted Ferret's body up in his broad arms and carried him away. Two young men followed him.

Still confused and agitated, the crowd wandered about, bickering over what had happened and why. A boy, eight or ten years of age, found the dagger on the ground, in the dirt where the prisoner had fallen. The boy picked it up. Its blade was stained red, but the blood was dry and hard. Puzzled, he glanced up and watched Ferret's body being carried to a hilltop cemetery. The boy ran to his father and showed him the dagger.

"You must return the dagger to the owner," the boy's father said.

"I do not know to whom it belongs." The boy began to finger the blade and discovered that it was dull. "Give me liberty or death—I liked what the old man said. Why did he say that, Papa?"

"Just return the knife," his father repeated.

Disappointed, the boy returned to where he had found the dagger and found the tall black man searching the ground. He towered over the youngster. Quickly, he spotted the dagger in the boy's hand and reached out for it. "I'm the rightful owner of that dagger."

The boy hesitated. Stepping back, he bumped into an old woman.

"You must give us the dagger, laddie," the old woman said gently.

The boy was flustered. "I think it came from the dead man, but the blood is dry."

The boy's father approached. He looked concerned. "Patrick, what's going on?"

"The laddie was returning our dagger," the woman said. "It belongs to us."

The father introduced himself. "I'm John Henry and this is my son, Patrick Henry." He took the blade from his son's hand and gave it to the woman. "You're kindred of his?"

"Aye," the woman said in a sweet, tearful tone.

"But the blood was dry on the knife," Patrick uttered again with a perplexed, solemn face. "How is that possible?"

"I appreciate your help," the old women said. Then she hurried back up the hill to the cemetery. The black man and dozens of other men, women, and children followed her.

Ferret's body had been placed into a shallow grave on top of the treeless knoll overlooking the fort. Several unwanted strangers peeked over the old woman's shoulder, gawking at the body. One teenage boy kicked a clod of dirt into the grave.

"Don't do that," the old woman said.

"He's dead, ain't he?"

The Negro's eyes twitched with annoyance. "Do you want to disturb the spirit world?"

"Nay, certainly not! But he is as placid as the night."

"Those who lie in wormy beds can be easily annoyed. Take heed. Something wicked this way may come. Alas, do you wish the night-crow to cry for your blood?"

The youth shook his head, backed up and bowed his head slightly. He scrambled down the knoll and joined the others at the fort.

As soon as the strangers had departed, the old woman turned to the Negro. "Is he?"

The Negro nodded. "Ready. Fill the hole, Darbee."

Darbee tossed small shovelfuls of dirt into the grave. He was careful not to cover Ferret's face. The old woman wailed, but no tears rolled down her thin, cracked face. Occasionally, she twisted around to see if anyone was watching them from below. Only a few men milled around the entrance to the fort.

She knelt by the grave and whispered, "Ferret." Her body was silhouetted by the setting sun. She smiled and took out a knife. With it she cut her finger and let a drop of blood fall into the grave. "You will never escape from me again, my sweetkin. Never. At long last, we will be free."

www.ingramcontent.com/pod-product-compliance
Lightning Source LLC
Chambersburg PA
CBHW030541260626
47157CB00006B/2145